# IN TOO DEEP

## Where else to find us!

**Anthologies featuring C. N. Buchholz:**

Festival of Crime

Cooked to Death Volume II: Lying on a Plate

Minnesota Not So Nice: Eighteen Tales of Bad Behavior

A Glass of Wine with Edgar

Hook, Line, and Sinker: The Seventh Guppy Anthology

It Was a Dark and Stormy Night, Doncha Know (Coming late 2024)

**Books by A. W. Powers:**

**The Psychic Guardian Angel Series:**

First Casualty (Book 1)

No Rest for the Dead (Book 2)

Flying Objects (Book 3)

Psychic Summons (Book 4)

Psychic Mission (Book 5)

Open for Business (Book 6)

Coming soon:

The Dead are Not Reluctant (Book 7)

And

Properly Dead

# IN TOO DEEP

## Kill Shot: Book One

C. N. Buchholz

and

A. W. Powers

Mayhem Books

Cover art by Jake at J. Caleb Design

http://jcalebdesign.com



Edits by Sonya Bateman



Published by Mayhem Books

an imprint of Wordwhipper Press, LLC

1021 Oakwood Terrace

Champlin, MN 55316

Version 1.0.0

Print ISBN: 979-8-9914430-1-2

eBook ISBN: 979-8-9914430-0-5

In Too Deep

is dedicated to Jody, my partner in all things and my biggest supporter as a writer.

Thank you. I love you.

It is also dedicated to Troy Buchholz, who believed in C. N.'s potential as a writer enough to support this endeavor and to push her to complete it, revise it, and follow her dream. And to Cathy. I would have completed this story someday. It might have been different than what we created, and it may have taken many more years. Working together made this project a priority. Thanks for the boost.

A. W. Powers

To my mother, who spent her career fighting crime. I miss you every day.

And to Tweedledum, a.k.a. Bill, who dragged me across the finish line.

C. N. Buchholz

# ACKNOWLEDGEMENTS

A big shout out to the Wordwhippers Writers Group who encouraged me in my writing career and helped improve my skills: Bill Anderson (a.k.a. A. W. Powers), Dale Butler, Marlene Chabot, Barb Danson, Joe Jubert (may he rest in peace), Liz Parker, Barbara Schmidt, Mary Rogers, and Mary Sebesta. Thank you to the writing community, specifically Twin Cities Sisters (and Brothers) in Crime members who have provided ongoing support and friendship.

I'd like to thank my family, especially my daughter, Brittany, who surpassed me early on with her writing ability and publishing credits. I am inspired by her talent and hope to co-write a book with her someday. Yes? Maybe? Thanks, also, to my son, Trevor. Although he avoids books and prefers a TV remote or game controller over a pencil, he respects my passion for words and appreciates my week-long visits to hammer out edits and lounge about his house in my pajamas. Finally, a big thank you to my husband, Troy. Like son, like father—another watcher of the big screen rather than reader of the printed page. Despite Troy's lack of interest in books, he's granted me space (sometimes two spaces) in every house we've owned for my 2000-plus book collection and for my late-night power writing sessions. He encourages me to stay focused, keep submitting, pursue my dreams, and come to bed already.

C. N. Buchholz

Special thanks to my wife, Jody, my daughters and grandchildren. They provide the diversions I need to avoid being a reclusive writer, hearing voices, hanging with spirits, and working in a poorly lit room. Thank you to the Wordwhippers: Daley Butler, C. N. Buchholz, Barb Danson, Brittany Jaekel, Mary Rogers, Barbara Schmidt, Liz Parker, Mary Sebesta, Marlene Chabot, and the painfully missed Joe Jubert. You made me a better writer, and you introduced me to Cathy, who was brave enough to join me in this endeavor. Thanks to the Florida Chapter of the Mystery Writers of America. After writing for a long time, it was nice to receive a bit of validation. Most of all, thank you, readers, for taking a chance on our book.

A. W. Powers

# CHAPTER ONE

The old man nodded to the hotel night clerk, lightly pressed his hand to the teen's back, and headed up the stairs toward the dumpy room at the end of the hall where he would offer her a new life. In the past month, all the girls' new lives began there.

With the cold Minnesota wind whipping its way up and down city streets, runaways and homeless were easy to lure into a toasty car, quick to accept the offer of a hot meal and a warm bed. No strings attached. He was a harmless-looking white-haired man with a worn Bible. An elderly man of God who shared scripture, helped the frightened and lonely, and spoke of his own daughter lost to the streets.

His efforts proved so successful the boss hinted at a pay raise. If he stuck it out for a few more years, squirreled away enough cash, he could return to the Keys and retire to a life of study and contemplation.

He missed the Florida weather. The tropical breeze on his skin, the hot sun on his leathered face. He missed his wife. Her watery death in Islamorada had shocked him to the core. It drove him from the ocean's depths, from the love of diving that brought them together in the first place. He hoped that if he someday returned and faced what had happened, he would find peace in his old age.

The man used a plastic card to open the keyless door. He flipped on the light, pointed to the king-sized bed. "You can sleep there. The sheets aren't the best, my friend, but they're clean. The mattress is comfortable."

Jo-Jo would arrive in an hour, and his part of the girl's salvation would be complete. He could collect his fee and be a step closer to moving on. One more hour to keep up the pretense. One more hour until the handoff.

# CHAPTER TWO

Wes Phillips believed he was about to die. The rooftop door had latched behind him, and his heart was already hammering. A slick layer of sweat covered his lean twenty-eight-year-old body, sticking to his running clothes. He closed his eyes, reached back, and pressed his gloved palms against the door.

No one hid in the early morning shadows. No one pointed a gun. At five A.M., the eighth floor's open-air patio of the South Minneapolis condominium complex appeared empty as usual. Only he and his overactive adrenal glands occupied the open space.

When he had been condo searching, his realtor had tried to get him to ride the elevator up to the eighth floor and explore the outdoor patio. She considered the rooftop community garden and the view of the Minneapolis skyline to be the complex's biggest selling points. He had refused and had waited downstairs in the lobby while she walked the roof's perimeter. She returned, breathless. "It's even more amazing than the pictures show."

He managed to smile in response. "I'll bet."

After purchasing a condo on the ground floor, he made it a goal to see the view for himself. Baby steps, he had thought. Weeks of walking up and down the stairs, then, finally, to the rooftop. He had stood at the door and fed out a tape measure until it reached the edge of the garden. A distance of twenty-five feet. Ten steps away with his normal stride.

Phillips took several slow, deep breaths and opened his eyes. He stared down and forced his long, muscular legs to move, his feet to shuffle across the open patio. *One, two, three…* His stride shortened as it always did on the roof.

Twin Cities temperatures had dipped below freezing, not uncommon but below average for mid-November. Winter arrived with its first dump of snow. The grounds crew cleared most of the patio, yet remnants of the white stuff still sat on the park benches as if gazing outward at the skyline and inward at what remained of the garden.

A flutter of wings forced him to pause in mid-step and look up. A crow perched on the edge of the raised garden. It shook and ruffled its feathers, then cocked its head, staring at Phillips.

A scene from Alfred Hitchcock's movie *The Birds* flew

through Phillips' mind. He reached for his weapon. "I'll shoot you before you can push me off the roof." His hand fumbled at the empty spot beneath his arm.

The crow blinked and cocked its head again.

Phillips bent down, gathered a snowball, and pitched it toward the bird. "Go on, get outta here."

With a slow flap of wings, the crow took off. Black feathers disappeared into the early morning darkness.

He used his jacket sleeve to wipe the sweat from his forehead, took off a glove, and checked his pulse. It was racing. He stared in the direction of the bird's exit. Lights blinked in the distance, a plane leaving the Minneapolis-St. Paul International Airport.

Phillips never walked the perimeter of the patio during his routine. Never stood too close to the edges. The early morning commuters on the streets eight stories below raced by with no time to slow down or stop for a falling body, intentional or otherwise. He tried not to think about how vulnerable he felt far above his ground floor unit. He glanced down again and resumed his steps, maneuvering directly toward the community garden, focusing on his breathing. *In, out.*

He made it in twelve steps.

The shrink at the police academy called it acrophobia when Phillips struggled with rope climbing, wall scaling, classroom seating near the windows on the upper floors. He didn't need some overpaid doctor to tell him he feared heights. For as long as he could remember, his mind had been vertically challenged.

Today felt no different. Neither did yesterday. Yet, each day, he continued to work on what he called his Twelve Step Program. Before his morning jog around the Lakes, he sprinted up the condo stairs to the top floor, walked twelve steps out on the open patio and twelve steps back. The unpleasant adrenaline rush kick-started his morning runs.

He vowed to beat the fear. He had to if he wanted to make it in the cop business.

# CHAPTER THREE

Minneapolis Police Chief Roxanne Dalestrom paced behind a massive wooden desk, a phone receiver with a long cord pressed to her ear. When Wes Phillips appeared in her office doorway, she flicked up her chin in greeting and pointed a long, blue-lacquered nail toward a chair in front of her desk.

"I know we've been over this. And I fully understand, Mr. Mayor." She turned her back to Phillips. "But I disagree." She stared at an oversized map of Minneapolis tacked to the wall behind her desk. "I'm going to have my officers set up a perimeter hours before the parade, so we have the entire route covered with uniforms. I'll borrow from St. Paul if I have to."

The mayor yelled back, and she tensed her shoulders. Phillips stared at the back of her head—her thick copper-red hair pulled into a messy bun. She smoothed her hand across the right side of her head and tucked a few loose strands behind an ear adorned with three large gold hoops. A hint of coconut and musk permeated the air.

She shook her head. "No, not possible." She gripped

the receiver, her knuckles white. "Listen, Mr. Mayor, if you want to get in a pissing match with me about what's good for the city and your damn public relations, by all means go ahead. I'm not here to make people comfortable. I'm here to make people safe. Even you.

"We've already received credible information regarding terroristic threats surrounding the Thanksgiving event. I'm not about to jeopardize the lives of my officers and parade-goers if things go tits up." She spun around and threw her pen on the desk. "Fine, sir. Call the governor if you'd like. I already know what he's going to say."

She slammed down the receiver. "Prick," she muttered. "Did you vote for him? Don't answer that. I don't care."

Phillips bounced to his feet and extended his hand. "Chief."

She ignored the greeting. "As you were." She pulled out her own chair and sat with a sigh, folding her arms over her starched white blouse. "The wannabe politician, first year of his first term, and he thinks he knows how to better protect the city than all the professionals working together. Pretty amazing if you ask me. And arrogant." She leaned back and crossed her legs, pointing a black pump at Phillips. "Are you arrogant, Officer Phillips?"

His brown eyes stared at her, unblinking. He opened his mouth to respond.

"Don't answer that either." Dalestrom yanked open a drawer to her right and pulled out a bag of Fun-Size candy bars from Halloween. She held out a Snicker's Bar. "Chocolate?"

"Ah, no thanks, ma'am." Phillips patted his flat stomach. "I'm watching my weight."

Dalestrom cracked a smile. "Yeah, right. That's a load of shit. You look like you could run circles around every officer in this department." She tore open the wrapper, releasing an aroma of peanuts, caramel, and cocoa, and took a wolfish bite.

"Tell me. How long have you been a cop?" she asked while chewing.

He sat with his back straight and both feet on the floor. "Four years, eight months."

"And five of those months with the Fourth Precinct," she noted.

"Plus three weeks."

"Hmph." She leaned forward. "You know why you're here today?"

Phillips knew most officers never had private meetings with the chief, especially during the training and probation period. His training officer seemed like a straight shooter who would have told him if he had screwed something up. And the chief didn't personally fire an officer. That was the purview of the human resources department and the union.

"No clue."

"Me neither." She paused to swallow. "Somebody asked for help and named you specifically."

Phillips raised his eyebrows. He didn't know anyone on the Minneapolis force other than the ones at the Fourth Precinct. "Who would do that?"

"The bigger question is why." She held up a manila folder and waved it. "I know all there is to know about you, Officer Phillips. Everything. You have no secrets. Nothing in your file suggests you should be requested for any kind of duty other than shit work. But apparently, you're one lucky man." She dropped the folder back on her desk.

Phillips shifted in his chair. "And that means…"

"A special assignment. A friend of mine from the Department of Homeland Security requested you." She played with the candy bar wrapper, tearing at its edges. "After I stopped laughing, he managed to convince me it was real. He was serious. Said he needed a warm body and a nobody. You're relatively new to our force, a no-name with no face. But somehow, DHS knows your name."

Phillips cocked his head. "I don't quite—"

"You're going undercover to play with the big boys," she cut in. She watched for his response and dug in the bag for another mini bar.

Phillips straightened. "What? Undercover?"

"Don't ask me why. I told him you have a history."

His mind took a few steps back to the rooftop helipad at Lino Lakes City Hospital. The suicidal girl staring over the edge. Both of them sweat-soaked and trembling. He shoved her from his mind before he could relive what happened next and jerked himself back to the present. "Aw, jeez. I'm just getting started at the Fourth."

Dalestrom shrugged. "It's the shits, ain't it? But my friend Martinez says DHS seems set. I said I'd send you over."

"How soon are we talking?"

She glanced at the clock. "You're already late. People are waiting for you at the BCA."

"Bureau of Criminal—"

"Apprehension," she finished. "Is that what I'm detecting? A bit of apprehension?"

He swallowed hard.

"Ask for Special Agent Eric Martinez. And remember, Officer Phillips, you're on loan. After your fun and games, you'll return to your current position and not divulge the nature and extent of your undercover activities to anyone. Including me."

Phillips released a long breath. "What should I tell my sergeant?"

"Nothing. It's already taken care of. You're off the schedule until further notice." Dalestrom chuckled. "It's like you don't exist." She crumpled the two wrappers into a ball and tossed it over Phillips' shoulder into a metal wastebasket.

"Can I ask what the assignment entails?"

Dalestrom dumped the candy bag in the drawer and slammed it shut. "Don't know, and I'm not supposed to. You're dismissed."

He rose and headed toward the door.

"Officer Phillips, two things."

He stopped and turned to face her.

"Don't screw up and make me look bad."

"Copy. And the second?"

She smiled. "Try not to get yourself killed."

# CHAPTER FOUR

The girl in ratty jeans and a frayed sweater sat cross-legged on one side of the hotel bed, flipping through TV channels. The old man perched stiffly on the other side of the bed, his back to her, his feet flat on the floor. He paged through his Bible. Every few minutes, he turned and asked her to mute the volume so he could read her a passage. The smell of his sour breath and unwashed body hunkered between them.

She jumped at the violent knock on the door.

The man stood, smoothed crease marks in his polyester pants, and walked across the stained carpet. He pulled off his reading glasses and peered through the peephole.

The girl's eyes widened. She scrambled off the bed and crouched out of view. "Don't open it," she whispered. Her dirty blonde hair hung in her eyes. Her nostrils flared from the stench of mold embedded in the carpet. "Please, mister."

The man waved his hand behind him. "It's nobody.

Relax." He swung open the door.

A pimply-faced teenage boy leaned against the frame, an extra-large pizza box in his hands. "Compliments of hotel management."

The man smiled. "Why, God bless you, son." He took the pizza, flipped up the cardboard lid, and sniffed. "Mmm. Just what the doctor ordered. Tell the management they've been too generous."

The teenager shifted from one foot to the other.

"Ah, hold on a minute. I might have something for you." The man set the pizza box on a small round table and reached into his pocket, pulling out a worn leather wallet. "Hmm." He stared at its contents and dug out a rumpled five-dollar bill. He handed it to the teen. "It's not much, but it might help."

The teenager took the bill, nodded, and left.

The man closed the door, and the girl's head popped up. "Is that food really for us?"

The man pulled out two chairs, the seat fabric ripped on one. "Indeed, it is. They treat me well here. Real well." He glanced at the clock on the nightstand and motioned to the pizza. "Come. Hurry up and eat. It'll do those scrawny bones of yours some good. And you're going to need the energy."

The girl sat on the ripped chair and grabbed a slice, stuffing the food into her mouth. She chewed vigorously, ignoring the grease and sauce smearing on her lips and chin.

The man chuckled and handed her a napkin. "You sure weren't fibbing when you told me you were starving."

When she reached for a third slice, another knock rattled the door. Her eyes darted toward it. The man sighed and stood. "Kid probably forgot something." Not bothering with the peephole, he turned the knob.

A hulk of a man with pale skin, greasy black hair, and dark brown eyes shoved his way into the room. He looked at the girl and smiled.

"You timed that well, Jo-Jo," the old man noted. "You always show up at mealtimes. Don't they feed you?"

Jo-Jo shrugged off his black leather jacket. He stood well over six feet with broad shoulders, a solid chest, and thick, muscular arms. He could've easily been mistaken for a Vikings linebacker or an escaped gorilla from Como Park Zoo.

Jo-Jo threw his coat on the dresser and sat beside the girl in the old man's chair. "Fuck you, Priest Man. A man's gotta eat." He grabbed a slice of pizza and shoved it into his mouth.

His eyes skimmed over the girl who perched on the edge of her seat, eyes wide, both hands gripping the sides of the chair. "Who's your little friend?"

The girl's eyes narrowed, and she frowned. "No one to you."

Jo-Jo laughed. "She likes me already." He leaned toward her. "You're gonna fit in good, little honey. Learn how to use that smart mouth like a real lady."

She jumped to her feet and tried to run past him. Without standing, he grabbed her thin arm and yanked her back over to her chair. "Rule number one," Jo-Jo warned. "Not until I say so." He grabbed another piece of pizza and turned his focus to the old man. "Sit down, Priest Man. You make me nervous."

"Yeah? Well, you make me nauseous. For God's sake, close your mouth while you chew."

Jo-Jo wiped a greasy palm on the front of his jeans. "Jesus Christ. Do you ever have anything nice to say to me, old man? Remember who pays you."

"Certainly not you."

"Whatever. Grab me something to drink outta that fridge." He turned toward the girl. "Let's get this party started."

# CHAPTER FIVE

Wes Phillips made good time getting to the Minnesota Bureau of Criminal Apprehension's headquarters in St. Paul. He entered the stark concrete building and headed to the counter separated from the front entry and the world by bulletproof glass. He wore civilian clothes and placed both hands where they could be seen. "I'm here to see Special Agent Eric Martinez."

The two agents behind the glass stared at him. The one on the left, a large man in a gray suit whose open coat revealed a shoulder rig and a semi-automatic pistol, asked, "And you are?"

"Officer Wes Phillips."

The other agent rose to her feet. She wore slacks and a blazer over a dress shirt. Her weapon was visible at her hip. "Identification, please." Phillips set his Minneapolis Police ID on the counter. "Thank you." She picked it up and looked from it to him. "I'll have your weapon, please." Phillips stood still for a moment. She set his ID on the counter and slid her hand to her holster.

Phillips lifted his hands. "Not a problem." His out-of-uniform weapon was a 9 mm Glock 43 in a holster beneath his arm. He slowly pulled open his jacket, released the strap, and removed the gun with two fingers. A drawer opened in the counter, and he set the gun inside it. It snapped shut.

"Is that your only piece?"

"It is today."

She removed her hand from her holster. "Meet me at the end of the counter, by the door. I'll escort you to your meeting."

They walked parallel to each other toward the end of the counter. She went through a door, and he stopped at the corner. Phillips looked back to see her partner at the counter, removing his Glock from the drawer. Another door opened around the corner, and she poked her head out. "Right this way." She held the door open.

Phillips stepped through and eyed the stairwell. He turned and looked at her. She made no motion until the door had closed and latched. "We're going down."

"No elevator?" he asked.

"Not for you." She started to descend.

The female agent was about his height. The body

armor beneath her dress shirt made it impossible to gauge her conditioning or her body. Her light brown hair was secured to the back of her head in a tight bun. Her makeup matched her nonexistent smile.

Phillips followed a few steps behind. “Having a good day?”

“Yep.”

“Been with the BCA long?” They turned the corner and started down another flight.

“Yep.”

“Do you like your job?”

“I do.”

“Not a big fan of small talk, eh?” They passed a door and descended another flight of stairs.

“People who have their weapons confiscated at the door and go down these steps rarely come back out the front. I don’t bother getting to know people I’ll never see again.”

“Wow. That sounds ominous.”

She looked at him with a tight smile. “It is what it is.”

He wanted to ask how people left if they didn’t go past her and out the front door, but he decided he didn’t want to hear the answer since it would be as short as the rest and equally ominous.

They reached the bottom of the stairwell. She opened the door, and they entered a long, dimly lit hallway with doors staggered along both sides. About half of the fluorescent ceiling lights worked. She stopped at the second to last door on the right and gestured for Phillips to go in.

"Make yourself at home."

"But—"

"They'll be along soon." She closed the door, and Phillips heard a key turn in the lock. Her footsteps faded away.

He jiggled the doorknob, then turned and glanced around the room. A small conference table bolted to the floor sat in the center. A single chair, also attached to the floor, sat on the other side of the table. The chair faced a one-way glass mirrored wall and two chairs with wheels. He knew he was expected to use the interrogation chair. How else could he be evaluated? And by whom? And for what?

He really didn't care. He was one of the good guys, and he had been requested. If he failed this evaluation, he'd simply be sent back to Minneapolis and continue his daily grind at the precinct.

Phillips pulled out the closest chair with wheels and sat, keeping his back to the mirror. *Let them watch nothing.* He did consider spinning around and picking his nose. He also considered reciting some poetry. Maybe Joyce Sutphen or Robert Bly would appeal to the local cops. He didn't believe they'd appreciate the beauty of it, though. He regretted not having his notebook. He could have used the idle time to write.

*Screw it.* After an hour of waiting, he rolled the chair backward and leaned his head against the mirrored wall. He folded his hands in his lap and let his whole body relax. His eyes accepted the semi-darkness, and his mind began to drift.

He was disturbed by the rattle of keys and the door opening. He swiveled the chair to face the door. Two men stared at him. The first, who stood about six feet tall with broad shoulders and a muscular build, filled the doorway. He reminded Phillips of a brick wall. His dark hair fell in waves, and he wore a medium-gray suit, white shirt, and striped tie.

The second man peered over the other's shoulder. Behind them, several people passed by and traveled down the hall, most likely toward the stairwell.

Phillips stood and yawned.

"Are we keeping you awake?" the man filling the door asked.

"Barely." Phillips rubbed his eyes. "Another few minutes, and I'd have been lost for the night."

"Take a seat. We'll see if we can get the blood flowing again." Phillips sat back down, and the man cleared his throat. He pointed at the stationary chair. "Over there. The one you're in happens to be mine."

Phillips stood, circled the table to face the one-way glass, and sat. The man sat opposite him. "I'm Special Agent Eric Martinez with DHS." Phillips only nodded. "Do you have a problem with authority, Officer Phillips?" Martinez lifted a folder that looked a lot like the one Chief Dalestrom had been reviewing. "It says here you do."

The second man stepped into the room and closed the door. He stood with his back to it. He wore a tired black suit, a white shirt, and highly polished shoes. His receding hair was trimmed short. His navy tie hung loose around his neck, and his five o'clock shadow bloomed early.

Phillips smiled. "If you've read that, you know I do. What it doesn't say is I have a problem only with authority that's improperly used."

Martinez raised his eyebrows. "By your definition, I assume."

"I'm not afraid to ask questions."

"There are places and situations where that could get you killed," Martinez stated.

"I'm sure there are," Phillips agreed. "I'll be sure to question my decision to ask questions should that happen."

Martinez snorted. "I've gone to your superiors and made a request they could not deny. You are now on a task force I'm leading. Any guess why?"

"None, sir."

"Because I need somebody expendable," Martinez continued.

"Expendable in whose eyes, sir?"

Martinez stifled a laugh. "Considering how quickly they agreed to unload you, obviously in the eyes of your superior officers."

"I'll be sure to thank them. But honestly, I don't feel very expendable."

"Good, because I need someone who's young in the game with high potential. Someone with superior critical thinking skills. And someone who's willing to do whatever it takes to resolve our little issue and still go home alive."

"Has there been a problem with that, sir?" Phillips asked.

"You'll learn soon enough."

"Great. More ominous and cryptic answers. Nothing makes my day better."

Martinez chuckled. "Yep. We're going to get along fine. The expendable charging to the cliff." He stood. "Let's see if either of us have a job after this. Assuming we're alive."

"Let's assume we will be, sir. The idea of a longer life makes getting out of bed more appealing."

Martinez shook his head and stood. "I have someplace I have to be. Two of my associates will continue this conversation and make a final decision. I hope you're the guy we're looking for." He nodded to the other man, handed him the folder, and turned back to face Phillips. "Whatever happens, Officer Phillips, good luck to you."

Martinez stepped from the room, and an older man walked in. He was soft around the middle and in the face with hanging jowls and eyelids drooping over sunken eyes. His skin was pasty, as if it never saw daylight. Phillips suspected he was the lurker behind the one-way glass. This was not the kind of situation where somebody important waited in the hall.

The man by the door moved forward. "I'm Special Agent Russell Malloy with the BCA." He set the folder on the table without looking at it and extended his hand. "Nice to meet you."

Phillips stood and returned the handshake. Malloy jerked his thumb at the older man. "He's with the DHS. Robert McNellis."

McNellis gripped Phillips' hand in a vise-like handshake.

"Gentlemen." Malloy gestured to the chairs. The men sat in silence while Malloy rifled through the folder. He stopped on a page. "Looks like you got your feet wet pulling security, then jumped into the police officer position at Lino Lakes." He looked from the paper to Phillips. "You put in your time at Lino and requested a transfer to Minneapolis."

Phillips nodded. "Lino Lakes seemed quiet, sir. Too quiet for me."

"Hmph," McNellis muttered.

Phillips glanced at McNellis.

McNellis leaned in. "Tell us about the girl in Lino," he growled, exhaling a hint of alcohol in Phillips' direction. "The one who jumped off the roof. You stood there with your thumb up your ass and watched. Did you have a brain fart?"

The girl's face flashed in Phillips' mind. He felt his color drain and his teeth clench. He hesitated, then bent forward as if to stand. Or to go over the table. "I didn't—"

Malloy held his palms out. “Relax, Officer Phillips.”

McNellis remained motionless, his stare burrowing into Phillips’ brain.

“I’d like to answer the question.” Phillips locked eyes with McNellis.

Malloy shrugged.

“To be clear, I was following protocol,” Phillips began. “I was moving toward the girl. Slowly. She was in distress. I wanted to get to her, but I didn’t want her to take me over the edge, too.” He paused. “Does that night have anything to do with why I’m here?”

“I need to know what kind of man you are,” McNellis replied. “There’s a lot riding on this.” He pointed a crooked finger at Phillips. “I need to know I can trust you.”

Phillips straightened. “Trust *me*? I know nothing about why I’m here or what the hell’s going on.” His voice rose. “Or why everybody’s so cryptic and ominous in their messages.”

Malloy closed the folder and pushed it aside. “Let’s take this down a notch, shall we, Officer Phillips?” He folded his hands on the table. “Let’s get a bit of background history in your own words. What can you tell us about your siblings?”

Phillips’ gaze flicked to Malloy. “I have two sisters, sir.”

"We know. Are you close?" Malloy asked.

"Yes, we are."

"What do they do for a living?"

"The oldest is a lawyer. But she's okay, she's a prosecutor." Phillips paused, waiting for the usual laugh. The two men gazed back in silence. Phillips cleared his throat. "My little sister is a stringer for the Associated Press."

"What would you do for your sisters?" Malloy pressed.

"Anything short of leaking confidential information or—"

"Unless, of course, the leak was part of your job," McNellis cut in.

Phillips nodded slowly. "If it was necessary for the job, yes, I could enlist the aid of my sisters. If it didn't jeopardize their credibility. Or their lives."

"Do you recall a student by the name of Katrina Malloy?" McNellis asked.

Phillips' thoughts slid back several years to a young woman he had spent a lot of time with while studying law enforcement. After they graduated from the academy, he lost contact with her. He pulled himself back to the present. "Yes, sir, I do."

"She requested your presence on this task force. She's integral to its success, claims you're the man we need." McNellis shook his head. "I can't imagine it, but her, I trust. So, I'm going along with it."

Phillips leaned in. "Sir, Katrina and I were close. I respect her judgment. If this assignment's going to help her succeed, I'm ready. What do you need me to do?"

McNellis rolled his chair back. "Save your energy for tomorrow." He got up and opened the door. As he left the interrogation room, he muttered, "We are so fucked."

Phillips and Malloy stared at each other. Malloy waited for McNellis to be out of earshot, then burst into laughter. "He's always a joy, a regular ray of sunshine." Malloy rubbed his stubbly face. "Let's get a drink."

"Alcohol for dinner?" Phillips asked, thinking about McNellis' breath.

"Nope. Only for the first course."

Phillips realized he was hungry. Talking about the past, both bad and good, worked up an appetite.

"Besides, this place is depressing. Unfortunately, I practically live here." Malloy stood and headed for the door. Phillips followed in silence.

Malloy retrieved Phillips' weapon from the security people. As they left the BCA through the front entrance, Phillips made sure he waved to the woman at the counter. She raised an eyebrow.

# CHAPTER SIX

Russ Malloy and Wes Phillips jaywalked across University Avenue and down the street to a place called Porter's. The sign on the door boasted the best steaks and drinks in St. Paul. Maybe Phillips could test that claim today. So far, his favorite steakhouses were in Minneapolis.

Phillips let his gaze roam the dim room, its lighting courtesy of old neon beer signs, a few newer LED designs, and the glow from the kitchen. The bar extended all the way back to the end of the narrow club. Most of the patrons' sweeping glances and confident stares suggested they worked as cops, BCA agents, or feds.

"Hey, Russ," the bartender called. "The usual?"

Malloy nodded. "Yeah, please." He turned to Phillips. "What about you?"

"What's the usual?"

"Jack. Neat," Malloy replied.

Phillips knew how stupid he could get if he drank the hard stuff. "I better stick with beer." He looked at the bartender. “Whatever you have that isn’t light.”

“Got it.”

Malloy led Phillips to a booth near the front wall. Plywood, painted matte black, boarded up the window facing University Avenue. Postings for roommates, benefits for ailing customers, and local band notices covered most of it. In the center, a menu laminated in plastic caught Phillips’ eye. He laughed as he passed it.

Malloy raised an eyebrow, sliding into the booth. “What?”

Phillips sat across from him and gestured toward the boarded-up window. “The front door says the best steaks in town, but I didn’t see any listed on that menu.”

“Every once in a while, Brian buys a case of steaks. They’re word-of-mouth to the regulars, and they’re great. I don’t know where he gets them or what he does, but they are the best. You have to earn one, though.”

“Huh. If they’re as good as you say, I’d love to try one someday.”

Malloy smiled. “Maybe you’ll last long enough.”

Phillips tensed. “No one’s said a word about what we’re after, what we plan to do, or anything to inspire confidence."

Malloy fiddled with a coaster. "You'll understand soon enough."

The bartender appeared and set down two drinks taller than Phillips expected. His beer looked at least pint-sized, and Malloy's Jack Daniels shot looked like a double.

"Thanks, Brian." Malloy handed him a credit card. "Start us a tab. It's going to be a long evening."

"Any food?"

"Not yet. But yeah, we'll eat before we leave."

"If I don't get back in time, give me a signal." Brian headed back to the bar.

They stared at each other over their drinks. Phillips tapped his fingers on the table. "Katrina's your sister, isn't she?"

Malloy took a long swallow. "Yeah."

"You wanted to know what I'd do for my sisters in hopes I'd do the same for yours."

"Pretty much."

"You said she asked for me?"

"Yep."

"Why?" Phillips asked.

"Evidently, she decided you could be trusted."

Phillips gazed into his glass. "I'm flattered."

"Is she right?" Malloy's tone was sharp.

Phillips' eyes snapped up. He stared hard at Malloy. "Yes, sir."

"Good. That's what I wanted to hear. And you can call me Russ."

Phillips eased a bit in his seat. "Okay, Russ. Tell me what's going on."

Malloy took another long swallow and looked around the bar. "We've been after a particular individual for a while now." He spoke in little more than a whisper.

"Who exactly is 'we?'" Phillips pressed.

"You met Martinez with DHS."

"Yeah."

"Like I said before, I'm with the BCA."

"Okay, that's two. I met warm and friendly Robert McNellis. DHS, as I recall."

"Correct, and he's okay. He's a family friend, so I've

known him a long time. He's mostly bluster."

"If you say so."

Malloy chuckled. "Give it time. If nothing else, he'll grow on you."

"I had a fungus once."

Malloy laughed again. "Anyway..." He held up a hand and counted off on his fingers as he recalled names. "Bruce Ellison, Minnesota DEA. Tom Caffrey, FBI. Dan Larkin is out of the Chicago DEA office. Then there's Curtis Blair with the ATF."

"Jeezus," Phillips remarked. "All but one of the acronyms. Where's the CIA when you need them?"

"You're taking their place, you and Katrina. You're both Minneapolis Police."

"Okay, I have a feel for the players." Phillips tapped his fingers again. "What's the game?"

"Our task force recruited Katrina straight out of the academy after you both graduated. She possessed the right assets to go under and has already proven herself on several assignments."

Katrina slipped to the forefront of Phillips' mind. She barely reached five feet and struggled to keep weight on. At the academy, she styled her pixie cut differently every day.

Spiked, flat, occasionally a mix, and often various colors. Her body was toned, her skin flawless, and she had a twinkle in her eye that let you know she was trouble. You'd find it difficult, if not impossible, not to go along with any fun plans she concocted.

He wondered which assets got her onto the task force. He focused back on Malloy.

"She was pretty intense," Phillips recalled. "Very intent on being a good cop. I'm not surprised she's done okay."

Malloy nodded. "Our target is Damian Reynolds. He enjoys a variety of young women, preferably teens and preteens. We hoped Katrina would be able to get close to him, find a way to stay around long enough to figure things out. Apparently, she did."

"What did she figure out?"

"We knew Reynolds was into drugs, stolen weapons, the kinds of things taken during home invasions. Enough of them to get the attention of all the agencies."

"But—"

"My sister found something bigger. She couldn't tell me what, though." Malloy exhaled a long breath. "The last time we talked, she said, 'This is huge. I need help. Get Wes Phillips.

Tell him our cover is we met at summer camp and used to fool around. He was a camp counselor named Stephen Mayer. He called me Izzy.'"

Malloy paused and sipped. "Listen, Phillips, to be clear, her cover name is Isabella Cantrell. You're evidently the only one who calls her Izzy." He peered around the bar again. "That's all I got."

"Shit."

"Yeah, shit. Not much to go on. But evidently, she thought you could help." Malloy rubbed his palm across his stubbly chin. "She said you guys used to be close."

Phillips looked down, then sipped his beer. "How deep is she under?"

Malloy shrugged. "We don't know. That's the problem with these undercover roles. Sometimes, they get too far under. People get lost that way."

"So, I'm supposed to go in, find her, and get her back out."

"Sounds easy when you say it that way," Malloy stated. "Are you game?"

"Yeah, I'm all in."

***

Brian swung by their table. “Ready for dinner yet? Or you gonna keep yackin’ until I threaten to close the kitchen?”

Malloy nodded. “Yeah, we’re ready. I’ll have a turkey club. Heavy on the mayo.” He pushed his empty glass toward the bartender. “And one more of these oughta do it.”

“Sure.” Brian picked up the empty. “What about you?”

“You got a French dip sandwich?” Phillips asked.

“One of the best.”

Phillips nodded.

“Another beer?”

“Nah, I better not. Water would be good.”

Brian raised his eyebrows. “Sure, bud.”

As soon as Brian walked away, Phillips propped his elbows on the table and leaned forward. “I know I haven’t been a Minneapolis cop long enough to know how things work, but how are you going to explain my being on a task force? I mean, aren’t there guys who have enough history and experience that they’d want to be on it, should be on it, and will be pissed they’re not?”

“Of course there are. Plenty of men and women,” Malloy replied. “That’s police work politics, though. You either gotta know somebody, shine enough to catch someone's eye, or understand the difference between brown-nosing and ass-kissing."

"And I do?"

"You know Katrina," Malloy stated. "If anyone asks, we say the job you have is the thankless, ruin-your-career spot doing shit work for all the agencies involved in the task force."

Phillips rolled his eyes. "Sounds swell."

"Believe me, every task force has one, and everybody knows it. Whoever hears you have that job will know you're not going to get any rest, any decent food, any help. Plus, when it goes bad, you'll be the one sacrificed. You'll be the next aggressive young officer working at the Mall of America, passing out strollers." Malloy laughed. "The problem is it's true."

"Marvelous. Sounds like the ideal job for a rookie. Good thing I spent my formative years working security. You know, just in case things don't pan out. It'll be like going home." Phillips tipped his glass back, downed the last swallows of beer, and pushed the glass to the table's edge. "Now, what about Katrina?"

"As I mentioned, Reynolds likes them young, and not many women on the force look younger than Katrina. She also hasn't worked as a street cop long enough to smell like one."

"We have a particular smell?" Phillips asked.

"You know how it is. After a certain amount of time, you look like a cop, no matter what you do. Truth is, all the agencies tried getting someone close to Reynolds. We don't know how close any of them got, but before they shared any intel with us, they ended up missing or dead. Almost as if Reynolds, or someone close to him, could smell cop on them."

"They didn't do or say anything stupid?"

"We don't know," Malloy replied.

"But you know Katrina's okay?"

"She was. Like I said, she cut the call short. I haven't heard back from her since."

Phillips cleared his throat. "Are you sure she's alive?"

Malloy looked away, then back at Phillips. "As far as we know, yes. With everything I've got, I believe my sister is still alive and working for us."

Phillips glanced around the bar. "Did we sign her death warrant, and mine, by having this conversation here? Should we have talked someplace more secure?"

Malloy laughed. "Two things. First, I'd vouch for

anybody here and for all the guys on the task force. Second, Brian's a paranoid old spy. The place doesn't have Wi-Fi, is swept, shielded, and insulated, so nobody can listen to anything here. He has a scrambler running, too. Have you seen anybody get a message or a call for as long as we've sat here?"

"No. And that's odd."

"No, that's Brian. The other places we meet, like the basement conference room or the interrogation rooms, I'm not so sure."

"That's comforting," Phillips muttered. "What's our timetable?"

"Unfortunately, we don't know. We don't know how deep Katrina is, how close she's gotten to Reynolds, what this big new thing is, and when whatever is going to happen will happen. We don't know if Reynolds made her and is keeping her around anyway or if he's playing her against us."

"Could he do that?"

"Maybe. She's acting differently. Perhaps she's falling for him."

"Shit. Not another one of those bonding cases."

"Bingo."

Phillips clenched his jaw. "When do I go in?"

"The others want a little time with you," Malloy told him. "They say it's to fill you in, but I think they're nervous and want to check you out. As soon as they're done, you go solo."

"Okay. So, when's my first meet and greet?"

"Seven A.M. tomorrow. We're going to a stakeout."

# CHAPTER SEVEN

The old man never stayed for what Jo-Jo referred to as "the interview." He could imagine the terror in the girl's eyes, the pleading voice, the cries and screams. Before it went too far, he picked up his Bible and left the room. He returned after the filthy, disgusting parts had ended.

This girl hadn't behaved any differently than the others, he reminded himself. He had seen her numerous times. She was another runaway, a young soul who shouldn't have been on the streets. He had warned her in the coffee shop about the evil ways of the world, pointing to Bible passages and quoting bits and pieces from the sermons at the Basilica. It wasn't his fault the girl didn't listen to reason. Or that she eventually thought she could trust him and had accepted the car ride.

He walked down to the lobby, running the numbers in his head. It proved a good month. Even Jo-Jo was acting giddy. Of course, it didn't take much to entertain a buffoon. As long as he didn't get too rough with the girl. The boss disapproved of receiving damaged goods. Every now and then, the boss knocked that into Jo-Jo's head, resulting in a few bruises for Jo-Jo and a pay cut for both of them.

The old man dug his readers out of his shirt pocket, perched them on his bulbous nose, and logged onto the hotel's guest computer in the lobby as Priest Man. He didn't mind Jo-Jo's nickname for him, but heck with letting him know it. He had worked as a minister in his earlier days, leading a flock of gray-haired Florida sheep and inspiring a small congregation. Jo-Jo had been one of his young rams.

He closed his eyes, remembering. If only he had refused to take Jo-Jo and those other men out on the boat. If only Suzanna hadn't insisted on joining them. The weather off the Keys was perfect that day. The water, clear as usual. The dive remained her decision. Her fault.

He forced open his eyes and straightened. Now, only he and his Bible remained. No commitments, no responsibilities. He answered only to the man upstairs. It's better this way, he told himself. There will never be another Suzanna. *Never.*

The old man sighed. Time to get on with it. See if the boss said anything new. His inbox stated no new messages. He logged out of his email and checked his favorite website, Words to Live By. The message for the day appeared.

**Be thankful for the gifts you receive.**

Not enough people did that. Especially the multitude of materialists. What they had was never enough and never quick enough. No patience, no gratitude. It was pathetic, sacrilegious. Jo-Jo certainly needed the day's lesson. If he possessed a few brain cells, the old man would pass the wisdom on to him.

The time on the bottom of the screen read eleven fifty-nine. He finished scanning the pages, logged off the computer, and tucked his glasses back into his pocket. He shuffled back to the room, stood outside the door, and listened.

# CHAPTER EIGHT

On the drive home from Porter's, Wes Phillips tried to distract himself by thinking about work. He had spent hours with Russ Malloy, talking about bar food, sports, family, life as a cop, and not enough about the case. As if specifics were not available or he didn't need to know. Yet.

He thought about Katrina Malloy and about his own sisters. During college, Katrina may have been closer to him than his siblings were, especially his oldest sister the lawyer. Even though she was a prosecutor, she had a dislike for cops. As if they weren't doing their jobs or weren't doing them well enough. As a result, she claimed her job was more difficult than it should be.

However, he'd lost contact with Katrina after graduation, obviously because she immediately went undercover. He'd gotten to spend more time with his older sister, but they had avoided all talk of work and politics other than agreeing the world was a mess.

He entered his condo, flipped on the lights, and tossed

his keys onto the entry table. A framed photo of his parents smiled at him. He kicked off his shoes and shed his heavy coat, hanging it on the hook by the door. The cold from the entryway's ceramic tile floor penetrated his socks. He cranked up the thermostat and went to the entertainment center to insert a CD.

"Time for some therapy."

B. B. King's distinctive guitar playing filled the room.

He strolled into the bathroom, relieved himself, washed his hands and face, and headed to the kitchen. He poured a glass of ice water and sat at the high-top breakfast counter.

Phillips looked around. The place was austere and tidy, almost as if the tenant had not brought any personality with him. The furniture was only months old. He had bought it after moving in. His old furniture, more to his style and substantially more comfortable, had too many memories attached and did not make the move with him. This was all affordable and utilitarian. If he were to have guests, they wouldn't get comfortable enough to stay long.

A flicker of light pulled his view to the side window. It looked out to an alley followed by a brick wall. The proximity allowed very little light to penetrate the shadows, and the alley kept its coating of ice much longer than the patio did.

Almost no one used the alley. He could sit in his underwear with little worry about being seen. He rarely did, however. It didn't seem right for a cop to be an exhibitionist, nor did he want to tempt his neighbors into voyeurism.

The light was probably a car passing along or turning around at the end of the drive. Maybe a dumpster-diver lighting a cigarette. He didn't bother to close the blind.

His notebook waited on the counter. It was a fixture there, and he spent as much time as he could writing in it. Some days, inspiration came easy. Other days, not at all. The wire spiral was bent and smushed. Little ears of paper stuck out, sticky notes he had added, and fragments from a page he had ripped out that didn't come clean at the perforation. He picked at a scrap, and when it didn't pull free, he opened the notebook.

Most of his poetry dealt with death. The death of his parents, the death of his dog, the deaths he had witnessed on the job. The trauma of seeing and surviving death every week. And some weeks, every day.

He read a poem from the previous week. It was about his younger sister, Alyse, and her up-and-down moods, quick outbursts, and struggles with being parentless. Her emotions all seemed to stem from one fateful day.

He turned to a blank page and stared at it, his thoughts slipping back in time. Their parents had decided to go on a road trip through the Colorado mountains. They rented a motorhome and invited their three adult children.

All had good reasons to decline, so they gave their parents a big sendoff. After all, it was their dream vacation, their first since reaching retirement age, and probably the biggest of their married lives. They laughed and smiled and held hands as they climbed into the motorhome. Phillips was happy for them.

A few days later, his older sister, Jen, called him before class. She delivered the news of the crash and their parents' deaths with a flat, matter-of-fact voice that betrayed no emotion.

Alyse, fresh out of high school, sobbed and screamed and threw anything within reach. The doctor prescribed Valium and supervision. Jen took her in. Somehow, the three of them managed to make it through those dark days, arranging the funeral and burial, the sale of their childhood home. Things hadn't been the same, though. Grief created a distance they hadn't been able to overcome.

Phillips found regrets easily. His excuse for not going

on the trip was two summer classes. He justified it by saying his parents had been raising kids since about a year after they married. They deserved time by themselves, a chance to get to know each other again, a chance to accept becoming empty nesters.

He should have skipped summer school and gone with them, helped his dad with the driving, medicated his way through the mountains. They'd be alive. It was his fault. Jen and Alyse never said it, had even denied it, but he knew.

Losing Bruno, a big, slobbery Great Dane of a lap dog, had been equally difficult. His dad would have laughed but agreed. His dad believed pets were simply kids we couldn't understand very well. He said many times that pet owners who claimed to be childless were delusional.

Dad never met a pet he didn't love as long as he wasn't the caretaker. He said after raising two daughters and putting up with a son, he was intent on being selfish and could not be a pet owner ever again.

Bruno had proved to be a comfort during Phillips' wandering years, his return to college, his security guard work, and his employment with Lino Lakes Police Force. Unfortunately, Bruno succumbed to organ failure at the ripe old age of eight.

At the memory of the dog, Phillips pulled his eyes from the blank page and glanced over to the corner of the living room, where the dog's oversized bed lay empty and unused. A ball and a well-chewed stuffed bear, minus most of the stuffing, lay beside it.

Bruno had died before Phillips had moved into the condo, but the dog's belongings made the move and took their places in the new home. Phillips clung to Bruno's memory as much as he held on to the loss of his parents.

B. B. King's *The Thrill is Gone* was playing when Phillips closed his notebook and looked at the wall clock. Over an hour had passed since he had left Porter's. He wondered where he might find Katrina Malloy. He wondered if Russ Malloy could sleep knowing, or not knowing, what he had gotten his sister involved in. Maybe that's why the man had ordered shots.

He crossed the living room and peered out the rear window. The view was supposed to match the view from the roof. It looked onto a ground floor patio with furniture and planters stacked in the corner for the winter. Lake Street, a busy main thoroughfare, was beyond the patio.

Minneapolis never slept. Phillips stared at the passing cars and wondered what the chief had told his training officer or the precinct sergeant about their newest rookie being snatched away for an undisclosed project. And how many years he would have to be a Minneapolis cop before he was no longer considered a rookie.

His training officer, Eric Waldron, was a seasoned veteran and decent guy who'd trained many cops. Partner shuffling always occurred. However, Phillips hoped when this undercover stint ended, and he had rescued Katrina from whatever shithole she had fallen into, Chief Dalestrom would be true to her word and partner him with Waldron again for at least a while longer.

The CD ended, and the condo fell into a deathly silence. "Everyone in the world is asleep except me," he muttered. Where was Katrina? What was she doing? Screwing? Sleeping, he hoped. He remembered how good she felt in his arms, their hugs of greeting, comfort, and goodbye. How they touched each other despite never dating.

Phillips had pushed her away the one time she held him for too long, had brushed her lips against his cheek. So, she shoved him away in return. It was the wrong time for a serious relationship. They both knew it. Not while he was grieving.

Phillips had thrown himself into graduating from the academy. He worked security gigs and channeled his energy into running. He lived day to day. Being single and dateless remained his fault.

He stretched out on his queen-sized bed and glanced at his phone one last time. Jen had texted.

**Call me.**

*Tomorrow*, he thought. He set the phone on the nightstand and tossed and turned until he fell into a deep sleep.

After what felt like minutes, he woke, covered in sweat. He bolted upright and shook his head, trying to clear the terrifying images.

His dream had revolved around Katrina. She appeared high above him, waving her arms out an open window of an old, rundown building. He stood below her in the dark parking lot. Russ Malloy appeared, standing beside him.

Malloy motioned toward the building. “Go on. She asked for you. Move your ass. Save her.”

Wearing only boxers, Phillips raced across the parking lot in his bare feet. Debris, glass shards, and broken concrete littered the ground. The building’s front door hung on one hinge, its doorknob missing. He pushed through the heavy door as it groaned and screamed in resistance. His feet felt like bricks as he ran to a winding staircase and climbed upward in slow motion.

Several floors above, Katrina peered over the railing. “Wes…” She was so far, looked so small being so high up, yet her voice cried in his ear.

After taking each step, the one below him disappeared. Phillips’ heart pounded. His mouth grew dry. He gripped the railing, his knuckles white, his breathing labored, and looked back at nothing. He forced his body to move. The only way was up.

He reached the top step. Katrina stood within reach. He extended his shaky hand to hers. “It’s okay,” he panted. “I’m here.”

The step he stood on fell away. He fell with it. Plummeting downward, he pumped the air with his arms and legs. Katrina grew smaller and smaller above him, her eyes wide with fear. Before Phillips hit the ground, Katrina’s face morphed into the face of the teenager from Lino Lakes.

# CHAPTER NINE

The girl curled up in a ball near the end of the bed. Zip ties encircled her wrists, and duct tape covered her mouth. Her hair hung in snarls around her face. The room smelled of sex and sweat. The old man noted blood on the fitted sheet, whistling from the bathroom, and Jo-Jo's smile when he emerged half-dressed. The old man gritted his teeth and threw the sheet over the girl's naked, shivering body, avoiding the accusation in her eyes.

"Back so soon?" Jo-Jo asked. "I was about to start the second course."

"Right. I'd say you already had your fill and then some. It looks like this one was a virgin, too."

"Yeah, so?"

"So, you screwed up. You know what the boss says about virgins. They're top dollar. You're not supposed to spoil the high-value goods."

"What? Am I supposed to ask for her sexual history first?"

"It's the rules," the old man returned. "And besides, you probably should. You never know what you'll catch."

Jo-Jo yanked his shirt over his head and tucked it into his jeans. "Blah, blah, blah." He thrust his arms into his jacket. "What the boss don't know won't hurt him."

"No, but if he finds out, he might hurt you."

"Wow, Priest Man. I almost think you care."

"I do. I care for everyone."

Jo-Jo stared hard into the old man's eyes. He could see it there. The man was sincere. "You know, you could have your fill, too, if you dropped your guard and your pants once in a while." He leaned over the bed and gave the girl a swat on the ass. "What do you think, little girl? Wanna do it with a man of God?" He laughed and swatted her again. "I bet he could take you for one helluva holy ride." He laughed harder. "Or you could take him."

The old man stepped forward and put out his hand. "Enough. You don't want to piss off the boss, do you? Show up late? He's expecting you, isn't he?"

Jo-Jo's eyes darted to the clock on the nightstand. "Fuck." He checked his pockets like he was searching for his keys or phone. "Next time, Priest Man, I'll let you have dessert.

On me."

"Sure," the old man muttered. "Sure."

Jo-Jo found what he was looking for in his jacket pocket. He pulled out a plain white letter-sized security envelope and dropped it on the corner of the bed. "Here's your finder's fee."

The old man picked it up, peered inside, and thumbed through the bills. "Don't forget to stop at the front desk."

"Don't worry, Priest Man. I already gave that asshole his cut." Jo-Jo picked up one of the pillows and shook it out of its case. "If it was up to me, that greedy little bastard wouldn't get shit."

Jo-Jo pulled the girl into a sitting position, and her eyes widened. He thrust the pillowcase over her head. She tried to scream through the duct tape. She swung her secured arms like a bat and tried to kick. He pushed her back down and wrapped her like a mummy in the sheet, then scooped her up and tossed her over his shoulder.

"Relax, little girl. We're going for a short trip." He started for the door, and she tried to flop away from him. "Keep it up, honey, and I'll knock you upside the noggin."

Jo-Jo and the girl disappeared toward the back hotel

entrance. The old man closed the door and picked up the phone. He pressed zero. “Yes, I need someone to come to Room 220 and do a little housekeeping.”

# CHAPTER TEN

The hotel's back parking lot appeared deader than normal for a Friday night. A few rusted cars sat covered in newly fallen snow. The smell of tacos from the late-night fast-food joint across the street filled Jo-Jo's nostrils. After burning off all that energy, he could go for a couple of Supremes, heavy on the hot sauce. But time was ticking.

He looked at the lone security camera and gave a thumbs-up with his free hand. The night clerk would be eying his exit, making sure Jo-Jo removed the new inventory before his shift ended. The clerk probably wished he could enjoy a sample, too. *Disgusting little prick.* He'd never be allowed near any of the girls. Too bad they had to fork over a cut to the guy to keep his yap shut.

Jo-Jo dug out his keys, unlocked the Cadillac Escalade's liftgate, and dumped the squirming girl inside the cargo area. "Relax. You'll be nice and comfy back here." He threw a heavy blanket over her and closed the gate.

He stomped a path with his heavy boots to the driver's door, sending up little clouds of flakes. "Fuckin' snow," he muttered. "Who chooses to live in an arctic wasteland?" He brushed the fresh flakes off the driver's window, wishing he had thought to wear gloves, then opened the door a crack and gave it a slam, knocking any remaining flakes to the ground.

He pulled the door open again and climbed behind the wheel. After cranking the engine and watching the windshield wipers clean a swath in the flakes, he decided he could see enough. The wind from driving would clear the rest. "To Grandmother's house, we go."

After twenty minutes of slipping and sliding on Interstate 94 and through downtown St. Paul, he pulled into the long, circular driveway of a massive three-story brick home on Summit Avenue, not far from the governor's mansion. Despite the late hour, lights flooded every level of the house. It was party time.

He eased the SUV past several Audis, Volvos, a four-wheel drive Lexus, and three stretch limousines. He shifted into park beneath a large brick archway that loomed over the front entrance.

The double doors to the house swung open, and a doorman hurried to open Jo-Jo's door. "Evening, sir."

Jo-Jo nodded. "Evening, Eduardo." He climbed out of the SUV, stretched his back, then opened the liftgate and scooped up the wriggling bundle.

Eduardo clasped his hands. “Another recruit. How delightful. The boss will be pleased.”

“Yep, he will. I’ll need the usual confirmation of delivery.”

“Of course, sir.”

The two men entered the foyer. A large chandelier, recently shipped from India, twinkled down upon them. Jo-Jo stood on the thick red carpet, the snow from his boots soaking into the thirsty material. Loud, bluesy music played in an adjoining room.

Eduardo cleared his throat. “Shall I take your coat, sir?”

“Naw, I ain’t staying.” Jo-Jo shifted the bundle on his shoulder and looked around. “Doc here?”

“Ah, yes, sir. He’s entertaining a client in the Burgundy Room.”

The girl on Jo-Jo’s shoulder kneed him hard in the chest. Caught off guard, he stumbled to his side and knocked his hip against a glass entry table. A vase filled with an assortment of brightly colored tulips rocked precariously. Eduardo caught it and steadied it. Jo-Jo swatted the girl through the sheets. “Damn it, bitch! Hold still.” He spun slightly and banged her head against the wall. It elicited a muffled groan, and he chuckled.

Jo-Jo leaned over the entry table and scanned the guest registry book. “Looks like a full house.”

Eduardo beamed. “It’s been a pleasant evening, sir.”

Jo-Jo winked. “For me, too.” He swatted the girl again. “Now, help me get this package downstairs. And don’t forget my receipt.”

“Of course, sir.” Eduardo set the book behind the desk counter and led the way down a narrow hall, snaking around to the back of the house. He stopped in front of a door near the servants’ kitchen.

The smell of grilled chicken wafted around them. Jo-Jo’s mouth watered. God, he was hungry.

Eduardo grabbed the key ring on his belted waist and unlocked the steel door to the basement.

# CHAPTER ELEVEN

The girl had lost track of time. Jo-Jo, or the big baboon, as she referred to him in her mind, rolled her out of the sheet and onto a narrow cot. He pulled the pillowcase off her head, tossed it on the floor, and reached for her. She tried to back away, but he grabbed the Zip ties and jerked her forward.

He pulled out a pocketknife and cut the ties. Another man, who she guessed was Eduardo, tried to pull off the duct tape from her mouth. His hands were gentler, but not much. After a few fumbles, she squirmed backward and pulled it off herself.

The smell of urine and mildew assaulted her nose. She shivered in the cool, damp basement air. Her gaze darted around and processed what appeared to be a six-by-eight-foot cell with two cots. She sat on one. Somebody who lay still, facing the other way, occupied the other.

She pulled the hotel sheet over herself, tried to move even farther from the two men, and shouted every swear word in her internal dictionary. Jo-Jo laughed, Eduardo ignored her, and they stepped from the cell, clanging the metal door shut behind them before they climbed the stairs.

A female voice from the other bed announced, "You can holler all you want. It won't do you no good." The woman rolled over. She was thin, dark-skinned, and looked old and tired. She was probably only a few years older than the girl. The woman sat up, pushed her back against the wall, and crossed her legs. "They ain't coming back to set you free."

The girl jumped up and slammed her body against the cell door. She shook the bars and pried at the lock, scraping with her fingers until they bled. "Get me the fuck out of here! Let me out *now*!"

She screamed until her voice turned hoarse, and tears took over. She wrapped the sheet tighter. "Let me go," she whimpered, pressing her face to the bars. Finally, she shuffled back to the bed, flopped down, and buried her face in the worn mattress. Her body shook as she cried.

"The first night's never easy, honey. I seen lots of first nights," the woman stated. "You'll find out this place ain't so bad, though. Not as bad as it could be. Hell, at least we got a bed and warm food. And a roof over our heads." She chuckled. "No more scrounging the streets, right?"

She paused and looked closer at the girl. "Shit, how old are you anyway?" The woman climbed off her cot and sat beside the girl. "Come on, honey, talk to me. We can be friends, you know. It's good to have a friend here." She set her hand on the trembling girl's shoulder. "I'm Jasmine. Everybody calls me Jazz." She tugged lightly. "Come on, sit up, girl. Come here, now. Let me hold you."

The girl rolled over and slowly sat up.

Jazz hugged her for a long moment. "I know, honey. I know. If you want, you can tell me all about it, what brought you here. Hell, we all have a story, ain't that right? One helluva sad, sorry story." She ended the embrace and gestured around the room. "This here is just another chapter." She lifted the girl's chin with her index finger, and they locked eyes. "That don't mean it ain't gonna have a happy ending. Hell, no. I've been working on that since they threw my fine ass in here."

"Who's they?" the girl whispered.

Jazz smiled and laughed. "Girl, I knew you'd talk to me. I'll tell you, but first, tell me your name."

The girl drew a deep breath. "Savannah." She looked around. "I'm only thirteen."

"Woo-hoo, girl, that is young. But hell, you ain't the youngest here. I shouldn't be surprised none. Those bastards like their babies. Shit, I turned sixteen last March. I guess that makes me an old lady."

Jazz stood and crouched by her cot. She fumbled for something beneath the mattress and pulled out an oversized tee shirt with the words *Be Happy* across the front. "Here, honey." She tossed it to Savannah, then reached under the mattress again and produced a pair of socks. "Get yourself comfy, and I'll tell you my story."

Jazz sat on the edge of her cot and inhaled deeply. "He said he loved me. Fool that I was, I believed him." She smiled almost wistfully. "He wined and dined me, took me dancing. He bought me this slinky cocktail dress, told me I was beautiful. And I was." Her expression turned cold. "One night, he says he's gonna introduce me to some friends. He brings me here. Next thing I know, he's long gone, and I'm a prisoner." She wiped a tear. "You could say I'm a prisoner of love."

Savannah leaned forward, eyes wide.

Jazz waved her hands around. "All this, it's like a giant, three-ring circus. We're caged like animals and taken out to perform on cue." She stood and began to pace. "They make it real clear if you don't do what they want, you'll get hurt. So, you do it. They parade you around, tell you to do a little dance."

"And after your act," Jazz continued, "the head honcho, Mr. Reynolds, auctions you off to some rich, high-class bastard in the audience. Highest bidder pays for a private performance on one of the upper levels. If you're lucky enough to get out of performing for the crowd, they drag you up to a private room anyway."

Jazz raised her hands and drew a set of quotation marks. "They call it a 'scheduled appointment with a special guest.' There is no way to go untouched." She laughed bitterly. "I tell you, I was one helluva naïve person before I ended up here. Didn't know nothing 'bout nothing. Shit, I had only kissed one guy, hadn't fucked him or anyone else. Just pretended I had to all my friends."

She looked down. "I sure wasn't looking for trouble, either. It came up, disguised as a prince, and sold me out." She glanced at several sheets of paper, mostly sketches, taped to the wall above her bed and pointed to one with numbers. "Nine months, one week, and four days."

Savannah gasped, her eyes filling with tears. "You've been here that long?"

"That ain't nothing. Dee-Dee's been here over a year." Jazz held her cupped hands in front of her chest. "Old Double Ds is what I call her behind her back." She dropped her hands and frowned. "The other girls say she's gotta be legal age by now. Only reason they keep her around is because she don't look it. Hell, she acts like this place is all fun and games. Like she's something real special.

"Stay away from her, is all I can say. Rumor has it the last girl who got too uppity for the house tried to strike some side deals with the customers. She was disposed of per Mr. Reynolds' orders. Dee-Dee's the one who ratted on her and told him about the deals."

Savannah shook her head. "I can't believe...I just...I've got to get out of here. There's got to be a way out." She jumped off the cot and rattled the barred door again.

Jazz leaped after her and grabbed her arms. "You don't want them coming back down here. Believe me. It's nighttime, it's show time. You cause a stir, and they'll haul your ass up there and start in on you early. You don't want that, now, do you?"

Savannah slumped against her, tears flowing freely. They sat back on Jazz's cot.

"You gotta learn not to cause any problems, no matter what they do," Jazz continued. "It don't take long before they know everything about you. They can make a lot of trouble for you, your family. They know where I used to live, that my little sister... Well, it'd be so easy for them to..." Her voice caught in her throat. "Anyway, the shit that goes on upstairs is what puts food in your mouth, keeps you off the street, keeps your family safe."

Jazz cupped Savannah's chin. "Girl, I know it's hard to understand. It's hard on everyone, 'specially in the beginning. But I'll tell you, when they come and haul you off to one of those rooms, it goes better if you don't fight whatever the hell it is they have in mind. And if a paying customer gets too rough, well, that's what Doc's for. Don't get me wrong, he can be as bad as any of 'em, but at least he threads a clean needle."

Savannah's body shook. She pulled her head away and covered her face with her hands.

"Shit, girl, I don't mean to keep making you cry. You just gotta hear it like it is. Get it straight in your head. The quicker, the better."

The door to the basement creaked open and slammed shut. Light footsteps sounded down the stairs. "That'll be Double Ds," Jazz whispered.

A tall, curvy figure with shoulder-length kinky black hair and heavy eye makeup appeared. She wore leather and lace in a combination that suggested dominatrix chorus girl. She sashayed in front of their cell and paused when she saw Savannah.

"Well," she purred. "I thought I smelled fresh kitty." She smiled and ran her fingertips along the bars. Her eyes bored into Savannah's. "Mmm, mmm, good. Just remember, little bitch, I'm the top feline here." She strutted off to a one-cot cell with an orange shag rug, a lava lamp, and the cell door propped open.

"She earned those privileges," Jazz declared. "The hard way."

# CHAPTER TWELVE

The rusty Ford Taurus reeked of greasy fried food and sweat. Wes Phillips had been introduced to two members of the task force and greeted with disinterested grunts.

Bruce Ellison sat behind the wheel, staring at a game on his cell phone, his fingers tapping furiously. When his fingers paused, his chin would lift as if he were looking out of the car. Dan Larkin sat in the passenger side front seat, a crossword puzzle from the Star Tribune in his lap. Phillips and Russ Malloy occupied the back.

They had avoided the early morning rush hour by weaving their way through the back streets to the location of the stakeout. They now watched a tall, skinny white male step out onto the front steps of a two-story house in St. Paul and sit down. The man wore an open Minnesota Gophers basketball jacket with a gold sweatshirt underneath, its hood pulled over his head. His hands remained stuffed in his pockets, and both knees bounced. Clouds of breath hovered around his head.

"That's Christoph Morton," Larkin remarked. "He spends a lot of time with Damian Reynolds."

Ellison slapped his phone against his thigh. “Shit. Died again.” He sighed and turned toward the back seat. “Old Damian is pretty sly. He doesn’t actually do anything himself.”

“At least, not that we can prove,” Larkin chimed in.

“Morton moves the drugs,” Ellison explained. “Either doing it for Reynolds, or they’re just best buddies.” He shook his head. “We don’t even know if either one uses.”

Larkin nodded and tapped his pen against his chin. He looked back down at the puzzle. “Morton talks to Reynolds a few times every day. Random times, no pattern in the calls.”

“How do you know?” Phillips asked.

Larkin and Ellison looked at each other. “We’ve been checking Morton’s phone logs,” Ellison revealed.

Phillips raised his eyebrows. “You have a warrant for that?”

Ellison made a slight head nod.

“Why don’t you get one for Reynolds, too?” Phillips suggested.

Larkin stared at Phillips. “Sometimes, it’s better not to ask too many questions.”

Ellison cleared his throat. “We’ve had a warrant for

Morton's phone for a while. We haven't been able to get one for Reynolds. The judge says our evidence is too thin."

"Is it?" Phillips asked.

"Not in our opinion," Ellison replied.

Larkin continued. "Anyway, a few minutes after they talk, Morton is on the road. He drives around town, stops often, goes into a couple of buildings, and comes out with grocery bags or small boxes. He drives to different buildings, carries said packages inside, and comes out empty-handed."

"None of the stops are more than a few minutes," Ellison explained.

"Have you talked to the people inside the buildings, the ones who receive the packages?" Phillips asked.

"Interesting suggestion," Larkin muttered sarcastically. "We've tried. We've gone in and found them empty."

"So, we resorted to thermal imaging," Ellison added. "We hoped we could see who he meets and how they leave."

Larkin scribbled a word on his puzzle. "All that does is prove no one is in the buildings when Morton stops by."

Phillips shifted in his seat. "The packages he carries in, can't you find them?"

Ellison and Larkin looked at each other again. “Man, we should have thought of that.” Ellison jerked his thumb at Phillips. “This newbie’s got smarts.”

Larkin made a noise. “Whatever the hell he carries in is either incredibly well-hidden or teleported to another location or dimension in time.”

Phillips shook off the sarcasm. “Who owns the buildings?”

“They’re all owned by a company we’ve managed to trace back to Reynolds or his family,” Larkin replied.

“Six layers removed,” Ellison added.

Phillips glanced back at Morton, the man’s knees still bouncing. “His family’s in the business, too?”

“Nah, they’re only another front.” Ellison tapped on his phone and started a new game. “As far as we can tell, they don’t have a clue what he’s really up to.”

“Then again, neither do we.” Larkin’s brow furrowed, and he leaned forward to scribble in another row of boxes. “We keep playing by the rules, at least as much as we have to, and they keep skirting the law. And we can’t prove a fucking thing.”

“Hopefully, when you get into the inner circle, you’ll be

able to provide us with a few insights," Ellison stated.

"Or enough evidence so we can finally get a warrant and actually look at things." Larkin jotted down another word. "All this waiting and wondering is killing me."

Malloy blew out a long breath. "Let's hope that's the worst it gets."

They sat in silence until Ellison pounded his fist on the armrest. Everyone jumped. "Damn it," Ellison growled at the screen of his phone. "Motherfucker got me again."

Phillips' phone chirped with a text.

**We need to talk.**

*Shit.* He'd forgotten to call Jen. She rarely called. He wondered what was so important.

Malloy glanced over. "You're undercover, remember? Leave your life behind. Wes Phillips no longer exists."

Phillips silenced the phone and slid it back into his pocket. "I know. Sorry."

Ellison cranked the engine. "Heads up. Our boy is on the move."

# CHAPTER THIRTEEN

Wes Phillips and Russ Malloy spent the rest of the morning riding in the back seat of the Taurus, accompanying Bruce Ellison and Dan Larkin as they followed Christoph Morton from one pick-up and drop-off site to another. Around noon, Morton returned to his home, and Phillips and Malloy climbed back into their own car.

Despite the bright sunshine, the air was chilly. Malloy cranked up the heat. "You wanna get burgers?"

"Sure."

"After inhaling the stink of old sandwich wrappers all morning, I'm craving a bunch of sliders," Malloy announced.

"You don't say."

"What? Your stomach can't handle it?"

"It's fine," Phillips replied.

They pulled into a White Castle drive-thru and paid for a ten-pack and two large Cokes. Phillips wrapped his hands around the warm bag in his lap. "At least they're good for something."

Malloy looked at him, then the bag, and gave a humorless "Ha."

They drove to a two-story brick building on Cedar Avenue north of Hiawatha Parkway, circled the block, and parked in back. With the engine running and the heat now set on low, they downed their food.

"What's with this place?" Phillips stuffed the last of the empty slider boxes into the bag and crumpled it.

Malloy reached for the door handle. "You'll see."

"Give me a sec." Phillips pulled out his phone and tapped a response to Jen's last text.

**Can't talk now. On assignment.**

He shoved it back into his pocket.

Malloy led him along the side of the two-story building to the front sidewalk. It ran tight against the brick façade. Plate glass display windows flanked the entrance. A cat sat in one, watching but obviously not caring, the way only a cat could. A display of action figures and models filled the other. They went in the front door, and Phillips found himself in a tightly packed and busy comic book and role-playing-game store.

Phillips followed Malloy through the musty-smelling

store, past a clerk who ignored them and a parrot who didn't. "Tell me a tale, Cap'n," it squawked. Phillips spun around and stared. The parrot stared back. Phillips turned to follow Malloy, and the parrot called after him. "You gonna pay for that? This ain't no library."

Phillips jerked his thumb at the parrot. "Who trained the bird?"

Malloy gave a half-smile. "I think it's watched too much TV."

They pushed open a warped door and started up a narrow flight of stairs. It creaked as if every board wanted to crack. The stairwell was well-lit by an ascending row of windows that looked out over the neighborhood.

Phillips' heart raced. "How long did you say we were going to hang out in here?"

Malloy paused on the third step and looked down at Phillips. "I didn't say. Why?"

"Nothing, sir." Phillips wiped sweat off his forehead. "Nothing I can't handle."

"You look like shit. Did the burgers do you in? You gonna puke?"

"Just a minimal case of vertical apprehension."

Malloy shook his head and laughed. “Well, fuck me. That’s a new one for a hotshot officer of the law. Looking at you, though, I’m not sure how minimal it is.” He continued up the stairs. “I’ll try in the future to keep you on solid ground.”

At the top, another door opened to a large room with a couch and TV. The far wall contained two doors. One hung open and revealed boxes of books. Malloy strode over to the other door, rapped twice, and turned the knob. Three members of the task force waited behind it.

Eric Martinez rose and greeted Phillips with a handshake. “Good to see you again.”

The closest agent rose. He stood about six-foot-four, his frame half as wide as Martinez’s. “This is Curtis Blair with the ATF,” Malloy announced. Blair shook hands with Phillips, his large, dark hand swallowing Phillips’ smaller, pale one, and sat back down.

“Nice to meet you,” Phillips stated.

“And you’ve met Robert McNellis,” Malloy continued. McNellis remained seated and raised a glass of amber-colored liquid.

“I have,” Phillips replied. “I’m looking forward to what you all can teach me.”

"Pfft. Won't be much," McNellis grumbled. "We've been doing this too long to know anything." Phillips wondered how much the man drank and how often.

"I hope you realize what you've gotten yourself into." Blair's medium tenor voice floated out and hung in the air. "Your life expectancy decreased substantially by joining our little task force."

Phillips stared at him. "Please enlighten me, sir. Let me know what I've gotten into."

"First off, you can drop the *sir* bullshit," McNellis told him. "There's no ass-kissing in here. Right, Agent Blair?"

"Yes, sir," Blair replied.

The men laughed.

"Want a drink?" McNellis tapped his glass. "Makes the bad news easier to accept."

Martinez narrowed his eyes at McNellis' glass.

Phillips shook his head. "No, I'm good."

Blair shifted in his seat. "Truth is, you're not the first person we've tried sending in."

Martinez nodded. "All our agencies have tried at one time or another."

"The last guy was one of mine, ATF," Blair explained. "Great kid. Would've been an excellent agent. He went undercover as a grad student. At the end of October, he got close. Next thing we know, he's dead.

"Official cause of death was exposure to the elements. Went to a party, drank too much, had a few recreational chemicals, and wandered off in the cold without a jacket. Even took a dip in a swamp. We found him a few days later, half-frozen in a ditch."

"Damn," Phillips grumbled. "That sucks."

"It gets worse," Blair continued. "Unofficially, he was only half as drunk as the published report said. He had Rohypnol in his system."

"He was roofied and dumped in the cold?" Phillips asked.

"It appears that way," Blair replied. "Officially, it looks like he wasn't undercover, and it was only a tragic accident."

"The reason we're intent on getting in close is someone has moved weapons into the area," Martinez explained. "AK47s, Uzis, all kinds of automatic firepower."

"Plus, a rumor about shoulder-fired surface-to-air missiles," McNellis added. "'Our continual failure to get close and bring closure to this case may result in a catastrophic attack and a public relations nightmare for the department. At least that's what the boss keeps screaming in my ear."

He emptied his glass and licked his lips. "The bad thing about this assignment is if we're successful, no one will ever hear about what we did. If we fail, our heads will be on public display, and our bodies will never be found. It's enough to make a person drink. And I think I will."

Martinez frowned. "Don't you think you should cut down?"

McNellis grabbed a half-empty bottle of Glen Moray off the shelf behind him and refilled his glass. "Probably, but what'll that accomplish? At least when I drink, I fully appreciate the sacrifices of people we've sent to their deaths." He held his glass high. "Here's to you, Phillips. Try not to be next."

# CHAPTER FOURTEEN

The morning floated in dark and thick with clouds. Snow was forecast, with a possible winter weather advisory. Wes Phillips shuddered from the ominous chill as he worked through his Twelve Step Program on the condo roof. The wind's bite tried to pull away a breath before it could be drawn in. He cut his morning jog short. Russ Malloy would be picking him up at seven. Phillips suspected his new boss was the punctual type.

After a quick shower and a breakfast of champions, he stood in the main foyer of the condo complex. He called Jen while he waited. Voicemail picked up, and he listened for the beep. "Hey, Jen. I'm gonna be off the radar for a while. I'll try to give you a shout this weekend." He paused. "I hope everything's okay."

Moments later, a five-year-old Lincoln Continental with a Hawaii license plate pulled up. Malloy climbed out and nodded to Phillips. "You drive."

At Malloy's direction, Phillips steered the car from the Uptown neighborhood of South Minneapolis toward downtown, avoiding the occasional bicyclist who veered into his lane. Rain, snow, and extreme temperatures did not deter Midwest adventurists who rode two wheels year-round. Phillips was not one of them. He didn't trust people in cars enough to share slick surfaces.

They turned near the Walker Art Center and into the Kenwood neighborhood that overlooked the city. Malloy pointed to the left. "There."

Phillips slowed and turned into the freshly plowed driveway of a huge house on Kenwood Parkway.

"Did I tell you you're moving?" Malloy asked.

"I am?"

"Yep, this is yours."

Phillips looked around. "What's mine?"

"The car, the house. Well, not the house, but the carriage house." Malloy pressed a button on the garage door remote that sat in the cup holder between them. Phillips pulled in and killed the engine. Malloy closed the door behind them.

The garage boasted three stalls, the other two empty. Sheetrocked and painted walls with grated, security-sensored windows surrounded an immaculate textured and sealed concrete floor.

They left the car, climbed a flight of stairs, pushed open

the door to a mud room and another door to a large living area. Through open curtains, Phillips could see the main house. It eclipsed the carriage house but did not block the elevated view of the city. "Is it okay if I sleep in the car?"

Malloy stared at him for a long second, then crossed the room and closed the curtains. He turned in time to see Phillips visibly relax and color return to his face. "How have you managed to live this long if you're afraid to even be up two floors?"

"I'm better if I'm distracted or concentrating or can't see how high up I am. But to stand still, high up, and admire the sights…" Phillips shook his head. "Not for me. I know what's below."

The carriage house was approximately twenty-four-by-forty, not much smaller than the Southeast Minneapolis home of his childhood. The main house, what he could see of it, was about four times the size, with a three-story center section. Phillips intended to look at it when he got the chance, but it wouldn't be from the window.

"When someone asks, who owns this place?"

Malloy looked between the drapes, letting a stripe of cloudy light into the room. "Your business associates."

"And when someone digs, who owns this place?"

"A shell corporation within a shell corporation within a conglomerate fronted by a shell corporation."

Phillips smiled and shook his head. "Do you think they'll give up before they find the truth?"

"We sure hope so."

Phillips pulled a small plastic tube from his pocket, opened it, and shook a small yellow tablet into his palm.

Malloy's eyes narrowed. "What's that?"

Phillips headed to the kitchen. "Daddy's little helper when it comes to heights." He laughed. "I know where we are. Curtains only do so much. Especially when you insist on opening them." He filled a glass with water and washed down the pill. "Otherwise, we continue this conversation in the garage, next to my new Continental bedroom."

"Jeez. You ever talk to a shrink?"

Phillips sat on the plush couch and fluffed a throw pillow. "Yeah. That's how I got the prescription. Give me twenty minutes, and I'll be as cool as you."

Malloy laughed. "That'll never happen." He moved to the love seat and sat across from Phillips. "I guess everybody has their secret demons."

Phillips exhaled a long breath and crossed his legs at

the ankles. "Yeah? What's yours, Russ?"

Malloy looked at his hands. He sat silent for a long time and twisted a gold band around his ring finger. "I was married for five years. Our last year together was when my wife was diagnosed with ovarian cancer. She was only thirty-one." He glanced at Phillips. "It was quick."

"I'm sorry. That's tough."

Malloy shifted on the couch and looked back at his ring. "Still can't believe she's gone. I keep thinking she'll walk back through the door someday."

Phillips thought about his mom and dad. The sold home in Southeast he occasionally drove by. He nodded.

"Anyway..." Malloy cleared his throat. "I found out the hard way that I don't do well with loss." He stood and walked to the kitchen. "Like hell will I lose my only sibling next," he said over his shoulder.

Phillips leaned his head against the back of the couch, the anti-anxiety medication loosening his neck and shoulders.

While Malloy rummaged through the fridge, Phillips breathed in and out, deep and steady. His pulse slowed to a normal rate.

Malloy returned with two bottled orange juices and a

box of doughnuts.

"So." Phillips changed the subject. "Tell me about my Lincoln. What's the story with the Hawaii plates?"

Malloy placed the food on the coffee table and sat again. "According to official documents, it's been yours for three years."

"I've lived in Hawaii for the last three years?" Phillips asked.

"No, for the last six, you've lived in Florida." Malloy held the bottle to his lips, took a few hard swallows. "But you've owned a car in Hawaii, so you could drive your own whenever you went there. Which you did a few times a year. Six months ago, you had it shipped over, and you picked it up in San Francisco and drove it here from there."

"Wow, I've been a busy man."

Malloy opened the doughnut box and peered at the selection. "You have, and your bank accounts reflect that. Unfortunately, none of it's real. So be careful." He removed a chocolate frosted cake doughnut with sprinkles, leaned forward, and bit in. "Mmm. I love sugar in the morning." He pointed the doughnut at Phillips' phone. "And get rid of that. This is your base now. Use it wisely."

# CHAPTER FIFTEEN

The old man worshiped the light rail. It whisked him from the Mall of America and the Minneapolis-St. Paul International Airport out through the northern suburbs and all the way to Big Lake. It made hunting easy. After all, what better way to run away than to take a train?

He climbed aboard in the morning and rode to the airport, where he spent a few minutes in Arrivals by the door that led to the parking ramp and the buses and cabs. He hollered out a few, "Welcome to Minneapolis," and "May the Lord bless and keep you," blessings, then rode the escalator to Departures, where he wished people, "Safe travels," and "The Lord travels with you."

He beamed when a young woman stopped, smiled, and replied, "Thank you, brother. He travels with you as well. Have a blessed day."

From the airport, he hopped back on the train for the short ride to the Mall of America, smiling and reading his Bible the whole time. The mall elevator carried him to his starting point on Level Four. The doors slid open and revealed a comedy club, its door closed and lights off. He once spent time in there and had been shocked to hear excessive profanity used in attempts to be funny. Blasphemy was not funny. He shook his head. "Please, Lord, find your way to help the foul-mouthed heathens find theirs."

He strolled the long walkway between Smaaash, the Adrenalin Adventure, and Cantina #1. The walkway widened, and he found himself between Recharge and Hooters. "Please, God, forgive all who patronize and manage this place. Give thoughtful guidance to the unfortunate young women who need to work in such abysmal conditions, akin to Sodom and Gomorra."

The host approached him, arms folded over her tight-fitted T-shirt. "Thanks for thinking of us, but you can't scare away the patrons. It'll only make our jobs and lives worse."

"I shall not be deterred, my child." He stared at the ceiling, waved his arms, and prayed louder.

A few minutes later, a call came from inside the restaurant. "Hey, Padre." He peered through the door. A young woman with long dark hair smiled at him. She yanked up her white uniform shirt and revealed a lacy black bra bulging with oversized breasts. "Bless these."

The place erupted in cheers and whistles.

His mouth dropped open. When he found his voice, he whispered, "Sinner, harlot, temptress." He pointed at her. Louder, he called, "Ruination upon you, Daughter of Satan," and scurried away. He continued past Rick's Last Resort to the escalators. He rode to Level Three and looked back to be certain the Jezebel hadn't followed.

He strode down a hallway that ran past Bubba Gump's Shrimp and behind Nickelodeon Universe to a food court of overpriced chain restaurants. He sat at a table and read from his Bible, flicking his eyes up frequently to people-watch. His target was a teenage girl who looked desperate and alone, on the run, or with a drug habit. A girl to extend a helping hand.

He glanced up and spotted a young black woman with thick natural hair, a round bottom, and wide thighs leading to thin ankles jammed into tight pants. Jo-Jo's favorite type. Her face appeared pleasant, and her top half proportional, although neither mattered to Jo-Jo. He was a butt-and-legs man. If he played his cards right, Jo-Jo would pay him extra on the side.

However, the woman moved fast, her expression confident and aware. A woman on a mission, without time for distraction. He sighed and turned a page.

By noon, the food court had filled with young mothers

pushing strollers of loud small children, whining, crying, and screaming. He closed his Bible. *God may favor the children, but I cannot.* He left his table and wandered into the concourse.

He moved on to Level Two, marveling at the chain stores. The same this, the same that. Was uniqueness no longer a desire? Finally, he arrived at something different. Mystic Lake Casino occupied a storefront. They sold hotel and gambling packages, concert tickets, and gave blackjack lessons.

Customers arrived at the casino ready to lose while they enjoyed their hotel package. The old man stood near the door and whispered a quick blessing for the dealer and the girl selling hotel packages.

He looked down one level and found another unique shop. The official store of the Minnesota Vikings. Two cheerleaders bounced around outside the door, smiling, cheering, and waving shoppers inside. He issued another blessing and headed to Santa Land.

Santa had begun his wheezy ho-ho-hoing last week. The overweight, red-faced man faced a long haul if he wanted to portray jolliness all the way until Christmas. The old man despised the holiday. Beyond the rampant commercialism and greed, holiday pictures always portrayed large, happy families. People with fake smiles and arms around each other.

He glared at the fat man in the red suit. “Forgive me, Lord, for wishing ill upon the liars and deceivers ruining the holiest day of all.”

He rode the escalator back up one level and arrived at the newest enticement, Culinary on North. Nothing special, nothing fancy. Merely another food court with the usual suspects. Mothers with children, old ladies, old men. He walked over to a railing and looked down to stare at the windows of Victoria’s Secret. Each displayed giant pictures of scantily clad supermodels.

He leaned over the railing and raised his hand to issue a blessing when he noticed someone. He stepped back, and his hand fell to his side. “It can’t be. It’s not possible. How did you… How could you…”

The woman passing in front of Victoria’s Secret was a vision from his past. Her hair, a silver mane parted an inch from the center and swept back. Her build featured broad square shoulders, straight back, narrow waist, long legs. Her attire was a long sweater dress with leggings and flip-flops. Suzanna always wore flip-flops, no matter the temperature or season.

He raced after her, separated by one level. When she stopped, he stopped. She led, and he followed almost halfway around the mall.

She stepped into a store. "No. Come back," he cried, his hands sweaty, shaky. He stood looking over the railing and waited. She popped back out. He released a long sigh. "Ah, there you are. Thank you, Lord." She walked on and disappeared from sight. He ran after her, looking over the level's railing. "Wait."

A man wearing a mall security badge stepped in his way. "Can I help you with something, sir?"

The old man tried to slip around him. Time was running out. He'd lose her. Again. "No. I'm fine. Thank you."

The guard raised a hand, blocking his exit. "Are you in a hurry, sir?"

"No… Well, yes. I'm following someone."

"We know."

The old man looked around. Two additional security guards stood close by. The first guard towered over him. "Who are you following?"

The old man pointed past him. "I think I know that lady."

"Know her how?"

"I think she's my wife."

"You *think* she's your wife? But you aren't certain. Sir, are you able to recognize your wife? Are you experiencing memory difficulties?"

"Of course I can recognize my wife," the old man snapped. "That woman's not my wife. My wife's dead. She *reminds* me of my wife, though. I must see her. I must speak to her."

The guard held his hands up. "I think you should leave the lady alone. It's time for you to go."

The old man's eyes widened. "Go? Go where?"

"Anywhere. As long as it's not the Mall of America."

"You're throwing me out?"

"No, I'm asking you to leave for the rest of the day."

The old man glanced around. A crowd of onlookers had gathered nearby. His mind darted away to the downstairs level, the aquarium. After Suzanna's death—his life disrupted, almost destroyed—he relished the times he visited aquariums. Mesmerized by the clear salt water, its brilliant colors of life, and its moving creatures, it proved the closest he came to having his wife back. "But I haven't been to Sea Life yet," he replied in a small voice.

"Please, sir. It's time to go." The other two guards

moved closer. Behind them, two Bloomington police officers approached.

The old man's shoulders sagged. "Of course, you're right. It's time for me to leave. I'll catch the light rail, ride it back into the city. You all have a blessed day." He spun on his heels, gripping his Bible in one hand and a metal cross that dangled around his neck in the other, its sharp edges digging into his palm.

# CHAPTER SIXTEEN

Wes Phillips pushed open the door to the basement bookstore on the corner of East Franklin Avenue and Park Avenue. The hinges squeaked. He entered in a gust of cold evening air and brushed the snow off his shoulders. A morbidly obese man with a round face, thinning black hair, and a bad comb-over glanced up from behind the counter.

Phillips walked across the scuffed wooden floor and rapped the counter once with his knuckles. “Hey, Leo. How’s business?”

“You late.” Leo reached into a half-empty jar of jellybeans next to him and shoved a handful of colors into his mouth. “They’s already started.”

Phillips looked past Leo toward the back room. Through the doorway, he saw a girl, roughly fifteen, hunched over a podium. From where he stood, he could barely make out the murmur of her voice. Her face turned in his direction, her green eyes connecting with his before flickering back to focus on her poem.

Leo shifted his weight on the extra-wide stool. "You got something to read tonight, Sally? Or are you back for shits and giggles?" Leo grinned.

Phillips leaned in close. "Hopefully, just giggles."

"Ha!" Leo stuffed another handful of candy into his mouth. "I don't care what them others say. You're okay in my world, kid."

Phillips slipped into the Reading Room. Twenty pairs of eyes looked him over. A few faces seemed familiar, yet he hadn't attended enough poetry readings to recall names. He took a vacant seat in the back row. An empty chair sat to his left.

Up front, the girl recited in whispers. She clutched a spiral-bound journal, eyes downcast.

"...his hand—an act of God...

"Made me want to die...

"No. Live..."

Phillips shrugged off his heavy coat and pulled a black knit cap off his head. He kneaded it between his hands while watching the girl. Her dark bangs hung in her eyes. The rest of her unwashed hair ended in a crop cut slightly below her shoulders. She wore layers, a tank top beneath a tight, threadbare T-shirt, a ratty gray unzipped hoodie. She had draped an army green down coat with a faux fur-lined hood over one arm.

"He said it was for my own good..."

The girl shifted her body slightly to the side of the podium. One leg peeked out, and Phillips noted her practically painted-on skinny jeans had holes in the knees and thighs. But that was the style. She wore scuffed black combat boots laced ankle-high. A well-worn, over-stuffed canvas bag with military patches and insignia was dumped on the floor next to her foot.

She was the same girl he remembered from other readings. The lost look, the meek voice, the quick show-and-go. He tried to recall her name. Jill? Joan? The girl's blackened right eye from last time had faded to a barely visible yellow-green. A fresh bruise on the left side of her jaw made up for it.

"That last push..."

A woman in the front row wiped her eyes. Others leaned forward; their heads tilted. Phillips strained to listen, and his phone chirped on his waist. "Damn it," he muttered, reaching to silence it.

The woman in front of him turned and hissed, "Cell phones off!"

"Sorry," he whispered.

The girl paused and found her voice.

"And out the door I flew...

"So high. My first high..."

Phillips had started visiting the bookstore after accepting the job on the Minneapolis force. He carried a folded, scribbled-on paper in his pocket to the readings but never read his musings out loud. He preferred to spectate, eavesdrop, learn the craft without taking the risk. He cringed, thinking what the guys at the station would say, given ammunition.

*Jane!* That was it. Phillips overheard someone ask the girl's name last time. She'd hesitated long enough for Phillips to know whatever name she offered would be a blatant lie. Jane, he thought. Little Miss Doe. How convenient.

Polite applause followed. Without glancing up, Jane shuffled down the rows of chairs and took the seat next to Phillips. She dumped the bag and jacket on the floor, then curled up in the chair, knees to chest. She wrapped her arms around her legs and rocked back and forth.

The woman in front of Jane turned and smiled. "Nice job, dear. But so tragic. Awful. Perhaps you might want to try a rhyming poem about something, say, a bit more pleasant. Maybe school or prom or a favorite pet." She reached out to pat Jane's hand, but the girl flinched and shrank back. "Hmph." The woman withdrew her hand and turned toward her neighbor. "I guess some people just aren't open to constructive criticism."

The other woman nodded. Jane uttered something unintelligible under her breath.

A heavyset man in the second row heaved himself from his seat and waddled up to the podium. His bald head shined beneath the ceiling lights, and he withdrew a large handkerchief from his front pocket and wiped his sweaty brow. He cleared his throat.

"I, uh, I, uh…would like to read from, uh…" The man coughed and cleared his throat again. He held up a thick book and pointed to the cover. "One of my, uh, favorite poets."

The man continued with his public struggle. Phillips enjoyed Frost, yet he winced hearing the poet's life work slaughtered. He glanced at Jane. She stared at the hole in her right knee, picking at the white frays around it. The clock on the wall pointed to eight P.M. In a few minutes, Leo would stick his greasy head in the door and grunt at everyone to wrap up. "I don't sleeps here, ya know," he liked to say.

Phillips' mind drifted. He wondered if Jane had a place to stay. A safe place. It looked like she carried all her belongings in her bag. He didn't want to pry, come across as some kind of creep, but he knew enough in his line of work that runaway Jane Does had no safe place. Even a shelter held danger. He thought of the bed back at the carriage house, the stocked refrigerator, the warm shower, and clean towels.

He reached into his pocket and pulled out a blank sheet of paper to jot down phrases that would or would not live to become a poem. Many of his scribbles ended up in the trash. A proper burial. He chuckled out loud, and the woman in front of him turned and gave him the stink eye. Mr. Baldy wasn't done with his butchering job.

Phillips thought of all the unsafe Jane Does. And Katrina. The underworld breathed foul breath into every city. Even small towns. He gripped his pen, tuning out all sounds in the room. He wrote a furious path across the sheet. The words, the lines kept coming...

***

"Hey! Alice!" Leo's fat hand waved in front of his face. "Wake up! Tea party's over."

Phillips looked around. Most of the others were heading to the door. A couple of gray-haired women with bright-colored scarves stood in the corner, pulling on long woolen coats and gabbing about the cold weather. Jane's chair was empty. He stuffed the paper in his pocket and slipped on his coat.

Leo reached for Phillips' chair, revealing large armpit stains on his shirt. "This place don't lock itself up."

"I can help." Phillips folded the chair and handed it to Leo.

Leo leaned the chair against the wall and grabbed another. "Naw," he grunted, breathing hard. "Doc says I need exercise. This is my exercise. All you artsy-fartsy people need to clear my workout room. I gotta make enough space on the floor for the heart attack that rich bum keeps threatening me with."

Phillips laughed. "All righty, then. Take it slow."

"Slow, schmo," Leo replied. "I've got a antsy female waiting for me back at the *el rancho*."

"Oh, yeah? Wife or girlfriend?"

"Neither, thank God. Lolita is my four-legged feline. She hates it when I'm late for dinner. Her dinner, that is."

Phillips stepped out into a heavy snowfall and remembered the disruptive call during the reading. He pulled out his phone and shuffled his feet through the slushy sidewalk, head down, tapping at the screen. He stared at a text from Jen.

**This is important!**

She answered on the first ring. "Wes, you're not going to believe what I found."

"I'm outside, walking through a snowbank, so talk fast."

"I can't. I have to tell you in person." She was breathing hard. "When are you off?"

"I'm working on an extended assignment. I can't meet up with you right now." He peered through the blinding whiteness up and down the block for any sign of Jane Doe. He made out a few stragglers. She wasn't one of them. "Just say what you have to say."

"For God's sake, it's about our parents. Their trip."

His throat closed at the mention of them.

"I finally decided to sort through some of those old papers. You know, the ones in the cedar chest?"

He nodded to the phone in reply as he trudged around the corner on Oakland Avenue South. He found the Lincoln covered in white flakes. Damn. The weather forecaster had got it right.

"Turns out...wasn't..."

"Jen, are you there? You're cutting out." He looked at the phone. No connection. "Damn." He pocketed the phone and searched the back seat and trunk for an ice scraper or snow brush, coming up empty-handed. He used his coat sleeve to brush away snow. Thank God for a frostless windshield. Phillips crawled into the front seat, turned the key, and cranked the fan and seat warmer to high. Hell if he'd freeze in all that luxury.

Too bad he couldn't say the same for that girl. He wondered if she booked it on foot to some warm place for the night.

What the hell was Jen revved up about? Phillips shook his head, tried to clear the runaway thoughts. Focus on the upcoming mission, he reminded himself. This was his big chance to prove himself to the department and the task force. Wipe his slate clean. He needed to lock the personal phone away, catch a few hours of sleep. Whatever was bugging Jen would have to wait. Soon, it would be show time.

# CHAPTER SEVENTEEN

Russ Malloy rapped his knuckles on the driver's window of the Taurus, knocking away an accumulation of snow. Bruce Ellison looked up and elbowed Dan Larkin in the ribs. "Open your eyes. Malloy's here."

Ellison rolled down the window, welcoming the remainder of the snowflakes into the car. "What's up?" He brushed off his jacket sleeve.

"Thought I'd swing by, see if there's been any action," Malloy replied.

Ellison flipped on the wipers to clear a thin layer of snow and peered out into the night through the foggy windshield. He and Larkin had sat parked for the last hour down the street from a boarded-up, unmarked building. They were supposed to be watching the back entrance where Christoph Morton disappeared earlier. "Only the usual." Ellison rubbed a large portion of the fog away with his glove. "It's a waiting game."

Larkin straightened in his seat. "How'd it go with

Phillips?"

Malloy skimmed the outer area surrounding the building. "He's set up in his new place. Excited to be living the life in his penthouse apartment."

Larkin raised his eyebrows. "Huh? What's that supposed to mean?"

Malloy glanced back at the two men and smiled. "Never mind. Anyway, I told him to get some rest, he'd be diving in soon."

"Gonna meet Reynolds?" Ellison asked.

"That's the plan." Malloy pulled his hands from his coat pockets, rubbed them together, and blew on them. He shoved his hands back into his pockets. "Hopefully, Katrina's still at the same location."

"If she doesn't fuck with us again," Ellison grumbled.

Malloy's smile disappeared. "That wasn't her fault."

"No? Funny how people tend to die in her vicinity," Ellison snapped.

"You have a problem with my sister, Ellison?"

"Just stating an observation."

Larkin leaned over. "Listen, Russ, I have to agree with

Bruce here. We honestly don't know if Katrina's trustworthy at this point. Whether you like it or not, she could be our leak over on the Dark Side."

Malloy averted his eyes.

"I only hope the boss isn't making another mistake by sending this rookie in and feeding him to the sharks." Larkin pulled out a handkerchief, blew his nose, and added, "Look what happened to the last guy."

Ellison nodded. "Exactly what I was saying, but there's no way around it. The boss said the higher-ups requested another dispensable body—"

"Dispensable body?" Larkin cut in. "Shit. Were those his exact words?"

"Well, something like that," Ellison hedged.

Malloy snorted. "Can you even spell that word, Ellison? Or did you see it in one of Larkin's crossword puzzles?"

"Fuck you," Ellison muttered. "Let's hope this new body can stay alive and handle things when they get hot and heavy."

"He better." Malloy stared at Ellison. "My sister's life is on the line."

"But will he be able to handle Menendez?" Larkin

laughed, trying to break the tension.

Ellison looked over at Larkin. "Who?"

"Sofia Menendez. That spicy-looking chick who lives down south. The boss borrowed her once before. Remember that fucked-up Mexican drug bust a few years back?"

"Ah, yes. Sofia." He grinned and looked back at Malloy. "Is that right? They gonna have the new recruit partner up with her?"

Malloy nodded. "She's on her way."

"Lucky bastard."

"Let's hope *she* doesn't kill him," Larkin added.

# CHAPTER EIGHTEEN

She was dead.

Wes Phillips straightened on his kitchen bar stool and stared at the girl's face in the *Star Tribune*. He skimmed the newspaper headline again. *Suicidal Teen Dies After A Year in Coma*. He dropped his toast, his heart racing, and wiped his hand on his boxers. "Fuck."

> ***Parents of 16-year-old Cassie Roberts claim Lino Lakes City Hospital is at fault for the death of their only daughter***
>
> *Roberts was being treated for severe depression, and after negligent supervision by mental health hospital staff and an unsecured unit door, Roberts escaped to the roof's helipad, where she threatened to leap to her death. After several attempts by hospital Security Officer Harry Clemons and Lino Lakes Police Officer Wesley Phillips to draw her away from the edge, she jumped.*

*Due to life-threatening injuries, Roberts spent the last year and several months in a coma while being treated for numerous broken bones, including fractured hips, internal bleeding, and swelling in the brain. A lawsuit is pending.*

He stared again at his name in print, the guilt fresh. His brain leaped back to that day on the helipad. The bright sun, the ungodly heat, the unrelenting wind pushing him toward the girl at the roof's edge.

She had stood trembling in a sweat-soaked yellow patient gown, her body turned outward, stringy brown hair whipping across her expressionless face. An old man in a rumpled security guard uniform stood several feet away, waving his hands, pleading, "Don't jump!"

In his gut, Phillips believed the girl was intent on dying. Her posture, her demeanor, the certainty of her voice. Despite dry swallowing a pill to calm his erratic nerves on the way up the staircase, there wasn't much he could do to help short of tackling her and hoping to God they both didn't tumble over the edge.

He had arrived too late in the game. Seconds after he initiated conversation, the girl simply stepped forward.

After he returned to ground level and stopped trembling, his heart back to its regular rhythm, he told himself to let it go. Hell, the chief had even said to him, “Sometimes shit happens.” Yet, over the past year, Phillips followed the news stories. Searched for words of hope. Maybe the girl would recover. Maybe…

He glanced at the clock. It was almost time to meet Katrina. He cut out the article, set it aside, and headed for the shower.

# CHAPTER NINETEEN

Wes Phillips followed a giant security guard into the depths of the closed restaurant, Louiselle's, and breathed in an aroma of garlic, tomato, bread, and cheese. In a recessed alcove along the back wall was a huge table illuminated with candles and one ceiling canister light.

Damian Reynolds, small and slender with chiseled cheekbones and tanned skin, sat at the canister light's edge, facing Phillips. He rested a hand sporting gold rings on several fingers on the back of a head buried in his lap.

Phillips drew in a breath and curled his right hand into a fist. He stared at Reynolds, fighting the urge to call him an arrogant piece of shit and grab him by the throat. "I'm supposed to meet Izzy here," he stated in a tight voice.

The head tried to rise. Reynolds forced it back down.

"Your people at the door don't know who I'm talking about," Phillips continued. "So, I asked to talk to the man who knew things. They brought me to you. Do you know things?"

"Who the fuck is Izzy?" Reynolds growled, shoving his dark bangs off his forehead. His green eyes drilled into Phillips'.

"Isabella Cantrell."

"Oh. Well, Isabella's busy." The head tried to rise once more. Reynolds forced it down again, and the person gagged.

Phillips shifted his stance. "How about I wait for her?"

"How about I have your ass thrown outta here?"

The security giant stepped forward.

Phillips stared at him, then looked back at Reynolds. "Your steroid-laden behemoth is too slow. I could grab the gun from behind his back and shove it up his ass before he lifts his arms."

Reynolds laughed. "I like you. Who the fuck are you?"

"Stephen Mayer."

"Like the author?"

"Which author?"

"The one who wrote those vampire and werewolf romances."

"That would be Stephanie Meyer. So no, not like the author."

"Well, fuck me. How do you know Isabella?"

"I know Izzy from summer camp. I was a counselor. Used to sneak her out of her cabin so we could canoe at sunup."

Reynolds squirmed in his Armani slim-fitted suit. His breathing quickened. He pushed at the head to increase the up-and-down motion. Phillips opened his mouth, and Reynolds raised his other hand, stopping him. After a minute, Reynolds stiffened and released a huge sigh. The security giant smiled and chuckled.

Reynolds grabbed a handful of purple-spiked hair and pulled the girl up from his lap.

Phillips stared at a disheveled Katrina Malloy.

His thoughts ping-ponged, and his stomach twisted. *For chrissake, not Katrina.* What kind of perverted control did this Reynolds have over her? What else was the prick making her do? He forced a blank expression.

Reynolds yanked Katrina's face around to look at Phillips. "Is this who you're looking for?"

Her eyes were bloodshot. "Hey, Steve," she slurred. "How's things?"

Phillips willed his voice to remain even. "I'm good, Izzy.

How are you?"

She fluttered her fingers to the front of her throat. A large port wine stain covered most of it. She typically hid the birthmark with turtlenecks or high-collared shirts. Today, it stood out against her low-cut blouse. "Never better."

Reynolds pushed her away. "Get yourself cleaned up. You disgust me. And take pretty boy with you. We can talk later."

Katrina slid from behind the table. She wobbled on platform heels that added six inches to her five-foot frame. She lurched toward Phillips, and he grabbed her, wrapping an arm around her shoulder and leading her away.

In the ladies' room, Katrina stumbled into a stall, not bothering to close the door. She shoved a finger down her throat and puked into the toilet. Phillips soaked a few paper towels in cold water and handed them to her.

"You okay?" He reached around her to flush the toilet.

She groaned, shuffled bent over to the sink counter, and leaned on it with both elbows. She waved her hands limply under running water. "Do I look okay?"

"Not really. I hate to see you messed up and doing what you're doing with that piece of scum. How deep under are you?"

"I've done all the things they tell you not to do." Katrina slumped against the wall, her fingertips dripping water. "I've fucked my way to the top, and I'm a drunk. I'm lost, Wes. But that's the job, isn't it?"

He shook his head and handed her a fresh paper towel. "No. We're supposed to go home alive at the end of the day with our morals intact."

"Good luck with that." Katrina half-wiped her hands. "Just you wait and see."

He held his hand out to her. She staggered close and turned it into a hug. "God, I'm glad to see you." She squeezed her eyes shut and breathed in his fresh cologne. "You always smell so good." She lifted her head and looked up at him. "Don't leave me this time."

His mind drifted back to graduation. "I'm sorry." He shrugged from her embrace. "I'm here to help with the investigation. Whatever you need me to do."

"That's the problem. I know something big is up. Real big, Wes," she slurred, grabbing the front of his shirt. "I can't find out what, though. I need a new angle."

He gently extracted her hand. "Let's see what we can

do."

"Right. From here, it's all improv."

"That's fine. Just remember not to contradict me no matter what comes up."

She shook her head vehemently. "No contradictions."

***

Katrina slipped into the chair beside Reynolds. Her black leather skirt rode up her thighs. He smiled and squeezed her leg. Her gaze wavered down to his hand, but she didn't bother to adjust her skirt. Instead, she placed both palms on the table and tried to keep her balance. Reynolds slid a full glass of booze toward her, and she gripped it eagerly.

"So, pretty boy, Isabella mentioned we should meet." Reynolds motioned for Phillips to sit across from him. "She says she was your first."

"Yeah." Phillips looked at Katrina. "She had a thing at camp about wanting to deflower the virgin counselors. Turns out I was the only one."

Reynolds interlocked his fingers, displaying manicured nails. "How'd you do it?"

Katrina leaned forward. "We canoed to the middle of the lake, and I told him to fuck or swim," she slurred, swirling the liquid around her glass.

Phillips nodded. "I was a good swimmer. Wouldn't have had any trouble making it to shore, but I'd been a virgin for too long. And she was a kid who thought she was all grown up. It seemed like a perfect opportunity. Besides, look at her. Who wouldn't want to be deflowered by Izzy?"

Katrina laughed. "We gave new meaning to the term 'rocking the boat.'" She lifted her glass and spilled some of the alcohol on the table. "Oops." She looked at Reynolds. "Sorry."

He smiled. "Lick it up, and I'll forgive you."

Phillips' body tensed. Katrina bent forward and wiped her tongue across the table, slurping the liquid until it disappeared.

"Good girl."

Phillips cleared his throat. "As I was saying, I'd been a virgin for too long. We only rocked the boat for about thirty seconds."

"Hah," Reynolds laughed.

Katrina smirked. "I didn't remember it being that long."

"As you can see, she's graduated from virgins," Reynolds remarked. "Her skills are quite impressive. She didn't get them from breaking in virgins."

With shiny eyes, Katrina looked away and said nothing.

Reynolds drummed his fingers. “So why are you here? It ain’t to bullshit about kiddie camp.”

“I represent a group of entrepreneurs looking to make certain acquisitions,” Phillips replied.

“Oh, yeah? And where did you meet this group?”

“Old family connections. My great-great-grandfather was a mover and shaker here in town, and the family nurtured all the connections he made way back when.”

“Who’s your great-grandfather?”

“Great-great-grandfather,” Phillips corrected.

Reynolds waved his hand dismissively. “Whatever. Who the fuck was he?”

“Salvatore Mayer.”

“And who the fuck’s Salvatore Mayer?”

“He’s one of the three who ran bootlegging into Minneapolis.”

“Nah, there were only two,” Reynolds returned.

“Kid Cann and Meyer Lansky,” Phillips agreed. “The two everybody heard of because they’re the two who got in trouble with the feds. Grandpa Sal managed to stay clear of prison, make money, share enough, and take care of his family. Now, I'm continuing his legacy."

"So, what do you want with me?" Reynolds asked.

"Izzy tells me you have multiple business interests. We'd like to discuss synergies, maybe take some inventory off your hands."

"I don't discuss things I can't pronounce. And who says I have inventory?"

Phillips straightened in his chair. "Lots of people confirm you have access to many things, have some available on short notice. That suggests an inventory, and that's what we'd like to discuss. See where our interests are similar and where we can help each other. That would be the synergies."

Reynolds leaned back and sat silent for a moment. "Isabella, he stays with you until I can check him out. If lover boy's okay, we'll talk. If he isn't, you both die." He grabbed her chin and squeezed. When she tried to pull back, he leaned over and mashed his lips against hers, then pushed her away, almost knocking her from the chair.

Phillips stood and extended his hand to her. "C'mon, Izzy, let's go. You can sleep at my place." She took his hand and rose from the chair. They started to walk away.

"Hey, Stevie," Reynolds called. "There's no leaving. Not until I'm done checking you out."

Phillips turned to face him with narrowed eyes.

Reynolds set a SIG-Sauer 9 mm on the table. "Hand over your phone. I'm gonna have my boys do some checking."

Phillips said a silent thank you to God that he'd locked up his personal phone in the carriage house. He set the police-issued phone on the table.

"In the meantime, I want you close. Just in case," Reynolds added. "You sleep in her room." He waved a finger at Phillips. "Don't touch her, though. You had your chance at Boy Scout camp. She's mine now."

Katrina led Phillips to the front of the restaurant, through a swinging door, and into the dark kitchen. He peered around. "Where are you taking me?"

"To my room. Upstairs."

"Shit," he muttered under his breath. "Why does everything have to be upstairs?"

They crossed the kitchen and slipped through another door. Behind it hid a narrow flight of stairs. A single bulb dangled at the top, and a long hallway boasting faded flower-patterned carpet and gold wall sconces led to several scuffed doors. Phillips breathed hard. Katrina snagged her heel on the frayed carpet, wobbled, and almost fell.

She squeaked open the third door on the right and flipped the light switch. Phillips closed the door behind him and sniffed. The small room reeked of mildew. Thin, shabby red curtains pulled to one side hung over a broken window held together with duct tape. A bed with a sleeping bag rested underneath it.

Katrina kicked off her shoes and rolled onto the bed. "Bathroom is at the end of the hall."

Phillips leaned against the closed door. "If you've screwed your way to the top, why aren't you sleeping someplace nicer than this?"

"I usually do, but he gave me a room so I can have my own space, and he can use his bed for other things."

*Other things.* Bile rose in Phillips' throat. "You haven't fallen for him, have you?"

"Jeezus, Wes." She stared at the ceiling, then back at him. "Fine. Maybe a little." She got on all fours and peeked out the window. She looked back over her shoulder at Phillips. "It's more like dependence. Besides acquiring a taste for booze, I need what he provides me."

"Which is what?"

"You know."

"No. I don't." Phillips pulled at his tie. "And could you…turn around and sit down?"

She turned halfway and sank onto the back of her heels. "He provides me with love." She closed her eyes and touched her exposed throat. "He loves me."

Phillips was sickened. "No, he doesn't. He's the bad guy, and you're supposed to be the good guy. Remember the assignment? He's using you, Katrina. Destroying you a little bit at a time. More every day."

"Oh, stop it, Wes. You're jealous." She extended her hand. "Come over here."

"I can't."

"Damian doesn't care. Believe me. He's whored me out lots of times." She waggled her fingers. "C'mon. What, are you afraid of me?"

He shook his head. "That isn't it."

"Then what is it?"

"Katrina, we used to be good friends, and it's killing me to see you like this." He swallowed hard. "Besides, I'm having one of my moments."

She laughed, pressing her hand to her stomach. "Oh, my God. You still have that phobia?"

He cleared his throat. "Maybe. Possibly. Okay, definitely."

Her laughs tapered away. She sighed and pulled the curtains closed. She sat cross-legged on the bed, her back pressed against the wall, forcing her skirt to ride high up on her thighs. The material strained against her skin. Phillips caught himself staring at her lower half.

"Deep, slow breaths, Wes, remember? In through your nose, out through your mouth."

He rolled his eyes. "Chrissake, I'm not in labor."

"Shut up and listen." She tugged at her skirt. It rode further up her thighs. "Try to imagine we're on solid ground." She patted the bed and scooted over. "And this is a nice solid anchor to that ground. Now, the next step is to lie down here and hold me. You don't have to do anything else. Concentrate on your rescue breathing."

He shook his head.

"Lie down, Wes. You said you'd do whatever I needed you to do."

"So now I'm enabling you."

"Yeah, you are." Her voice fell to a whisper, and her eyes began to close. "And right now, I need some sleep. So come enable me to sleep."

"Give me a minute. I'll be right back."

Phillips left the room and walked down the hall to the bathroom. He flipped on the light, and a small army of cockroaches scattered. "Nice place," he muttered. He closed the door and noticed the missing lock. "Figures."

Peeling yellow wallpaper decorated the walls, and rings of scum and mildew stained the sink, tub, and seatless toilet. He pulled the toilet lever. At least it flushed. He glanced in the cracked mirror at his tired eyes and splashed cold water over his hands and face. After wiping his hands on the front of his pants, he sighed, reached into his pocket, and pulled out his pill bottle. "One oughta do it." He'd be asleep soon, anyway.

By the time he returned to Katrina's room, she lay sprawled out on the bed, one arm dangling over the edge. "I started thinking you were only a dream," she slurred, her eyes slits. "An old memory to tease me, then *poof*."

"Not hardly. Do you want me to turn out the light?"

"No," she mumbled. "I don't like the dark."

# CHAPTER TWENTY

After a brisk, escorted morning walk, Wes Phillips headed back to Louiselle's in his rumpled suit and coat, a behemoth in front, a slightly smaller behemoth behind.

"Hey, I appreciate the company. I would've normally broken into a run, but I wanted to be polite." Phillips grinned. "You guys having a good day? I'm having a great day. It's beautiful outside. Isn't this air crisp? The snow clean and white? Life's wonderful."

The behemoth in front turned and glared at him.

"You should try smiling," Phillips added. "It's an automatic uplift to your day, your mood, and, not surprisingly, your face." When the behemoth looked again, Phillips widened his smile.

Inside Louiselle's, Damian Reynolds sat at the same table as the night before, dressed in another Armani suit, this one a shade darker. His tie shimmered with a satiny emerald hue. A gourmet breakfast surrounded him.

Phillips stared at a stack of crisp bacon. Maybe he should skip his daily run, use the excuse of the walk, and enjoy a long, leisurely breakfast. After business with the egotistical pimp, he would decide.

Reynolds held a cell phone, talking between bites. “Look, Christoph, I don’t care. This guy can’t see what all’s in the warehouse on 26th. Get there early, move the crates to the storefront on 29th. It’s clean, it’s private. It was swept yesterday. The screen-printing machines make the right amount of noise to make anybody’s parabolic microphones worthless.”

He stared at Phillips, who waited across the room. “*Parabolic.* Look it up. Shut up for once and do it my way.” He listened for a minute. “No. That’s not right. I said ten.” He listened again and waved his fork around. “Quit trying to work yourself out of a job. Be there, be ready, and keep this guy happy without him learning more than he already knows.”

He disconnected and waved Phillips over. “So, Stevie, you’ve checked out okay. So far.” Reynolds dug in his suit coat and slid a phone toward Phillips. “But now the checks get serious.”

Phillips pocketed the phone. “Can I go back to my place now?”

"You can, but we'll be watching," Reynolds warned him. "Gimme your address."

"You don't need it."

Reynolds smiled. "We'll see about that."

Phillips stared hard. Katrina was still asleep upstairs. "Can I take Izzy with me?"

"Nope. She's my property."

"Uh-huh. And what's next for us?" Phillips asked.

"You introduce me to your friends."

"It's my turn to say nope."

"Why is that?"

"Because if you met my friends, they'd kill you, then they'd kill me. For now, you'll have to be content to do business with me."

Reynolds set down his fork. "That's not how I work."

"In that case, I'll offer you a hundred grand for Izzy, and we'll leave."

"Hah. You're a funny guy. Who says she's for sale?"

"Everything's for sale. We only have to find the right number."

Reynolds gazed at Phillips for a long moment. "True enough. So, let's talk a little more business. After all, you're still on my watch list, and I haven't decided if my not meeting your friends is going to be a big deal. Maybe even a deal-breaker."

"Let's start simple," Phillips suggested. "Provide us with a list of your overrun items, your excess inventory. We'll look through it, pick what we want, and come back with an offer."

Reynolds cocked his head. "What makes you think I have excess inventory?"

"Because I've, or more correctly, we've been checking you out as well," Phillips replied. "You don't think we'd enter negotiations without a solid knowledge base and an understanding of what benefits you can provide, do you?"

"Depends how bad you want to get into the neighborhood."

Phillips smiled. "If we wanted into the neighborhood, we'd just kill you."

Reynolds' eyes narrowed.

"You're familiar with the term infrastructure, right?" Phillips asked.

"Of course."

"If we killed you and everybody who fought to replace you, we'd have to build all that over again. But if we can partner with the business leader in the area, we can avoid the time and expense necessary to rebuild the infrastructure we destroyed to get rid of you."

"It all sounds so simple, Stevie."

"We're businesspeople and pragmatists," Phillips told him. "But like everyone else, we'd prefer to do things the easy way. Working with you, not against you. If we have to work against you, you won't profit ever again, and it'll take some time for us to maximize ours. Simple logic and good business."

Reynolds picked up a slice of bacon and waved it at Phillips. "I'll consider it. In the meantime, you leave. Isabella stays."

***

Phillips brushed Katrina's purple bangs off her forehead. "Hey, Izzy. How you doing?"

She stirred and opened her eyes. "Okay."

"I gotta go for a while. But I'll be back. Will you be okay?"

"I'll be fine. Did you talk to Damian?"

"The opening discussions have been hopeful."

She sat up on the bed and looked past Phillips. "Stop spying on us, Kong."

Phillips turned. The steroid-laden behemoth leaned against the doorframe. "Your name is Kong?" Phillips asked.

The man grunted. "No. It's Dennis."

"I call him that because he's big, like King Kong," Katrina replied. "Except, with Damian around, he'll never be king."

Dennis glared at her.

Katrina pulled the sleeping bag tighter around her body and glared back. "You can leave."

"Not until he does." Dennis spoke in a deep but soft tone, a little too scratchy for voice-overs. "As long as he's here, I'm his babysitter. Yours, too."

"I don't need babysitting," Katrina muttered.

"Don't matter what you think. The boss says babysit, I babysit."

Phillips shook his head. "I've gotta take care of some business. You sure you'll be okay?"

"I'll be fine," Katrina insisted.

"Anything you need or want when I come back?"

She tapped her finger against her lips. "Do you know Hauser's Wings and Fish on University?"

"No, but I can find it."

"Bring me a combo platter. Catfish and strips. The food here's good, excellent really, but I miss Hauser's catfish. I could use a fix."

"Consider it done."

"You can make that a double order, *Stevie*," Dennis added with a smirk.

# CHAPTER TWENTY-ONE

Wes Phillips changed into running clothes, fried up a half pound of bacon and one egg over hard. He wrapped a few large lettuce leaves around the egg and bacon strips, grabbed a water bottle, and headed out of the carriage house. It took a few blocks of walking to eat his improvised breakfast sandwich before he could run.

He took Kenwood Parkway to Vineland Place, ran between the Walker Art Center and the Minneapolis Sculpture Gardens, turned south onto Hennepin Avenue, followed it to West 26th Street, and west to Penn Avenue. However, he didn't enjoy the run, didn't see the sights because as fast as he ran, his mind raced faster.

Back at the police academy, Katrina Malloy had tried to fit in but didn't. Neither did Phillips. Most of the macho tough guys at the academy swallowed too many supplements to enhance their musculature. The air around them swirled with false bravado and open hostility toward women.

Some women in the class sported muscles comparable to the men. Those who didn't possess strength or size backstabbed other classmates, sabotaged their work, laughed at their failures.

Small-statured Katrina chose the path of proper communication. She used her brain to deescalate situations rather than bludgeon through them. She claimed proving one cop was tougher than another destroyed teamwork mentality.

Phillips believed the same. The two found each other, studied and exercised together, and had each other's backs when the rest of the class decided to gang up.

They both arrived at the academy with knowledge not included in the curriculum. She used a pressure point to put their largest classmate on the floor. Phillips ducked under a frontal attack, went for the knees, and dropped another man with so much force the student bit through his own lip.

They spent a lot of time talking about why they wanted to be cops and if they could or couldn't make a difference in the world. They both wanted to believe they could. They also talked about books and music and places they yearned to see. Yet no words were spoken about the Colorado mountains, that fatal day, Phillips' tucked-away grief.

At graduation, Katrina remarked, "You know, if we'd have been at any other school, pursuing any other degree other than law enforcement, I would've expected you to pursue me with all your heart."

"Believe me, sometimes I wish I had," Phillips replied. "Maybe things will be different down the road. Either way, if you need me, I'll be there."

Now, as a cop, she had dug herself so far undercover, in so damn deep, that she used and drank and blew and banged the target with no end in sight. Phillips quickened his pace, remembering the image of her head in Reynolds' lap. He had to pull her out of that hellhole and away from that sonofabitch. She was debasing herself for an assignment. *A job.* A lousy government paycheck.

He thought about last night, her warm body and soft, even breaths as they slept crowded in bed. His arms had ached to hold her. Could he save her from herself? Would she be the Katrina he remembered?

Phillips finished his run back on Kenwood Parkway and slowed to a walk. He should go knock Katrina's brother around. Get this resolved. Or kill Reynolds. Hell with it. If Reynolds took advantage of Jen or Alyse, the prick would suffer immense pain for an extremely long period of time with no end in sight.

He stomped into the carriage house, stripped off his sweaty clothes, and stood in front of the bathroom mirror. He leaned close enough to count his pores.

"What are you gonna do, smart boy?" he asked his reflection. "You're a cop." He raised his fist as if he was going to punch his reflected image and stopped. "This is wrong. Fucked up. It's not why we became cops." He closed his eyes, shook his head. "We're supposed to go home at night, live our lives without worrying about becoming one of the bad guys. Or worse." He stepped back. "So, what are you gonna do? You're gonna take your shower and go do your job." *Dumbass.*

He climbed into the shower, turned the hot water on full, added a splash of cold. After he scrubbed his skin clean, he shut off the hot water and counted a hundred and twenty seconds before he shut off the cold. His body shivered, and his teeth chattered. Suitable penance for doubt.

He slipped into a freshly pressed suit, prepared another lettuce-wrapped sandwich, and opened his laptop. He Googled Damian Reynolds and read while he ate.

Reynolds graduated from Lakeville South High School, where he had been voted most likely to succeed, been the debate team captain and chess club president. He went on to Normandale Community College and transferred to the University of Minnesota Carlson School of Management. After graduation, he studied pastries at one of the cooking schools and took a job at Louiselle's. Where he used more of his management skills than culinary techniques.

Next, he looked up Louiselle's. Most of the reviews were positive. The website described it as affordable fine food for real people. The menu listed burgers and steaks, a few pasta dishes, some fish and chicken dishes, and an extensive wine list. Nowhere did it list pastry of any kind.

His third Google search found Hauser's. It did not have an internet presence or a place to like it on social media. Most of the posted reviews gave it four or five stars and thumbs-up, saying, "Tacky but wonderful" and "Don't look too close, just enjoy, it's the best."

Phillips glanced at the bottom corner of the screen for the current time. Eleven A.M. If Hauser's behaved like a normal restaurant, which he couldn't tell from the internet, it should be open. Time to get Katrina's lunch.

# CHAPTER TWENTY-TWO

Wes Phillips parked the Lincoln a few blocks north of University Avenue and walked to Hauser's. The State Capitol loomed within sight, about a block east and across University.

He entered Hauser's and inhaled the heavy aroma of fish and chips. Three chairs lined up against the plate glass window, facing a short counter sitting on faded and yellowed linoleum. An antique cash register sat on the counter. Behind it, a large pass-through window opened to the kitchen. Suspended in the window hung an aluminum wheel with paper orders clipped most of the way around.

Two people stood behind the counter, a young girl on the phone and a middle-aged woman at the cash register, digging through a pile of tickets. Without looking at Phillips and in a gravel voice, as if she'd spent years preparing to give life to animated monsters, the woman stated, "Be right with you." She rifled through a few more tickets, pulled one out, and slammed it on the counter. "Here's the bastard. I knew I'd seen the son of a gun in here."

The girl on the phone ripped a slip of paper off a small

tablet and punched buttons, changing to a new call. "Hauser's," she answered as she pushed a paper menu toward Phillips.

Two men stood in the kitchen, visible through the pass-through window, wearing paper hats. One had a mask stretched over his beard. The other wore a scowl and sang along with a radio blaring classic rock. He watched Phillips as if assessing a threat but didn't stop moving his hands.

"What'll ya have?" The woman stuffed the slip of paper into her pocket and slid the rest off the counter and into a drawer.

"Two catfish and strips combos," Phillips replied.

She met his eyes for the first time. After a long moment, she grunted. "That all?"

"Well...yeah. Isn't that enough?"

"Probably not. How many you feeding?"

"Two."

"Might be enough. Might not. Sure you don't want more, just to be safe?"

"I think that'll be enough. Your food comes highly recommended. I can increase my order next time I come."

"Hey," the cook in the beard mask yelled. "Management wants to talk to you."

Phillips looked around. "Who? Me? Why?"

"How should I know?" the cook growled. "Go 'round the counter. Come through the kitchen."

Phillips shrugged his shoulders and walked across the sticky floor, his dress shoes squeaking with complaint.

The woman smirked. "I'll wait to hang your order. See if you come back out."

Phillips looked through the window and sized up the cooks. "Why wouldn't I come back out?"

She chuckled. "Never know."

Inside the kitchen, the odors of deep-fried meat grew more intense, and the floor slick. The two men stood at a metal table, fresh breading fish and chicken. Behind them, a row of deep fryers bubbled madly, baskets submerged. Vents roared full blast. Flour and breading covered the floor except where feet had slid and created a smear of clean.

The masked cook pointed to a door. Phillips pushed it open and entered a shadowy dining room.

Of six tables, only one was occupied. Robert McNellis, Russ Malloy, and a small Hispanic woman with striking dark eyes and long raven hair pulled into a ponytail sat at the table, surrounded by food.

"Hey, Wes," Malloy called. "Join us. There's plenty."

McNellis raised a beer bottle. "It's excellent, too. Best there is. But you already know that."

Phillips raised an eyebrow. "How would I know that? The woman at the front hasn't even turned in my order."

Malloy smiled. "My sister told you. She's alive and well, or you wouldn't be here."

"And she obviously trusts you," McNellis added in a conspiratorial voice. "Or she wouldn't have told you about Hauser's. It's a closely guarded secret."

Malloy waved at an empty chair. "C'mon. Sit."

Phillips grabbed the chair and sat opposite them. "The secret must not be kept too close. The place sure looks busy from out there."

"It's a neighborhood joint," Malloy stated. "The neighborhood supports it well."

"So does family. Speaking of family…" McNellis pointed to the woman. "This is Sofia Menendez. She'll be moving in with you tonight."

Phillips looked closer at Sofia, and his pulse quickened. She wore a tight-fitted midnight blue sweater with plenty of curves in the right places. A gold chain dangled around her throat. She saluted him with a chicken wing.

He looked back at McNellis. "I work alone. That was the plan."

"Plans change," McNellis informed him. "Higher-ups decided you need a girlfriend."

"Ah, jeezus."

Sofia set down the wing. "What? You don't like women? You think we're too dainty for this type of work?"

Phillips rolled his eyes. "That's not what I meant."

"She'll help protect your cover," Malloy put in.

"And your ass," McNellis added.

Sofia giggled. "Especially your ass."

"I think somebody needs to tell me what's really going on," Phillips grumbled.

Sofia handed him a clean plate and flashed her eyes. "I think you should eat first, darling."

Food started coming in Phillips' direction. Within seconds, his plate overflowed with catfish, wings, French fries, and coleslaw. "I'll need—"

"We don't talk business or sports while we're eating," McNellis interrupted. "It screws your appreciation."

"I was going to ask for a napkin. And if I have to go out front to pour my own beer."

"My mistake." McNellis reached into a cooler beside his chair and produced a bottle of beer. He passed it over. "Hauser's doesn't have a liquor license."

Phillips gripped the wet bottle in his hand and paused before opening it. "Can they get in trouble for us drinking here?"

"Nah," McNellis assured him. "This room doesn't exist."

"Neither do we," Malloy added.

Phillips kept the rest of his thoughts to himself and enjoyed Hauser's finest. The others finished before him, then sat back and watched.

"Not bad, eh?" McNellis asked.

Phillips wiped his mouth with a napkin. "Not bad at all. It's easy to understand why you eat here. I promise not to talk it up too much."

"Good idea," Malloy agreed. "Keep it in the family."

Phillips pushed his empty plate to the side. "So, why did Katrina send me here?"

"This is our unofficial office," Malloy replied. "It's secure and bug-free."

"And no one else knows about it," McNellis added. "Despite our coming here for years."

Phillips leaned forward. "No one's followed you or figured it out yet?"

McNellis shook his head. "Evidently not. Or else they don't take us serious enough to figure out what we know and what we do."

"Why would that be?" Phillips asked.

McNellis snorted. "I'm a drunk, and Malloy got his job because of family connections, namely me. No one understands how good of a cop he actually is."

Malloy stared at McNellis. "Gee, thanks."

Phillips focused on the dark-haired woman. "What about you?"

"I'm DHS," Sofia replied. "But not from here."

"I had her imported from Dallas-Fort Worth," McNellis

revealed. "Like with you, we needed more unknowns." He winked at Phillips. "Ain't she a beauty?"

Sofia kicked McNellis under the table. "Shut up, old man. You're drunk and obnoxious."

McNellis grinned. "She's feisty, too."

Sofia grabbed McNellis' bottle and moved it across the table. He leaned over and grabbed it back.

Phillips' eyes narrowed. "Let's back up a sec." He pointed at McNellis. "How much of a drunk are you? Will I be able to trust *you* when I need you?"

McNellis frowned. "First of all, that's 'how much of a drunk are you, *sir*.' I'll allow ass-kissing this one time.

"Katrina is my goddaughter," McNellis continued. "I won't let anything happen to her. You can damn well trust me."

# CHAPTER TWENTY-THREE

Sofia Menendez carried a small suitcase and followed Wes Phillips into the carriage house. "This is all right. I could be happy here." She dropped the suitcase on the couch and flopped down beside it.

Phillips remained standing. "Wonderful. I worried you wouldn't like my decorating."

She smiled. "I know you didn't decorate. You can't fool me."

"How could you tell?"

"It doesn't have that tough-guy motif."

"Do I come across as a tough guy?" he asked.

Sofia played with her necklace. "No. You're one of those guys who has trouble saying what he feels. You want the sensitive side to stay hidden."

"Is that such a bad thing?"

"Maybe. Maybe not." She pulled her hair loose, slid the ponytail holder onto her wrist, and massaged her scalp. "But at some point, you'll have to let someone in. Or you're going to die alone and crabby."

"We all die alone."

Sofia dropped her hands. "I don't believe that for a minute. Just like I don't believe you're alone after you die. I guess that would be your choice, though."

He stared at her for a second, then pointed down the hall. "Your bedroom's to the right."

She cocked her head to the side. "Avoidance. Well done." She stood and picked up the suitcase. "We'll share the same bed."

"We will?"

"In case somebody snoops, we need to keep up appearances. Don't worry, darling. I'll force myself to sleep in flannel pajamas."

He swallowed hard and followed her into the bedroom. She threw her suitcase on the bed, found an empty drawer, and unpacked.

The doorbell rang, and they froze.

She looked at Phillips. "Expecting someone?"

"No. You?"

She shook her head. "Hell, no. Everybody I know knows better than to stop unannounced. Good way to get shot."

The bell rang again. "I guess I'll answer," Phillips conceded. "You might want to stay hidden for now." He pulled the bedroom door shut behind him.

***

Damian Reynolds and Dennis stood downstairs in front of the garage's entry door. When Phillips unlocked the door, Reynolds pushed his way in. Dennis turned and faced the driveway and street beyond, hands clasped loosely before his bulk.

"I wasn't expecting you." Phillips followed Reynolds' quick stride up the steps.

"I like surprises," Reynolds replied. "Don't you?"

"No. How did you find me?"

Reynolds turned and smiled. "I have sources. Everywhere."

Phillips followed him through the mud room and into the living area. "Yeah? So, what do you want?"

"I decided it's time to talk business." Reynolds peered around the room. "And I wanted to check out your pad. It tells me more about you as a man." He sat at one end of the couch.

Sofia emerged from the bedroom, barefoot and clothed in boxer shorts and a tight red T-shirt. Her legs appeared well muscled, and the shirt clung to her breasts, nipples erect. She strode into the kitchen, found a glass from the cupboard, filled it with water, and returned to the bedroom.

Reynolds stared after her and jerked his thumb in the air. “Who’s the chick?”

“Nobody,” Phillips responded from his chair next to the couch.

“Oh, yeah? What’s this so-called ‘nobody’ doing in your bedroom?”

Phillips drummed his fingers on the armrest. “I’m stuck with her. She’s a gift from my business associates.”

Reynolds nodded. “Quite a gift.”

“You have no idea.” Phillips crossed his legs at the ankles. “So, let’s talk business if that’s what you want.”

Reynolds pulled a slip of paper from his pocket. “Here’s some of the info you asked for.”

Phillips unfolded the paper and began to read.

Sofia stormed from the bedroom and stopped in front of Phillips. She released a torrent of Spanish, her hands providing accents and a few gestures Phillips didn't think were lady-like. She turned, glared at Reynolds, and stomped back to the bedroom.

Phillips cleared his throat and looked back at the paper. "A lot of things are missing on this inventory."

"Nah, it's everything."

Sofia returned and issued another stream of rapid-fire Spanish. She pumped up the volume, her hand movements more intense, as if conducting an orchestra as fast as it could play. She returned once more to the bedroom and slammed the door.

Phillips looked over at Reynolds. "Did you catch any of that?"

"Nah, I don't *hablo* Spanish. Besides, I never got past her tits. What about you?"

Phillips shrugged his shoulders. "My Spanish isn't good. I think I heard the words for kiss and ass. Maybe we're supposed to kiss her ass." He lifted the paper again. "As I was saying, this is incomplete."

"It's everything."

"I can buy this crap from a twelve-year-old on any Minneapolis street corner. AKs and Saturday night specials.

Does it look like I need that?"

Reynolds frowned. "What were you expecting?"

"MP5s, a few Steyrs, maybe a Barrett or two," Phillips replied. "And toss in an RPG or ten."

"What makes you think I've got an arsenal lying around?"

"I have sources, too."

Reynolds rubbed his chin. "None of them work for me."

Phillips shrugged. "People talk. They've told me what they've seen. And yes, they work for you."

Reynolds reached over and snatched the piece of paper. "Bullshit."

"People are willing to gossip for cash. I'm sure they told me things they thought you'd be telling me anyhow. Or maybe already had. Common knowledge is meant to be shared, especially when someone waves dollars."

Reynolds stuffed the paper into his pocket. "You can't be going around me. Not if you think we're gonna work together."

"I'm not going around you. This is an independent confirmation. Kind of like calling an applicant's references."

Reynolds rose and started toward the door to the mud room. "I don't know, man. I gotta think about this so-called partnership." He stopped and faced Phillips. "For starters, how about a trade? I'll give you Isabella, and you give me your little present in there."

"I'll consider your generous offer." Phillips got to his feet. "I just got Sofia and need to show my associates my appreciation. Plus, if Izzy knew I was discussing her like a piece of property, she'd kill me."

"Nah, Isabella'd be okay with it."

"Not the Izzy I know."

"Maybe she's changed. Maybe she's no longer the little innocent Izzy you knew."

***

After Reynolds and Dennis left, Sofia plopped on the couch next to Phillips. She no longer wore the tee. Instead, she wore one of Phillips' extra-large shirts. He scowled at her.

She smoothed the material over her ample breasts. "You don't mind, do you?"

"Kind of, yeah."

"But I'm your girlfriend. I'm supposed to run around in your shirts."

"In case you didn't hear, you're my property."

"Yeah, I heard."

"I hoped you were listening."

"Hell, I recorded it," Sofia stated. "In case he said something we really needed."

Phillips nodded. "He came close. What he showed me and what he said could get him for something, but it isn't enough."

"We need his suppliers," Sofia agreed.

"What was up with all the Spanish?"

"I needed to know if he spoke Spanish," she replied. "He doesn't."

"How do you know?"

"Because I said some things guaranteed to get a reaction."

"Like what?" Phillips asked. "What did you say?"

She smiled. "I said you could kiss me, you could fuck me, and you could share me. But if either of you tried to fuck me in the ass, I'd kill you both."

Phillips blushed. "Why would you say something like that?"

"If that didn't get a reaction out of him, either he was dead or didn't understand a word," Sofia explained. "I had to be sure because some of his employees do speak Spanish. Maybe it will help us get to them."

He bit his lower lip. "Reynolds said he would trade for you."

"Should we go for it? Could I get closer than Katrina is now?"

"I don't know, but it may be an option to consider."

"Why?"

Katrina's inebriated image stumbled through his brain. He looked at Sofia. "She's struggling undercover. I'm not sure we'll get her back alive."

# CHAPTER TWENTY-FOUR

Dan Larkin and Bruce Ellison camped in the Taurus a few houses down from Christoph Morton's home. Larkin sat behind the steering wheel, staring at the day's crossword puzzle. Ellison slouched in the seat as if hiding, his coffee cup beneath his nose, where he sniffed and inhaled deeply. It looked like he was using the cup as a shield.

Larkin tapped his pen against the paper. "And we begin another busy day of indescribable business."

"I'd like to believe this isn't a waste of time, but I can't," Ellison grumbled. "It's almost like somebody knows we're watching, so they pay him to wander around, lead us nowhere and everywhere."

Morton stepped out of the house and over to his Mercedes SUV, parked in the short driveway. He opened the back, dug around, slammed the door, and went back into the house.

Larkin glanced back at his puzzle. "So much excitement for nothing."

Morton lived in the top half of a duplex owned by his mother. He always used the private entrance on the second level to go in and out. He often ran the stairs and stood at the top as if checking for movement or a tail. Which he pretty much always had. The question was, did he know it?

"Do you think his mom charges him rent?" Ellison asked.

"I sure hope so. If we're right about him, he makes good money. Too good not to share with Mom."

"I'm pretty sure he makes better money than either of us."

"We're the good guys," Larkin reminded him. "Pretty much everybody makes better money than we do."

Ellison sighed. "Sad but true. Almost enough to make a good cop turn bad."

"Almost."

"Better not to think about it."

"Definitely better," Larkin agreed.

They fell silent, each to their own thoughts about equity and justice.

A half-hour later, Morton came out again. "Damn."

Larkin folded his newspaper and tucked his pen in his pocket. "Must be something special today. He's all dolled up."

Ellison sat up in his seat, trading his coffee cup for his binoculars. Morton wore a nice navy-blue suit, a white dress shirt, a tie with diagonal red and navy stripes, and dress shoes. Ellison whistled low. "He's got a hot date."

Morton climbed into his SUV, primped in the rearview mirror, and backed out of the driveway. Larkin put the car in gear and followed at a safe distance. Morton turned right onto a busy street, and Larkin trailed behind.

"How much do you think that snazzy Mercedes cost him?" Ellison asked.

Larkin snorted. "Maybe that's why he lives with Mommy. Of course, it could be despite being a courier for a slime ball, he might be a good son."

"Yeah, living at home is how he affords the Mercedes."

Morton stopped every morning at the Starbucks drive-thru. Larkin and Ellison waited across the street in the parking lot of a food cooperative. Morton received his coffee and pulled away.

Ellison peered through the binoculars. "Hey, where's his doughnut?"

"Hmm. First a suit, and now no doughnut. Maybe our boy's changing his ways." Larkin pulled into traffic with a few cars between him and Morton.

"Maybe he does have a date," Ellison suggested. "Doesn't want to risk messing up his suit."

Morton's habitual second stop was a print shop and copy center. He parked in front, in the tow-away zone with the emergency flashers on, went inside for two minutes, and walked out carrying a business-sized envelope.

The third stop was a bakery. Morton carried the envelope inside and emerged empty-handed.

"Do we need to break his taillight?" Ellison suggested. "Or toss a bag of pot on his seat?"

"What would that accomplish?"

"It would give us enough probable cause to find out what the hell he's couriering all over the Cities. Unless he does something stupid, we're never going to find out."

Larkin lifted his coffee cup. "Here's to stupid." He drank, set it back in the cup holder beside Ellison's, and sighed. "We have to hope and wait to get lucky."

Ellison waggled his eyebrows. "Or we make our own luck."

They followed Morton into St. Paul, onto West Seventh Street. "This is new, isn't it?" Ellison asked.

"Actually, it isn't. I followed him over here on one of the first days we tailed him."

"Where was I?"

Larkin pointed to the cell phone face down on Ellison's lap. "Right next to me, playing one of your little phone games. Said you were on Level Five and not to bother you unless it was life or death."

"Hmm. I guess I can understand that. Level Five is a bitch."

They pulled into the parking lot of a strip mall containing a dozen businesses. "Now, this is definitely new," Larkin stated.

Ellison nodded. "A break from routine. Never a good thing."

Morton circled, looking for a parking space. He found one at the end of a long row. Larkin pulled into a space two rows over. Morton climbed out of his SUV, looked around, and headed away from the strip mall to the sidewalk along the street.

Larkin killed the engine and shoved the keys into his

pocket. "We better get moving." They scrambled from the car and cut through the rows, staying parallel to Morton instead of using the sidewalk and following him down the busy street in plain sight.

Behind the strip mall, a building stood by itself. A big sign hanging above the door said, *Thrillers*. The fine print clarified: *Real Girls, Real Fine.* With another furtive glance, Morton slipped inside.

Larkin and Ellison looked at each other. "I guess we risk it," Ellison remarked. "We need to know what he's up to."

"Okay. One at a time or together?" Larkin asked.

"Let's try together. If we're made, it won't matter."

They pulled open the door and stepped into a mostly dark room. Neon lights hung around and above the bar and the three long runways extending from the front wall toward the back of the room.

"He brought us to a titty bar?" Ellison muttered.

Scantily clad young ladies strutted to the ends of the two outside runways, paused at the end by striking a pose, pivoted, and strutted back. They walked along the front wall and repeated the parade at the other end.

The middle runway had a brass pole at the end. A

limber and athletic young woman, wearing nothing but a nearly invisible G-string, swung her body around it.

Larkin looked at Ellison. “Let’s go with it. See where this takes us.”

The host approached, dressed in a fur bikini. She was tall, mostly leg, and had bleached-blonde hair. Her breasts threatened to spill from her bikini cups. “Good afternoon, gentlemen. Welcome to our lunchtime lingerie show. Would you like to sit up front or at a table to the rear?”

“We can’t stay long, so I think a table in back,” Larkin suggested. “We won’t miss anything, will we?”

She winked. “Not a thing. We’ll make sure. Lunch menu?”

“I don’t know that we have time,” Ellison replied. “But yeah, let’s have a look.”

She grabbed two menus and waved them to follow. “Please, right this way.” They followed her to a table in the back, between the first and center runway. She stopped, made sure she had their attention and leaned over extra far to set out the menus. “Enjoy your lunches.”

Larkin smiled. “I’m sure we will.”

They circled the table so their backs were against the

wall. Before he sat, Larkin made sure he could still see Morton.

Larkin held the menu high enough so he could study it and Morton. Ellison watched the fashion show. A server appeared next to them. She wore short shorts, fishnet stockings, and a mesh shirt. She displayed flat abs and plenty of curves.

"See anything you like?" she asked.

Ellison scanned her. "Most definitely."

She gave a practiced smile. "Thank you, but I was referring to the menu." She tapped a long finger with a bright red nail against his menu. "Shall I come back?'

Ellison picked up his menu. "Yes, please."

Morton stood, moved his chair, said something to someone close, and sat back down.

"Wait," Larkin blurted. "We'll each have a tap beer. I'm thinking we don't have time for lunch."

"Two tap beers coming up." She grabbed the menus and left.

The pole dancer finished her act to a smattering of applause. She disappeared through a curtain and reappeared seconds later near the front door. She had draped a fine mesh coverup over her bare skin and nude-colored G-string. She sashayed past their table. As she moved, light reflected off her glitter-covered breasts. She smiled at the two men. “I hope you enjoyed the show.”

Larkin grinned. “Yes, ma’am. We sure did.”

She waved and walked over to Christoph Morton. He stood as she approached the table. From beneath his coat, he produced a flat brown envelope and a small box wrapped in bright red paper and tied with a gold ribbon. He handed them to the dancer and said a few words as she opened them.

A smile lit up her face, broadening into a big, toothy grin. She screamed and threw her arms around him. He stood stiff-armed as she almost lifted him off the floor and rocked him side to side. She released him, kissed him, clutched the envelope and the box to her chest, and ran from the room.

A loud laugh came from behind the bar, followed by a roar of “Good luck.”

Morton straightened his suit, finished his drink, tossed some greenbacks on the table, and headed for the door.

“Shit,” Larkin grumbled. “We need to leave.”

The server appeared with two frosted mugs. “Here you are.”

Larkin stood. “Thanks, but we gotta go.” He threw

some fives on her tray and ran for the door. Ellison took a quick gulp from one of the beers and followed.

By the time they reached their car, Morton was nowhere in sight.

***

Russ Malloy slammed his fist into the dashboard of his black Land Rover, parked down the street from Christoph Morton's home. "He breaks routine, and you lose him."

Ellison stood on the passenger side, leaning forward to look in the window and across the empty seat. "It was the break in routine that threw us."

Malloy narrowed his eyes. "You think maybe it was the naked women?"

Larkin stood at the driver's side window, a safe distance from Malloy's reach. "Yeah, you could say Morton exploited the distraction. We'll keep searching for him, see if he returns to his routine."

Ellison nodded. "If not, we'll get back on his tail in the morning."

"In the meantime, we don't know what he's up to," Malloy complained. "He could be anywhere, doing anything. Goddammit, morning might be too late."

"We'll keep looking," Larkin suggested.

"Did you go back and shake down the dancer?" Malloy asked.

"Uh, we tried," Larkin told him. "As soon as we lost Morton, we went back into Thrillers to find her. We hoped she'd tell us about the package, if it was from Morton or if he was only the delivery boy."

"But she was already gone by the time we got back in," Ellison added. "The amazing thing was none of the customers knew her name. They all claimed they'd never seen her before."

"No one wants to admit to the cops that they're spending their lunch hours looking at strippers," Malloy grumbled. "You two probably should have been smart enough to do that, also."

# CHAPTER TWENTY-FIVE

Wes Phillips sat on a cold park bench, facing the icy water of Lake of the Isles and its running trail. He wore dark glasses and tilted his face toward the bright sun.

Damian Reynolds and Dennis strolled across the white lawn, their boots crunching across the thin layer of crusted snow. Dennis took in the scenery and found a thick-trunked tree to lean against. Reynolds walked over to Phillips. He held a hand above his eyes and squinted through the sun's glare. "Why are we meeting out here?"

Phillips remained seated. "Two reasons." He paused and gazed at a pair of young women jogging past on the trail. "The view and the privacy."

Reynolds hunched his shoulders and stuffed his hands in his coat pockets. "It'd be better if it wasn't so fucking cold."

"Be glad the sun's out. A rarity for November."

"So again, why are we here?" A dark-haired woman jogged by. Reynolds stared at her, and she gave him the finger. "Isn't that—"

"Yep." Phillips nodded. "She doesn't like me any more now than before."

"I wondered how that was going."

"Still sleeping with my eyes open," Phillips admitted. "Anyway, we're here to talk specifics."

"What kind of specifics?"

"We're looking for specialized tools for one of our favorite clients."

"What exactly are you looking for?" Reynolds asked.

"The party in question wants to take an airplane out of the sky. Rumor is, you have a connection who can find such a toy."

Reynolds shook his head and gazed at the partially frozen lake. "I don't support terrorists."

"This isn't terror. Only a personal matter. A divorce of sorts."

"Kind of extreme, isn't it?"

"Probably cheaper than a real divorce in the long run," Phillips replied.

Reynolds peered around. "You know, you people are beginning to make me nervous. We haven't concluded a single transaction, yet you keep pushing me to find costlier toys. Maybe you should make some kind of good-faith deposit into one of my accounts."

"You're extorting us?"

Reynolds chuckled. "Nah, consider it a down payment. Like earnest money when you buy a house. Prove you're serious."

"We've never done that with our other partners," Phillips insisted.

"There's always a first time."

Phillips drummed his gloved fingers against his leg. "I'll see what I can do."

Reynolds smiled and leaned in. "In the meantime, you want me to find a home for that present of yours?"

"What kind of home?"

"A nice one. Probably in Russia or the Middle East. They like them with a bit of fire."

"You can do that?"

Reynolds laughed. "Shit, that's nothing. Finding a piece like that a home is easier than some of the other things you've asked."

# CHAPTER TWENTY-SIX

Wes Phillips and Sofia Menendez parked outside the Subway sandwich shop near Hennepin Avenue South and 24th Avenue and went in to order a late lunch. They carried their food to a back booth, where Russ Malloy waited.

Malloy drank from his cup and set it beside a rumpled napkin. An empty sandwich wrapper sat in a ball in front of him. "Any progress on Reynolds?"

Sofia scooted onto the booth seat while Phillips shook off his coat. "Well," Phillips stated in a low voice. "He didn't say no, per se, when I asked to get my hands on a weapon that could take out a plane."

"Then what did he say, per se?"

Phillips sat beside Sofia and unwrapped his sandwich. "He wants us to make a deposit into his account first. Make sure we're on the up and up."

Malloy leaned back, folded his arms, and watched Phillips bite into the sandwich. "What was your response?"

Phillips chewed for a while and swallowed, then wiped

some mayo off his lips. "Told him I'd see."

"He was okay with that?"

Phillips nodded and sipped his soda.

Sofia elbowed Phillips in the ribs as he was about to swallow. She waved her flat wrap sandwich around. "Tell him about me."

Phillips coughed and sputtered. He grabbed his napkin and covered his mouth, choking. One of the Subway employees leaned over the counter and looked his way.

Malloy gave a wave of dismissal. "He swallowed wrong."

Sofia gripped Phillips' arm, bent her head down, and peered into his watery eyes. "Are you all right? Can you talk? Do you need help? I can help you."

Malloy grinned and watched Phillips shake her off.

"I swear you'll be the death of me. Not this assignment," Phillips managed between coughs. He blew his nose on a napkin.

"He's okay!" Sofia shouted over Phillips' head. "He can talk." She smiled at Phillips and bit into her wrap.

Malloy shook his head. "Sofia, you better do the

talking. What were you going to say?"

"Mmm-mmm." She took another bite. "I love flat wraps. Not so much bread, you know? Bread fills you up. Makes my stomach full for hours." She patted her flat abs. "Not that I have to worry about gaining weight." She looked at Phillips. "Do I?"

Phillips pointed at Sofia. "You see?" he told Malloy. "This is who you sent me for a partner. This is who I have to deal with."

Sofia elbowed him again. "Be glad it's me. You could be sleeping in that bed every night with some boring old plain-faced agent, one who's not pretty and vivacious like me."

Phillips looked up at the ceiling. "If only."

"Or worse yet, you could be sleeping with a man. Someone like Russ, perhaps." She smiled and winked at Malloy.

Phillips rubbed his side. "So? At least he wouldn't run around the carriage house modeling my T-shirts and boxers."

She tilted her head. "You think?"

"Okay, okay," Malloy cut in. "I don't want to hear any more lovers' quarrels. You're both scaring me. Tell me what I need to know so I can be on my way."

Phillips smiled. "Actually, it's about getting rid of

Sofia."

Sofia raised her fist and punched his shoulder. "That's not how you said Reynolds worded it."

"Damn." Phillips slid as far as he could away from her. "I should get workers' comp just for sitting next to you." He turned to Malloy. "Reynolds said he could find a home for her if I was interested. In Russia or the Middle East. Sounded like he's made that kind of arrangement before."

"Wow. This could be bigger than we thought." Malloy stood. "Keep on him. It'll be interesting to see where this goes."

"What about the money deposit?"

Malloy slipped on his jacket. "I'll discuss it with Martinez. Any word about my sister? She still doing okay?"

Phillips straightened. His hands balled into fists beneath the table. "Barely." His tone turned serious. "Listen, Russ, if she was my—"

"Don't even go there," Malloy interrupted, warning him with his eyes. "I didn't choose this profession for her. She's the one who followed my footsteps. Always competing with me, her big brother. Had to do everything I did just as well, if not better."

His voice grew louder, angrier. “Don’t think I didn’t try to talk her out of this assignment. Don’t think…” He paused, gathering his composure. He looked away, then back at Phillips. “It’s killing me inside. Eating me up. I want to protect her, but there’s only so much I can do.” He zipped up his jacket and pulled a black knit cap over his ears. “I hope to God she knows what she’s doing.”

# CHAPTER TWENTY-SEVEN

Wes Phillips dropped Sofia Menendez off at the carriage house with a flimsy excuse of needing some alone time to think. He headed toward Mayhem Books, dialing the car radio to a classic rock station. Stevie Ray Vaughan was wailing on his guitar to *Look at Little Sister*. As he drove, Russ Malloy's words rolled around in his head. He felt sorry for the guy. He tried to imagine Jen or Alyse following him through the academy, onto the streets, underground.

His last encounter with Katrina Malloy resurfaced in his brain, her bloodshot eyes, her hungover body, her matter-of-fact voice. She was drinking herself to death, offering her body to a scumbag criminal and his criminal friends, all in the line of duty. If Jen or Alyse... He shook his head, trying to clear it. Thank God they picked safe careers.

He entered the bookstore, dusted snowflakes off his shoulders, and stamped his feet. A warm, musty smell greeted him. He glanced at the counter as he removed his gloves, shoved them into a pocket, and unzipped his coat. Leo's perch sat empty.

"If you're a customer, make yourself comfy," a deep voice growled from the back of the store. "If you're here to rob me, cash register's behind the counter. The drawers are loaded just like the gun on my hip."

Phillips smiled and headed over to a round table that displayed an array of mystery and suspense novels. A sign saying *We Love Local Authors* was propped in front of them. Phillips picked up a hardcover titled *Break Every Rule*. He flipped open the cover and turned to the copyright page. "Is this Freeman's latest?" he called.

"That you, Sally?" Leo shouted back. "Come here and gimme a hand."

Phillips set the book down and headed toward Leo's voice. The man sat on the floor, his body wedged between two aisles. Several stacks of books towered precariously beside him.

Leo extended two fat palms. "Help me up. My ass is killin' me. I don't think I gots any circulation left in either cheek."

Phillips grunted as he hefted the man upward. "Where's your helper?"

Leo reached out to steady himself. "Philosophy class. Little prick's always disappearing when I gots work to do." He drew a few ragged breaths. "Thanks for showing your ugly mug." He jerked his thumb at the books behind him. "Thought I'd be stuck here in the land of romance all night." Leo waved to follow and waddled toward the front of the store.

"Not sayin' I ain't a romance kind of guy. If you know what I mean." Leo stopped and swung an elbow lightly into Phillips' ribs. "Heh, heh."

The bells over the door chimed, and a small figure dressed in an army green coat entered the store. She pulled back the fur-lined hood, revealing green eyes and dark hair.

Leo furrowed his brows. "Ah, if it ain't my favorite top-paying customer." He turned and looked at Phillips. "She's granting my store another good-for-nothing visit."

The girl stared at the ground and stomped snow off her boots.

Leo shook his head and squeezed behind the counter. "That's Miss Browser," he told Phillips as the girl slunk past them into the stacks. "You'd think she'd buy something one of these days coming in as often as she does. Hell, no. Uses the john, then wanders up and down the aisles, enjoying the bennies of my high heating bill. 'Just looking,' she always claims." He leaned forward and whispered, "Thinks I'm a stupid fuck."

Phillips smiled. "Well? Are you?"

Leo grinned back. "Aw, screw you. If I had half a mind, I'd double the price of your purchases due to lousy customer attitude." He pulled a thin book off a shelf labeled *For Customer Pick Up* and set it on the counter. "But I'm a nice guy. Ain't I a nice guy?" he yelled toward the book stacks. He shook his head again. "Kid won't answer. Doesn't like to converse."

"Maybe it's with whom she's conversing."

"Yeah? Ain't you mister know-it-all."

Phillips leaned close, lowering his voice. "I've seen her at some of the readings. Name's Jane. How often does she come around?"

"Too often. If I wasn't so nice, I'd kick her out for loitering." He rang up the book and waited as Phillips dug out his wallet. "Kids should be in school!" he yelled toward the stacks again.

Phillips set a twenty-dollar bill on the counter, then rapped it with his knuckle. "Hold on." He walked back to the display table and picked up *Break Every Rule*. He handed it to Leo. "Add this to my bill."

"Gotta love Freeman. Ever meet him?"

Phillips shook his head. "I heard he's a nice guy. Easy

to talk to."

Leo smiled. "Coming for a book signing early December. He's gonna be a Christmas present for business."

As they exchanged money, the girl hurried by. She yanked her hood up and reached for the doorknob.

"Thanks for supporting local businesses!" Leo shouted. *"And good riddance!"*

The door closed, and all Phillips saw through the basement window next to the stairwell was a flurry of legs. Leo tucked the books into a plastic bag marked *Mayhem Books: The Suspense Will Kill You* and handed it to Phillips. "Kid'll be back tomorrow."

***

Phillips reached the corner on foot, the Lincoln less than a block to the south, and noticed the girl sitting in the bus shelter across the street. A bus pulled up, its sign blinking *Franklin Avenue*. Two young, dark-skinned men hopped out, and the bus pulled away. The girl remained on the bench.

*I should talk to her*, he thought, tugging at the collar of his coat. *Jeezus, I'm crazy for doing this.* He looked both ways and crossed the street, the bitter wind blowing in his face. The snow swirled around him, falling thicker and faster. The past few winters proved mild. Not much snow, not much cold. This year would be a polar bear, per the weatherwoman. "So much for global warming," he muttered as he neared the shelter.

He paused several feet away, deciding what to say, when an old Buick Riviera pulled up next to the shelter and lowered its passenger window. Phillips turned away and stared through the barred window of a jewelry store at the expensive display of diamond rings.

The girl headed to the car. She leaned in, and Phillips strained to hear their conversation. He couldn't make out any words but got a blurry glimpse of the driver's face in the store window's reflection. An old man. Phillips guesstimated seventies. The man smiled and waved a thick black book at the girl. She rushed to the shelter to grab her large duffel bag, scurried back to the car, and crawled in.

*Shit.* Phillips spun around and memorized the license plate as the car rumbled away through the slushy downtown street.

# CHAPTER TWENTY-EIGHT

Dennis flashed a fake badge at Leo. "I'm with the Feds."

Leo focused on Dennis' cold, humorless, dark eyes. "Which part of the alphabet?"

Dennis pressed his bulk against the counter and leaned on the glass with greasy palms. "Been tailing that guy who just left your store."

Leo turned away to rifle through some receipts. "Fella's got a secret admirer, eh?" He clucked his tongue. "Some guys have all the luck."

Dennis straightened. "Yeah, sure. Luck. We could all use a bit of that. Some more than others." He glanced around. "Especially on a day like today when one finds oneself quite isolated."

Leo turned back, eyes narrowed. "That some kind of punk-ass threat? 'Cause I don't do well with threats."

Dennis smiled. "Let's just say my higher-ups are in need of information, and I'm in need of a long-overdue promotion."

"Right." Leo grunted. "And I'm in need of kicking some smart-mouth in the hind end if given the chance."

Dennis' right hand twitched. He puffed up his chest. "Listen, Mister…" He glanced at Leo's name tag. "…Mayhem. I'm the little guy, if you know what I mean. I'm here to collect a name. That's all. Gimme that fine customer's name, and I waltz out of here like the end of a fairy tale. We on the same page?"

# CHAPTER TWENTY-NINE

Chief Roxanne Dalestrom closed her office door and sat at her desk. She punched in the number for the DHS and asked the high-pitched voice who answered to transfer her to Special Agent Eric Martinez.

"May I ask who's calling, please?"

She tapped her nails on the desktop. "Tell him it's Chief Dalestrom."

"Chief who?"

"Oh, my God." Dalestrom sat forward in her chair. "Dalestrom," she repeated loudly, enunciating each syllable. "Minneapolis Police Chief Roxanne Dalestrom. Do you need me to spell it?"

"One moment, please."

Christmas music played in her ear, and she waited for Martinez to pick up. "Chrissake," she muttered. "It's not even Thanksgiving yet. Can't the world enjoy one holiday at a time?"

"Martinez."

"Hey, Eric. This is Roxanne. How goes the life of a crime-solver?"

Martinez chuckled. "I could ask you the same question."

"And you'd probably get the same answer. It's the shits." Dalestrom paged through her desk calendar. The Saturday after Thanksgiving was circled in red. "Not to mention I've got both the mayor and the governor chewing my ass."

"About the Thanksgiving Parade?"

"You got it. The mayor chooses to slap his sweaty palms over his ears whenever the words 'terrorist' and 'potential threat' are thrown around, then he cries to the governor that I'm blowing things out of proportion."

Martinez sighed. "I hear you. Some people want to look the other way, even when a gun's waved in their face. They refuse to deal with the reality of our violent world."

"Glad we're on the same page. Hey, speaking of guns, how's my rookie doing? Phillips shoot anyone or fuck anything up?"

"I like him. Seems to be a good guy. One of our agents who's working closely with him says he's pretty sharp. No nonsense."

"Well, damn. Here I thought Phillips was cocky. Too green to go under."

"Sometimes green can be good."

"For his sake, let's hope so. I don't want him to come back missing an ear. Or worse." She swiveled in her chair and peered at the map on the wall. "Any chance he'll be back on my schedule in time for the parade?"

Martinez cleared his throat. "To be honest, Roxanne, I don't know. The mission's more complicated than we had hoped."

"Crap. That's what I was afraid you were going to say. What about your other agents? Can I rent a few for the day to help cover the parade route? I've got some hot spots where our caller threatened to create holy havoc."

"There always has to be one crazy caller out there," Martinez remarked. "Then again, you don't know what kind of crazy, do you?"

"I can speculate, but then I'd be written up for profiling. I hate to say it, but in this day and age, I have to believe everything I hear. Or not hear." Dalestrom shook her head. "I wish the mayor and governor felt the same way."

"Tell me the locations. I'll see what I can do."

Dalestrom stood and focused on several red tacks placed along the parade route through downtown Minneapolis. "Caller claims he's going to start his mass murders at the beginning of the parade where Dunwoody Boulevard meets Hennepin Avenue. The area surrounding the Basilica, in other words. Farther down the route, he's going to annihilate the corner of Hennepin and South 12th Street right where Beccah's Bible and Books is located."

"And a damn good restaurant. Butcher & The Boar," Martinez added.

"Hmm. Never been, but I'd be delighted to go. Hint, hint."

Martinez laughed.

"Next hot spot is the Scientology Outreach Center of Minneapolis on Hennepin and South 6th."

"Shit, Murphy's Steakhouse is right there, too. Another one of my favorites. A bit pricey, but worth every dollar."

"For God's sake, Eric, quit mentioning food. I'm getting hungry as hell, and it's not even lunchtime." She squinted at the map. "Okay, now, if you follow 6th Street further south, you'll run into Jacob's Bakery and Bistro. Definitely a nice location to wipe out a group of innocent Kosher gatherers."

Martinez scribbled down the information. “Got it.”

“Not done yet. Caller wants to take out the Hennepin Bridge over the Mississippi at the end of the parade route. We figure he wants to cut off any possibility of police, fire, and rescue from that direction.”

“Shit. This could be bad. After we hang up, I’m talking to my boss. I guarantee you, Roxanne, he will personally sit down with the governor.”

Dalestrom closed her eyes and exhaled a long breath. “Thanks, Eric. I owe you.”

“Two tickets to the Minnesota Wild game?”

“Only if I can come.”

“You got it.”

She smiled. “Oh, and Eric?”

“Yeah?”

“Dinner’s on you.”

# CHAPTER THIRTY

Katrina Malloy sat in the back seat pressed against Damian Reynolds as Dennis eased the Cadillac Escalade to a complete stop. "This is it, honey." Reynolds slid his hand out from beneath her dress. He squeezed her thigh. "Home, sweet fucking home."

She stared out the window at the massive brick house while Dennis heaved his large body out of the front seat and came around back to open their door. Strings of red, green, and blue lights adorned the exterior of the house and lined the full length of the driveway. The bulbs blinked on and off, displaying the same proper pre-holiday cheer as the surrounding homes. A man who appeared to be of Mexican descent, dressed in a white dress shirt, red vest, and black bow tie and slacks, hurried out the front door to greet them.

Dennis held the car door open, and Reynolds climbed out.

"Welcome, sir." The man first bowed to Reynolds, then to Dennis. "Sir."

Reynolds slapped the man on the back and motioned to Katrina. “Eduardo, this fine, upstanding young lady will be dining with me tonight and touring the facility. See that she’s well taken care of.” He winked at Eduardo.

“Yes, sir. Of course.” Eduardo reached for Katrina’s gloved hand and helped her from the car. A rush of cold night air breathed its way up Katrina’s short red velvet dress, swirling between her legs, blowing across her exposed skin. She shivered, clutching a high-waisted fur coat tighter around her upper body.

Eduardo guided her toward the door, his hand lightly on her lower back. Happy hour drinks ran through her bloodstream, and she wobbled across the recently shoveled driveway in spiked heels. Reynolds walked alongside her, holding her left arm, and surveyed the parked cars in the drive. Dennis walked several paces behind Katrina, his hands casually tucked in his jacket pockets, his eyes enjoying the occasional glimpse of a bare cheek.

They reached the front steps. “Another busy night, eh?” Reynolds asked.

“Yes, Mr. Reynolds,” Eduardo replied, helping Katrina up the steps and through the door into the entryway. “We’ve had an abundance of guests this past week.”

Reynolds dropped Katrina's arm, unzipped his jacket, and strolled to the entry table. He picked up the guest registry book. "Tis the season." He carried the book to the reception desk and opened it. The small print, written in Eduardo's handwriting, was not intended for public consumption.

Dennis closed the front door and wandered to the self-serve bar.

"No problems, I assume?" Reynolds asked Eduardo.

Eduardo shook his head. He joined Reynolds behind the reception desk and pulled at his starched collar. He watched the man's index finger slide across the recorded names. "No. None, sir. Everyone has been most gracious and satisfied with this week's entertainment and their individual appointments."

Reynolds flipped the page. "Uh-huh."

Dennis set out two highball glasses. "Your usual?" he called to Reynolds.

"Yeah. And don't make it pussy weak this time."

Eduardo looked at Katrina and raised his brows. "Would the lady like a chair?"

Reynolds didn't look up. "She don't need one." He closed the book and slid the top desk drawer open, pulling out a three-ring notebook marked Inventory.

Eduardo peered over Reynolds' shoulder. "It's all in order, sir. As you can see, we've had a few new employees delivered earlier this week." He cleared his throat. "Doc entered their deceptions and measurements into the computer."

Reynolds looked at him. "*Descriptions*, you mean." He pointed at two blank spaces. "I don't see no pictures."

Eduardo shifted on his feet. "I, uh, haven't had the opportunity, sir. Several guests requested the recruits immediately. They've spent a lot of time entertaining upstairs."

"I don't give a fuck if these girls are sucking off the President. Get their photos. I want them on the Web, pronto."

Eduardo nodded. "Yes, sir, Mr. Reynolds. Right away, sir."

Dennis headed to the reception desk and set Reynolds' drink down. He sipped from his own glass and meandered around the entryway, admiring the nude paintings and sculptures.

After several minutes, Reynolds snapped the notebook shut and looked at Katrina. She wavered on her feet. His gaze raked her from the ground up. "I'm famished."

Dennis smiled.

Eduardo hurried around the desk and opened a door to a large walk-in closet. Expensive men's coats lined the rack. He grabbed an empty silver-plated hanger. "May I take your coats before you enter the dining room?"

Reynolds picked up his glass. "Just the lady's."

Katrina reluctantly slid her coat and gloves off and handed them to Eduardo. Eduardo smiled and nodded at her.

Reynolds reached for Katrina with his free hand. He slid it up and down her bare arm. He smiled. "A nice, strong drink oughta warm you up, eh?"

She smiled back. Even in her inebriated state, she could tell the kind of establishment she stood in. The foyer, its lavish carpet and furniture, the art décor of naked women. A steady pulse of music radiated through the walls. An occasional far-off cry sounded above, accompanied by a man's laughter.

She wondered how many women, how many *girls*, turned tricks here and how many names were listed in that book. She doubted they performed willingly. If only she could get her hands on those two books. Somehow, some way, she would have to get Reynolds to invite Wes to this place.

"Right this way, sir." Eduardo scurried ahead, leading

them down a narrow corridor and to a set of double doors. Painted above the doors in metallic gold stencil were the words The Burgundy Room. Eduardo motioned them inside.

A dimly lit, smoke-filled room greeted them. The walls were papered in metallic gold and silver speckles, the plush carpet and floor-length drapes a deep burgundy. An ornate candelabra occupied the center of each white-linen-covered table, the flickering lights casting dancing shadows on men's faces while they dined.

The room pulsed with surround-sound speakers as a young woman, bathed in a neon spotlight, danced provocatively across a small stage. Her body, costumed in a black G-string, nude pasties, sheer black nylons that stretched thigh-high, and spiked heels, gyrated to the music. Long black gloves reaching to her elbows adorned her hands. She held them above her head, playing with her kinky black tresses. A studded collar encircled her neck and was attached to a leather leash that dangled between her ample breasts.

Eduardo pointed to an empty table near the front. "Will this be to your liking, Mr. Reynolds?"

"Perfect." Reynolds sat, his gaze never veering from the woman's body. Eduardo pulled a chair out for Katrina.

The woman smiled when she caught sight of Reynolds

and blew him a kiss. She spun around, bent over, grabbed her ankles, and stuck her ass out in his direction. She looked over her shoulder, locked eyes with Reynolds, and moved her hips in a slow, circular motion. Men seated at other tables whistled.

Eduardo turned and looked at Dennis. "And you, sir? Will you be dining as well?"

"Yes, he will," Katrina answered for him. She patted the chair on her other side. "Sit down, Kong. Right here next to me." Reynolds glanced at Katrina, his eyebrows raised. She smiled back.

Eduardo handed out three menus.

Reynolds raised his index finger. "One more. Tell Doc to get his butt in here."

"Yes, sir," Eduardo replied. "I believe he is engaged at the moment, but I will let him know." He smiled. "Enjoy your dinner. Your server will be here shortly." He bowed and stepped away.

The song ended, and the woman exited the stage while another girl took her place. A new song began, this one slower, sultrier. Dressed in a skimpy outfit made of lace and feathers, the girl moved her hips from side to side, both arms hugging her body. She closed her eyes and wore a drugged smile.

The woman sashayed toward their table, ignoring everyone except Reynolds. He watched her every step. She stood behind him and purred in his ear. “That dance was for you.” She draped both arms around him in a hug and pressed herself against the back of his chair.

Reynolds smiled, reached back, and tugged on her leash. “Come here, Dee-Dee.” He patted his lap. “Let me look at you.”

Dee-Dee laughed and wiggled as she sat on his lap and put one arm around his shoulder. She pressed her pasties against the front of his shirt. “Better?” She nibbled his ear.

“Mmm. Much.”

Katrina looked at Dennis and pretended to stick a finger down her throat. Dennis laughed, then cleared his throat when the topless server approached their table. She leaned over and filled their water glasses. He stared at the girl’s breasts.

“Mr. Reynolds,” the server greeted politely. “Would you like to order now, or should I come back?”

Reynolds peeled Dee-Dee away from him and smiled at the server. “Bring three house specials for now. No, actually two.” He pushed Dee-Dee in Dennis’ direction. “Dennis, you can join us later. Take Dee-Dee upstairs and keep her busy for a while. Isabella and I are gonna talk business. Doc, too, if he ever decides to join us."

Dennis smiled and stood, reaching for Dee-Dee's leash. "It would be my pleasure."

Dee-Dee pouted. "But Damian, I thought you and I would—"

"You thought wrong, sweetheart. Not tonight." He waved her off. "Go on. I promise Dennis will show you a good time."

Dee-Dee sneered at Katrina, scrutinizing her. She mouthed the word "bitch." Dennis pulled on the leash, and she turned to follow him.

Reynolds motioned to the server, pointing to his highball glass. "Bring me one more. And the lady would like a double shot of Vodka on the rocks."

After the server left, Katrina turned to Reynolds. "Your friend Dee-Dee's a lovely girl." She jerked her head toward the girl on stage who danced provocatively against the pole. Most of her feathers lay scattered on the floor. "It looks like you're surrounded by lovely girls."

Reynolds followed her gaze and laughed. He reached for his glass, enjoyed a long sip, and moved his chair closer to hers. "You're my number one beauty, though. Ain't that right, Isabella?"

"Sometimes, I'm not so sure."

He smiled and gazed into her eyes. "These girls mean nothing to me. You're different. You're mature for your age, and you've got smarts to go with it." He leaned close. "I could use your help in my business."

The server returned. She leaned over to set down the drinks and brushed her bare breast against Reynolds' arm. He grinned. "Thanks, hon."

Katrina clenched her jaw, grabbed her glass, and took several large gulps.

"Whoa." Reynolds reached for her glass, pulled it from her hand, and set it down. "Either you're awfully thirsty or jealous as hell." He placed his hand on top of hers. "Like I was saying, I think it's time to shift your responsibilities from pleasing me and my close associates to broadening your horizons here at the house."

She pulled her hand away. "What? You want me to pole-dance and fuck the gawkers? Or let me guess. You want me to walk around topless and serve food, then fuck."

"Isabella, no. I didn't say—"

"Your dinner, Mr. Reynolds." The server set down two salad bowls and two steaming plates of steak and lobster.

Reynolds rubbed his hands together. "Looks good. My compliments to the chef." He picked up his knife and fork and cut into the steak. "Now, what was I saying? Oh, yes, ramping up your work. Increasing production." He tried a bite of steak and looked at Katrina.

She sat with her hands in her lap, staring back at him.

He pointed his knife at her plate. "Eat. You got nothing in your stomach but booze." He waited until she picked up her fork. "Good girl. You want to move up in the business, you'll do what I say. No questions." He sliced off another piece of steak. "I need someone I can depend on to keep an eye on my merchandise. Help with marketing and distribution. Someone who follows orders. Think you might be that girl?"

Katrina nodded and started on her salad.

Reynolds lifted his fork, about to take a bite. "After dinner, I'll give you a private tour of my little warehouse downstairs. Just you and me." He winked at her and popped the steak into his mouth, his focus turning to the food and the girl onstage.

# CHAPTER THIRTY-ONE

Wes Phillips knelt on one knee in the mud room of the carriage house, tying a shoe, when Sofia Menendez stepped in front of him wearing short shorts and a tank top. Her bare legs smelled like a mixture of lemon and sugar. A few fine, dark hairs below her kneecap poked from her skin. Phillips held his gaze at knee level, not allowing his eyes to travel any higher.

"Going somewhere?" Sofia asked.

"A run."

"Are you trying to get away from me?"

He stood and closed his eyes. "No, I'm not trying to get away from you. I'm having a lot of trouble with this sit-and-wait B. S. I need to burn some energy. A run would be the best way."

"Can I go?"

"Not dressed like that."

"You didn't even look. You don't know how I'm dressed."

He snapped his eyes open. “Not dressed like that.”

“Will you wait for me? Five minutes?”

“Three minutes.”

“See you in five.”

He closed his eyes again so he wouldn’t see her bounce away, then decided his imagination was worse.

***

They ran along his usual route, starting on Kenwood Parkway, past the Uptown sites, and back to Kenwood. Ten minutes from the carriage house, they came to an octagonal tower built on top of a hill. Steel rods protruded like ribs, encircling the brick and stone medieval-like structure at four different intervals. An eight-foot wrought iron fence surrounded the grounds.

Sofia jogged through the snow to the gate, lifted the heavy latch, and entered.

Phillips frowned. “Sofia, what are you doing?” He waited on the sidewalk, jogging in place.

She smiled over her shoulder and circled behind the tower, out of his sight.

“Sofia.” He continued to jog in place. After a few

minutes, he followed her tracks across the lawn to the gate and pushed it farther open. “Sofia,” he called louder, stepping inside the fenced area. “Where are you?”

She emerged from around the other side of the tower. “Here.” She walked slowly, peering upward while dragging gloved fingertips across the bricks. She held her phone in her other hand.

“Don’t disappear like that.”

“Sorry. I was looking down the hill,” she replied. “It’s a pretty good drop at the edge, mostly straight down to the highway.”

“I trust you. I don’t need to see.”

“Did you know this is a water tower?” Sofia tucked her phone in her pocket. “I Googled it and found an article about Minneapolis water towers. This was the first one the article talked about.”

“It’s amazing what you can learn on Google,” Phillips grumbled.

“How tall do you think it is?” Sofia asked.

“Don’t know. Don’t care.”

“Look. Take a guess.”

Phillips shrugged.

"Come on, Wes. Your fear of heights is so bad you can't even look up to see how tall a building is?"

He nodded. "Some days. Most days."

Sofia removed her gloves and tossed them to him. She stepped up to the base of the tower, clawed her fingers into the half inch-deep mortar seams between the bricks, and started to climb.

"Wait, wait, wait. What are you doing?"

She looked down, placed her foot, and moved upward. "Helping you."

Phillips threw the gloves at her. They hit her in the back, then fell into the snow. "Helping me how?"

"By showing you there's nothing to be afraid of."

"Only heights, the fall, and the rapid acceleration. Oh, yeah, and the abrupt stop at the bottom." Phillips glanced back at the sidewalk and the empty street beyond. "Jeezus, Sofia, will you get down from there?"

She clawed her fingers between the bricks and laughed as she continued to climb. "Are you afraid of heights? Or of falling?"

Phillips stared directly ahead, refusing to look up. "I get dizzy when I look at things from above or below. I lose my balance, lose consciousness, and, if I'm lucky, I fall on the person who made me look up or down."

"Are you paying any attention to me?" Sofia called from above.

He heard her moving around. "I'm listening."

"You should be looking at my ass. It's spectacular."

"I'm a professional. I don't look at asses."

"Bullshit. I've caught you looking. You're alive. You notice."

"Well, you kind of flaunt it."

Sofia laughed. "That's because I'm also alive, and I enjoy the attention."

"Well, you've earned it. It is spectacular."

"Then why aren't you looking at it right now?"

Phillips sighed. "Because it's above my head. I'd have to look up. And if I look past you, I'd see clouds or stars or whatever is up there. Trust me, the results won't be good."

"Well, I'm going to cure you."

"Oh, for God's sake, Sofia. Come down now. Let's go. I

burned my energy already, and now my shoes are wet."

"I'm going to throw myself off this water tower, and you're going to catch me."

He snuck a glance up. She remained poised on the first rung of steel rods. He returned to staring directly ahead. "How is your dying here today going to cure me?"

"I'm not going to die. You're going to catch me. That will teach you with a good spotter, the right tools, or the right mindset, you can be higher up and not die."

"That is not a good plan."

"I know," she agreed. "But I trust you."

He looked up, and she pushed herself away from the wall and fell backward. Phillips took a step, raised his arms, and caught her, staggering under the sudden weight. He crushed her body to his chest, his heart pounding, and released a deep breath. "Are you okay?"

She smiled. "Of course I am. I was never in any danger."

He dropped her to the ground.

"What the hell?" she sputtered.

He stared down at her. "I didn't like your cure. Maybe

you'll learn not to play games."

"If you'd looked, you'd have seen I was only, like, seven feet off the ground. I wasn't going to get hurt, but you saved me anyhow."

He closed his eyes and exhaled another deep breath.

"What did you see, Wes, when you looked up?"

"I saw you falling. And I couldn't let you get hurt."

"You didn't see clouds or stars or pigeons waiting to crap on our heads?"

"No."

"That's how you approach heights." She tugged her gloves on. "You focus on what you need to do. You don't even see the rest. It's not there." She reached out a hand.

"I still don't like your cure." He ignored her hand, turned, and jogged back through the gate.

"No, but you like my ass," she shouted after him.

"I love your ass," he called back. "It's spectacular."

She scrambled to her feet and chased after him.

# CHAPTER THIRTY-TWO

Damian Reynolds held Katrina Malloy's arm and helped her maneuver the basement steps. He had decided to wait on dessert, wait for Doc to finish whatever the fuck he was doing and whoever the fuck he was doing it with. In the meantime, he and Katrina had finished their meals. He was eager to take her on that private tour.

He paused on the bottom step and turned to face her, waving his arms around. "This is where I keep my precious goods."

She gave a curt nod and waited, holding onto the rail behind her for balance.

"I envision you, Isabella, as a team leader. A Heidi Fleiss of sorts. I need someone with smarts who can keep a semblance of order with my employees. Make sure they're performing as required, following the house rules, not causing any trouble. You'd report any problems, and I'd follow up with proper disciplinary measures."

He stepped down and offered her his hand. She took it

and stumbled after him past the first row of cells. Most of them stood empty. The girls were either entertaining scheduled guests or taking turns on stage.

While paging through the appointment book earlier, Reynolds had noted that one of the dark-skinned girls, the one who called herself Jazz, was scheduled for a private appointment. He liked her. Her obedience, her willingness to do whatever a guest asked of her. Many of the girls fought the rules, fought the men. But not Jazz.

Dee-Dee also held his interest. She was willing, almost too willing. Reynolds had no respect for hookers and whores. Every day, Dee-Dee slid a little further into that category. When he had enough of her, he'd sell her ass out of the country.

Katrina looked right and left in disbelief, trying to focus on what Reynolds was saying.

"I'm looking for someone with the same organizational skills as Dee-Dee. I think you'd do well in that capacity. I'd even let you perform on stage if you asked nicely. Be the main act." He stopped and smiled. "All women like that sort of attention. I bet you're no different."

Katrina shook her head. "From what I saw—"

He held a finger up to her lips. "Let me finish." He swung an arm around her shoulders and started walking again.

"This is big business, Isabella. Any of my employees would jump at the opportunity I'm offering you. With a little training, you'd be surprised at what you can accomplish. And if I like what I see, if you fulfill all the duties I ask of you, I may consider you for a special marketing job in the works. We're talking serious money."

They turned the corner and headed down another row of cells. "How does traveling to a nice, warm place for the winter sound to you?"

"I—"

"Don't answer that," he interrupted, squeezing her shoulder. "I'm looking for the right person who can schmooze with my southwestern clients, work out lucrative deals when renting out my merchandise. Upon that certain someone's return, she would be promised a top management position here at the house. Or perhaps at one of my other locales." He winked. "That would be a whole different venture, though."

They passed a cell where a naked girl with heavy breasts and a large, distended belly lay on a cot. Her eyes were closed, and her hands rested on her abdomen. Reynolds hitched a thumb toward her. "You wouldn't believe the price men pay for banging a chick who's prego."

They walked by Jazz's empty cell. Her cellmate, the

new girl named Savannah, was upstairs as well. Reynolds made sure earlier in the week that Eduardo scheduled the girl for an appointment with him tonight. He liked to check out the new goods. According to the week's reviews, this one apparently had looks to kill for. And she was young. Barely thirteen, according to the book.

"A warm room, a comfortable bed, free food." Reynolds waved his hand around and smiled at Katrina. "These girls got it made."

Katrina leaned against the wall, listening to Reynolds go on and on about the benefits of the job. *Yadda, yadda, yadda. Does he really think he's fooling me?* For a moment, she imagined herself locked in one of the cells, at the mercy of men who only wanted to—

A girl's hoarse scream from a cell at the end of the row caught Katrina's attention.

"Let me out of here!" The girl banged on the bars. "Someone unlock this goddamn door!"

Katrina straightened and took a wobbly step in the girl's direction.

Reynolds grabbed her arm. "No. Leave her alone. She's one of the new ones. Apparently, she's not adjusting well."

"But—"

"She's high on something. I'll have Doc come down and give her a little calming medicine. It'll ease her withdrawals." He walked Katrina back toward the staircase at the opposite end of the basement. "Now you see why these girls need our help. So often, they come to us hooked on all sorts of nasty street drugs. They're dirty, sick, undernourished. Part of what I offer them is a new beginning. A clean start."

The girl's cries sobered Katrina up. *Remember the mission.* Despite what Reynolds said, these girls were prisoners. Drugged or frightened into submission, forced to perform lewd sexual acts against their wills. This was clearly sex trafficking, and Reynolds was ultimately responsible.

She glanced into the last cell. A young girl, who couldn't have been more than seven or eight, sat on a bed with a pillow pressed to her chest, rocking back and forth. She stared at the wall with a blank expression.

Katrina jerked a thumb in the girl's direction. "And her? How does that little girl fit into your business venture?"

Reynolds stopped and looked at the girl. He licked his lips and turned toward Katrina, pulling her close. He grabbed the back of her head and forced her mouth to his. When he pulled away, Katrina was breathing fast.

"That little girl is extra special to me," he whispered. "I'm keeping her out of the screwed-up foster care system while her meth-head mother spends time here convalescing. Doc has her in one of our luxury rooms upstairs so he can keep a close eye on her." He motioned toward the girl. "I've become a father figure to her." He traced his finger down Katrina's cheek and over her lips. "Don't worry about the kid. She's in excellent hands. No one's allowed to go near her but me."

He smiled and spun her to face the steps. "Now, come, Isabella. Let's go have dessert."

***

Reynolds and Katrina emerged from the basement. Eduardo stood in the hallway, a fresh drink for each in his hands.

"Thank you, my good man," Reynolds told him.

As Eduardo escorted them back to their table in the Burgundy Room, Katrina drank from her glass, trying to wash down the images from the basement.

An older gentleman with thinning gray hair stood as they approached. Even with slumped shoulders, he loomed above them. His body, with its long arms and legs, pushed almost seven feet. He wore dark slacks, a dress shirt, and a tie. Despite a protruding belly over his belt, he appeared muscular under all the flab. An oversized white doctor's coat was draped over the back of his chair. A plate scraped clean sat on the table.

He peered over his glasses at Katrina. "Well, well, well. Who have we here?"

Reynolds smiled and pulled a chair out for Katrina. "Doc, this is Isabella. The girl I was telling you about."

Doc reached down and took Katrina's hand, lifting it to his mouth and pressing his lips against it. "Glad to meet you, my dear. What a beauty, if I may say so myself. You sure know how to pick them, Mr. Reynolds."

Dennis and Dee-Dee had returned from their romp upstairs and were already seated at the table. Dennis glanced up, then continued to plow through his food as if it was his last meal. A slice of chocolate lava cake sat in front of Dee-Dee. She had draped a fringy shawl around her body and sat across from Dennis, beside Doc's chair, her legs crossed, one heel swinging back and forth. Her hair was disheveled and her lipstick smeared. She licked her fork and eyed Reynolds with Katrina dangling on his arm, then snorted at Doc's comment.

Reynolds nodded for Doc to sit, then seated himself between the two women and rubbed his hands together. He looked around the table. "Now that we're finally together, I'd like to announce that Isabella is considering an opportunity here at the house to help further our mission."

Dee-Dee dropped her fork with a clatter onto her plate. "What?" She grabbed Reynolds' arm.

Reynolds extracted her hand. "Business is growing, honey, and I've got plans in the works for pre-Super Bowl season. You know that's a busy time. Look what happened last year. This time, you're gonna have help managing the girls."

"But, Damian, you said—"

"Shut it." He turned his gaze to Katrina. "Besides assisting Dee-Dee, I also got another venture that may require your help. One of my other houses needs a pretty face to help with administrative work." He lowered his voice. "I'm talking weapons and pharmaceuticals. No tricks at that house. Only one man to please, namely me." He winked. "Of course, we could hold off on that position until you return from the southwest."

Dee-Dee scowled at Katrina. "I don't believe this," she muttered. She jumped from her chair, almost knocking it over. "You're gonna pick this drunk-ass bitch over me?"

Several men at nearby tables glanced over. Dennis rose from his chair, his hands twitching.

"Sit your ass back down," Reynolds ordered Dee-Dee, his eyes drilling into hers, "before I have Dennis take you upstairs again. This time, it'll be a lesson in manners. I guarantee you won't like it."

Dee-Dee opened her mouth, then closed it and eased back onto her chair. Dennis sat down again.

Katrina struggled to remain vertical, but her body was refusing. She slumped to one side, leaning toward Dennis. While Reynolds' lips moved, all she could think of was the little girl in the basement. Her face, her vacant eyes. She wished she had never seen her. She tried to focus on the heated conversation at the table, but the room kept spinning. She rested her head on Dennis' shoulder. She had reached her drinking limit. If she didn't lie down soon, she'd puke, pass out, or both.

"Well, I think that's a splendid idea, welcoming Isabella into our endeavors. You always have such a business sense, Mr. Reynolds." Doc raised his wine glass, his pinky extended. "Hear, hear."

Reynolds lifted his glass and motioned to the others.

Katrina dragged herself upright, grabbed for her glass, and missed. She didn't know what she would toast to, but what the hell, she thought.

Dennis picked up the glass and handed it to her with a smile.

"Thanks, Kong," she slurred.

They all sipped. Reynolds waved over the server. "Get the lady her dessert. She's celebrating."

The server nodded and hurried off.

"So, Isabella, what do you think?" Reynolds leaned toward her and whispered in her ear, "Are you ready to play some serious ball?"

*Yes,* she thought, *whatever you say. Just give me a few minutes to...* She leaned back onto Dennis' shoulder and closed her eyes. As she started to drift, she heard Reynolds laugh beside her.

"Keep an eye on her until I get back," Reynolds told Dennis as he stood. "I'm going upstairs to take care of a little matter."

"Sure thing, boss," Dennis replied. He pulled Katrina's glass from her hand and set it back on the table.

"Doc, while I'm up there, I want you to take care of a certain young lady downstairs," Reynolds stated. "One of the new employees is in need of a little something to make it through the night."

Doc nodded fervently. “Yes, sir, Mr. Reynolds.”

Reynolds squeezed Dee-Dee’s shoulder. “Be a good girl and help Doc out. Otherwise, you’re going back in your cage.” He leaned over and kissed her hard on the cheek.

Dee-Dee gave him a fake smile.

# CHAPTER THIRTY-THREE

Savannah, her hair shampooed and body washed, sat on the edge of the bed in Room 203. The man they called Eduardo told her Mr. Reynolds would see her soon. She knew from mysteries and movies their casual use of names meant she wouldn't get out of here alive. Unless she took drastic action of her own.

At least she hadn't been drugged tonight. She had her wits about her, memorizing every detail of the house as Eduardo escorted her to the second floor with a group of girls, including Jazz. No one fought to get away. They followed in a line, dressed in flimsy lingerie, oversized high heels clumping up the ornate wooden staircase, eyes downcast. Eduardo smiled politely and nodded, motioning each one to wait in a separate locked room for their scheduled guest.

She smoothed her hand over the red velvet bedspread. It was certainly not her pink comforter with polka-dot sheets. Nor were there any stuffed animals propped next to the pillows. She'd survived much in her short life in the foster care system, learned about survival sex early.

When her foster mother worked second shift, her foster father worked on caretaking, especially around bedtime. He taught her everything she needed to know about a man and his needs. On the weekends, when her foster mother was around, he called her “his little buddy” and asked her to help him in the garage, in the yard, on the roof.

That last day, she pushed back and witnessed his tragic fall. After the hospital stay, he returned, his body hunched in a wheelchair, his memory clouded. Despite his new demeanor, she ran for the streets.

She’d escaped one system to end up in another, trading blowjobs for meals and places to stay. The skills got her by until the night that big bastard violated her in ways she never imagined. All of her still hurt.

But she was a survivor. She’d make it through.

She stood and paced the plush white carpet, her mind wandering to the locked basement. From what her handyman foster father taught her about construction, the cells were an afterthought, designed long after the old house had been built.

Yet because the construction was crude did not mean it was easy to escape. She had examined where the bars went into the concrete. There wasn’t much cracking, didn’t appear to be much give. Almost as if the bars had been stood in place and the floor poured in after. They certainly weren't placed on existing concrete and bolted down.

This room on the second floor was nice. Large, fancy, quiet. Exactly what guests of this hellhole desired and what she had always dreamed of. But that dream also consisted of a loving family and a safe home.

Savannah shook the thoughts from her head and examined the lock on the door. It required a skeleton key. The one above it was electronic and needed the right combination.

She snuck around, checking the dresser drawers. She found no metal she could form into a tool. She was about to crawl under the bed, see if the springs or frame might yield a suitable weapon, when she heard someone working the lock.

The door opened, and a well-dressed man walked in. He wasn't an imposing physical specimen, not like the brutal ape who had brought her here. He wore a dark suit, a shiny blue tie, polished shoes, and heavy cologne. He could've modeled in a men's magazine.

He smiled. "You must be Savannah."

She sat back down on the bed and avoided eye contact. She nodded.

"I'm Mr. Reynolds." He stared at her. "You really are

lovely. We'll have to get your picture taken soon. I hear you've had quite a few visitors since your arrival. That's good. I'm sure others will want to enjoy seeing you, too. You're model quality." He swung the door shut. After it latched, he took a step in her direction. "Do you know why you're here?"

She shook her head.

"We offer protection, safety from the outside world. Out there, as you know, it's a mean, nasty place. Too many girls like you are abused and homeless, runaways from bad situations beyond their control. Destined to die early, never having known what love really is." He stepped closer to the bed. "We're here to make sure you're loved and cared for."

He took off his suit jacket, draped it over a chair, and loosened his tie. "We want you to have everything you need to lead a healthy, productive life." He held her chin, tipping her head back to look into her eyes. "We want to teach you the necessary skills."

"I have skills," Savannah mumbled, staring back.

"Really?"

She nodded.

"Will I be impressed?"

She nodded again.

He dropped his hand. "Show me."

"Take off your pants and lie on the bed."

"Ooh, a take-charge type. Interesting." He stepped from his shoes, opened his pants, and sat on the bed next to Savannah. She playfully pushed him back to a lying position, then knelt beside him.

"Close your eyes," she whispered. She would close hers as well. And imagine herself far, far away.

"You're on. Impress me."

***

By the time Doc returned from the basement with Dee-Dee, Katrina was resting her head on the tablecloth next to an untouched slice of cake. He shook her shoulder several times, but she was difficult to rouse. "Leave me alone," Katrina slurred in response. "Let me sleep."

"Sorry, my dear, but it's not quite time for bed." Doc rested one sweaty palm on her thigh. With the other, he lifted a water glass to her lips, his hand shaking, and forced her to drink. "The night is still young. Very young indeed."

She tried to push away the glass but finally gave in. Some of the water dribbled down her chin and onto the front of her dress. Doc hummed as he dabbed at the wet material with his napkin.

Dennis gave Doc a disgusted look. The old man was always sweating up a stink, especially around the girls. He acted like a teenager on his first date, with his nervous talk and armpit stains. Dennis wondered if the man could even keep a hard-on for five minutes before exploding all over himself.

Dennis' knees bounced. He twitched, fidgeted, and finally got up to pace. His eyes never stopped moving. He scanned the dining room and stared down any man who looked at Katrina. He watched Dee-Dee finish Katrina's dessert, and Doc's hands roam dangerously close to Katrina's plunged neckline. One of these days, Dennis thought, he'd take that whiny, oversized weasel out back and kick his ass.

Dennis glanced at the girl on stage, her slanted eyes, jet-black hair, and light brown skin. He figured she was part of the group delivered last week, fresh off the boat. Reynolds mentioned receiving a bunch of non-English-speaking girls. He looked back in Katrina's direction. Doc was smiling, his face inches from hers.

Dennis shook his head. He wanted to get this night over and get back to usual business. Just me, he thought, and Reynolds and Isabella.

Reynolds entered about twenty minutes later, wearing

a big smile. He swaggered over to the table. "It's going to be a wonderful auction," he told Dennis. "And it's going to be a wonderful night." He leaned down and kissed Katrina on the forehead. "You've got some work to do."

She pulled herself up in the chair. "What kind of work?" she asked groggily, her eyes glazed as she looked around.

Reynolds smirked. "You'll figure it out. Doc, get Savannah ready for the auction. She's in Room 203. I want her to be the picture of perfection and in her happy place, but not too happy. I don't need her falling off the stage. While you're at it, take her picture. Eduardo fucked up and was supposed to have done it already. Tonight, at the auction, she's either going to net us a record amount or she's going to move into my home so I can thoroughly enjoy her company before she flies off to warmer weather."

# CHAPTER THIRTY-FOUR

Behind a closed velvet curtain, the girls lined up on the wooden stage in the Ruby Red Room. They swayed back and forth, drunk or drugged, holding on to themselves and each other. Savannah stood at the end of the line, her mouth open and her eyelids heavy. Her brain refused to recall how she had traveled from the room upstairs to the brightly lit stage. She couldn't see past the edge of it, but she had a feeling several people were staring back at her.

Dee-Dee strutted around, preening the girls' skimpy outfits, touching up their hair and makeup. She towered over all but one of them, a young teen with long, skinny arms and legs and a flat chest. Despite how many times Dee-Dee fixed the girl's makeup, the tears started again, leaving lines of mascara running down her cheeks.

Dee-Dee slapped her hard. "Want me to give you something to cry about?" she hissed. "Stop your damn sniveling. I'm sick of it."

The girl choked back her tears. "I'm sorry," she blubbered. "Please. Let me go home."

Dee-Dee laughed. "This is home, bitch. Get used to it."

Doc waved at Dee-Dee from stageleft. "Two minutes." He turned on the stereo system surround sound and pressed play. Soft jazz music filled the room. Dee-Dee moved off to the side, and Doc opened the curtain and grabbed the cordless microphone.

Several men from the Burgundy Room now reclined in the plush theater seats. Wining and dining were over. They no longer wanted to watch a girl dance out of arm's reach. They wanted to bid on her and buy her for the night.

Damian Reynolds sat next to Katrina Malloy in the first row. She rested her head on his shoulder, fighting sleep. Dennis stood in the shadows at the back of the small theater, arms folded, legs shoulder-width apart, staring at the backs of the audience's heads.

The lights in the room dimmed, except for the spotlight on the girls. "Welcome, gentlemen," Doc announced, beads of sweat dotting his forehead. "On behalf of Mr. Reynolds, I'd like to thank each and every one of you for joining us this evening."

One by one, he announced each girl's name and age and told her to step forward. Dee-Dee prodded those who were too dazed to follow directions. After spinning in a circle, each girl wobbled back into line.

Reynolds nudged Katrina. “Hey. Pay attention. This is gonna be your job someday.”

Katrina raised her head and squinted at the girls. They looked so young and out of it. She wondered why the tall girl was crying. “What’s going on?” She pointed to the girl with the runny mascara. “What’s wrong with her?”

Reynolds grinned. “That girl may be teary-eyed right now, but as soon as she gets upstairs, she’ll find a happiness she never knew existed.” He leaned toward Katrina and whispered, “Kind of like you did with me.” He lifted his hand and cupped her chin, then danced the tips of his fingers down her throat, resting on the port wine stain.

Katrina smiled, moved her head forward, and kissed him full on the mouth.

Reynolds squeezed her thigh and settled back into his seat. “That’s my girl.” He glanced back at the stage, his eyes landing on Savannah. He smiled and gave Doc the thumbs-up to begin the bidding. “Now, keep your eyes open, Isabella. Watch how the money rolls in.”

# CHAPTER THIRTY-FIVE

Dee-Dee pressed her face against the bars. "Wake up, my little kittens. It's din-din."

Jazz rolled over on her cot and watched Dee-Dee slide a tray with plastic bowls, cups, and spoons under the door. The tall girl smirked. "Breakfast for my little pretties. Fruit Loops and OJ."

Jazz picked up the tray and set it on her cot. She tugged on Savannah's arm. "Hey, you okay? Get up, girl." She pulled Savannah to a sitting position. The girl's hair hung in knots, her bleary expression smudged with makeup. "You feeling any better?"

Dee-Dee laughed as Savannah winced, then lay back down. "Too much fun your first few nights, eh?" She stared at Savannah. "I heard a certain someone has been needing a pop of encouragement in her drink every night. Don't expect that to continue. Your fragile little pussy ain't more special than anyone else's."

"Leave her alone," Jazz snapped.

"Don't tell me what the hell I'm supposed to do or not do," Dee-Dee replied, twirling her kinky black hair around her index finger. "You mean shit around here. If I wanted to, I could send a message to Mr. Reynolds about your attitude. He'd make sure your ass got passed around all night long tonight." She smiled at Savannah. "Or your ass."

Savannah hid her face, her shoulders shaking. Jazz sat on the edge of her bed and rested a hand on her back. "Come on. You gotta eat something. Cereal's getting soggy, and you know we don't get fed again until afternoon."

"That's right," Dee-Dee snarled. "Coddle the little bitch. Word has it she's destined for Las Vegas anyway. Gonna be a game attraction."

Savannah jerked her head up.

"You like football, little kitty? I hope so. Men out there pay good money for a whole lot of star action. Those hotel rooms get booked up quickly come Super Bowl time."

Jazz glared at Dee-Dee. "You don't know that."

"Hell, if I don't," Dee-Dee retorted. "Mr. Reynolds told me himself he's getting a group of girls ready for pre-season shipment. Another one was dumped in here last night while the two of you were playing with your boy toys upstairs." She pointed down the hall to a cell room out of their view. "Jane's her name. Wouldn't stop screaming and carrying on. Doc finally had to come down here and shoot her up with his magic syringe. Haven't heard a whimper from her since.

"And we had a visitor," Dee-Dee continued. "Some bitch named Isabella. She was draped all over Mr. Reynolds' arm. They came down here for an inspection. She ain't nothing to worry about, though. That girl was either sloppy drunk or high in the sky. In fact, Mr. Reynolds whispered in my ear that she's only temporary. You know what that means."

Savannah sat up and limply motioned for the tray of food.

Jazz handed her a bowl, and she slurped up the cereal greedily. "That's it, girl. Eat and drink."

Dee-Dee straightened and puffed out her chest. "As soon as that bitch is gone, Mr. Reynolds is gonna make me his number one girl. I won't have to live in this hell hole with the likes of you any longer, and I'll get to go everywhere with him. He mentioned something to that Isabella bitch about another house. Guns and drugs only, no tricks. Just one man to please."

# CHAPTER THIRTY-SIX

Wes Phillips walked through the darkened restaurant and wondered if Louiselle's was ever open. The small man in the ill-fitting suit, his two weapons molded by the material, led him to a back office where Damian Reynolds sat at a desk, staring at a computer screen. Reynolds glanced at Phillips. "Ah, it's the pretty boy. Are we scheduled for business today?"

"Nope. I came to see Izzy."

"She's not here," Reynolds told him.

"Where is she?"

"With Kong."

"You call him Kong, too?" Phillips asked.

"Isabella taught me that. I think it's funny." Reynolds smiled. "Pisses Dennis off."

"I can imagine. So, where's Dennis?"

"Escorting Isabella."

"And where would that be?"

"Out," Reynolds snapped. "You're putting your nose

where it don't belong."

"Just looking out for Izzy's best interests."

Reynolds glanced back at the computer screen. "She's fine. She's with Kong."

Phillips leaned over the desk. "I'm detecting a hesitancy to communicate here."

Reynolds pushed his chair back and stood. "You don't need to know. Unless you want to die an early death."

"Be careful you don't bring that about for yourself. We're partners, but that doesn't mean it can't become temporary."

"Ooh. You've set me all a-quiver. All this tough talk." Reynolds turned and smiled at the guard by his side. "Are you shaking in your shoes?"

The guard smiled back at Reynolds.

Reynolds sat back down. "Listen, Stevie. I'll tell Isabella you were checking on her. If she wants to talk, and I want to let her, she'll call you. So, if we're not doing business today, get the fuck outta my face."

Phillips turned and began to walk out of the office, the small man still close. When he was within reach, Phillips stopped, turned, and jabbed his right elbow into the man's nose. Blood squirted out. The man's eyes rolled back, and he wavered on his feet. Phillips grabbed him by the shirt collar and slammed his face into the file cabinet. The unconscious man melted to the floor.

Reynolds jumped out of his chair. "What the fuck was that for?"

"He touched me."

"Fuck if he did. I was watching."

Phillips shrugged. "I thought for sure I felt something. My mistake. I guess that was my way of telling you I'm serious and I'm not worried about dying. Izzy better be okay, and you better work on your communication skills."

"Yeah, whatever," Reynolds exclaimed. "I can't wait until you try that on Kong."

"Dennis," Phillips reminded him. "Remember, we're serious. And I'm the easiest to get along with. My other partners, who are watching you, aren't nearly as gentle."

***

Phillips almost made it to Louiselle's exit when he heard a familiar male voice. "Hey, *Steve*, you gonna leave without saying hello?"

Dennis and Katrina Malloy sat at a table for two next to

the kitchen. Her spiked hair had morphed from its deep shade of purple to a midnight blue.

"Hey, how you doing?" Phillips asked.

"Lunch, man. Time to feed the monster."

Phillips wandered over and looked at their loaded plates. "How's the food here?"

"Not like Mom's, but not bad." Dennis stared hard at him. "Say, you read any good books lately?"

"Hmm? Why do you ask?"

Dennis smirked. "No reason."

Phillips looked at Katrina and raised his eyebrows. "Hey, Izzy. I've been looking for you."

She set her drink on the table, only ice cubes remained. "I've been meaning to call you."

"She can't," Dennis clarified. "All communications go through Mr. Reynolds."

"Did you make It to Hauser's?" she asked.

"I did. It was excellent. I bought you what you asked for, but when I couldn't find you, I ate it. I could easily go there again."

She smiled. "I'm glad you liked it. "It's special."

Dennis patted her hand. "Maybe I should take you there. Try it for myself."

"That would be nice. Thank you, Dennis, I'd like that."

Phillips looked at Katrina. "No more Kong, eh?"

"Dennis and I have come to an understanding. A friendship of sorts."

"Okay." Phillips nodded. "How have you been, Izzy? I haven't seen you for a while."

"I'm fine. I've been busy. Damian gave me a job."

"I thought you had a job."

"Kind of," she replied. "Now I'm more than his squeeze or fluff or whatever position I was in. I'm going to be leading marketing and distribution for one of the product lines. Isn't that exciting?"

"Yeah, very. What's the product line?"

Katrina glanced at Dennis and back to Phillips. "I'm not supposed to talk about it. Confidentiality and all that. You know, proprietary business practices. I don't want to lose my new job already, so I have to be careful."

"That's good. You should be careful, but I need to talk to you." Phillips shifted his stance. "I need to know you're okay.

Our business with Reynolds can't move forward if you're not okay."

She set her fork down with a clatter. "Steve, I already told you I'm okay. The success of this endeavor cannot rest on my health. You need to detach from me and you. Do what you have to."

"I can't. For me, business is personal."

She got out of her chair. Dennis started to rise. She put her hand on his shoulder and stopped him. "You relax and eat. I'm going to walk Steve to the door. I'll be back in thirty seconds, and you'll be able to see me the whole time."

"I don't know," Dennis grumbled. "Mr. Reynolds won't like it."

"So don't tell him. It'll be between the three of us. It'll be okay. I won't do anything to get you in trouble."

"Promise?"

"I promise." She took Phillips by the arm and steered him toward the door. "Dennis is helping me learn my new job. He's been a great help, but there is so much to know. It's overwhelming." Katrina looked back over her shoulder and smiled at Dennis. Quieter, she added, "And he's like a different person when it's just the two of us."

"You can handle it," Phillips whispered. "I know you can. Watch your back, and be careful around Dennis."

They stopped at the door. Katrina waved to Dennis and turned to whisper to Phillips, her breath a mixture of alcohol and fruit. "I'm finally getting deep enough to get what we need. Don't blow this by making it personal."

"I can't help myself."

"Well, get over it. Now, give me a hug and hold it until Dennis starts to get up, then get the fuck out of here. Let me do my job, and go do yours."

He wrapped his arms around her and squeezed. She squeezed back just as hard. They heard the scrape of a chair across the floor and released each other. Phillips took Katrina's hand, raised the back of it to his lips, and kissed it. "See you soon."

# CHAPTER THIRTY-SEVEN

Wes Phillips followed Leo down the aisle marked *Mysteries and Suspense*. "Describe the guy."

Leo reached up and pulled out a paperback. He waved it at Phillips. "Nice young woman, this Chandler chick. Local. Comes in for signings and sometimes to shoot the shit. Yeah, her books always make me chuckle."

"Leo—"

"Okay, okay, Sally. Big. Kinda like me. Maybe a little beefier in the biceps, but hell, sure not as handsome." He winked.

"And all he asked for was my name?"

Leo grabbed a book from the shelf with last names beginning with D. "And Deese. Woo-hoo." He caressed the cover with his chubby fingertips. Whistled softly. "Tall, beautiful, elegant. If I could only have one night with that babe. Yowza. She don't know what she's missin'." He waggled his eyebrows.

Phillips cleared his throat.

"Sorry, Alice. These Sisters in Crime get to me, you know?" He headed back toward the front of the store. "Now, what was so golly-gee important? Oh, yeah. Yous's name. No worries, Sally. I don't know what yous's into, but mum's still the word. Told the goon your last name was Spade. Couldn't recall your first name. Something like Sam or Sim." He chuckled. "Guy didn't even blink an eyeball."

# CHAPTER THIRTY-EIGHT

Wes Phillips stood in the carriage house kitchen, freshly showered and shaved after his morning run. His police-issued cell phone rang. He recognized the number. "Good morning. Are you ready to do business?"

"In a manner of speaking," Damian Reynolds replied. "By the way, Stevie, did you hear about Rico?"

"Rico who?" Phillips asked. "Rico Royal clarinet reeds? Ricardo Tubbs, affectionately known as Rico on *Miami Vice*?"

"What the fuck is *Miami Vice*?"

"An old TV show, recently made into a movie."

"Jesus Christ, your mind wanders. You should probably get that checked," Reynolds advised. "No, Rico, the guy you assaulted in my restaurant."

"Never knew his name," Phillips replied. "But no, I haven't heard any news."

"The man couldn't handle the shame of failing to protect me. Word on the street is he went for a swim in the

Mighty Mississippi late the other night and disappeared."

Phillips rubbed his chin. "Yeah, hypothermia can set in pretty quick. Underwater currents can be tricky, too. I know a guy who almost lost his dog to currents. He found the dog a few miles downstream, exhausted but alive."

"That's good. I hate stories where animals get hurt."

"Sorry to hear about Rico," Phillips added. "Did you want me to recommend a replacement?"

"Funny," Reynolds replied. "The point in all this is that I'm serious, too. And none of us are afraid to die. You might want to keep that in mind before you go all Clint Eastwood or Mel Gibson or whoever the fuck you're supposed to be again."

# CHAPTER THIRTY-NINE

Sofia Menendez sat on the bed in the carriage house, propped up by two pillows and engrossed in something on her laptop. She wore boxer shorts and one of Wes Phillips' white cotton undershirts. When he walked into the bedroom, she looked at him, set the computer aside, and slid down onto her back and stretched. Her long, dark hair fanned out behind her.

"Lord, give me strength," Phillips muttered. "Do you mind?"

"Not at all. Can't you tell I'm dressed for success with all your wonderful friends?" she teased.

"C'mon, we need to go for a walk." He went into the closet, shoved the clothes to the side, and opened the safe. He extracted a small Beretta in a strap-on holster, secured it to his ankle beneath his pants leg, and pocketed his personal cell phone. He stared at Sofia. She stretched again. "Put some clothes on. You can't go like that."

She smiled and batted her lashes. "I don't think you appreciate your partner."

"I appreciate you fine. But if I teased you like that, you'd punch my lights out."

"How true."

Phillips left the bedroom and strolled around the living and dining rooms, peeking out the windows. The ground was too far down. Satisfied that no one was lurking outside, he began to pace. When Sofia entered the room, wearing jeans and a gray hoodie, he asked, "Do you think the air conditioner works?"

"What are you talking about? It's the wrong time of year. It'll freeze up," she replied. "And no, you can't freeze me into wearing more clothes. I am just too hot."

"It was worth considering. Let's go." He put on his heavy coat and led her from the house.

They walked a few blocks, stopping occasionally to admire the manmade architecture of the neighboring houses and the natural architecture of the yards where the snowbanks had melted. They inhaled the clear air, nonchalantly checking their surroundings for a tail. Another block later, Sofia tugged on Phillips' coat sleeve. "Put your arm around me."

"Are we being watched?"

"Maybe by a neighbor. No, stupid, I'm cold."

Phillips sighed. "You saw me put on my coat. Shouldn't that have been a sign?"

"I'm not from around here. It looked nice outside."

"In Minnesota, looks are deceiving."

"More than you can even imagine. Now, put your arm around me. Unless you want to give me your coat."

He put his arm around her. "Better?"

"Yes, much. Now it even looks as if you like me."

He tilted his head back to look at the sky. "The things I have to do to be me."

She slugged his shoulder. "You're terrible."

After a few more minutes, they came to the brick tower and entered through the gate. Following Sofia's old snow tracks, they circled behind it. Sofia looked over the North Cedar Lake Regional Trail and Highway 394 while Phillips faced the tower. "No climbing this time," he warned.

Sofia laughed.

He took out his personal cell phone and called Jen.

"Sorry about our last call. It must've been a bad connection," he told her when she answered.

Jen sighed. "Yeah, right. What about the other days in

between?"

"Like I said, Jen, I'm busy with work right now. I'm not even supposed to be talking to you."

Sofia tilted her head toward the phone, straining to hear the conversation. Phillips gave her a slight push away.

"What do you mean? What kind of crazy work detail do they got you doing? Remember, it's only a job, Wes. It pays the bills."

Phillips glanced around and lowered his voice. "I'm undercover."

A moment of silence. "Oh, my God. You're worrying me now."

"Listen, there's nothing to worry about. What did you want to tell me the other night?"

Jen hesitated and drew a breath. "Our parents. They went to Colorado to meet with…to see…"

Phillips held the phone tighter to his ear. Sofia waved her hands and mouthed, *"What's going on?"*

"We have a brother, Wes. An older brother. Those papers I found, they gave him up. Our parents were only teenagers. God, they never even told us."

The words swirled around him. A buzzing sounded in his ears.

"Are you there? Did you hear what I said?"

Phillips swallowed. "Does Alyse know?"

"No. Shit. I don't know. I think she'd flip out."

"Don't say anything to her yet. Let me… I need time to think about this." He ended the call, tucked the phone in his pocket, and grabbed his police-issued phone from a different pocket.

Sofia batted his shoulder. "Who was that? What did they say? Who's gonna flip out?"

Phillips scrolled down to find a number and pushed the call button.

"Hey, Wes," Russ Malloy answered. "You okay?"

"Yeah, fine."

"Is Sofia okay?"

He glanced at her. "I think so. Did you want to ask her?"

"Later. What's up?"

"I'm gonna put you on speaker so she can hear, too." Phillips pulled the phone down and pressed a button. "You still with us?"

"Yeah. Hey, Sofia."

"Hi, Russ."

"Wes treating you okay?"

She narrowed her eyes at Phillips. "Yeah, he's a real gentleman."

Malloy laughed. "Sorry to hear that."

"Hey, wait. What do you mean?" Phillips asked.

Sofia patted his arm. "Cop humor. It's okay."

"I didn't know cops had senses of humor," Phillips grumbled.

"We don't, and you're living proof," Malloy retorted. "Okay, so once again, what's up?"

"Did you fish somebody out of the river?"

"Yeah, early this morning. You know something about it?"

"Possibly," Phillips replied. "What can you tell us?"

"The guy had been in a fight. Hit a doorframe or something with his head."

"It was a file cabinet," Phillips clarified.

“Uh-huh. There were no defensive wounds.”

“Nope. He didn’t know what hit him. Never had time to react.”

“Yeah, well, what killed him were the two holes in his chest.” Malloy rustled papers in the background. “His name was Richard Olson. Went by the name Rico. Small-time stuff. Mostly, the guy was a pain in the ass.”

“He was working his way up,” Phillips explained. “Doing close security for Reynolds. I popped him to send Reynolds a message. He had Rico killed to send one back.”

Sofia leaned closer to the phone. “Any chance Reynolds pulled the trigger?”

Phillips shook his head. “I doubt it. The guy’s not the type to get his hands dirty. Killing would be the job of somebody who wants to keep theirs.”

“Any prime candidates?” Malloy asked.

“Maybe Dennis,” Phillips replied.

“Dennis who?”

“Don’t know his last name,” Phillips told him. “Probably Menace, as he’s been following me around and threatening anyone I talk to.”

"Fuck." Malloy's voice grew louder. "Have you been careful with your cover?"

"Yeah, it's all good."

Malloy exhaled. "What about Katrina? Any word on her?"

"I saw her yesterday. She sounded okay, but—"

"But what?"

Phillips stood silent for a moment. "Let's just say I think she's playing with fire."

"Shit," Malloy muttered. "And the game only gets hotter. I'll pass the word on. Anything else?"

"Yeah, when was the last time you had our place scanned for bugs?" Phillips asked.

"Last night, while you were at dinner. The place is clean."

"Are we sure Sofia's internet access is secure?"

"Yep," Malloy replied. "Best encryption available."

"Any signs of somebody close with parabolic microphones?"

"No. We know the neighbors, and everyone's been checked out. We've scanned the area for passive and active recording equipment, and we've done a few drone flights."

"Our team has drones?" Phillips asked.

"Of course. Why are you asking about all this stuff?"

"Reynolds made a comment when he told me about Rico that suggested our cover has been blown already. Obviously, Dennis has been sent to check me out."

"We're still alive," Sofia pointed out. "Could it have meant something else?"

"Yeah, it could have meant Reynolds is a fan of movies where the hero doesn't always follow the rules," Malloy added.

Sofia jabbed a finger at Phillips' chest. "Wes, have you been playing by the rules?"

Phillips grunted. "Not entirely. I keep telling him we're serious about doing business, but I threatened Dennis the day we met, and I smacked Rico around to prove a point."

"Maybe Reynolds likes you," Malloy suggested.

"It's possible," Phillips offered. "He once suggested as much."

"I agree." Sofia spoke into the phone. "Reynolds may perceive himself as a hero, a Robin Hood, willing to do whatever he has to do. And he thinks Wes is like him."

Phillips nodded. "Let's hope that's it. I'm not ready for the river yet."

***

An hour later, Phillips lay on the couch in the carriage house, nursing stomach cramps and occasionally running to the toilet. Sofia, wearing dark glasses and Phillips' coat and hat, had insisted on taking the car and staking out Louiselle's entrance. "I have to do something. We can't both waste time." He waved her away, too miserable to protest.

She smiled. "I promise to play doctor with you when I get back."

"Don't tell Malloy I'm sick," he managed.

The stereo surround sound made doing nothing bearable. Big Joe Turner sang *How Long, How Long Blues* while Phillips cradled his stomach. He should've learned to play the guitar or a brass instrument when he was a kid. Why didn't his parents insist he join the school band? Alyse was the musical one. Classically trained. Played for hours on the old upright piano. Until… The last time he heard her play was at the funeral service. She had cried all over the keys. "Chopin," she had told him. Like it was an excuse.

He listened to Big Joe, glad Sofia wasn't around to complain about his choice of music. "Too depressing." She had popped out his CD and inserted one with loud salsa music. Despite her shimmy moves across the floor, he refused to get off the couch and join her.

"The tempo's too upbeat," he had insisted.

His thoughts turned to Jen. A brother, she'd told him. Why the secrecy? Were their parents shamed into giving up that child? Was it their decision? He tried to imagine his parents as teenagers, his mother—the missing pictures from her junior year. God, she had been tough on them about dating, especially tough with his sisters. And his father's repetitious words to him, "First you go to college, and then you find a nice girl."

Had their parents finally found their firstborn? Or had he found them? Who did this guy think he was, inviting himself into their lives now? Luring them to Colorado, the mountains, the sharp cliffs.

Phillips' stomach spasmed. He groaned and headed for the toilet

# CHAPTER FORTY

The next day, Wes Phillips, his stomach still tender, and Sofia Menendez were backing out of the garage when Dennis and Damian Reynolds pulled into the driveway in the Escalade. "Get in," Reynolds called from the open window. "I got something to show you."

Phillips shrugged, closed the garage, and locked the car.

Dennis exited the Escalade and opened the back passenger door. Reynolds slid to the other side, Sofia sat in the middle, and Phillips sat against the door. Phillips put his arm around Sofia, and she leaned into him. A few minutes down the road, she began to speak in Spanish. She used a sweet voice none of them had heard before. After a couple of minutes, Dennis burst into laughter. "Oh, my God. This is hysterical."

"You understand Spanish?" Reynolds asked.

"Yeah. Too bad you don't. You'd both be laughing your asses off. Well, maybe not you, Mr. Mayer."

"What did she say?" Phillips asked.

Dennis peered in the rearview mirror at Phillips. “Sounded all lovey-dovey, didn’t it?”

“Yeah,” Phillips agreed. “I’m beginning to think she likes me.”

“Ha. She said your dick is so small, not even the size of her little finger. She can’t even feel you inside her. She pretends to get excited so you’ll get excited. And you don’t last more than a minute.”

Reynolds laughed. Phillips removed his arm from around Sofia.

Sofia smiled and spoke more Spanish.

Dennis listened and laughed again, wiping his eyes. “Now she said after you die in your sleep, which might happen soon, she’ll find a real man to please her.” Dennis looked at Sofia in the mirror and said, “Ah, *bonita. Te amo*, baby. *Me haces reir. Si se cansa de el, usted debe venire a vivir conmigo*.”

“*Quiza lo haga*,” Sofia replied.

“Hey, what did you say to her?” Reynolds asked Dennis.

“I called her beautiful, told her I loved her and that she made me laugh. And I told her when she gets tired of Mr. Mayer, she should come live with me.”

Phillips stared at Sofia. “And she said?”

Dennis grinned. “Maybe she will.”

Reynolds looked at Phillips. “*Now* do you want me to ship her off somewhere?”

Phillips’ eyes narrowed. “No. I’ll return her to my friends. They can fix her.”

Sofia slid forward on the seat until she was right behind Dennis. She whispered something, and he reached a hand back over his shoulder. His gaze reflected puzzlement in the rearview mirror. She took his hand, looked at the palm, traced the lines as if she were reading it. Then, she extended one of his fingers, rolled the rest into a fist, and slid the finger in and out of her mouth, sucking loudly. Sofia twisted on the seat so Phillips and Reynolds could watch, then turned and fixed her eyes on Dennis’ reflection in the mirror.

“Shit, man, watch where you’re going!” Reynolds yelled.

Dennis looked back out the windshield and jerked his hand from Sofia. They had drifted out of the lane and headed toward a parked U-Haul truck. He yanked on the wheel. Sofia chuckled and slid back between Phillips and Reynolds.

Reynolds threw an elbow into Sofia’s ribs. She

slammed into Phillips and lost her wind. He pulled his elbow back for another jab. “Fucking bitch. Trying to get us killed.”

“Hit her again, and you die. Right here, right now,” Phillips declared.

Sofia crumpled forward, gasping for breath. Dennis tried to see her in the rearview mirror. When he couldn’t, he adjusted the mirror downward until he could.

Reynolds shrank closer to the door. “Just fucking drive. Let’s get this over with. And no more Spanish.”

***

They drove to an industrial complex in Plymouth and arrived at an unmarked building at the end of a cul-de-sac. Dennis pressed a button, a door opened, and he drove inside. He parked the car near a stack of crates along a side wall, close to a spotless silver Toyota Land Cruiser.

All four got out. Reynolds pointed at Dennis and Sofia. “You two lovebirds stay here.”

Sofia scooted closer to Dennis.

Reynolds led Phillips to a stack and flipped open the top crate. It contained a shoulder-fired surface-to-air missile. “Will this do?”

Phillips nodded. “I believe it will.”

"Good. I've shown you mine," Reynolds returned. "Now show me yours. Transfer some fucking money so I know you're for real."

"You'll have proof tomorrow morning," Phillips replied.

Reynolds slammed the crate closed. "About fucking time. Yanking my chain, threatening me in my own car. Asshole." He walked over to the Land Cruiser and swung open the driver's door. "Dennis, give them a ride home." Reynolds climbed in the Cruiser and peeled away.

While Dennis helped Sofia into the front passenger seat of the Escalade, Phillips snapped a picture with his cell phone of the label on the missile's side, making sure the model and serial numbers were legible. He hurried back to the SUV and climbed into the back. Dennis closed the door.

Pretending to check messages on his phone, Phillips sent the picture to Malloy, and after verification of delivery, he deleted it. He also sent the license plate number of the Land Cruiser. Up front, Sofia and Dennis spoke softly in Spanish, each with a hand on the other's thigh.

# CHAPTER FORTY-ONE

Wes Phillips and Sofia Menendez stood again behind the tower. Phillips faced the brick, keeping it within arm's length. Sofia looked down on 394 and the Trail. She wore a heavy designer winter coat with fur trim and thigh-high boots. "So, Russ, what have you learned?" Phillips asked.

Russ Malloy chimed in on speakerphone. "I have people looking into it, but it appears the surface-to-air missile was destined for the Middle East when it apparently fell off the truck and disappeared."

"Well, we know where it turned up. Now, we need to figure out how it got to Minnesota," Phillips suggested. "What about the Plymouth warehouse?"

"We've got eyes on it," Malloy replied. "It's not one that Morton frequents."

"Reynolds must have other people traveling between his locations," Phillips remarked. "How do we find out who and how many?"

"That's part of why we're only watching this one.

Maybe we turn whoever shows up."

"Morton is sticking to his normal routine?" Phillips asked.

"Not entirely." Malloy proceeded to tell Phillips and Sofia about Ellison and Larkin and their brief lunch at the strip club.

Sofia laughed. "Men and their brains in their dicks. It's why women will one day rule the world."

Phillips rolled his eyes. "I thought these guys were professionals."

"They are," Malloy stated. "That doesn't make them infallible."

"Have we talked with the dancer?" Phillips asked.

"Not yet."

"What are we waiting for?"

"Justifiable and easy access," Malloy replied.

"That's bullshit," Phillips grumbled. "Other than that, Morton's been visiting his usual spots?"

"Yeah."

Phillips rubbed a gloved hand over his face. "Are we staking out any of those?"

"Not yet, but it's coming."

Phillips shook his head and kicked at the tower.

"What's next?" Sofia asked.

"Keep watching and learning," Malloy replied. "We almost have enough to ask for warrants."

"I think you should hold off on that," Phillips ventured. "There's still too much we don't know. But Katrina's right—there's something much bigger going on."

"We better find out soon so she can come home." Malloy disconnected.

Phillips pocketed the phone and pulled out his personal cell. Jen had texted him.

**He wants to meet us.**

He swore under his breath and tapped her number. Sofia folded her arms and shuffled her feet.

"What should we do?" Jen asked upon answering.

"How the hell does he know about us? What happened?"

"Evidently, Alyse keeps secrets, too," Jen informed him. "She said Mom accidentally let the news slip a long time ago and swore Alyse to secrecy."

"Jeezus."

"And apparently, Alyse and this guy have been FaceTiming for a while now," Jen added.

Phillips blew out a long breath. "Well. I, for one, have no feelings for this guy whatsoever."

"You're not even curious?"

"I don't have time to be curious. As far as I'm concerned, he's the reason our parents died."

"Wesley Phillips! Don't even say that. He had nothing to do with the accident."

He stared up at the tower. "Oh, yeah? Do you know that for a fact?"

She stayed silent.

He wobbled on his feet, and Sofia reached out to steady him. He lowered his gaze and centered it on her. "I gotta go."

"Right. You always immerse yourself in work or running or whatever else is convenient when things get tough."

"Jen—"

The phone went dead.

# CHAPTER FORTY-TWO

Wes Phillips sat at the kitchen table in the carriage house, scribbling notes. He had just finished speaking with Eric Martinez. "It's ready," Martinez had promised him.

Phillips tapped in Damian Reynolds' number. "I've created an account. There are two names on it, yours and mine."

"I never agreed I was going into business with you," Reynolds argued. "Why the fuck would I want a joint account with you? Unless you're going to load it up and die and leave it all to me."

"Nah, that won't work," Phillips replied. "It's kind of complicated, but if something happens to me, it all goes to the Animal Humane Society, and everything I know about you goes to the Attorney General. So, you better hope there isn't some cat lover at the adoption center willing to kill me."

Reynolds was silent for a moment. "You still haven't told me why I'm on 'our' account."

"If we're able to conclude the deal we were discussing

the other day, the account becomes yours."

"You were supposed to put money in *my* account," Reynolds insisted. "Not some bullshit account with all kinds of strings and threats attached."

"There are no threats attached," Phillips assured him. "If we conclude negotiations, the account becomes yours. If we can't come to terms, the account disappears, and nobody knows it ever existed."

"Still seems like a lot of bullshit, but hey, it don't matter anyhow. The other day didn't feel right. So, I sold your divorce proceeding to someone else."

Phillips threw his pen down. "Jesus Christ, man, what's wrong with you? We were doing so well."

"It's shit like that, asking what's wrong with me," Reynolds exclaimed. "There's nothing fucking wrong with me. You better look closer to home to see the problem. Asshole."

The call ended.

Phillips bolted from his chair. He stormed back and forth, growling as he rubbed his temples.

# CHAPTER FORTY-THREE

Katrina Malloy stood outside Dee-Dee's room, rested her head against the bars, and watched with glazed eyes as Eduardo and Doc yanked the girl off her cot. Dee-Dee screamed and spat in Katrina's face as they dragged her by. "Fucking cunt! No bitch is gonna replace me. Especially some drunk-ass one."

Katrina wiped the spit off her cheek with a clumsy hand. A cell door clanged shut from down the hall. "You keep me locked up with this newbie Jane whore, and I swear I'll choke the life out of her with my bare hands," Dee-Dee continued her rampage. "Tell that to Mr. Reynolds. Do you hear me, Eduardo? Open this door back up. I'm not fuckin' around."

"No worries, young lady," Doc's voice smoothly replied. "According to his plans, you won't be in here long."

As Doc and Dee-Dee continued to exchange words, Katrina staggered into the girl's former room. The blankets looked cotton-soft, the cot inviting. She needed to lie down for a few minutes. Give her brain a rest. Straighten out her thoughts.

"What's so special about that bitch, huh?" Dee-Dee's voice turned into a whine. "Please, Doc. You know I'm his favorite. He counts on me to keep the girls in line. Damn it, you know he loves me!"

Katrina's body relaxed. Her mind drifted. She hadn't drunk that much this morning. Maybe Doc slipped something into her glass. Maybe...

Somewhere in her dream state, she imagined a knight in shining armor leaning down to caress her face, her body. His lips pressing against hers. The clang of a cell door. The click of a lock. A man's voice telling her to sleep well.

# CHAPTER FORTY-FOUR

Wes Phillips' phone rang slightly after midnight. Sofia Menendez nudged him with her elbow, and he rolled over in bed to grab the phone from the nightstand. The screen displayed Damian Reynolds' name.

"You ready to redeem yourself?"

Phillips sat up. "If you think I need to, sure." He tapped Sofia's arm, and she grunted and moved away.

"Meet me in twenty in the parking lot between the old Rudolph's building and the Purrniture Store," Reynolds demanded.

"Purrniture?"

"Sign says it's for cat lovers or pussy lovers, or I don't know. Come alone. And don't be late."

The call ended, and Phillips climbed out of bed and headed to the closet.

"Am I going somewhere?" Sofia mumbled from beneath the covers.

"Nope." Phillips slid on a long-sleeved shirt over his white T-shirt and buttoned it partway. He tugged on a pair of jeans over his boxers. "Just me, myself, and I."

"Good. Make sure the three of you don't get into trouble. I need my beauty sleep."

***

Phillips sat at the far side of the parking lot when Dennis pulled the Escalade alongside. Phillips opened his window.

The Escalade's back passenger window slid down, and Reynolds looked out and around, then into the car where Phillips sat. "Open your trunk."

Phillips reached down and pressed a button. The Lincoln's trunk lifted. He opened the driver's door, leaving the engine running, and circled to the back of the car.

Dennis popped the Escalade's liftgate. He climbed out and opened Reynolds' door. Reynolds motioned toward the cargo area. "Here's your chance to prove your dedication to our endeavor." He smirked. "See? I can use big words, too." He reached inside and pulled out a pair of bare legs secured at the ankles with duct tape. The young woman was shoeless. After her legs were straightened, she started kicking.

Reynolds motioned for Dennis to drag the woman out of the SUV and drop her to the icy pavement. "Here. She's yours." The woman's hands were secured with duct tape behind the back of her short dress. She had a matching strip of tape across her mouth. Reynolds tapped Phillips' chest. "Redeem yourself to me. Kill her and dispose of her."

"Uh, can I ask why?"

"You shouldn't, but I'll tell you anyway. 'Cuz I like you. And I want you to know who you're dealing with." Reynolds kicked the woman's shivering body. She groaned. "She's a cop." He kicked her again, and she tried to scream through the tape.

Phillips glanced around the empty parking lot. "You abducted a female police officer just to have me kill her?"

"Nah, she was undercover. Cozied up to one of my guys, tried to get inside information, you know. But I have sources. They revealed her true self to me." Reynolds smiled. "Now, I'm giving you the pleasure of killing her."

Phillips nodded. "Okay. Put her in my trunk." Nobody moved. "I'm not going to do it here. I'll take her somewhere else. That way, you can establish your alibi. She'll be feeding the alligators by morning."

Reynolds scoffed. "We don't have alligators here,

dumbass."

"Did I say she would be feeding local alligators? You don't want to know where she ends up. It's better that way. Take comfort in knowing she won't be a problem anymore. Put her in the trunk."

"Fine, but I want proof."

"What kind of proof?" Phillips asked.

"I don't know. Surprise me."

Dennis lifted her from the ground as if she weighed nothing and dropped her into the trunk of Phillips' car. She kicked and thrashed. Dennis hit her, and she stopped moving. He grabbed her heels from the Escalade's cargo area and tossed them in with her, then slammed the Lincoln's lid.

***

Phillips drove to the carriage house, the heater cranked on high and the vents aimed toward the back, and parked in the garage. He left the garage door open and the car running. After racing up the steps, he popped a pill without any water. Sofia lay in bed, eyes closed. One hand poked out from beneath the covers, clutching her phone.

Phillips shook her shoulder. "C'mon. We need to go."

She looked at him, wiped her eyes, and glanced at the

time on her phone. “Go where?”

“I don’t know, but we can’t be here. We need to go now. I need to think. I need some questions answered.” He paced wildly. Sofia mumbled something in Spanish and dragged herself to a sitting position. He stopped in front of her. “Hurry up.”

“Okay,” she grumbled. “Five minutes.”

***

They sat in the most isolated corner of the parking lot of the Brooklyn Center Walmart, waiting, silent. Russ Malloy finally pulled up and parked next to them. All three got out of their vehicles. Malloy looked at Sofia, who shrugged.

Phillips strode to Malloy, his face inches away. “What have you gotten us into? What kind of shitstorm is this?”

Malloy stood his ground and stared at Phillips. “What are you talking about? You know what we’re up against. Your intel has been the best we received.”

“Who else are you receiving intel from? How many other people are working this case?”

Malloy raised a hand in surrender. “It’s late. You’re tired. So am I. You’re not making any sense, and I’m about to go home and go to bed if you don’t start soon.”

Phillips jerked open the trunk. “Is she yours?”

Sofia’s eyes darted from the woman’s body to Phillips. “What the fuck, Wes? What have you done?”

“Nothing yet. I’m supposed to kill her and send Reynolds the proof.”

“Jesus Christ. Why would you do that?” Malloy asked. “Who is she?”

“You tell me. Reynolds said she’s a cop.”

The woman in the trunk moved. They stood and watched as her eyes slowly opened, and it dawned on her where she was. She started flailing. Malloy held his badge in front of her face. “You’re okay. You’re safe.” Her struggling slowed. “If you’ll stop, I’ll get you free, and we can talk.”

She stopped moving.

Sofia stepped up to the trunk, pulled an ivory handle from her pants pocket, and pushed a button. A blade flicked into place. She slipped the blade between the woman’s wrists and ankles and slit the tape.

After her hands were free, the woman slowly pulled the tape off her mouth. “Where are those bastards? I want to kill them.” The woman scrambled from the trunk. She stood on one foot, then the other, shivering as she shoved on a high heel. “Are you really a cop?” she asked Malloy.

“Yeah,” he told her. “I’m with the BCA.”

“Are *you* really a cop?” Phillips asked.

The woman straightened and stared at Phillips for a long moment, then at Sofia. “Who the fuck are you two?”

“They’re with me. They’re okay.” Malloy dug in the back seat of his SUV for a blanket and handed it to her.

“I don’t know, man.” She wrapped it around herself. “I’m not sure I can trust you. I mean, I was with people I didn’t trust, and look at the shit I’m in.”

“What shit are you in?” Sofia asked. “Because the way I see it, you got out of a lot of shit and put us in the middle of it.”

The woman looked at Malloy. “Do you know how to work your phone? Can you use FaceTime?”

Malloy raised his eyebrows. “What do you think I am?”

“An old guy, a technophobe, a Luddite,” she answered.

Sofia pulled out her phone. “I can make it work.”

“Call this number, get him on the screen.” The woman recited a number, and Sofia punched it in.

“That’s Eric Martinez,” Malloy snapped.

Phillips stared at Malloy. "Our fearless leader is working another angle?"

Martinez answered the call. "Sofia. I didn't realize you had my number."

"It was just given to me," Sofia replied.

"By who?"

Sofia turned the phone. The woman smiled back at the screen.

"Oh, shit. Meet me at the Roseville Lunds. Get off the line. Now." Martinez disconnected.

"That was rather rude." Sofia pocketed her phone. "I guess we have to go. Should we take one car or two?"

"I'll follow you," Malloy stated.

The woman jerked her thumb at Malloy. "I'll ride with him." She bent to adjust the high-heel straps.

Sofia held the switchblade in front of her nose. The lights from the parking lot reflected off the blade. "I wish I'd brought my gun."

***

Martinez was at Lunds when they arrived. "Did introductions get made?" he asked.

The woman wrapped the blanket tighter. "No. It was a silent drive here."

Martinez motioned to her. "This is Veronica Colburn."

"Roni for short," Colburn added.

"She's with DHS," Martinez continued.

Phillips frowned. "How many angles are you working? Are there other undercovers waiting to get found out and killed, or get us killed?"

Malloy slid his eyes over to Martinez's.

"Roni is working a different case," Martinez explained. "It's run into ours."

"That sounds like bureaucratic bullshit," Malloy scoffed. "Who is it you're covering for this time?"

Martinez's eyes narrowed. "Nobody. The chief called and asked for help."

"Remind me never to trust my boss," Phillips grumbled. "Oh, yeah, I don't."

"Chief Dalestrom has credible evidence of a terrorist threat happening at the Thanksgiving Parade. I've got people looking into it. I decided to send Roni in, see if she could find anything."

Colburn leaned forward, waving her hand as she spoke. “I find this guy, Bart Gibson, who’s into incendiary devices, and find a way to get close. I send word back. It might be enough for a warrant. Before I hear if a warrant is coming, Gibson tells me I need to meet a friend of his. We go see his friend Reynolds. The next thing I know, I’m wrapped in tape, punched in the head, and tossed in the back of an SUV.”

“How did Reynolds know you were a cop?” Phillips asked.

“No idea.” Colburn looked at Martinez. “Who went for the warrant?”

“Our friend in the FBI,” Martinez admitted.

“Caffrey?” Malloy asked. “Is he the leak? Is he why all our people have been killed?’

Martinez shook his head. “No. I’ve known him for years. He’s above reproach.”

“Who did he have to go to for the warrant?” Phillips asked.

“He probably went to the FISA court and saw Judge McIntire. He’s been helpful in the past,” Martinez explained.

Phillips looked at Colburn. “Okay, so that means our new friend Roni here gets to stay alive for the moment. I still need to submit proof of her death, though. And I don't think pictures of her in bloody makeup are going to suffice."

"What do you propose?" Malloy asked.

Sofia smiled. "Anybody got a knife? Oh, yeah. I do."

Phillips stepped toward her. "Sofia, don't do anything rash."

"Oh, c'mon, you know me better than that. No, wait, you really don't. No one does, but hey." She poked Phillips in the ribs, making him jump. "You're the closest."

***

Phillips strolled into Louiselle's carrying a small plastic cooler. The lid was blue, the box was faded white. It was dirty and beaten and might've earned a quarter in a garage sale. Reynolds sat at his usual table, surrounded by his tough-guy friends. They stared at Phillips, got to their feet, puffed up their chests, and moved close. Katrina Malloy was nowhere to be seen. Phillips set the cooler on the chair next to Reynolds.

"A present? For me?" Reynolds rubbed his palms together. "You shouldn't have."

"Oh, but you insisted," Phillips returned. "It's the proof you wanted."

"So, you took care of our little problem?"

"I told you I would," Phillips replied. "You really shouldn't doubt me."

"Where is she? What did you do?" Reynolds asked.

"Beyond seeing the proof you requested, you don't want to know. Remember the political term 'plausible deniability?'"

Reynolds nodded. "I was never really sure what it meant, but okay."

"As long as I tell you nothing more, you have plausible deniability. That and the people you were with providing an alibi, and you're safe." Phillips looked at the others. "Right?"

Reynolds nodded and lifted the lid. He peeked inside and jumped to his feet. The lid went flying. So did his chair and breakfast. "Jesus Christ, what the fuck is that? What did you do?"

One of the other men peered inside the cooler and grimaced.

Phillips smiled. "You wanted her dead, and you wanted proof. Her heart should be sufficient proof."

"You're fucking sick," Reynolds declared. "Get that thing out of here."

"As you wish." Phillips picked the cooler lid off the floor

and slid it back on top. The tough guys gave him a wide berth as he strolled from the restaurant.

***

The cooler rode in the Lincoln's back seat. A Mossberg pump shotgun with a short barrel and extended magazine rode between Sofia's legs in the passenger seat. "Where have you been hiding that?" Phillips asked. He turned the Lincoln off White Bear Avenue and onto South Shore Boulevard. To the left was White Bear Lake, and a few blocks the other way was the business district of the city of White Bear Lake.

"I have a large purse," Sofia replied. "Where are you taking me? Someplace special?"

"I don't know how special. We're going to where Martinez stashed Colburn."

"Why?"

"We're returning her heart."

"Oh. Is that all?" she drawled. "How's your heart?"

He looked at her, wondering at the sentiment in the question. Her face betrayed nothing. He watched her fingers slide on the short barrel of the shotgun. "Do you really think you need that?"

"After your midnight *rendezvous* with Reynolds and his

kill order, it might be prudent of us. Besides, that Roni chick makes me nervous. Until she has her heart back and leaves town, yeah, I think I want my little metal friend between my legs."

He stole another glance, and she laughed.

"What?"

She shook her head. "Nothing." She peered out the window at the dark neighborhood. "Where the hell are we, anyway?"

"Apparently, unfamiliar territory to you. I could leave you here and make my getaway."

"Nope. I'd find you."

Phillips sighed. "I have no doubt."

Sofia smiled, laid her head back, and closed her eyes. When Phillips pulled the car into a driveway and shut it off, she whined, "A few more minutes and I'd have been out."

"I hurried the last bit because I knew you weren't sleeping yet."

"How could you tell?"

"You weren't snoring."

She hit him on the shoulder. "I don't snore."

***

Martinez let them into the house. Phillips carried the cooler, and Sofia carried the shotgun. Martinez pointed at the gun. "Is that necessary?"

"Girl Scouts are always prepared," Sofia replied.

They followed Martinez into the living room. Malloy and Colburn sat on the ends of the couch. Another man, heavyset with thin dark hair, gray creeping into his mustache and neatly trimmed beard, sat in a chair near the fireplace. He wore slacks a size too short. The leg cuffs revealed dark socks and darker leg hair. His dress shirt pulled tight across his middle, and his tie almost covered a stain riding high on his belly.

"Is that my heart?" The man heaved himself from the chair and moved toward Phillips. He stopped when he saw the shotgun. "Um, is that thing loaded?"

Sofia smiled. "Of course. Seven shells and one in the chamber."

The man glanced at Malloy.

Malloy stood. "This is Professor Edward Canton. He's with the University of Minnesota Medical School. He was generous enough to help by providing the heart."

Canton kept an eye on Sofia and the gun as he stepped to the cooler. “Some first-year is going to dissect it tomorrow. Assuming you haven’t ruined it or let it spoil.”

“No, it’s fresh,” Phillips assured him.

“We kept it on ice,” Sofia added. “It’s about as cold as my partner’s heart.”

Phillips looked at her and the shotgun. “I’m not the cold-hearted member of this team.”

“Ah-ha! You do think I have a heart,” she exclaimed.

“Kids,” Malloy muttered.

“Relax, Dad,” Sofia sniped.

Canton lifted the lid off the cooler and peered inside. His brows furrowed. “What did you people do?”

“What do you mean?” Martinez asked.

Canton waved his arms around. “It wasn’t covered in blood when I gave it to you.”

Sofia jerked her thumb at Phillips. “My partner here tried putting it into a guy, but he rejected it. Not before he made it a bloody mess, though.”

Canton blew out a loud breath. “This is serious. You may have contaminated a perfectly good practice specimen.”

“That makes no sense.” Phillips shook his head. “How can you contaminate something a student is going to butcher?”

Canton tightened his jaw. “Biohazards. It was clean. Now, it’s covered with biohazards. What if the student cuts himself and gets this into his system?”

Sofia shrugged. “He dies. If his knife skills are that sloppy, he probably shouldn’t be performing surgery.”

Canton’s eyes closed briefly, then snapped back open. “Where did the blood come from?”

Phillips opened his mouth. “Well—”

“Let me tell him,” Sofia interrupted, bouncing on her toes.

Phillips nodded.

“It’s his.” She pointed at Phillips. “It was only a little cut, but it was a squirter.” She smiled.

“I’m sure I’ll be fine.” Phillips played along. “At least physically.”

“Jesus H. Christ.” Canton turned red. Sweat appeared at the edge of his mustache. “You didn’t?”

“Of course she didn’t.” Colburn slid back on the couch, rested her head, and closed her eyes. “It couldn’t be from only one person. We each had blood drawn and poured it into the cooler. You know, shared responsibility. I mean, I had to be in on it. They saved my life." She opened her eyes and looked at Canton without lifting her head.

Canton's mouth opened and closed. He blinked rapidly. "You're killing me."

"Relax, Edward. This is how cops have fun." Martinez looked at Sofia. "At least the sane ones." She smiled at him and batted her eyes. "My daughter is an intern at the Guthrie Theatre," Martinez continued. "She set us up with some stage blood. It's glycerin, food coloring, and a bit of alcohol. It'll rinse off. Your specimen's fine."

Martinez put a hand on Canton's shoulder and steered him toward the door. "I know you're busy, so we won't keep you with any more cop jokes." Canton nodded. "Just let me say we appreciate your help. As Roni said, you and your specimen helped save her life tonight. So, thank you very much."

Canton picked up the cooler. "Fine, but I never want to see you people again."

# CHAPTER FORTY-FIVE

Jazz lay silent on her cot, eyes closed, waiting for Doc and Eduardo to climb the stairs and lock the basement door. When she heard the door shut, she bolted upright. “Hey.” She turned to face Savannah. “It’s safe. Get your ass up, girl. Come sit by me.”

Savannah rubbed her eyes and hobbled over. She sat gingerly on the edge of Jazz’s bed and pressed her thighs together.

“You still hurtin’ from last night, honey? Hell, ’course you are.” Jazz patted the girl’s shoulder. “It’s always tough in the beginning.”

Savannah stared at the floor and sniffed. “When I get out of here, I’m gonna kill every one of those bastards.”

Jazz laughed. “Yeah, honey, you and me both.”

“I’m not kidding.” A hard edge laced Savannah’s voice. She turned and looked Jazz in the eyes. “I know some people. And they’re not the kind you have cookies with.”

Jazz stared back. “Okay, then. I bet you do. And for

both of our sakes, I hope you get out of here sooner than later."

"First on my list is that old fake preacher who claimed he was gonna help me." Savannah nodded. "Yeah, he helped me all right. Fed me pizza and handed me over to some big-ass baboon. Guy went at me for hours, it seemed." She stole a glance at Jazz. "I had never before, um, exactly..." She paused.

"It's okay, honey. I know what you mean. Go on and let it out," Jazz urged.

"Well, I felt like I was gonna die. And, and...when that bastard finally..." Her voice faltered, her body trembling, and she drew a deep breath. "Anyway, they're only the first ones to be dealt with."

Jazz leaned back against the wall and sighed. "Girl, we all been writin' a list in here. Some of us just have longer ones."

Someone moaned from a few cells down.

"You hear that?" Jazz jerked her thumb in the direction of the noise. "Somethin' big is goin' down soon. They didn't move Old Double Ds to a different cell for nothin'."

"What do you mean?"

"Little Miss Privileged has been replaced. That Isabella girl is the new head bitch around here. You saw them lock her up in Double Ds' room."

Savannah frowned. "So, is this good or bad for the rest of us?"

"Hard to tell, but definitely bad for that new Jane girl. I've seen Double Ds pissed as all hell before, but nothin' like today. I tell you, honey, it ain't gonna be pretty when that happy juice Doc shot her up with wears off. She's true to her word, and she meant it when she said she was gonna take out her new roomie. All Jane can hope for is that she's quicker on her feet and faster with her fists than Double Ds."

# CHAPTER FORTY-SIX

Wes Phillips and Sofia Menendez strolled into Hauser's. A gesture from the gravel-voiced woman sent them through the kitchen and to the room where Russ Malloy and Robert McNellis were eating. Several empty beer bottles rested beside McNellis.

"You're just in time," McNellis announced. "Hot and fresh and perfect as always."

Sofia sat next to him and grabbed a big, deep-fried filet. McNellis dug into the cooler and handed her a bottle of beer.

Phillips sat, hands clamped to the edge of the table, and stared at the two men.

"What's eating him?" McNellis asked.

"I don't know," Sofia replied. "He's been kind of pissy since this morning. Gave me the silent treatment all the way over here. Either it's that time of the month, or we're having our first lovers' quarrel."

Phillips ignored Sofia's comments and continued to

stare at Malloy and McNellis. "I can't stop thinking about Colburn. How Reynolds wanted me to off her. One wrong move on my part, and she and I would've been easily disposed of that night."

"Tell us about it," Malloy stated.

"And I haven't heard from Katrina. It's been a while."

Malloy glanced at McNellis. "Do we need to worry?"

"Not yet," McNellis replied and sipped his beer.

"Did you learn anything from that picture I sent you? The one from the warehouse?" Phillips asked Malloy.

"The surface-to-air missile in question shipped out of the country according to plan, then went missing six months ago from an American air base in the Philippines. If the military let the ATF or the FBI in on the investigation, they don't seem willing to share and might be getting better at pretending to be stupid."

"Or they're not pretending," McNellis suggested.

"And the warehouse itself?" Phillips asked.

"No action that we've seen. No one in or out," Malloy confirmed.

"Have you sent any agents in to look around?" Phillips

asked.

Malloy shook his head. “We couldn’t get a warrant with the little we had.”

“Ah, shit.” Phillips released a long breath. “You may want to break in, then. I don’t believe you’ll ever be able to get a warrant now.”

Malloy dropped his piece of fish on his plate and wiped his hands. He looked at Phillips. “Why is that?”

“Reynolds told me the missile deal won’t be happening. He sold it to a different buyer.”

McNellis slammed his beer bottle on the table. “Goddammit. We’ll get into that warehouse tonight. One way or another.”

“On top of all that, I think Reynolds is into something worse,” Phillips added. “I can’t prove it yet, but he said a few things that imply he’s in the people business.”

McNellis leaned forward. “What did he say?”

“He asked if I wanted him to find a new home for Sofia. Outside the States,” Phillips replied.

Sofia pulled at her necklace and looked at Phillips. “Again, he wants to get rid of me? You said no, didn’t you? You said you want to keep me around, right?”

Phillips smiled at her across the table. It wasn't a happy smile. "I didn't take the idea out of consideration."

Sofia kicked him under the table. "You bastard."

Phillips grabbed his shin. "Hey, if I get one more bruise, I swear I'll report it."

Sofia laughed, and warmth crept into Phillips' smile.

"She does grow on you, doesn't she?" McNellis remarked.

# CHAPTER FORTY-SEVEN

"Go someplace private," Russ Malloy insisted. "I'll call you in two minutes."

"Make it five," Wes Phillips replied and disconnected. He looked at Sofia Menendez, who was sitting on top of the bed covers, propped up by both pillows and dressed in boxer shorts and another one of his T-shirts. Her eyes were glued to her computer screen. "Grab your coat," Phillips told her. "And pants. Time for a walk."

Sofia looked up and smiled. "Ah, a midnight stroll with my lover."

Seven minutes down the street toward the tower, Malloy called back. Phillips put him on speaker.

"One of our associates made it into the warehouse tonight," Malloy reported. "It was clean. Looked as if it had been professionally scrubbed."

"Nothing at all?" Phillips asked.

"Well, not nothing," Malloy replied. "We did find two hairs in the sink of the restroom."

"And?" Phillips prompted.

"One was Sofia's."

"I was never in the restroom," Sofia protested. "We weren't there long enough."

"I guessed that," Malloy stated. "It was obviously planted."

"Did they plant some crazy woman's hair to throw you off or because they know she's not some crazy woman but a cop of some type?" Phillips asked.

"I'm a crazy woman now?" Sofia kicked at his shin with her boot. "That doesn't sound very loving, my darling."

Phillips groaned and grabbed his leg in pain.

"I might make you sleep on the couch for that," she quipped.

"Good." Phillips checked for blood.

"What the hell's going on?" Malloy asked.

Phillips gritted his teeth. "Nothing." He glowered at Sofia.

Sofia smiled. "Wes was telling me how much he enjoys working undercover with me."

"Wonderful," Malloy intoned. "Anyway, like I was

saying, that's what we don't know. I think we should pull you out of there, Sofia. It's not safe anymore—"

"Wait," Sofia interrupted. "You said two hairs. Who did the other hair come from?"

There was a long pause. "My sister, Katrina."

"She wasn't with us." Phillips shook his head. He had lost all color. "Katrina was never there. I told you before, I haven't heard from her. She's the one you need to pull out."

"We know that. Why the fuck do you think we hired you?" Malloy drew a deep breath. "Wes, right now, you're the only one who can get close enough to do that."

Sofia waved her hands. "You need to let me in. I need to get all the way inside. I need to be the one who gets close to Katrina. Wes is going to have to trade me for something. I have to be there until we figure out how to get her out."

"We can't take that risk," Malloy declared. "We don't need Reynolds shipping you off to who-knows-where."

Sofia grabbed Phillips' phone and spoke directly into the receiver. "Russ, we don't have a choice. I need to get in there. Wes needs to figure out what's going on, and we need to get your sister home. Alive."

# CHAPTER FORTY-EIGHT

Doc leaned over the young Asian girl who lay supine on the examining table beneath a white sheet. She held an icepack against her bruised cheek in one hand and several wadded-up tissues in her other hand. She trembled as Doc stitched her lower lip. Although he had injected the site with Lidocaine, the girl flinched every time he came at her with the needle.

Doc's humming filled the quietness of the tiny room. The last guest had left the house, leaving the injured girl for Doc to fix up. But Doc didn't mind. He enjoyed working on the girls. It kept his skills sharp since he retired from the clinic. And, of course, the lucrative pay padded his pockets. Damian Reynolds was a smart businessman, Doc thought. He paid Doc good money to keep the girls healthy and patched up.

He smiled at the girl. "A few more sutures, and you'll be pretty as a peach."

A rap on the door distracted his thoughts. Eduardo burst into the room, wringing his hands. "I'm so sorry, sir, but you must hurry downstairs."

Doc held a needle holder in his shaky right hand and

bloody gauze in the left. He turned and peered over his glasses at Eduardo. "It can't wait?"

"No, sir. It's those two girls. They're fighting again. Please come quickly."

"Damn it." Doc tied a knot, cut the suture, and threw his instruments onto a sterile tray. "I'll finish later," he muttered, tearing off his gloves. He leaned close to the girl's face and taped a piece of clean gauze over the site. "You're going to wait here and not move. *Capiche*?"

He took the icepack away from her and strapped her arms and legs to the table. He never liked to use constraints unless a girl was combative. He liked to give them the benefit of the doubt. Trust them until they proved him wrong. He knew underneath all those screams and cries, they enjoyed his examinations and administrations.

However, this was a new girl, and she didn't seem to understand a word of English. He waggled a finger at her. "Stay." He turned to follow Eduardo.

***

Blood dripped from Dee-Dee's left nostril and from a cut above her left eyebrow onto her white silk nightie. Scratch marks raked her cheeks and both arms. Her upper lip was swollen, and the skin around her left eye was puffy and already changing colors.

"You little bitch!" Her screams bounced off the basement walls. She swung again at Jane. When Dee-Dee's fist missed her target, she staggered forward and landed on the cement floor, bruising her knees. On all fours, she looked up, her face contorted with rage. "I'm gonna kill you for that, you goddamn cunt."

Jane wore what was left of a ripped T-shirt and torn panties. Scratch marks grazed her upper chest and thighs, her knuckles bled, and her throat sported red blotches the shape of handprints. Choking and coughing, she backed away and pressed her body against the far wall. "Stay the hell away from me," she sputtered.

"Girls, girls!" Doc shouted as Eduardo unlocked the cell. "That's enough." The two men pushed their way inside. Doc grabbed Dee-Dee and twisted her arms behind her. "No more fighting. Mr. Reynolds is not going to be happy with you."

She squirmed in Doc's grasp, knocking the two of them onto the cot. "Get the fuck off me, old man!"

"Goddammit, hold still." Doc was breathing hard and half-sitting on her. Eduardo cuffed her hands to the bar at the head of her bed. Doc pulled a syringe out of his coat pocket.

"No!" Dee-Dee screamed. "I'll stop. I promise."

"That's what you said last time this happened. Now, it's too late." Doc jammed the thick needle into her thigh and injected half of the syringe's contents. "You asked for that, sweetie."

Dee-Dee groaned and curled into a ball. Her hair lay plastered against her face in sweaty clumps. "I didn't do anything wrong," she moaned.

Doc stood, smoothed out his white coat, and looked at Jane. "I'm afraid you're next."

Jane shook her head. "I didn't start it." She pointed at Dee-Dee. "She was choking me in my sleep. I could barely breathe." Jane's gaze darted toward the open cell door. She made a lunge for freedom.

Eduardo was quick on his feet and blocked the door with his body. Doc moved in from behind her. The two men wrestled her to the other cot and cuffed her hands to the bar at the head of the bed. "Please," she cried when she saw Doc hold up the syringe. "No drugs. I don't want any drugs."

"It only hurts for a second." Doc stabbed her thigh and injected her with the remaining medication. "Then you'll be feeling good." He waited a few minutes for the drug to take effect. Dee-Dee was already breathing slowly and steadily. Doc looked back at Jane and ran his hand down her leg. She tried to pull away. "I'll be back later when you're both nice and relaxed. Then I can clean the two of you up properly."

The men walked by Dee-Dee's old cell room before they returned upstairs. Katrina Malloy lay on the bed, her eyes half open. She dragged herself up to a sitting position. "What's going on?" she slurred. "Why am I locked up?"

Doc smiled, his hands wrapping around the bars. "Are you comfortable, Isabella? Warm enough?"

Katrina narrowed her eyes. "Where's Damian? Does he know you have me caged down here like an animal?"

Doc turned and gave a nod to Eduardo. "I'll be upstairs in a minute. Could you check on my patient? Make sure she stays put?"

"Yes, sir." Eduardo headed to the staircase, the keys on his key ring jingling with each step.

Doc looked Katrina up and down. "Mr. Reynolds insisted you'd be happy to stay with us. He even gave you the luxury suite."

She stood unsteadily and wobbled toward Doc, grabbing the bars when she got close enough. "I don't believe a word you say." She looked up at him, his face high above hers. "I'd like to hear that from Damian himself."

Doc licked his lips and bent down. He could feel Katrina's breath on his mouth. "Maybe I'll pass the message along. Maybe for a favor." He placed his sweaty hands over hers and squeezed.

Katrina pressed her body against the bars, closed her eyes, parted her lips. Doc's mouth came at her hard, his tongue forcing its way inside. "Mmm," she hummed with satisfaction, then bit down hard.

Doc let go of her hands and sprang backward. "You bitch!" He grabbed his mouth, felt his tongue, tasted blood.

Katrina laughed and fell back onto her bed. "Consider the favor accomplished."

Doc glared at her and slammed his palms against the bars. "You can rot in here with the rest of these dirty whores." He turned and walked away, Katrina's laughter echoing behind him.

***

Doc's tongue throbbed by the time he returned to his exam room. He could taste blood every time he swallowed. Damn that sneaky bitch. *To hell with helping her.*

He pulled off his doctor's coat and hung it up. Glanced at the girl lying on the table. At least *she* wasn't causing any problems. He looked in the mirror and opened his mouth, staring at his tongue. It didn't seem too bad. The damage could've been a heckuva lot worse. He'd seen some nasty human bites in his day.

Beads of perspiration riveted down each temple and the center of his back. He turned on the faucet, rinsed his mouth out, washed his hands, and splashed water on his face and forehead. He grabbed paper towels and dried off as best he could.

"All righty." He pulled on a fresh pair of gloves. "We're going to have to hurry this along, little lady. I have two more patients waiting for me downstairs."

The girl shook as he reached forward and removed the bloody gauze from her lip. "First, a bit more numbing juice, then two more stitches should do the trick." He injected the Lidocaine and thought about his years at the clinic and hospital. The long hours. The overnights, the weekends, the holidays.

At least here, he was free to do as he pleased. Within reason, of course. He had no clinic director or medical board looking over his shoulder, reprimanding his actions. No investigations on the behalf of false patient accusations. No nurses to give him the stink-eye or complain of his supposed crude remarks, lewd suggestions, or improper touches.

Doc smiled at the girl and picked up the needle holder. Yes. Here, he had it damn good.

# CHAPTER FORTY-NINE

Wes Phillips entered Louiselle's and peered around the restaurant for Damian Reynolds. The place appeared empty until he spotted Dennis sitting alone at a corner table near the kitchen door, eating lunch. Phillips swore under his breath and headed toward him. "Where's Izzy?" He loomed over him.

Dennis looked up, continued to chew his food, swallowed, and set down his fork. "I am not in a position to provide that information."

"Nicely done. Well-rehearsed," Phillips sneered. "I thought you were watching out for her."

"I was." Dennis wiped his mouth with a folded napkin. "That part of my job is over. The boss said I didn't need to worry about Isabella anymore, and I know enough to do what I'm told." He placed the napkin back in his lap and picked up the fork.

"Are you saying she pissed off Reynolds, and he did something to her?"

Dennis concentrated on his plate, stabbing his food

with the fork. “I am not saying that. I’m saying I know enough not to ask.”

“I don’t,” Phillips grumbled. “Tell Reynolds I want to have a chat. Sooner than later.”

“Sure, *Steve*.”

# CHAPTER FIFTY

Morning clouds had dumped a few inches of snow across Minneapolis' Thanksgiving Parade route until noon, then tapered off. As the late afternoon event drew near, the temperature remained a steady thirty degrees.

Bruce Ellison and Dan Larkin had been tailing Christoph Morton in St. Paul since the beginning of their shift. It was business as usual until Morton picked up a passenger with several packages and headed toward Hennepin Avenue. He and Larkin looked at each other, thinking the same thought.

Ellison maneuvered the Taurus around a group of adults dressed in parkas and children bundled up in snowsuits who trudged on foot toward the parade. The adults carried folding chairs and thermoses, most likely full of alcohol. "Get the hell out of my way," Ellison growled over the steering wheel. He strained to see through the windshield whether Morton's Mercedes was still three car lengths ahead or if he had turned off.

Larkin tapped a number into his cell. "Martinez, Morton's heading straight toward Hennepin with a car full of packages. He's got a guy with him in the passenger seat."

Ellison tapped the horn at a group of teenage girls who were laughing and shrieking as they stepped out into the slow-moving traffic, holding arms and shuffling in high boots on the crunchy ice. One of the girls turned and gave him a dirty look and the finger. "You think these girls can penguin-walk any slower? Fuck, they don't even look when they cross the street."

Larkin pressed the phone harder to his ear and listened for a moment. "Yes, sir, I believe so. From Agent Roni Colburn's description, it looks like Bart Gibson. Does Minneapolis have snipers on the roofs? Just in case—"

"Ah, shit!" Ellison pounded on the dashboard. "They dumped the car. I'm double-parking. Let's go. Let's go!"

Larkin yanked off his seatbelt and bolted from the car. "In pursuit on foot. Heading north on 5th Street," he breathed into the phone. "Where's the rest of our guys?"

***

Eric Martinez gripped his cell phone and threaded his way through a crowd of parade-goers six blocks from Larkin's location. He couldn't make out Larkin's last words. A marching band from Champlin, dressed in heavy wool uniforms, black boots, and white gloves, pounded out patriotic music.

"Say again?" Martinez shouted.

The phone turned silent. "Damn it." He entered the number for an agent positioned outside the Scientology Outreach Center of Minneapolis on 6th Street and Hennepin.

"We got trouble heading your way," Martinez shouted when the agent answered. He glanced around and cupped his hand over his mouth. "Keep an eye out for Agents Larkin and Ellison. They're on 5th Street heading toward Hennepin, and they could end up at your location. They're trailing two suspects who may be armed with explosives. Call the bomb squad. Tell them to head over there and be on high alert. And to dispatch that chopper."

After the marching band passed by, a convertible Hummer with the top down followed. The Minneapolis mayor, dressed in a heavy coat, earmuffs, and gloves, sat in the back seat next to his wife, who was dressed likewise minus the earmuffs. She wore a rabbit-skin hat with white fur trim that matched her gloves. The two waved to the crowds, smiling for photos.

Several Minneapolis police officers on horseback escorted the Hummer. While the officers scanned the crowds for potential problems, the horses wearing blinders stared ahead, snorting and breathing out puffs of white. A police car with flashing lights and its front windows rolled down inched behind the procession. Chief Roxanne Dalestrom waved from the passenger seat.

Martinez's heart thudded as he imagined deadly chaos waiting for them six blocks ahead. "Oh, fuck me." He rushed through a maze of smiling, cheering people, children with runny noses and red cheeks riding on parents' shoulders, dogs on leashes wearing sweater vests and booties. Vendors with long customer lines sold turkey legs, yams on a stick, cranberry and stuffing cups, coffee, cider, and who-the-hell-knew what else.

Martinez continued down Hennepin, nearing 9th Street. Several people dressed in turkey costumes marched in his direction and blocked his way. They waved signs that read, *Stop the senseless slaughter*, *Save the turkey*, and *Eat more vegetables*. One of the turkeys shoved a flyer into his hand. "Do you know that forty-six million turkeys are killed each year for Thanksgiving Day dinners?"

Martinez crumpled the flyer and tried to push past him. "Tell the other turkeys I'm sorry. Now excuse me."

"Hey, man." The turkey shoved back. "Do you realize the horrors these birds endure just to end up on your plate? The unsanitary, cramped living conditions? The pain of having their beaks and feet clipped? The inhumane killing methods?"

Martinez raised his hands in surrender. "Got it. You go save turkeys. I gotta go save humans." He slipped past the feathered flock and bolted down Hennepin.

***

Ellison and Larkin trampled a block behind Morton and Gibson through the somewhat cleared sidewalks. "Why did we not wear boots again?" Ellison asked.

The two agents tried to blend in with the crowds heading toward the parade. So far, Morton and Gibson seemed oblivious to their tails. They each carried several small packages in their arms, occasionally joking and jostling each other around. At one point, Morton knocked one of Gibson's packages from his hands and into the slushy street.

Larkin stopped in his tracks. "Holy shit." Several people walked around him.

Ellison froze and stared at the package. "Uh, you think those two know what's in those packages?"

"I don't know what they think. Or if they think."

"And maybe it's not what *we* think."

The two agents watched as Gibson shoved Morton, then ran into the street to retrieve the package.

"Well, let's see what Martinez thinks." Larkin held the phone to his ear. When Gibson and Morton started to walk again, he stepped forward and motioned for Ellison to follow. "No answer." He pocketed the phone.

"Probably too much parade noise. Hey, did I tell you my feet are cold?" Ellison whined.

"Yeah. Twice now."

The groups of people heading toward Hennepin had grown thicker. They filled the streets. Ellison and Larkin sped up, weaving around slower pedestrians. Ahead, Morton grabbed Gibson's hat and darted forward. "You fucker," Gibson yelled over the ever-increasing blare of brass instruments from up ahead. He gripped his packages and chased after Morton.

"Fuck is right," Ellison muttered. "These guys are a couple of knotheads."

"C'mon." Larkin started to sprint.

***

Martinez stood in front of the Scientology Center, staring at Ellison and Larkin. "You what?"

Ellison averted his eyes. "We didn't lose them until we hit Hennepin. They both seemed to vanish in the crowd."

Robert McNellis stood beside Martinez, his arms

folded. “Jesus Christ,” he grumbled.

Martinez rubbed his five o’clock shadow and blew out a long breath. “Okay. We have everyone on high alert. Snipers and a chopper. No one’s seen anything.” He glanced behind him at the Scientology Center’s front entrance. “Bomb squad cleared the building as well as our other hot spots. For now, that is.” He narrowed his eyes at the two men.

“I gotta tell you, sir,” Larkin protested. “Morton and Gibson sure didn’t act like they were carrying explosives. They had no fear for their lives, even after dropping one of the packages. The job seemed like a game to them.”

Ellison nodded.

“I want you two to go back and keep an eye on Morton’s vehicle. If, for some reason, hell breaks loose, I want to know where they are. And where you two are.”

# CHAPTER FIFTY-ONE

"Where's Izzy?" Wes Phillips demanded, his right knee bouncing beneath the white linen cloth-covered table.

Damian Reynolds smiled. "Well, now, wouldn't you like to know?" He held up an empty wine glass and motioned to the waiter across the room.

Phillips gritted his teeth. A man in a white shirt, black pants, and red dinner jacket emblazoned with the word *Murphy's* above the breast pocket flitted toward them, smiling at several customers seated at crowded, candle-lit tables on the way. "Is everything to your satisfaction this evening, sir?" The man refilled Reynolds' glass.

"Perfect as always," Reynolds replied with a curt nod.

The waiter smiled. "Good to hear, sir."

Phillips waited until the man scurried to another table, then he leaned forward. "I haven't heard from Izzy or seen her in a few days." Phillips jerked his thumb at the entrance. "And your pet Kong over there seems to have lost his tongue."

"He called you, didn't he, after I agreed to this little

chat? I'm allowing you to interrupt dinner at my favorite steakhouse. You better not mess up my digestion." Reynolds unfolded his napkin, draped it over his lap, and sighed. "Tell you the truth, Steve-O, I got tired of Isabella. It happens." He took a long sip. "One day, you're the kitten's pajamas. Next day, you're dog meat. Get what I'm sayin'?"

Phillips' shoulders tensed, and his hands curled into fists. "I'm going to ask you one more time, and if I don't get an answer I like, I'm gonna come across this table and beat it out of that smartass mouth of yours. Get what *I'm* saying? Now, tell me. Where's Izzy?"

Reynolds set down his glass, leaned back in his chair, and folded his arms. "Don't worry, Steve-O. Your little girlfriend is safe and resting comfortably at one of my houses of pleasure."

"You're keeping her captive in a whorehouse?"

"Not quite. I decided she needed a vacation from winter this year, and she agreed. Truth is, Isabella volunteered to be the squadron leader for a select group of cheerleaders-in-training heading southwest."

"Human trafficking," Phillips muttered.

Reynolds' gaze slid toward a couple seated at a nearby table and back to Phillips. "Do we need to engage in this conversation elsewhere?"

Phillips shook his head, his lips pursed.

"So," Reynolds continued in a low voice. "Some VIPs are flying in from Las Vegas on a private jet soon. If they like what they see, Isabella and the girls accompany them back. They'll enjoy Christmas and New Year's fun in the sun parties, the pre-games, then the big finale."

Phillips stiffened. "No, I can't let that happen."

Reynolds laughed. "Right." He straightened up in his chair. "Listen, I'll make a deal with you. Only because you're such a tough guy. If you're still gung-ho about purchasing Isabella, I'll let you join us at the sale." He grinned wolfishly. "Bring a lot of money and that hot little number."

***

On his way out, Phillips stopped near Dennis' table, stared at him, and slid into the chair beside him. Dennis set his fork on his plate next to a double slice of cherry cheesecake and leaned back, his giant hands resting on the table's edge.

"I need your help," Phillips declared.

Dennis stared back.

"I know you care about Izzy. I can see it. I don't know if you think of her as a sister or a daughter or a favorite pet. It doesn't matter. What matters is that she's okay. I need your help making sure she is, and she stays that way."

Dennis remained silent.

"When things fall apart, which I suspect they will, please make sure she's protected. Do what's right by her."

Dennis gave a slight nod and reached for his fork.

# CHAPTER FIFTY-TWO

Images of Katrina Malloy, drunk or drugged, strapped to a bed in a whorehouse, ran through Wes Phillips' brain. He slammed the carriage house door behind him and stomped up the stairs to the upper level. A yip and low, throaty rumble greeted him. A one-eyed ball of dirty white fluff attacked his pant leg. "What. The. Hell. Are. You?" Phillips asked.

Sofia Menendez sprawled on the couch. A cardboard tray from a TV dinner, licked clean, lay on the floor. A crushed diet Coke can sat on the coffee table. She glanced at Phillips and back to her *People* magazine. "His name is Lucky, and don't growl at him. He only has one eye."

"I can see that." Phillips yanked his leg away and kicked off his shoes. The dog wagged its tail and pounced at him again. "And I wasn't growling."

"You were growling."

Phillips walked to the loveseat. The dog followed, nipping and scratching his legs. He slumped onto the cushion, and the dog jumped into his lap. Phillips' nostrils flared. "Sofia, why is there a dog—a stinky dog—in this house? What happened while I was gone?" His hand hovered over the dog's head. Finally, he patted a few tufts of ratty fur.

Sofia sprang off the couch and threw the magazine onto the table. "I'll tell you what happened. While you were out wining and dining at a fancy steakhouse, I was surviving on frozen shit food from the freezer."

"I wasn't—"

"Yes, you were. You left me out of the loop."

"I thought Reynolds would tell me—"

"There. Right there." Sofia glared at him and waggled her finger. "That macho attitude where you're more productive than me. You call the shots and ask the questions and leave me home to wash your clothes and cook your meals."

Phillips straightened. "What the fuck? For your information—"

"So, I went out. Had a nice jog in the goddamn snow. And Lucky found me." She stalked to Phillips, plucked the dog from his lap, and carried him into the kitchen. She sat him in front of a bowl of water and a plate of bologna and cheese. "Some jackoff dumped him in the park. In the cold. Without food or shelter or love." She stood and glared at Phillips through the doorway. "I knew you'd feel sorry for the little guy.

So, here he is."

Phillips sighed and stood. "I hope he's at least house-trained." He walked into the kitchen and filled a glass with ice and water.

Sofia leaned against the fridge, one hand on her hip, the other playing with her necklace. "Well? Lucky stays?"

Phillips downed most of the water and shook the ice cubes around. "Sure. Why the hell not? Everything's going to crap anyway. We could use a one-eyed guard dog around here. Might come in handy." He squatted and peered into Lucky's eye. "Whaddaya say there, little fella? Wanna be Secret Agent Number Three?"

The dog licked its chops and pounced on Phillips' stocking feet, scratching his toes.

Sofia smiled. "He likes you. I don't know why, but he does."

"It's because I'm such a tender-hearted badass."

Sofia rolled her eyes. "Whatever. Tell me what happened with Reynolds. Why is everything going to crap?"

"I'll tell you while you shampoo that thing. His fur reeks of shit and piss and who-the-hell-knows-what."

Sofia bent over and sniffed Phillips' hair. "After a day's

work, you don't smell so hot either."

He stood. "By the way, while you were here cooking your gourmet meal, did you wash my underwear?"

She socked him on the shoulder. "You're such a bastard."

# CHAPTER FIFTY-THREE

Katrina Malloy balanced a breakfast tray in one shaky hand and held onto the railing with the other as she hobbled down the basement steps of the Summit house in high heels. She wore one of Dee-Dee's transparent black negligees with a lacy V-neck collar, a high-cut hem, and a matching thong. The negligee was long on her petite body and roomy in the chest, but Eduardo insisted Damian Reynolds would be pleased. A master key to the cells dangled from an expandable wrist bracelet.

This was her fourth trip up and down the steps. Eduardo already gave her enough food to feed roughly half the girls. Katrina swallowed hard, her throat parched from stair-climbing. A large Bloody Mary, heavy on the vodka, waited for her when she finished. Although Eduardo kept strict house rules, at least he understood her needs. When this was over, she kept telling herself she'd sober up. *No more booze*.

Dee-Dee eyed Katrina. "I see you're enjoying my outfits."

Katrina ignored her and slid the tray under the cell

door.

"Too bad you can't fill them out like a real woman." Dee-Dee smiled as she lifted and squeezed her own breasts. "Mr. Reynolds told me he finds you lacking in bed as well." She laughed. "I suppose it can't help your self-esteem being cursed with an ugly ink spot, either."

Katrina fought the urge to cover her throat and glanced at Jane. The girl's eyes were still closed. At least Dee-Dee wouldn't pick fights with her anymore. Reynolds had stopped by the night before and personally warned the two of them.

"Keep it up, and I'll ship you to the Far East," he'd told Dee-Dee, then pointed to Jane. "And you could become a desert princess."

Katrina stood outside the cell, watching Dee-Dee cry on his shoulder, begging to have her own room back. "I'll be good," she whined. "I want to be your special girl again."

"Enough." Reynolds disentangled her arms. "Save the act for the customers."

Katrina pulled herself back to the present. She needed to finish breakfast duties and oversee group showers. She hated staring at the girls' naked bodies, the old scars, the new wounds.

If only she could get in touch with Wes Phillips. Get hold of anyone. Even Dennis. She nodded. Maybe Dennis would be sweet enough to call Wes for her. She had no idea when his next visit would be, though. Chrissake, maybe she was in over her head after all. According to Reynolds, the Las Vegas auction was coming up soon. She would be flying southwest, in charge of the girls. She needed to act strong, competent, and businesslike around these men. And prepare for self-preservation.

# CHAPTER FIFTY-FOUR

Wes Phillips stepped through Hauser's kitchen and nodded to the two cooks. He headed toward the hidden dining room in the back. Russ Malloy and Robert McNellis sat at the table, plates empty, beers in hand. The men stood, McNellis wobbly on his feet. They all shook hands.

"Heard things are still a little shaky with my goddaughter," McNellis slurred. He sat back down, eyes narrowing. "I thought you were getting everything under control on your end."

Phillips pulled up a chair. "It was until recently." He glanced at Malloy. "Katrina is officially MIA, but according to my conversation with Damian Reynolds, I'm pretty sure we'll locate her shortly."

McNellis pounded the table with his fist, accidentally knocking over his bottle. Half of it spilled across the table in Phillips' direction before McNellis could grab it and set it back up. "Damn it! *Pretty sure* doesn't cut it in the Bureau. It's time for you to stop dicking around. Do what you've been hired to do. Get in there and get her out. This is my goddaughter we're talking about. Enough with the games."

Malloy grabbed McNellis' arm. "Wes is doing the best he can. We all are. I have a lot riding on this as well. My sister—"

"Hold on," Phillips interrupted. "Let me talk."

McNellis jerked his arm away. "Let's hear it. And it better be good." He gulped the rest of his beer and reached into the cooler for another.

Phillips leaned forward. "Reynolds is going to hold a private sale soon. He's got a group of girls he's auctioning off to some Las Vegas bigwigs."

"Aw, jeezus," McNellis muttered.

"He mentioned cheerleaders and pre-game parties," Phillips continued. "I assume he's talking Super Bowl."

"Shit." Malloy shoved his plate away. "If my sister and these girls get transferred out there, we'll never see them again."

Phillips held up his hand. "Reynolds knows Katrina—well, *Isabella* to him—and I used to be a thing. I've come on pretty strong about wanting that to happen again, that I want her back. So, he's offered to let me attend his auction."

McNellis belched. "It all comes down to who wants to

fuck who."

"And how bad," Phillips added. "I've been instructed to bring money. A lot of money. And Sofia."

Malloy rubbed the stubble on his chin. "What does Sofia say about being a tradeoff? Is she still willing to get in that deep?"

Phillips nodded. "It's what she's been waiting for."

# CHAPTER FIFTY-FIVE

Wes Phillips and Sofia Menendez lay supine on the king-sized bed, fully clothed yet shoeless. Lucky lay at the end of the bed, snoring. He was bathed, shaved, and resembled a pampered white rat. Sofia curled onto her side and faced Phillips. She stuck out a stockinged toe and gingerly rubbed it against his injured shin. "When is this big auction party?"

Phillips looked down at her foot, then at the ceiling. "Reynolds didn't give me a date. Not even sure when these suits fly in from Las Vegas, but I gather it's soon." He released a loud breath. "The Super Bowl's only two months away, and it sounds like these assholes want to have their inventory beforehand for—"

"Inventory such as me?"

Phillips rolled onto his side to face her, his brow furrowed. "I'm not sure. I get the feeling Reynolds wants to keep you for himself. Like I said before, you for Katrina."

She pulled her foot away, rolled onto her back, and folded her arms. "I can hardly wait to be Reynolds' new sex toy."

"That's not part of the job. I won't let it go that far."

"Goddamn fuckin' pricks. I want to puke every time I think about what these men do. Use 'em and abuse 'em, then throw the bitch away." She paused and lowered her voice. "We take Reynolds down, and there'll be another john ready to jump into his place." Her voice cracked. "Sometimes it seems this job's not even worth it."

Phillips grabbed her arm. "Don't say that. Don't even think that." He continued to grip her arm tightly. "We do what we do to help the victims. Get these girls off the street. Away from scum like Reynolds. Offer them a better life, a safe life. Prevent more young girls from walking the street or being trafficked.

"The harder we work, the more criminals we put behind bars." He loosened his grip. "Sofia, you're a big part of making that happen. You know that. The whole team knows it and appreciates what you do."

She looked at him with a small smile. "Thanks. You're right. I was having one of those moments."

"We've all been there."

She caught his hand and moved toward him, her

breath on his neck. He turned his head toward her, and they stared at each other.

"Forgive me." He pulled her close and pressed his lips to hers.

She moaned, her breath quickening, her hands stroking his face. He fumbled for the buttons on her blouse. He made a noise of his own, then slid his fingers beneath her bra and cupped her breasts. "We shouldn't be…" he breathed between kisses.

"Quiet."

Lucky sprang up and jumped on Phillip's leg, yipping and panting. Phillips pushed the dog away with his foot. Lucky jumped again, clawing at him and humping his calf. Again, Phillips shoved him off.

Phillips' cell phone alarm beeped from his back pocket. They both froze. For a moment, neither one spoke. They stared into each other's eyes, their breathing fast, heavy. Lucky resumed his pumping. Phillips kicked hard, and the dog squealed.

Sofia looked down toward their feet. The dog sat on his haunches, tongue out, tail wagging. "What are you doing to Lucky? Remember, he only has one eye."

Phillips sighed. “Yeah, I know. You keep reminding me.” He entangled his hands from beneath her shirt, pulled out his cell phone, and checked the time. “Shit.” He pulled himself to a sitting position. “We gotta get moving. McNellis doesn’t like it when people are late.”

“Yeah?” Sofia sat up and buttoned her blouse. “Well, I don’t like it when a team member drinks himself stupid on the job.”

“Tell that to McNellis.”

“Somebody should.”

# CHAPTER FIFTY-SIX

The task force had been gathered around a long conference table in the basement of the BCA for thirty minutes. Wes Phillips and Sofia Menendez slipped into the room and sat beside Russ Malloy. Robert McNellis glanced up from his notes and gave the two a dirty look. "Glad you could join us. Hope we didn't interrupt your *siesta*."

"Oh, no, sir," Phillips replied. "We're delighted to be here."

Malloy elbowed Phillips in the ribs.

"Right," McNellis grunted. "Here." He slid a pair of dirty athletic shoes down the table in Sofia's direction. "Courtesy of the FBI."

Sofia picked up one of the shoes, sniffed the inside, raised her eyebrows, and looked at Phillips. "Smells like your shoes."

Malloy smirked.

"Runaways don't believe in spending money on new shoes," McNellis added. He pointed at the rubber soles.

"We've installed a tracking device in each one. Now put 'em on."

Sofia tilted her head and batted her eyelashes. "*Por favor*?"

"Goddammit," McNellis growled. "Put the fuckin' shoes on. Please."

Several of the men suppressed smiles.

Eric Martinez stood at the other end of the table from McNellis. He cleared his throat. "Okay, people. Now that we've been brought up to date, we need to discuss our next move." He pointed at Sofia. "Tomorrow night at eight, I want you looking young and vulnerable, camped out at the bus stop where Jane Doe was last seen." He looked at Curtis Blair.

"East Franklin and Chicago, sir," Blair added.

"Right," Martinez continued. "Let's hope the same predator swings by and is enamored by your Miss Smartass looks. Malloy and Phillips will cover the street on foot. McNellis, you cruise the neighborhood in the unmarked squad. If we get lucky and the guy picks up Menendez, let's not lose them. If we do, we have our trusty trackers." He motioned to Bruce Ellison and Dan Larkin. "Meanwhile, I want a continuous tail on Christoph Morton and anyone he meets. And find someone other than you two to talk to that dancer."

Ellison and Larkin nodded.

"Blair, I want you to keep an eye on that warehouse. If—"

"Excuse me, sir," Phillips cut in, hand raised. "I thought we were going to wait for the auction and trade—"

"If you'd been here thirty minutes earlier, Officer Phillips," McNellis interrupted from the other end of the table, "you'd know plans have changed. We've decided it would be safer for all parties involved to come at this from a different angle. The task force will continue to survey and follow any suspects. Hopefully, we'll discover where Reynolds is holing up and keeping these girls before this auction takes place."

"But—" Phillips protested.

"He's right," Martinez insisted. "Every day we wait for these Las Vegas hot shots to fly in puts these girls and Katrina in further danger." Martinez looked around the room. "We're no longer only talking about the sale of weapons. We're now talking about human lives."

# CHAPTER FIFTY-SEVEN

"I want to apologize for my behavior earlier," Wes Phillips told Sofia Menendez from the passenger seat of the Lincoln after leaving the task force meeting. "I was out of line."

Sofia clutched the steering wheel. "Yes, you were. Lucky has had a hard life. He only wants to be loved. Not kicked." She turned on the blinker and looked over her shoulder. They remained silent as she changed lanes.

"I meant about the kissing."

"I know what you meant. I'm sorry I kissed you back, but I'm even sorrier we were interrupted."

Phillips turned in his seat to face her. "What?"

"Yeah, I'm sorry." She stared ahead at the traffic. "I was about to let you get further out of line and get me out of my clothes. We were saved from ourselves at the last second."

"Sofia, we were risking everything. The investigation, our jobs. We were unprofessional. Lives are at stake."

"We're going to risk it all for each other anyhow. Why

not reap the benefits while we're at it?"

"Are you serious?"

"I am. And when this is over, if you're lucky enough to still be appealing to me, we can further explore this subject."

"Well, okay then." He shook his head and realized where they were. "Drop me off over there." He pointed to the entrance of the Minneapolis Public Library.

She stared at the building. "Are you for real? I didn't know they held story time this late."

"Whatever. I've got something important to do."

She pulled the Lincoln to the curb. "In the middle of an undercover investigation, you have a dire need to read a book? Really, Wes?"

"Yeah." He opened the door, climbed out, then he poked his face back in. "The book's called *The Idiot's Guide to Catching Criminals*."

She stared at him. "Okay, now I know you're joking. I saw a copy on your nightstand, and it already looked well-read."

He smiled. "Go have a mocha latte or one of those other fancy drinks they serve at Caribou. It's around the corner. I'll meet you there in an hour or so."

She waggled her fingers. “Okay, Mr. Secret Agent Bookworm.”

# CHAPTER FIFTY-EIGHT

An hour later, Wes Phillips walked out of the library and onto the sidewalk of the Nicollet Mall. He headed south and almost reached the corner when a Cadillac Escalade in the right lane of Fourth Avenue slammed its brakes and turned left onto the mall, cutting off three lanes of one-way traffic.

Dennis hopped from the SUV and opened the back door. Damian Reynolds stepped onto the sidewalk. “Hey, Steve-O. Fancy meeting you here.”

“You following me?” Phillips asked.

“No. This is a chance meeting. Dennis saw you, and I thought we should chat.”

Phillips jerked his head toward a no parking sign next to the Escalade. “You know you can’t park there, right?”

“It’ll be a short conversation.” Reynolds pointed at the book in Phillips’ hand. “You a big reader?”

“Sort of. A poet I wanted to hear had a reading.” Phillips held it up. “I bought his latest book.”

“Poetry, huh?” Reynolds reached for the book. “I’m a

poet, but nobody knows it." He laughed. "See how I did that? Pretty clever, eh?"

Dennis laughed.

"Very," Phillips deadpanned.

Reynolds held the book toward Dennis. "You're into poetry, aren't you, Dennis?"

Dennis peered at the cover. "Yeah, I like it. Some of it calms me. Some of it pisses me off."

Phillips held out his hand. "Well-written poetry has that effect on me, too. Especially when it's about subjects that piss me off."

"Hold on, hold on." Reynolds flipped the book over and examined the back cover as a short, muscular Hispanic man stepped up beside them.

"Hey, you fellas can't park there." The man jerked his thumb at the sign.

"You the parking police?" Reynolds asked.

The man puffed up his chest. "I start with Chicago PD next week. I'm home visiting *la familia* on my last weekend of freedom. So right now, I'm trying to be a helpful citizen by telling you to move your vehicle before a real cop comes along."

Reynolds looked at him with furrowed brows. “Thanks for your help, *Officer*. We’ll be moving along now.” He threw the book to Phillips, and it bounced off his chest. Phillips caught it before it hit the wet sidewalk. “See you soon, Steve-O.”

“Looking forward to it. And I’m looking forward to seeing Izzy.”

Reynolds smiled and gave him a big wink. He and Dennis climbed inside the Escalade and took off.

Phillips turned. “Thanks, man. You saved my life.”

“Oh, yeah? Glad I could help. How did I manage that?”

“Are you really going to be a Chicago cop?”

“Sure as shit.”

“So, you happened to be coming out of the library when I needed you?” Phillips asked. “You’ve never seen those two men before?”

“What is this? An interrogation?”

“I’m also a cop.”

“Ah. You’re undercover, and them two are suspects you’re working.”

“Yeah.” Phillips held out his hand. “Wes Phillips.”

The man shook Phillips’ extended hand. “Michael Ortiz.

You gonna tell me how I saved your life or not?"

Phillips held up the book. "I like poetry, try to write it on occasion. Tonight, one of my favorites had a reading in the library. I bought a book and had it signed. That guy was about to open it up and see it inscribed to someone he doesn't know. I'd have been dead or trying to come up with a whole new set of lies to cover my ass."

Ortiz laughed, flashing white teeth. "How fast are you at improvising bullshit?"

"Not very. I'd like to think I'm a good cop, not that I've been one all that long, but I'm no actor."

"It's probably a lesson we should both learn. Once under, don't let any of your real life sneak out. It could be your last poem."

"You a poet, too?"

"Nah, not so hot with words. But sit me behind a sweet set of drums..." Ortiz pantomimed holding a pair of drumsticks and let loose with a silent performance.

Phillips smiled. "Well, maybe someday I'll get to hear you play."

"Yeah, and if you ever need me, look me up. Next week, I'm officially one of you."

"Good luck in Chicago. Keep your eyes open."

"You, too. Hope to see you alive next time I'm in town."

Phillips walked toward the corner, stopped, and turned around. "Hey. Ortiz. You interested in helping me with something?"

# CHAPTER FIFTY-NINE

Michael Ortiz and his brother Antonio entered Thrillers loudly and boisterously. They spoke in rapid Spanish until the host in the fur bikini approached them. Michael, being the tallest, came up to her chin.

"Good evening, gentlemen. Welcome to Thrillers, *home of the finest*."

Antonio adjusted his baseball cap so the miniature camera he wore got a good look at the woman's body. Bruce Ellison, Dan Larkin, and Russ Malloy sat outside in an unmarked van, listening and watching.

Michael ogled her. "Thank you. We're happy to be here. Other than you, home of the finest what?"

She made a partial turn. "The finest everything." She smiled. "Let me show you to your table."

They followed her down an aisle along the ends of the runways. On the center runway, a woman dangled upside-down by one knee on the dancing pole.

Through the wiretap in Antonio's ear, Ellison

announced, “That’s her. The pole dancer. She’s the one.”

The host stopped at an empty table. “This okay?”

Michael flashed his teeth. “*Perfecto*.”

“Let me know if you’d like anything special before your server arrives.”

Antonio raised his hand. “A lap dance for my brother.” The host smiled, and Antonio pointed at the pole dancer. “With her.”

She stopped smiling.

“Hey, you’re gorgeous and all, but this is his going-away party. Unfortunately, you aren’t his type. He wouldn’t appreciate your beauty and would tip lousy.” He looked at the pole dancer. “She’s his type. I don’t understand, and I can’t believe we’re related, but she’s the kind of girl he’d want to take home to Mother. She kind of looks like our mother. Maybe that’s his problem.”

The host moved so her chest was mostly in Antonio’s face. “I’ll see what I can do.”

When the server appeared, Antonio leaned forward, elbows on the table, chin on his hands. From the view of the hat camera, he was trying to see past the gauzy material and around or beneath the strategically placed strips covering too much.

The server shimmied, drawing attention to her face. “What can I get you?”

“*Dos cervezas, por favor,*” Antonio replied.

“Anything special?” she asked.

“Something strong to make me forget your beauty and the fact that I’ll be going home with my brother.”

She laughed. “Wow. That was one of the better lines I’ve heard. Usually, the drunken assholes wave cash and ask when I’m dancing. Or when I’m getting off. But I don’t dance, and no one I meet here gets me off.” She leaned closer. Antonio’s breathing deepened. “You’ve come the closest.” Antonio’s elbows slipped, and he almost slammed his face into the table. In his ear, the task force laughed.

The server returned a few moments later with two frosty mugs. Antonio smiled and handed her a twenty-dollar bill. “Keep the change.”

The pole dancer, wearing transparent pink mesh and a G-string with blinking lights, stepped over to the table. “Someone here believes they’re man enough for a lap dance from Mandy.” She did a curtsy.

Antonio jerked his thumb at Michael. “My brother’s

your man. It's his going-away present. He needs something special."

"I. Am. Special." Mandy writhed her way closer to the table. "Do you deserve special?"

Michael cleared his throat, blinked hard, and nodded quickly.

Mandy swung a muscular leg over his head and stomped her heeled shoe on the tabletop. The frosty mugs rattled. She thrust her pelvis forward three times rapidly, lights blinking a runway that led between her legs. "I don't think you do," she countered.

"I do," Michael insisted. "I exercise just so I can keep up with lovely dolls like you. I dig strong women. I love your tone, the way your muscles ripple."

"Do your muscles ripple?"

He nodded.

"Open your shirt. Show me."

Michael undid the first button.

"You think I got all night?" Mandy grabbed the front of his shirt and ripped it open, sending buttons flying.

"That's why Antonio is wearing the wire," Malloy told

Ellis and Larkin.

Mandy stared at Michael's well-developed pecs and six-pack abs. "Well, hot damn, boyfriend. You ain't kiddin'."

Michael looked down at his ripped shirt. "That was my favorite shirt. It was a gift from my mother."

"I'll make it up to you," Mandy cooed.

Michael licked his lips. "I'm looking forward to it."

She placed a platform heel in the center of his chest. "You better sit back and relax. In a few minutes, I'll have you so worked up, every muscle will be screaming for release."

Michael slid back in his chair and placed his hands on his knees. "Enough with the teasing, honey. Let's get to it."

Mandy began to dance, a series of spins, twirls, and kicks. Then she stopped, her back to Michael, looked over her shoulder, and smiled. The mesh disappeared to cheers from everyone at surrounding tables. She smacked her hands to her ass, slid them down her spread legs, and clamped them to her ankles. Her hair dragged on the floor, her nipples pointing between her knees. She smiled at Michael again.

Michael nodded and smiled back.

She straightened and bent backward, arms over her head, until her hands rested on the edge of the seat between his legs. Mandy ran her tongue around her mouth, her lip gloss glistening.

Michael released a deep breath.

She straightened up again and looked over her shoulder once more. Her legs and feet tapped out a rhythm, flamenco-style, and she backed closer to him. The muscles in her ass quivered until they looked as if they'd never stop.

"You like my ass?"

"I love your ass," Michael declared. "But how can I be sure those are toned muscles with a mind of their own?"

She huffed. "What would they be if they weren't toned muscles?"

"Fat."

All movement stopped, and she stared at him. "There is no fat on me. Not a bit. Anywhere."

"It's okay, honey. Some guys are into fat, jiggly asses. I'm not." Michael pointed at her backside. "We need to prove that this is an ass I can stay in love with, an ass I can burn into my memory to enjoy for all time."

"What do you suggest?"

"A little side venture."

Mandy glanced around the room. “Are you a cop?”

“Nope,” Michael replied.

She looked at Antonio. “What about you?”

“*Chica,* we’re the kind of guys cops like to beat up,” Antonio insisted. “We’re good enough to clean their chickens and their turkeys but not drive through their town. Every traffic stop ends in a broken rib.”

She looked at them through narrowed eyes for a long moment. “We have another dance studio where we can settle this. It’s expensive.” She pointed at Michael. “And it’s only you. Your brother waits here. But I’m telling you…” She jiggled her ass again. “There is no fat here.”

“No deal.” Michael jerked his thumb at Antonio. “My bro has to come. He’s paying for the dance, and this needs at least one witness.”

“Fine. He can watch. *Only* watch.”

“Good.” Michael rubbed his hands together. “Let’s conclude negotiations and get to fat testing.”

Mandy led them across the club and through a doorway filled with suspended strings of beads. They followed her down a hallway, past loud music, private dances, and a few noises associated with a different kind of late-night dance. She motioned them to enter a small room separated from the hall only by another beaded curtain. It contained a couch and a chair. Neither was close to new, both stained lots of different colors.

Antonio sat in the chair and leaned back, locking his hands behind his head.

"How do you propose we test this?" Michael asked.

"I'll let you squeeze my ass." Mandy turned her ass in his direction and smiled over her shoulder.

Michael shook his head. "I want more than an ass-grab. I want the experience of a lifetime."

She peered down at him. "Sure. All the guys want that. So, what do you suggest?"

Michael looked at the couch, then back at Mandy. "I propose riding you like a little doggie, then reaching down and giving that fine ass a slap. That'll tell me everything I need to know."

"We can do that. Are you prepared to pay the price?"

"What's the price?"

"A grand. That allows one ass slap. Additional ass slaps are a hundred bucks each."

Michael looked at Antonio, who held up two fingers.

"Two slaps," Michael negotiated. "One per cheek."

"Okay, but I refuse to be spanked."

"Deal," Michael stated. "One more condition."

"No conditions or no deal."

"Nah, wait, humor me and hear me out," Michael continued. "This is a special occasion, and for that kind of money, I want it to be *really* special."

Mandy placed her hands on her hips. She cocked her head and looked at him through suspicious eyes.

"I saw it in a movie. It's not weird at all," Michael assured her.

"I don't think I'm going to like it. What is it?"

Michael grabbed a handful of bills from Antonio and held them up. "I don't want to just hand you money and fuck. First, I want you to lie on the couch on your back, then I want to lay these out across your fine body. Cover your skin with C notes like I'm papering a wall. I'll be turning you into a piece of monetary art."

She stared at him. "I let you do that, I scoop up the money, we fuck, you slap my ass and go away, right?"

Michael nodded. “That’s it. I’m sure turning you into art will take longer than the fat ass test.”

Mandy stretched, her body rippling like a cat. She lay back on the couch, one knee up slightly, one arm over her head. “Time is wasting. Make me art.”

Michael counted out fifty-dollar bills as he spread them across her chest, starting near her chin, and trailed the money between her breasts. He went back to place one bill on each nipple, then he resumed zig-zagging the money trail to her blinking G string.

When Michael had the money spread across her torso, she plucked the bills from her body and stood. “Was that as good for you as it was for me?” She straightened the bills in her hand.

Before Michael could answer, Malloy stepped into the room. “Time for some pillow talk.”

# CHAPTER SIXTY

Russ Malloy flipped the dimmer switch, illuminating the private room. Mandy quickly rolled the bills up and stuffed them into her G string. "You can't be back here."

Malloy held up his badge. "Why not?"

"I haven't done anything wrong."

"You've done enough wrong to get arrested."

She pointed at Michael and Antonio Ortiz. "They said they weren't cops. I asked."

"They're not cops." Malloy looked at Michael and Antonio Ortiz. "Gentlemen, thank you for your help. You can leave."

"*Si,*" Antonio replied.

Michael smiled over his shoulder at Mandy as he turned to walk out. "It's a fine ass."

Mandy raised her middle finger. "It's a shame you'll never know. And don't ever come back here. I'll tell Lucas to kill you."

"Terroristic threats," Malloy warned. "Keep adding on the charges."

"I told you. I've done nothing wrong." She spun around, sat in Antonio's empty chair, and tried to cover herself with her arms.

"I only want to talk," Malloy replied.

"Even that has a price."

Malloy nodded. "I know. I agree, and I'm willing to work that out."

"What are you offering?"

Malloy ran his finger along the arm of the couch. "You talk, I leave, you get to go back to work or home or wherever you'd like."

"I don't know anything." She met Malloy's stare, then looked away. "Fine. What do you want to know?"

He held up a picture of Christoph Morton. "This person of interest was in here recently, to see you."

"Don't know him."

"I have witnesses who say he handed you something, and you gave him a hug. Hardly seems like something you'd do to someone you didn't know. Unless he handed you money."

Malloy paused and stepped closer. "Tell me about this man you don't know."

"For God's sake. He's a friend of a friend of my boyfriend. He does us all favors."

"What kind of favors?"

Mandy waved her hands around. "Runs errands, makes deliveries, finds things. He's one of those helpful, resourceful friends we all wish we had."

Malloy pulled out a pen and notepad. "What did he bring you the day he was in here?"

"A package for me and my boyfriend."

"What was in the package?"

"Tickets."

He scribbled something on the pad. "What kind of tickets? I need specifics if I'm going to help you."

She sighed. "Airline tickets, tickets to a football game."

"Which football game?"

"The Super Bowl."

"This season's Super Bowl? In Las Vegas?"

"Yeah," she replied. "Nice, huh?"

Malloy tapped Morton's image on the photo. "And why did this man deliver them?"

"Remember that friend I mentioned?"

"Yeah."

"Well, he put the package together. He got the tickets, made the reservations, everything. Like our own travel agent. Christoph brought me the tickets so I could give them to my boyfriend."

"Who is this travel agent friend?" he asked.

"Damian Reynolds."

"And your boyfriend?"

"Harold McIntire."

"Would that be Judge Harold McIntire?"

"Do you know him?"

Malloy ignored her question and scribbled more notes. "How did you meet the judge?"

"Damian introduced us."

"How long ago was that?"

"Christ. I don't know. Six months."

"And how is it going? You and Harold?"

She grinned. “Great. We’re in love. After the Super Bowl, I expect Valentine’s Day will be extra special.”

Malloy flipped his notepad closed. “I’m happy for you.” He pocketed the pad, pen, and photo. “I really am. I hope everything works out for you and Harold. You should come see me if you make it back to Minnesota alive.”

# CHAPTER SIXTY-ONE

Chief Roxanne Dalestrom stared out her office window at City Hall and waited for her call to be picked up.

"Roxanne," Eric Martinez answered. "To what do I owe the pleasure?"

"I wanted to thank you for your help."

"You thanked me before, back on parade day when we got lucky and nothing happened."

She laughed. "This is the only situation I can think of where lucky and nothing happened can be considered a good thing."

"We take what we can get," he replied. "So, why did you really call?"

"What are you doing dragging my favorite nephew into your shitstorm?"

"What nephew? No, wait a sec, more importantly, what shitstorm? Everything is going according to plan."

"Really? You send my civilian nephew in to set up a

hooker, have him take his brother with him, and you tell me this is your plan?"

"Michael and Antonio Ortiz are your nephews?" Martinez asked. "They never said anything, and they shouldn't have talked to you."

"They are, and they didn't. They're not my only sources."

"Listen, Roxanne, you should know this deviation from plan, this short-notice improvisation, was the work of your rookie. This was not me."

"You're going to blame Wes Phillips?" Dalestrom snapped. "Don't you have control over your task force? You're letting inexperienced people make command decisions? I'm shocked."

"Shit. I can't believe I'm going to say this." Martinez paused. "Phillips is a good cop. He's creative and resourceful. He's getting us the best results of anybody on the task force."

"Wow, Eric. Complimenting one of my officers? That's unheard of from people in your department."

"Yeah, well, the way things are going, I may not be in the department much longer," he admitted. "I might as well do something positive before I go."

"Problems?"

"One of the judges has been complaining to my superiors that I'm sending him warrant requests so flimsy they should be criminal," Martinez replied. "He said he doesn't want to see another member of my task force in his courtroom unless we have something solid."

"Which judge?" Dalestrom asked.

"McIntire."

"Huh. McIntire is always on our side. I never have a problem. It's gotta be you. Kind of like dragging my nephews into your shitstorm. Yeah, it's you."

# CHAPTER SIXTY-TWO

"Get a hit on that license plate?" Wes Phillips asked Russ Malloy over the phone. He peered out of the bedroom window of the carriage house, then turned to watch Sofia Menendez slip from her clothes and wrestle on a pair of tight, faded jeans with holes. Lucky lay on the bed beside her, his head resting on his paws. The dog's eye shifted back and forth between them. Phillips turned away.

"We did," Malloy announced. "Guy's name is Richard Carmichael. Last known address is Palatka, Florida."

"He must have a Minnesota address," Phillips insisted. "He has Minnesota plates on his Buick. You can't register plates without an address." He glanced over his shoulder at Sofia. She was lying supine on the bed, wriggling her hips back and forth, groaning as she tugged at the jeans.

They slipped over her hips. "Finally!" she shouted in triumph. Lucky sat up and woofed. She smiled at Phillips and zipped them up. "I guess my booty's bigger than I thought."

Phillips covered the receiver with his hand and ducked out of the room.

"Nobody at the DVS has time to verify anything," Malloy continued. "Carmichael's address is for a warehouse converted into storage units."

"Jeezus. Does he even have a unit?"

"Evidently not," Malloy replied.

"Does he get his mail at the storage place, then?"

"No, he has a post office box at one of the pack-and-ship stores in Islamorada. I suppose we could have someone stake it out."

"We could, or maybe we'll get lucky, and he'll show up at the bus stop." Phillips turned and saw Sofia model-posing in the doorway. He cleared his throat. "Sofia's ready."

"Good. McNellis said he's already in position and is starting on his first cup of coffee."

"Hopefully, that's all he's got in his cup," Phillips muttered. "What about warrants on Carmichael?"

"One from Florida. His wife died under suspicious circumstances. He split for parts unknown before it could be resolved."

Phillips grabbed his coat and nodded to Sofia. "How long has he been in Minnesota?"

"No clue. It appears nobody is looking too hard."

"Then it's time we find him and have a little chat," Phillips stated. "See you in a few."

# CHAPTER SIXTY-THREE

Sofia Menendez stood at the bus stop at East Franklin and Chicago. She wore her hooded sweatshirt, tight jeans, and the dirty athletic shoes with the trackers. She had a microphone tucked inside her sweatshirt collar. The earpiece was small, state-of-the-art, and its signal was clear. "Why can't I be a homeless runaway who was smart enough to take a coat?"

"We want you to look miserable," Russ Malloy answered.

Sofia shivered. "Well, it's working. Let's hope this doesn't take too long."

"It won't," Robert McNellis chimed in. "The surveillance video from the store across the street shows Carmichael driving by each day like he was on a scheduled route."

"This is a popular bus route," Malloy added. "Goes downtown, goes to the Hiawatha light rail line, which goes to the airport and the Mall of America. Prime hunting ground for a scumbag."

“Tell me his story again.” Sofia’s teeth began to chatter. “I can’t help but think I missed something.”

“Richard Carmichael from Palatka, Florida,” Malloy began. “An actual minister, evidently of his own fanatical Christian church in the Keys. About twenty years ago, one of his parishioners died under suspicious circumstances.”

“How suspicious?” Wes Phillips wore a microphone and stood tucked into the dark corner of a nearby storefront, his back to the street.

“According to eight bystanders, she died during a religious ceremony,” Malloy explained. “They all insist it was due to natural causes, enhanced by the presence of the Holy Spirit. The reverend, under what he calls extreme duress, says she died while they were performing an exorcism. Based on the coroner’s report, it was an exorcism like I’ve never heard of. She had been suspended a few feet above the floor, spread-eagled, tied at the wrists and ankles, wearing only a necktie.”

Phillips snorted. “And they claimed she was the one possessed.”

“Wait. It gets stranger.”

“What can be stranger than an exorcism?” Phillips asked.

"Based on what I read, it looks more like a bondage-style gang bang with strangulation," Malloy informed them.

"Somebody was having too much fun and pulled too tight on the necktie," McNellis quipped.

"Evidently," Malloy conceded. "Then, a few days later, after the woman's funeral and before the district attorney can decide on charges, the church conveniently burns, and the reverend disappears."

"And made his way to Minneapolis," Phillips grumbled. "Where he ministers to the homeless runaways by selling them into slavery."

"That would be my working theory, too," Malloy agreed. "The other weird thing is that slightly before that woman's death, the reverend's own wife supposedly died in a freak underwater accident off the shores of Islamorada. Supposedly ran out of air during a dive with a group of fine church-going men from the same parish."

"Oh, jeezus," Phillips muttered.

"Here he comes," Sofia announced. "Let's ask him about it."

***

The old Riviera crept up to the bus stop. The passenger

window slid down, and Richard Carmichael leaned across the seat and smiled. “Hello, my child. Can I offer you shelter and warm food?”

Sofia rubbed her hands up and down her arms. “I don’t know, man. What’s the catch?”

“No catch,” Carmichael assured her. “There’s never a catch when one is doing the Lord’s work.” He lifted his Bible and beckoned her forward.

Phillips stepped from the shadows, his police-issued .45 Auto Glock 21 in hand. Malloy came up to the driver’s side window and knocked. Carmichael lowered the glass and looked at Malloy’s badge.

“Is there a problem, Officer?” Carmichael asked.

“Let’s go somewhere and talk about the Lord’s work,” Malloy stated.

# CHAPTER SIXTY-FOUR

Sofia Menendez jogged along Lake of the Isles Parkway, carrying Lucky in a front-pack dog carrier. The dog's head bobbed with each stride, and his mouth stretched in a smile.

After riding earlier in the unmarked car with Robert McNellis and Richard Carmichael, she had begged out of the interrogation. She refused to watch Russ Malloy and Wes Phillips play bad-cop, crazy-cop while McNellis stood guard. Drama was okay, it would be amusing, but it was more respect than the slimy minister deserved.

Considering he was the one who recruited girls into slavery, the interrogation techniques Sofia wanted to use would make the CIA's extreme methods look tame.

Sofia had driven Phillips' car back to the carriage house. She ditched the clothes and grimy shoes and ran bathwater. Still, after a half hour of soaking in bubbles and adding more hot water, she still felt slimy. She pulled on shorts, one of Wes' sweatshirts, her regular running shoes, then packed Lucky in the carrier, and headed outside for fresh air and exercise.

Halfway through her jogging route, she rounded a corner and saw Dennis pull the Escalade into a parking space ahead of her. He got out and stood next to the front passenger's door. In Spanish, he called, "Hello, beautiful. How are you?"

She slowed to a stop, breathing hard. "Fine." Sofia continued in Spanish. "What brings you here?"

"We need to talk." He glanced at Lucky. "Cute mutt. Climb in and bring him along."

Sofia looked over her shoulder at the deserted jogging path. "I need to get back. My piece of shit is waiting for me to cook his food."

Dennis laughed. "This won't take long. C'mon." He opened the door.

She slid into the front seat and glanced at her shoes. *Shit*, she thought. *Shit, shit, shit*.

Dennis closed the door, circled the SUV, and climbed in behind the steering wheel. They crept along the Parkway, and he reached over and took her hand. It almost disappeared in his giant fist. "I've been wanting to see you."

Lucky squirmed in his carrier, trying to lick Dennis'

hand.

“I’ve been hoping to see you again, too,” Sofia lied.

He lifted her hand to his mouth and kissed it. “You are so beautiful.” He smiled. “I’ve been wondering what it would take to make you mine.”

Sofia laughed. “Like any woman, I like a little romance, a little passion, and a lot of love. Beyond that, get away from your boss and get me away from the piece of shit who thinks he owns me, and we’ll see where we go.”

He took his hand back and fidgeted with his ring. “I’m loyal to Mr. Reynolds. How can I be sure you’ll be loyal to me if you can’t even be loyal to Mayer?” He reached into his coat pocket, then set his hand on her bare thigh. She felt a sharp poke and gasped. “As much as I would love to run off with you, that’s just not how things work,” he added.

Sofia scrambled for the door handle, her vision beginning to blur. Her arms and legs grew heavy. She sagged against the door and rolled her head to the side. Beside her, Dennis morphed into a giant dark blob. Lucky whimpered, and everything faded to black.

# CHAPTER SIXTY-FIVE

Russ Malloy held his hands in front of the kerosene-powered space heater. It blew like a jet engine into the center of the single-car garage. The exhaust pointed out the overhead door, cracked six inches. Outside, Robert McNellis, the owner of the rental property, waited in the car, watching the alley and the neighboring houses.

Malloy and Wes Phillips had handcuffed Richard Carmichael to a chair facing the heater but beyond its warmth. Despite wearing a coat, the old man shivered.

Malloy turned and stared at Carmichael. "Are you gonna help us, or should I let my friend work you over?"

Phillips stood in the corner, playing with a battery-powered Dremel tool. He pressed the Dremel's spinning wheel against a piece of scrap metal. The tool released a metallic whine and threw off a shower of sparks.

Malloy continued. "After that, I'll let him dump you in some deep, dark hole you'll never get out of."

Carmichael's face paled. "I'm happy to help." His voice

was shaky. “All you have to do is ask.”

“Good,” Malloy told him. “Let’s start by you telling us about your friends.”

“They’re not my friends. Only business associates.”

“Oh, well, excuse me. *Business* associates.”

Carmichael stole a glance at Phillips, then looked back at Malloy. “They’re not nice people, but I don’t sit in judgment of them. Only God does. And I have no loyalty other than to God.”

Malloy nodded. “Uh-huh. Keep talking.”

Carmichael shifted in his chair. The handcuffs rattled. “Jo-Jo hires me to get runaways off the street. I deliver them to him at a hotel in the Midway district.”

“Which hotel?” Malloy prodded.

“A different one every so often.”

“And what does Jo-Jo do with the girls?”

Carmichael looked away. “I don’t know.”

“Bullshit.” Phillips held up the Dremel. “I’m ready. It’ll be like a warm knife in butter. Those appendages will drop to the floor clean as a whistle.” He gave the button a click, and the wheel at the end whirred rapidly. “We just have to lean him over a bit so he can watch."

Malloy bent down, his face inches from Carmichael's. "I'm gonna ask you one more time. What does Jo-Jo do with the girls?"

Carmichael's head spun between Malloy and Phillips. "He promised me they'd be well cared for. They'd be off the streets and safe."

"And you really don't know what happens next?" Malloy asked.

Phillips walked over to Carmichael. He grabbed the man's cuffed hand and pulled at each finger. "Eenie-meenie-miney-mo. Pick a finger, grind it off nice and slow, serve it up with cocktail sauce." He gave the power tool a spin and looked at Malloy. "Hey, you know what I've never done?"

Malloy stood and folded his arms. "No, what?"

"Sliced them the long way, from the nail to the elbow."

Malloy grinned. "Ouch."

"Sweet Jesus, you can't," Carmichael protested, a bit of spittle on his chin. He looked at Malloy. "You're an officer of the law."

Phillips nodded. "Oh, but I can. Nobody knows where you are. Florida thinks you left the country, and no one we know saw you come here." He gave the grinder a spin. "You don't exist. Even less of you will exist when I'm done." He tugged at the man's pinky finger. "Here we go..."

"No. Oh, God, please. Stop."

"How many girls have you heard say the same thing?" Malloy asked.

"None. Good Lord, I swear." Carmichael's breath grew ragged. "I'm never in the room when...when whatever happens, happens. I'm telling you the truth. I don't know."

"But you suspect," Phillips pressed.

Carmichael nodded. "Yes. I suspect."

"Did your parishioner say to stop?" Malloy asked.

Carmichael frowned. "I don't know what you're talking about."

"The woman at your church," Malloy clarified. "How did she die?"

"That...that was years ago. During an exorcism."

"And how did your church burn down?" Malloy asked.

"God told me to purify the place," Carmichael explained. "Fire purifies."

Malloy shook his head. "How the hell did you go from

exorcism and purification to human slavery?"

Carmichael glared at Malloy. "I have nothing to do with slavery."

Phillips held the grinder in front of Carmichael's face. "I'll start with the nose, right up the center, so you can see it coming. Then, between your eyes and into your forehead. I can lobotomize you before you make another denial."

Carmichael scrunched back in his chair.

"I have to admit, he hasn't been much help yet," Malloy muttered. "Maybe you should do your thing."

Phillips moved the grinder a half inch closer to Carmichael's nose.

"No. Wait," Carmichael cried, his eyes crossing as they focused on the grinder. Beads of perspiration dotted his forehead. "What do you want to know?"

"Everything," Phillips whispered, stretching out the word.

"Start with Jo-Jo," Malloy stated. "How did you meet him?"

"He was young. Late teens. Always getting into trouble. I convinced him to become a member of my church. He was there when my wife died in a terrible, horrible diving accident."

Carmichael shook his head; his eyes filled with tears. "He helped me through the pain of losing her, my poor Suzanna."

Phillips kicked his chair. "What else?"

Carmichael sniffed. "Then, the night of the exorcism. It was plain to see that woman needed our help. She needed God's help. Jo-Jo was there when the woman passed on to eternal hell. Killed by the hand of Satan." He stared at the men. "I have witnesses to that. Of course, all you heathens wouldn't understand. Wouldn't believe in the sanctity of what we were doing. So, Jo-Jo helped me purify both the woman and the church. Then I moved here. He's helped me adjust since."

"Adjust," Malloy muttered. "How many different hotels did you use to meet Jo-Jo and sell young girls?"

"I don't sell young girls," Carmichael insisted.

Phillips kicked his chair again.

"It's hard to say. I move to a new location when things get sticky."

"And lately?" Malloy asked. "Which hotel?"

Carmichael cleared his throat. "The Setting Sun Motor Inn."

"Why there?"

"Jo-Jo had an in at the desk."

"And who would that be?" Malloy demanded.

Carmichael shrugged his shoulders. "I don't know the man's name."

Phillips exhaled a loud sigh. He looked at Malloy.

Carmichael scowled. "Fine. He's the night clerk. He has a tattoo of an ugly cartoon bird on his arm."

"Where do we find Jo-Jo?" Malloy questioned.

"I don't know. After a few meetings, he gives me a new phone and takes my old one. Says no one can track us that way. It has a number programmed into it. When I have a girl, I text him. He sets it up with the night clerk, and I go to the hotel. The clerk makes sure the hallway's clear and the room's ready. I wait in the room with the girl, and Jo-Jo shows up and takes her."

"What do you get for your efforts?" Phillips asked. "Playtime with an under-aged, unwilling girl?"

"No," Carmichael snapped. "I would never..." He shook his head and looked up at the men. "He gives me some cash and leaves."

"Where does he go?" Phillips asked.

Carmichael shrugged. “I don’t know. I don’t want to know.”

“Okay, so Jo-Jo gives you a phone, and you text him,” Malloy verified. “Do you know the number? Do you remember it?”

“I don’t bother. I compared the numbers of the first few phones. You know, just in case. But they were different. He must change phones, too.”

“The phone from Jo-Jo, is that the one we took from you?” Malloy asked.

Carmichael nodded.

“Let’s text him now.” Phillips gave the Dremel a spin.

## CHAPTER SIXTY-SIX

Robert McNellis headed to the station to book Richard Carmichael while Russ Malloy drove himself and Wes Phillips to the Setting Sun Motor Inn just off University Avenue. It sat surprisingly close to the BCA offices.

The two men entered the lobby and stopped at the front desk. Malloy smiled at the man behind the counter. The night clerk was soft in the middle and may have been medium height. It was difficult to tell with the way he slouched in his chair. His shoulder-length hair was a dirty red, thin and greasy.

He wore a white tank top under a tired red-and-black flannel shirt that hung open. The rolled-up sleeves revealed a tattoo on each forearm. On the right arm was the Mr. Hyde version of Tweety Bird. The tat on the left arm was a pair of snakes coiling around something scepter like. Malloy couldn't decide if it was a dagger, a garden stake, or a pointy dildo. He suspected the tattoo artist had missed the objective.

Phillips circled behind the counter. The night clerk spun his chair to face him. "You're not allowed back here."

"Why not?" Phillips asked.

"Well, it's the rules."

"Rules are nice things to have. Too bad they don't apply to me." Phillips gestured at Malloy. "Ask him. He'll tell you I'm an insubordinate sonofabitch."

"A mean one, too." Malloy flashed his badge.

Phillips grabbed the night clerk by the flannel shirt, lifted him from the chair, and pinned him against the wall. "Have you ever had one of those days that's so bad you hope someone, anyone, will say the wrong thing so you can reach down their throat and remove their appendix?"

The night clerk shook his head vigorously. "No. Um, never. And, and I've already had my appendix removed."

"You wouldn't lie to me, would you?" Phillips sneered, his face inches away.

"No. Not me," the clerk replied. "Wanna see the scar?"

Malloy leaned against the counter. "You want to help us, don't you?"

The clerk nodded just as vigorously. "Absolutely."

Phillips released him, and he slid a few inches down the wall.

"What's your name?" Malloy asked.

"Douglas Jeffries."

"Okay, Douglas, you have a few friends we're interested in," Malloy began. "One has the nickname of the Priest Man."

"I've never called him that, but I know who you mean," Douglas replied.

"The other one is Jo-Jo," Malloy continued.

Douglas' eyes darted around. "I don't like him."

"Why not?" Phillips asked.

"He's hiding a mean side," Douglas stated. "Worse than yours. He wants to hurt people. You know, use them, hurt them, throw them away."

Malloy waggled his index finger at him. "But you're in business with him, aren't you, Douglas?"

"No, not really. Well...sort of."

Phillips poked Douglas in the chest. "Sort of you are, or sort of you aren't? Like, do I sort of like you, or would I sort of like to remove your tongue?"

"No, no, nothing like that."

"Then like what?" Malloy asked. "Tell us and save

yourself a lot of agony."

Douglas straightened. "You can't hurt me. I got rights."

Phillips snorted. "Do you know the penalty for sex trafficking? Or for modern-day slavery?"

Douglas shook his head.

"Are you familiar with the term domestic terrorism?" Phillips asked.

"Everybody is," Douglas replied.

"Your business partners are using the money they raise selling girls into slavery to pay for weapons and explosives. They're preparing a campaign of domestic terrorism."

"Aw, that's bullshit." Douglas scoffed. "Man, you should be writing movies."

"Are you familiar with Guantanamo?" Phillips asked.

Douglas nodded. "What about it?"

"After I finish explaining the difference between your rights and the rights of the girls you helped sell into slavery, where the money is being used, and how you provided physical support to a terror network, they're going to send what's left of you to someplace far worse than Guantanamo," Phillips explained.

"But—"

"But nothing," Phillips interrupted. "The Priest Man has been talking to us. He's told us how many girls have been sent into slavery through this hotel, with your assistance." He bounced Douglas against the wall again. "There are two hundred and six bones in the human body. For every girl that Priest Man tells us about, I will remove, not break, but remove, one bone from your body." Phillips shook his head. "I'm telling you, the way Priest Man describes business, you won't be able to sit up, and your limbs will flop like they're jelly."

Malloy cleared his throat. "What do you know that might save you, Douglas?"

"I swear, I don't know anything," Douglas sputtered.

Malloy turned to the door. "Assuming you ever get out of wherever they send you, I hope there's something left for your family to identify." He waved. "It's been nice knowing you, Douglas. Enjoy being one of those people never seen again." He nodded to Phillips. "Call me later." He pushed the lobby door open and began to step outside.

"Wait, wait. Please, God, wait," Douglas called. "What do you want to know?"

Malloy turned back. "When was the last time you heard from Jo-Jo?"

"About a half hour ago. He sent me a text. Told me to have a room ready. Priest Man should be here any time with a delivery."

"Except we already told you we have Priest Man in custody, and he's singing like a bird," Malloy reminded him.

"Like a canary that comes into the light, out of the coal mine full of noxious gases," Phillips added. "Like the fat lady at the opera who sings until she passes out or somebody kills her with a prop sword because her aria is two days too long."

"There's definitely something wrong with you." Douglas turned from Phillips to Malloy. "You should have this guy evaluated, probably kept away from the public. He's going to hurt someone."

"You are my next 'someone,'" Phillips growled.

Douglas stepped toward Malloy. "Hey, you've got to protect me from this guy."

Malloy nodded. "Sure, but you've got to keep helping me. It's the only way I can help you."

Phillips moved closer to Douglas. "I love opera. Don't you?"

Malloy rapped his knuckles on the counter. "What's the procedure, Douglas?"

"Jo-Jo texts me. I get the room ready. Priest Man comes in with some chick, and they hustle up to his room. He already has a keycard. Been staying with us for a while now. Then I text Jo-Jo. He comes, pays for the room, pays me, then he joins them. A while later, Priest Man says the room needs housekeeping."

"Do you get a good look at any of these girls?" Malloy made his question sound like an accusation.

"I try not to. By the time I get up there to clean up, Jo-Jo and the chick have split."

"What about before, when the girls are sitting in the car with Priest Man?" Malloy asked.

"Well, sometimes I can sorta see them," Douglas admitted. "They're sitting there, you know, like they have no idea what's happening. Like they believe Priest Man is really helping them."

"You mean he isn't?" Phillips asked.

"I don't know, man." Douglas cringed. "I doubt it."

Phillips raised his eyebrows. "You mean you don't know what's actually happening?"

Douglas looked at the wall clock. "No, man. I don't have a clue."

"C'mon, man. You never go to the room?" Phillips winked. "Sample the merchandise?"

"No. Never. I...I'm not allowed."

"Your story is so difficult for me to believe," Phillips complained. "I'll bet where you're going, they'll favor a redhead with extra attention. Won't the extra attention be nice?"

Douglas raised his hands in surrender. "Please, man, I'm trying to help." He looked at Malloy. "You gotta protect me."

"I'm thinking like my partner," Malloy answered. "I gotta do nothing. Like you've done nothing for all these girls. Except, of course, make money off their misfortune. Pisses me off. Makes me think about hurting you myself. But I don't wanna spoil my friend's fun. He's really an artist, and that thing about removing bones..." Malloy smiled. "He's done it before."

"Look, maybe you can get Jo-Jo's number off my phone and trace it or something." Douglas' whole body trembled. "That's what they do on TV." His gaze flicked between Phillips and Malloy. "My phone is on the floor, plugged into the wall, charging."

***

Phillips dragged an orange vinyl-covered chair from the lobby to the hotel desk and sat across from Douglas Jeffries, staring and drumming his fingers on his knees. He bounced his feet like he was playing drums, the double bass going non-stop. But he was not the drummer. That was his new friend Michael Ortiz. Phillips was the poet, but the motion calmed him. And there was no poetry for what he wanted to do now. Needed to do now.

He needed to be moving, finding whoever had Katrina and using them for a punching bag. Or as filler in the foundation of a tall building.

He wondered if he would always be this out of control. It was no way for a cop to be. Or a poet.

Malloy sat beside him, talking on the phone. "Do not take it to the FISA court if you can avoid it. Find another sympathetic judge, someone who hates sex trafficking. We have a reliable witness who gave us the phone number. We only need a warrant." Malloy paused, gripping the phone tight. "Yes, yes, we already have someone working to find the phone. He won't give us the information unless we can present a warrant before he's done."

Malloy listened and frowned. He held the phone away from his ear long enough to give the person on the other end the finger, then returned the phone to his head and smiled. "Yes, sir, I understand. I also understand the rest of the task force has been strangely silent, as if we'd been cut loose.

"I understand their reluctance. This has been a tough one, but you need to rally them, get everybody on board. Because I also understand we have an undercover cop deep inside, now missing and possibly dead, and this phone is our best lead. We need that warrant *now*."

# CHAPTER SIXTY-SEVEN

Sofia Menendez woke with a dry mouth and a pounding headache. The bare mattress she lay face-down on smelled of sweat, urine, shit, and possibly vomit and semen. She fought a wave of nausea. Her arms were positioned over her head and secured at the wrists with fur-padded handcuffs. Her legs were pulled tight and apart. She tried to move them, but they wouldn't budge. Something rope-like was tied around each ankle and fastened to the bed.

She winced. Her body hurt everywhere. Parts of her were damp, as if things were seeping out. She suspected some of it might be blood.

She turned her head. One view was a concrete wall, and the other was six feet of air and a wall of iron bars. How had she gotten into a cell, and where was Lucky? She remembered the needle poke when Dennis touched her. *That motherfucker.* He had drugged, abducted, and imprisoned her.

She pulled again at her restraints, and her limbs contracted. She heard a chuckle. "Oh, goody, you're awake," Dennis called in Spanish. "Time for more fun."

Sofia felt the bed sink as he sat beside her, his hot breath when he leaned over and licked her cheek. Her eyes slid shut, and she shuddered.

"I'm going to kill you," she announced in English.

"Wow, a new you," Dennis exclaimed. "What happened to the little Mexican spitfire who *no habla* English?"

"What did you do to my dog?"

He laughed. "You have more important things to worry about right now than a mutt."

Sofia gritted her teeth. "I'm going to kill you slowly, and I'm going to enjoy every minute of it."

He grabbed a handful of her hair and yanked her head back. He stared hard into her eyes. "The first four times I fucked you, you were silent. I hate fucking silent bitches." He pushed her face back into the mattress, smothering her. "This time, you're gonna scream."

***

Wes Phillips stared at his phone. "Sofia's not answering."

"Maybe she's in the shower," Russ Malloy suggested. "Women take long showers."

"She told me she'd stay close to her phone in case something came up," Phillips insisted.

"What do you suspect?"

"Reynolds wanted to trade for her. He kept asking about her. Maybe he and Dennis are at the carriage house right now. Another impromptu visit. Or maybe they took her."

"Would Reynolds do that?" Malloy asked. "Kind of risky."

"I wouldn't put it past him. He hasn't been taking us too seriously. He sure doesn't seem afraid of pissing us off."

Malloy lifted his phone. "I'll call McNellis. See if he's finished at the station."

***

Blood dripped from Sofia's split lip to the mattress. Her right eye swelled partially closed. She knew the dampness between her legs, which was more than last time, was definitely blood.

Dennis sat on the bed, looking at his phone. "Sorry, doll, I have to work." He slapped her ass. "Wait here for me. We ain't done yet. When we are, you'll tell me who you really happen to be."

"I'll tell you now." Sofia's voice was gravelly and dry.

Dennis leaned closer. "I'm the bi-lingual Mexican spitfire who is going to kill you." She chuckled. "Then I'm going to resuscitate your ass and kill you again."

Dennis raised his head and laughed. "Ah, *bonita, te amo*." He swatted her again. "I may let you go just so you can try." He pulled her hair, licked her cheek again, then pressed her into the mattress one more time. "Rest up, bitch. From here, it gets rough."

# CHAPTER SIXTY-EIGHT

Jo-Jo grabbed the plastic hotel keycard from a jittery Douglas Jeffries. He was about to walk to the room when he thought better of it. "You okay, man? For a nervous guy, you seem particularly jumpy today."

Jeffries shrugged. "I got some bad stuff. I'm coming down hard. I'd love to go home, take something to mellow me out, but I can't. I gotta work."

Jo-Jo dug out his wallet. "Maybe this will help." He threw a fifty-dollar bill on the counter.

"Thanks, man. Appreciate it." Jeffries shook and twitched and glanced toward the lobby door. He looked back down at the bill, snaked out a shaky hand to grab it, and slid it off the counter and into his pocket. "That will help a lot. Always a pleasure."

"Sure." Jo-Jo studied him, shook his head, and left the lobby. He climbed the stairs and walked down the hallway to where Priest Man and another morsel waited, whistling a tune from *Snow White and the Seven Dwarfs*. *Hi ho, hi ho, it's off to work we go...*

Jo-Jo didn't have time to screw around knocking and waiting for the old man to shuffle to the door. He wanted to get back to the Summit house. *Go in and get to it.* He slid the keycard into the electronic lock and got a green light. He swung the door open, stepped inside, and closed the door. The shower ran full blast. Some insipid reality show played on the TV. But no old man, only a stranger sitting in the chair. "Who the fuck are you?"

"I'm your new partner," Russ Malloy intoned.

"Fuck that. I ain't got a partner."

Malloy gestured with his hand. "Come and sit down. Let's talk."

Jo-Jo turned for the door. "I'm done talking."

Malloy rose. "You need to stay here."

"You tell me one more time what I need to do, and I'm going to kill you," Jo-Jo spat over his shoulder. He opened the door.

Wes Phillips stood outside in the hall.

Jo-Jo's eyebrows shot up, and his mouth opened. He gathered himself.

"Hello, Dennis," Phillips drawled. "Or is it Jo-Jo? I'm surprised. I thought you were brought up better." He looked down the hallway. "So, this is what you do in your spare time."

Dennis' face flushed red, and his body stiffened. "A fucking cop. I should have known. You're dead, and so is everyone you know."

Phillips crossed the four feet between them in a run, grabbed Dennis by the jacket, and drove him back into the room. Dennis grabbed Phillips' wrists, peeled him away from his jacket, and swung him like a tennis racquet in a two-handed backhand, slamming him into the wall. Phillips dropped to the floor and lay still.

Malloy jumped from the chair and charged at Dennis. He hit him waist-high with his shoulder and wrapped his arms around his wide girth. Dennis backpedaled out into the hall with Malloy still hanging on. He picked Malloy off the floor, wrapping his big arms around Malloy's mid-section, squeezed him hard, and threw him against the metal reinforced fire door of the unit across the hall. Malloy landed in a crumpled heap.

Dennis took a last look into the room, then turned and sprinted like a running back toward the exit. He barreled through the door at full speed and down the stairs.

Phillips stumbled into the hallway and bent to check

Malloy, who struggled to breathe. He pointed toward the exit and waved Phillips into pursuit.

Phillips ran like a drunk on high heels, wobbling and bouncing off the walls, almost going down on one knee as his leg threatened to give out. When he opened the exit door, the door at the bottom of the steps leading to the parking lot clicked shut.

He searched the hallway for a window, hoping to see where Dennis went or what he drove when he was working solo, but it only opened to hotel rooms. He slammed the side of his fist into the door, turned, and kicked the carpet. Then, he looked back at Malloy, who was slowly getting to his feet. "This is bad." Phillips walked toward Malloy. "This is really bad. He's Reynolds' right hand."

"I know," Malloy panted. "We need to get the rest of the team." He pressed a hand against his ribs and grimaced. "I think I've got cracked ribs."

"Shit." Phillips scanned the hallway again. "Let's take you in, get you checked out."

"No time. I can heal when Katrina's safe." His phone rang.

Phillips walked back into the room and pulled open the curtains while Malloy answered the call. He could see the parking lot, but didn't see any cars tearing away or Dennis coming back for round two.

"Sonofabitch." Malloy disconnected the call. "That was McNellis. He went to the carriage house. Your car was there, but no sign of Sofia. Only a dog with a gold chain around its neck, sitting on the doorstep, whimpering."

Phillips spun to face him. "What?"

Malloy shook his head. "Her shoes were inside. The pair with the trackers installed. She must have been wearing her own shoes. And we've lost Katrina. Jeezus, what a cluster fuck."

Phillips swallowed hard. "We have to assume the worst about Sofia. Our inability to take down Dennis may have just gotten her killed."

"Did anybody tell us how big Jo-Jo was?" Malloy asked.

"No," Phillips replied. "But I knew how big Dennis was."

"Did you know Dennis and Jo-Jo were the same person?"

"Hell, no," Phillips replied.

"Then how could you know? It was my call not to have more people here to assist. We should have assumed the worst and had a small army."

"You couldn't know, either," Phillips pointed out.

"No, rookie, I couldn't. But I've got the big title and years of experience. I should've been prepared."

"At least you didn't say you get paid the big bucks," Phillips retorted with a slight smile.

Malloy gingerly touched his ribs. "Getting tossed like we did, no amount of money prepares you for that."

"Um, do you know what McNellis did with the dog?"

"He brought it into the house. Said you could deal with it."

Phillips breathed out. "Lucky dog."

# CHAPTER SIXTY-NINE

Dennis drove directly to the Summit house. Inside, he stormed to the front desk. "Give me a set of keys for the basement," he barked. *"Ahora!"*

Eduardo dug in a drawer, then held out a duplicate ring of keys with a shaky hand. Dennis grabbed it and headed down the hall. Eduardo waited for him to turn the corner, then he picked up the phone and dialed a number. "Your bird is landing."

Downstairs, Damian Reynolds pocketed his phone and stood outside Sofia Menendez's cell, several feet away, staring at her through the bars. Doc stood a few feet behind him, his hands fidgeting inside his coat pockets. Sofia's restraints were gone, but she was still naked, curled into a ball in the center of the mattress.

Dennis clomped down the steps and joined them. "Hey, I got something you gotta hear."

Reynolds turned to look at him, his eyes narrowing. "What the fuck happened, Dennis? Why is Sofia here? Why is she in this cell? And why is she covered in blood?"

"I can explain," Dennis replied. "But listen, I gotta tell you—"

"No. You can't explain," Reynolds interrupted him. "I was negotiating for her. It was going to be a trade. She was *mine*." He pointed. "Look at her. She's damaged. She'll never be the same again."

"Aw, fuck. Give her some time. She'll be fine," Dennis replied. "Right, Doc?"

"Walk over there." Reynolds motioned with his hands. "Close to the bars."

Dennis looked at him.

"Do it. Walk over there."

Dennis breathed hard and stepped forward.

"Now, look closely at her." Reynolds paused. "And tell me how she's going to be fine."

Dennis clenched his jaw and stared at Sofia's motionless body. He turned back to face his boss. Reynolds pulled the trigger to a Taser gun, and two darts shot out, trailing wires. They stuck in Dennis' chest and pumped fifty thousand volts into him.

"Are *you* going to be fine?" Reynolds yelled, watching Dennis twitch. He released the trigger, and Dennis drooped back against the bars. The ring of keys fell from his hand.

Sofia sprang off the bed and across the floor. She snaked her arms out between the bars and wrapped them around Dennis' massive neck. She put everything she had into strangling him. She adjusted her grip and pulled tighter, grunting with effort. When Dennis sagged and she was unable to hold up his dead weight, she let go.

"Wow. I'm impressed." Reynolds bent down and scooped up the set of keys. "Such passion. No wonder I want you."

"Thanks for not stunning him while I had a hold." Sofia's breath was ragged. "The shock would have passed into me."

Reynolds frowned. "Hey, that's English."

"*Si*, bitch. That's English." She stumbled backward and sat on the bed. "Now, give that trigger a little squeeze and restart his heart so I can kill him again."

"Doc, check him." Reynolds jerked his head toward Dennis.

Doc stepped forward, hesitated, and looked back at

Reynolds' hand holding the Taser. "Okay, but, uh...make sure that woman stays away from me."

"Don't worry." Sofia smirked from her seated position. "I won't kill you until later. After I kill Dennis a few more times, then your pimp boss."

Reynolds laughed. "She is indeed a feisty one."

Doc stepped closer to Dennis, keeping an eye on Sofia, and bent down to check Dennis' pulse. "He's alive."

Sofia rose. "I can fix that."

"Leave him be," Reynolds insisted. "You can have another shot at him after I'm done. Assuming you live long enough to get out of that cage." He ejected the Taser cartridge and let it drop to the floor, the wires still leading to Dennis. He pulled another cartridge from his pocket, loaded the Taser, and pointed it at Sofia. "How much of what I've heard has been a lie?"

Sofia rocked her head from side to side. "All of it. None of it. I might be lying now. I might be telling the truth. I get confused, especially after an out-of-control gorilla rapes and beats me."

"Yeah, he did that on his own. I had other plans." Reynolds stepped closer. "Tell me about Stevie Mayer and his partners."

"There are no partners. Steve is my public stand-in and private sex toy. I'm the operation. The beauty with the brains. I run everything."

Reynolds lifted the Taser higher. "Fuck, I don't believe you."

"It doesn't matter what you believe because you'll be dead." She laughed. "That's the only thing in all this you can be sure of. Believe me. I'll see you dead." She stepped toward the cell door. "Release me, and I may make it less painful."

He shook his head and lowered the stun gun. "You amuse me. I'm not going to panic because some naked bitch in a cell threatens me." He laughed. "I've been threatened before, once by your boyfriend, and I'm still here."

Sofia faked a lunge for the door. Reynolds jumped back.

"You've never been threatened by me. I only make promises."

"Sure, honey." Reynolds sneered. "Why don't you rest up? You're gonna need it where you're going." He looked at Doc. "Get her cleaned up. I know a Saudi prince looking for wife number sixty."

***

Dennis regained consciousness ten minutes after Doc left without doing more than staring. Sofia reached between the bars and grabbed a handful of his hair. “That’s one, asshole,” she whispered in his ear. “One death at my hands. Now, you’ve been resuscitated.” She pushed his head forward, then slammed it back against the bars. His hand came up, but before he could grab her, she let go and fell away from the bars. “I’m going to kill you again.” She got to her hands and knees and leaned forward, ready to spring at him. “Even slower next time.”

Dennis struggled to his feet, searching his pockets for the set of keys. He looked around and rattled the door to her locked cell. “You bitch.”

“Mr. Dennis, please don’t.” Eduardo stepped forward from the shadows. “Mr. Reynolds said you are not to touch her. You are not to go into her cell. He said if you do, I must shoot you in the head.” He held up a .380 Walther. “I like you. You’ve been a friend to me.” He shook his head. “I do not want to kill you. Don’t make me.”

Dennis patted under his arm for his Ruger. The holster was empty. “Aw, jeezus. Why didn’t you shoot her when she was strangling me?”

"She is small. You are not. And Mr. Reynolds said not to." Eduardo looked at his gun. "Don't make me kill you now."

Dennis sighed. "I won't. But do me a favor."

Eduardo nodded.

"Next time somebody is giving me a shock or choking the life out of me, shoot somebody. Even if it's me."

Eduardo nodded again and smiled. "Next time, I will not hesitate. I will shoot. Somebody." He nodded again. "Hopefully not you." His smile broadened. "Or me." He held the gun out in front, fingertips on the barrel. "I don't like these. Too noisy. Someone could get hurt."

Dennis extended his palm. "Should I take that from you? Help keep you safe?"

"Oh, no, no. No need for that," Eduardo insisted. "It was a gift from Mr. Reynolds. I need to have it in case he asks. But thank you. I know you have my best interests at heart."

"That I do. Now tell me, where's my gun?"

"Mr. Reynolds said you can't have it until you calm down. He brought it upstairs."

Dennis turned and rubbed his throat, glowering at Sofia. "I'm leaving. Got some business to attend to. But I'll be back."

Sofia smiled, both hands clenching the mattress, her legs curled tight beneath her. “I’ll be waiting.”

Dennis pounded up the staircase. He needed his gun, and he needed to make a call.

# CHAPTER SEVENTY

Wes Phillips' phone vibrated. He glanced at Russ Malloy, who was pasty white and hunched over in the Land Rover's driver's seat, holding his side. They had been hanging out in front of the hotel, discussing their next move and arguing about medical attention while they waited to see if Dennis would reappear. Phillips looked back at the phone and the name of the caller. He swiped the button on the screen. "Sofia?"

"No, asshole, it's Dennis. Yes, this means I've got your girlfriend. We've had great fun, right up until she tried to kill me."

Phillips pretended to laugh. "That's my girl." His jaw tightened.

"Is she a cop? 'Cause she don't act like a cop, but neither do you."

Phillips turned the SUV's heater fan to low and pressed the phone to his other ear. "She's not a cop, and I'll take what you said as a compliment. So, why are you calling?"

"I'd like to leave town," Dennis replied.

"You're looking for my permission?"

"No. I'm looking for a deal."

Phillips looked at Malloy. "What kind of deal, Dennis?"

"I'll tell you what I know, tell you where to find Sofia and Isabella, and you let me leave. No pursuit, no warrants. I go start over as somebody different."

"You believe you can do that?" Phillips asked.

"I have before."

"And what makes you think I'm the one to make a deal?"

"Probably the way you try to look out for Isabella and Sofia," Dennis returned. "You radiate honor. You'll do what you say you will. And I was kind enough to drop off that mutt at your house. That alone gives me bonus points."

"What if I say I will hunt you forever?"

"That's...that's what I'm trying to avoid. Because I know you would, and so would Sofia. At least this deal would keep you off my back."

Phillips was silent for a moment. "Did you hurt Sofia?"

"I might've got a little rough with her," Dennis

admitted. "I suspect she resents it, and I suspect she holds grudges."

Phillips forced a laugh. "I would guess Sofia makes me look forgiving."

"Yeah, I'd suspect that, too. Do we have a deal?"

"You and I do," Phillips agreed. "But I'll have to work on my bosses."

"Do that. But really, I'm not too worried about them. We've been operating under their noses for a long time. Almost like they don't give a fuck."

Phillips glanced at Malloy. "Maybe they're in on it."

"Could be," Dennis replied.

"So, why the sudden need for flight?"

Dennis sighed. "It's all coming apart. Reynolds has been running loose for so long he thinks he's untouchable. His greed and appetites are getting out of control. It's all going to come down soon, man. Whether it's from you or somebody else doesn't matter. I just know I don't want to be around when it does."

"Let's say we have a deal." Phillips pressed the speaker button. "Tell me what you know."

***

Malloy was still seated behind the steering wheel of the Land Rover, the seatbelt loose over his rib cage. The team had joined him. Eric Martinez sat next to him. Curtis Blair and Robert McNellis huddled in the back seat, and Phillips scrunched between them. They faced the house on Summit Avenue and kept the engine running so the windows wouldn't steam up. They wore Kevlar vests and had a small arsenal in the far back of the SUV.

McNellis turned and looked at Phillips. "Are you sure? Do you really think we can trust this Dennis character?"

McNellis hadn't had a sip of alcohol since the previous night when he had been paging through photos of his goddaughter. "I'm done with it," he had announced, setting down the glass of whiskey. He stared at the smiling face of a teenage Katrina. "I promise." By late morning, his hands shook, and his head felt like it was being squeezed between cell bars. Now, what little he ate for dinner threatened to come up. But he didn't tell the team. He didn't need their pity or snide remarks.

"Maybe it's a trap," Blair added.

"Of course I don't think we can trust him," Phillips answered. "And yes, it could be a trap." They sat for a moment, watching the property. "Reynolds did something to piss him off. So, in effect, they're all trapped. Dennis wants revenge and his freedom. So, he's our informant. He said the auction's tonight. Lots of high-powered people will be here, and most of the girls, including Katrina and Sofia, will be gone by sunrise."

Phillips looked at each team member. "I'm going in. What you guys do is up to you."

McNellis held up his hand. "Settle down, cowboy. You're not going anywhere alone."

Martinez turned in his seat. "Here's the plan. Dalestrom is going before a judge in Ramsey County. One who should know nothing about us. She has Colburn with her and a lawyer, too. They're asking for a search warrant for this location based on a tip from a reliable source. They're also asking for an arrest warrant for Reynolds for the arranged murder of Colburn. We also believe Reynolds will be at this address, another reason for the search warrant."

Blair nodded. "Sounds solid enough."

"We have SWAT two minutes away," Martinez continued. "We're ready to move."

A Mercedes SUV pulled through the gate and into the driveway. "That would be Christoph Morton," Malloy pointed out. A rusted Taurus drove past, continuing down the street.

"And that would be Larkin and Ellison."

"The circus clowns," McNellis muttered under his breath.

Martinez's phone buzzed. "Yeah. Okay, thanks. Stay out of sight for now. I'll give you the signal." He disconnected. "That was Ellison. They're going around the corner."

"All the players are coming together," Malloy murmured.

Blair reached between his legs and activated a tablet. The glow reflected off his highly polished combat boots. He tapped a few times and brought up an app. Phillips leaned forward, trying for a peek. "The drone shows four stationed around the house. Probably sentries. Most of the windows are curtained off, but infrared from the satellite shows roughly forty people total on four different levels."

"Roughly?" Phillips asked.

"Some of them are close together," Blair explained. "Their images blend."

"Horizontally?" McNellis asked.

"Not all of them," Blair replied. "There's some vertical blending as well."

"Shit, we're going to need another van." Martinez

stared at Blair. “What did your source say about the layout?”

“Captives are in the basement,” Phillips replied. “The auction will be on the first floor, toward the back. Sampling of merchandise is on the second and third floors.”

“Okay,” Martinez stated. “We’ll let SWAT breach and secure the building. Their instructions are nobody leaves, no matter who they claim to be. Everyone gets put in vans, victims separate from unknown offenders. McNellis, you accompany SWAT and secure the second and third floors. I’ll signal Ellison and Larkin to take the main floor and shut down that auction.

“Blair and I will split up. He’ll watch the staircase, and I’ll cover the front door, making sure no one enters or leaves. Malloy and Phillips, you head for the basement. Find our people, save some lives.” He looked over his shoulder. “And play it safe. If you’re not around for me to buy each one of you a drink later, I will be pissed. Understood?”

The other four made noises of assent. Martinez’s phone buzzed again. He looked at the display. “Message from Dalestrom. She has the warrants. She’s on her way.”

“About damn time,” McNellis grumbled. “We’re good to go.”

“Let’s saddle up,” Martinez said.

"Do me a favor." McNellis leaned toward Martinez, his voice gruff. "Forget the cowboy references. It was a mistake. You'll only encourage the rookie."

Martinez gave him a crooked grin. "Fair enough." He raised his voice and motioned to the others. "Let's go, people. And let's be careful." He reached for the door handle.

# CHAPTER SEVENTY-ONE

The selected girls stood in a straight line in the basement for inspection. Doc stood at one end, and Dennis, his throat bruised and swollen, stood at the other end, staring down its length. Dennis folded his arms, his right hand close to the Ruger hanging beneath his arm. He glared back and forth at Sofia Menendez and Damian Reynolds.

Sofia's lip was puffy, but it no longer looked split. Or like she had recently been punched. She tried to ignore the throbbing ache between her legs and the pain of standing. She held her head still but let her eyes roam around the room, searching for a weapon or something she could turn into a weapon.

The girl next to her—Sofia believed her name was Jane—wore a lace-up bustier. If Sofia could get her hands on the laces, she'd have a garrote. And if she could make it to an upstairs window, she could use her floor-length negligee as a rope and escape. Then she could return with Wes Phillips and kill everybody who needed it. Or maybe only Dennis and Reynolds. Or maybe everyone in the whole fucking house.

She shifted on her bare feet, the hem of her negligee dragging on the floor. It would've fit better if they had given her spiked heels. However, Dennis reminded Doc that a heel through an eyeball and into a brain would not be good for business. Sofia smirked. With or without shoes, she could kick Dennis to death.

Sofia snuck a look at Katrina Malloy. She stood at the far end of the line, near Dennis. When they first let Katrina out of her cell to help babysit the girls, they always gave her something to drink, and she sucked it down like her life depended on it. Yesterday, Katrina refused the booze. Maybe she knew something Sofia didn't. Today, she looked stoned, kind of dreamy, and slightly smiling. Doc must have slipped her something to keep her compliant.

Reynolds stepped in front of Katrina and traced the port wine stain down her throat with his fingertips. "You'll do fine. You're beautiful. Now go out there and make me proud." He squeezed her mouth so her lips would pucker. "Use that mouth the way you have on me, and you'll make anyone forget their troubles."

Dennis clenched and unclenched his fingers. He lifted his hand toward his gun.

Reynolds patted Katrina's cheek and started to move

away when his phone buzzed. He pulled it from his pocket and put it against his ear. Dennis dropped his hand. Beads of sweat dotted his forehead.

"What is it?" Reynolds growled. He listened, sweeping his gaze down the line of girls. "I'm almost done checking the merchandise, but I'm still waiting on Samantha and Jazz. Where the fuck are they, Eduardo?" He pressed the phone tighter to his ear, his brow furrowed. "As soon as they're done, I want them down here pronto."

He shook his head and spoke louder and slower. "I don't give a crap about the VIP. Let me know when our Las Vegas guests finish dinner, but don't rush them, *understando*? I'll be up shortly." He pocketed the phone and stepped to his right.

Dee-Dee stood second in line. The dissolvable stitches Doc had put in her eyebrow barely showed. Reynolds looked closely. "Nice work, Doc. If she goes for enough, there will be a bonus for you."

Doc nodded and smiled. "Thank you, sir. I appreciate it."

"Please, Damian, don't do this to me," Dee-Dee pleaded. Her mascara ran down her cheeks. "I've been loyal to you. Only you. Please, let me keep working here."

Reynolds waved his hand dismissively. "Time for you to move on, sweetie. Think of it as a new chapter." He pointed to her face. "And clean up your mug." He moved on to the next girl.

Dee-Dee's eyes narrowed, and her body tensed. "You fucking bastard." She leaped at Reynolds, her fingernails going for his eyes. "I'll kill you!"

Dennis stepped in and, with the back of his knuckles, hit her in the temple. She dropped to her knees. She held the side of her head with one hand and cried harder. "Damian, please. Don't do this. The customers always pay top dollar for me. I can make you even more money, I swear." She reached for him with the other hand.

Reynolds knocked her hand away. "Yeah, you should have been in the movies. So, I'll make sure you perform for an appreciative audience. For attacking me just now, you'll be sucking off prisoners in some frozen gulag in Siberia."

"For God's sake, Damian. I...I love you."

He laughed. "You're like me. You don't know what love is. You'll do whatever it takes, say whatever you have to, to get what you want. That's why you have to leave. You remind me of myself. Except you have the kind of oral skills I don't need, sweetie."

Dennis lifted Dee-Dee from the floor and dumped her back in line. She stood, and sobs shook her entire body. She began to wilt. Dennis grabbed her and straightened her up again. "Pull yourself together, bitch," he whispered. "Don't make him decide to kill you. Not now."

A noise, a scuffle, came from the top of the basement stairs. Christoph Morton pounded down the steps, out of breath, with Eduardo chasing after him. "Sir, please," Eduardo pleaded. "You need to wait."

Dennis started toward Morton, but Reynolds held up a hand. "What's going on?"

"I'm sorry, sir," Eduardo began. "He grabbed my keys and—"

"Mr. Reynolds, we need to talk." Morton threw the key ring back at Eduardo and brushed past Dennis. "It's Mandy."

Reynolds motioned him away from the line. "What about her?" he asked in a low voice, his eyes narrowed.

"She solicited some guy not too long ago. He ended up being a cop," Morton explained.

Reynolds leaned forward, his face inches away from Morton's. "Why the fuck did you wait so long to tell me?"

Morton stepped backward and raised his hands in

surrender. “I just found out today.”

“Did they arrest her back then?”

“No.”

“Well, what did she tell them?” Reynolds asked.

“About the gift, about the tickets.”

“Jeezus.” Reynolds stood silent for a moment. “Is she still seeing the judge?”

Morton nodded. “Yeah.”

“So, he doesn’t know?”

“No. He still thinks they’re in love.”

“Huh. Well, he must be spreading that love around.” Reynolds jerked his head toward the line of girls. “He’s a frequent flyer here.”

Morton smirked.

Reynolds straightened. “After tonight, I’m done with him. Whatever happens to him and Mandy, I don’t know either of them. I don’t care. Plausible deniability.”

Sofia’s laugh echoed loudly in the basement.

Reynolds turned around. “What’s so funny, bitch?”

“It’s all falling down around you, and you’re too stupid

to see it." She stepped out of line and limped over to Reynolds. She planted her hands on her hips, her feet shoulder-width apart. "I'm gonna make sure you die before it's over."

Doc crept up behind her and stabbed a needle through the thin material of her gown into her right buttock. She cried out as he emptied the drug-filled syringe. "That kind of behavior will not be tolerated, young lady." He withdrew the needle and shoved her back into line.

Reynolds pointed at the syringe. "Hey, how much of that shit did you give her? I don't want her passed out."

Doc smiled. "Only enough to make her compliant, Mr. Reynolds."

Reynolds turned back to face Morton. He was about to speak when a crash sounded above. He peered up at the ceiling. "What the fuck?" Another crash above, toward the rear of the house, made him swing his head in the other direction. He reached behind his back and produced a SIG-Sauer 9 mm.

"I think we need to go, sir." Doc motioned toward the rear of the basement. "This way."

"Gimme a sec." Reynolds rushed to a mounted gun safe hidden under the steps, pressed his palm against the electronic keypad, and opened the safe. "Morton, make yourself useful." He handed him an AK47 and an extra magazine. "I want a safe path." Morton grabbed the rifle, stuffed the magazine in his jacket pocket, and darted ahead of them.

Reynolds pointed at Dennis. "You're gonna follow and watch our backs." He spun around and barked, "Eduardo, slow them down."

"Who?" Eduardo asked.

"The cops," Doc hollered over his shoulder.

Eduardo stood at the bottom of the steps and, with shaky hands, pulled his .380 from his inside vest pocket. His gaze traveled between the unlocked basement door at the top of the stairs and his semi-automatic pistol. "Oops." He switched the safety off. After a moment, he switched the safety back on. He stepped to the side of the landing, set the gun on the floor, and raised both hands.

As Doc and Reynolds stormed past Dee-Dee, she leaped at Reynolds again. He hit her with his SIG, and she stumbled backward and collided with the bars of the nearest cell.

She looked back at Katrina. "You little bitch. This is all your fault." She launched herself again, this time in Katrina's direction. Dennis stepped between them and grabbed Dee-Dee by the throat with one hand. He lifted her until her feet no longer touched the floor and slammed her head into the bars. Once, twice. She flopped to the ground like a cloth doll.

Jane stepped over and kicked the limp Dee-Dee in the ribs. A redheaded girl dressed in a baby doll nightgown grabbed Jane by the hand. "Let's get out of here."

"No." Jane clenched the girl's hand. "Not the stairs. We'll wait in the corner until it's safe. We're victims. They're coming to help us." They held hands and hurried into the shadows. Two other girls, both Asian, scrambled after them. The four girls looked like a huddle for the lingerie football league as they ducked and tried to be invisible. The remaining girls scurried to a nearby cell and slid beneath the beds.

Sofia staggered after Reynolds, but Dennis, who was now carrying Katrina, hip-checked her into the concrete wall. She scraped her bare shoulder and elbow, the blood dotting her skin, and bounced off it, lunging for Dennis. She scrambled onto his back, reached under his arm for his gun, and yanked the Ruger from its holster.

"Get the fuck off me," Dennis yelled, twisting and turning. Sofia clung to his back and jammed the muzzle into his side, praying a round was chambered and the safety was off.

Dennis dropped Katrina and fumbled for the gun. His hand closed on Sofia's, and they toppled to the floor. She pulled the trigger, again and again.

Out of breath with her vision blurring, Sofia looked at the spent gun still in her hand and the growing bloodstain on the front of her negligee.

Dennis stared at Sofia. “What did you do, bitch?”

Sofia pointed at his body and smiled.

He looked down and pressed his hand to his side. It came away bloody. “You shot me? With my own gun?”

“I told you I’d kill you.” Her voice slurred. “Again.”

He glared at her. “I ain’t dead yet.”

He picked up Katrina and followed after Doc and Reynolds.

Sofia dropped the emptied gun. It clattered on the cement floor, and she collapsed face-forward.

# CHAPTER SEVENTY-TWO

Male voices shouted from the first floor of the Summit house. Several girls screamed. Someplace far below, a gun fired repeatedly.

In Room 206, Savannah lay naked with a customer. "For God's sake, what the hell's going on out there?" The man shoved her away, and he heaved himself out of bed. He stood, and his folded and wrinkled skin rearranged itself. He grunted and pulled on pressed slacks, not bothering with his boxers. He pointed a knobby finger at her. "Stay put."

He punched in the code for the door and cracked it open. Several customers ran by, heading toward the staircase. He opened the door wider and grabbed one of the customer's arms. "What's happening?"

The customer tore his arm away, his face red, sweat trickling from his temples. "We're being busted, dude. Get outta here."

"Oh, God, no. No, no, no." The man stepped back and started to turn when a lamp collided with his balding head. He staggered, spinning, and collapsed on the plush white carpet.

The ceiling spun in his eyes, and everything went black.

Savannah stood over him, naked, holding the lamp. Several shards of glass lay scattered near her feet. She kicked the man hard between the legs, fracturing her small toe. She didn't notice the pain. She stepped over him and fell onto her knees by his head, ignoring the glass that cut her, and smashed the broken lamp into his etched face repeatedly. "Bastard!" she screamed.

The man groaned. He raised his liver-spotted hands, reaching, searching. Savannah grabbed the lamp's long cord and wrapped it tightly around his neck. She sat behind him and placed her feet on his shoulders. "I'm gonna kill you!" She gripped the cord and pulled back as hard as she could, legs and back straining as she grunted.

"Jesus, Mary, and Joseph," Jazz whispered from the doorway, wearing her negligee inside out. With wide eyes, she stared at Savannah, the bloody bite marks trailing across the girl's chest, to her stomach, and down both inner thighs. "Girl, you're gonna… You're gonna…"

Savannah had a wild look in her eyes. Her breathing was labored, and her body rigid with effort.

Jazz reached for the doorframe, tried to steady herself, and slumped to a sitting position on the floor. Her mouth hung open, and she watched as the man slowly ceased moving.

# CHAPTER SEVENTY-THREE

In front of the unlocked basement door, two heavily armed and armored SWAT members stood, facing Russ Malloy and Wes Phillips. “We lead, you follow.” The lead SWAT member twisted the knob. Five gunshots from somewhere in the basement echoed up the stairwell to greet them.

Malloy looked at Phillips. “Remember, *we* follow.”

Phillips, palms twitching, followed the two large men down the steps, their bodies like a brick wall. Malloy grimaced with every breath as he crouched behind Phillips, watching the rear.

Eduardo greeted them at the bottom, hands up, bent at the waist. “Don’t shoot. Look.” He motioned at his .380 on the floor. “I am an unharmed man.”

The lead SWAT waved his gun and shouted, “On the ground. Face down. Move it!” The second SWAT swept Eduardo’s pistol from the floor and pocketed it.

“I am innocent. I do only as told,” Eduardo cried. “Please, I want to return to my home.”

The second team member pinned his arms, stood him up, and cuffed him to the basement railing. "You'll be going to a home, all right."

Jane and the three other girls screamed from the corner when the lead SWAT member pointed an assault weapon at them. "Show me your hands."

All four raised empty hands. Dressed in flimsy outfits, they had no place to conceal a weapon.

The lead SWAT spoke into his shoulder mic. "Need officers and EMTs in the basement. Female victims and one male suspect need extraction." He pointed at them. "Wait here. Someone will come get you." Jane and the others bobbed their heads. The men moved on to the first row of cells.

The second SWAT waved his weapon at a group of girls in one of the middle cells. Some hid beneath the beds, others huddled on the floor. A pregnant woman wrapped her arms around a young girl and held her close. The young girl squeezed her eyes shut and hid her face from the officer. "Show me your hands. Are you okay?" One after another, they nodded. "Someone will come for you. Stay here for now."

A few steps farther, they came to a young woman in a heap against the bars. The lead SWAT touched her, and she tipped to the side. Blood had seeped into her hair. He looked closely. There was a crease in the back of her head where the skull had dented and folded in.

He looked from her head to the bars and followed them to where pieces of hair clung to the metal. He knew it was pointless but checked her bruised neck for a pulse. Into his shoulder mic, he reported, “One deceased female, basement. Moving on.”

Phillips looked around and called, “Sofia.”

Both SWAT members spun and glared at him, raising fingers to lips.

Silence. Then, a weak, “Wes...”

Phillips turned and took a step in the direction of the voice. One of the SWAT members grabbed his arm. “Wait. It’s not secure.”

Phillips shrugged off his hand and raced ahead.

Sofia lay face down, a pool of blood beneath her. Phillips dropped to the floor and gently rolled her over. “Hey, I’m here.”

“I knew you’d come,” Sofia slurred. “I hate for you to...to see me like this. I’m a mess. They dolled me up. Injected me with some shit.”

Phillips wadded up the extra gown material and

pressed it against the wound, applying steady pressure. "I like you in anything or nothing," he told her. "Even my clothes. They look better on you anyhow."

Sofia tried to laugh and winced. "They'd have looked better lying on the floor that day if...if you'd have taken them off me."

"Someday." Phillips wiped the damp hair from her forehead, leaned over, and lightly kissed her lips.

"I don't think we're going to get that chance. This...this feels bad."

Phillips gripped her hand. "You stay with me. We're going to get through this."

The SWAT members came up to them. "This part of the basement's secure," one announced.

Malloy arrived. "Ah, shit." He stared at the blood. "This wasn't supposed to happen."

Sofia pointed a limp arm toward the basement's dark area. "Reynolds went that way. With Morton. And someone they call Doc." She coughed, and blood trickled down her lip and chin. "Go get the bastards."

"Wes, stay with her," Malloy ordered, his jaw tight.

She pointed again. "Dennis carried Katrina off that way,

too. After I… After I shot him."

The SWAT members moved. One barked into his mic, "Undercover officer down. She's a gunshot victim. Location, basement. Needs immediate attention. Moving on."

Malloy took a step, following the SWAT members. "Stay with her," he repeated to Phillips over his shoulder.

"No. One of you…" Sofia paused and drew a ragged breath. "…save Katrina. One of you get Reynolds." She coughed again. "Sit me up. I'll wait here."

"Sofia." Phillips' voice cracked. With the gown's neckline, he wiped the blood from her lips and chin. He leaned closer and touched his forehead to hers. Stared into her half-closed eyes.

"Wes," she whispered. "You need to hurry."

He slid her to the wall, ignoring her groans, and sat her against it. He pulled his small Beretta from his ankle holster, chambered a round, and pressed it into her palm. He kissed her again, this time with more force, then pulled away. "Give me a sec."

Phillips sprinted back to the second group of female victims. He motioned for them to come out of the cell. "Hey, I need help. Please. A woman's been shot." The victims emerged and followed him to Sofia. He grabbed one of the girl's hands and pressed it against the makeshift bandage. "Press hard. Don't stop. EMTs will be here soon."

"Go," Sofia insisted, her voice hoarse. "I'm... I'm fine."

He ran into the darkness and stopped. He looked back but could not see Sofia or the girls. "I'm not fine." He raced back, leaned over, and kissed her once more.

Sofia smiled and closed her eyes.

He straightened up, drew a deep breath, and headed back into the darkness.

# CHAPTER SEVENTY-FOUR

Damian Reynolds and Doc reached the dark area of the basement and stopped. “Where’s the light switch?” Doc asked.

“Don’t turn it on, stupid. Use your phone.”

Doc pulled out his phone and turned on the light function.

Christoph Morton stepped from the shadows, gripping the AK47. “Clear so far.”

“What the hell happened back there?” Reynolds asked. “Where’s Dennis?”

Footsteps pounded overhead. From the other side of the basement, a man’s voice shouted orders.

Doc aimed his light ahead. “Not now,” Doc insisted, his voice an octave higher. “We get to safety first. C’mon.”

He and Morton grabbed Reynolds by the arms, gave him a pull, and the three of them raced through the unlit hallways. They reached a door, pushed through it, and headed up a secret flight of stairs.

***

Dennis turned the corner around the last cell, voices shouting behind him, and entered the dark section of the basement. He had walked through the seldom-traveled hallways a long time ago. He remembered lights, but he didn't know where the switches were located.

Reynolds, Doc, and Morton hadn't bothered to turn them on. Either they knew the way out and had already left, or they waited in ambush. He imagined Morton standing in the shadows, poised in a shooter's stance, pointing the AK47's muzzle at him. Reynolds, smiling next to Morton, giving him the go-ahead.

A click sounded from the far end of one of the hallways. A door somewhere. They must have already gone through it. *Damn this day.*

He didn't know what to do, but he knew his body was weakening. His heart pounded, he was drenched in sweat, and his breaths were ragged. Although small in stature, Isabella was getting heavy. He carried her into the safety of the darkness, felt for the support of the wall, and stood her against it.

"What kind of shit did Doc slip you?" Her body was like a rag doll, and her head flopped to the side. "Isabella." He shook her gently. "How you doin'? Are you hurt?" She moaned and began to slide out of his arms. He set her on the floor and braced her against the wall.

"I'm such a screw-up," she murmured. "I quit drinking, but...I don't know what's wrong with me. I feel so tired. I can't... I can't..."

"You're gonna be fine," he insisted. "You need time to sober up properly. A good long sleep. Hell, you're fine all the time. One of the finest females I've known. No matter what, you've always treated me with kindness and respect."

He sniffled in the dark. "You're the only one I know in this whole fucked-up world I can say that about. And I appreciate it." He wiped his eyes. "Before I go find a light switch and get you help, I want to say one thing. I love you, Isabella. I should've said it before when...well, I always will."

"Katrina," she muttered.

"What?"

"Katrina. My real name is Katrina."

"Huh. Well, it's a pleasure to meet you, Katrina. I'm Kong."

She laughed. "Sorry about that, Dennis."

He slumped down beside her and put an arm around her shoulders. "Whaddaya think about running away with me and leaving all this behind? We could escape to somewhere safe and warm. You and me, Isabell—I mean, Katrina. Just us."

"Dennis, I—" She pressed her hand to her stomach.

"No, don't answer me yet." He pulled his arm away. "Just...just wait here. I'll be back real quick. I'm gonna turn on some lights." He rose to his feet, wincing in pain, one hand against his wounded side, and staggered away.

***

Malloy and the two SWAT members moved through the basement, the shadows growing with each step. The lead SWAT flipped down the scope to his night vision optics and continued ahead. The second SWAT gave his team member about five steps, then moved forward. Malloy followed in the rear, his right hand gripping his pistol and his left hand running along the wall.

Up ahead, voices murmured. The second SWAT darted across the hall. All three men shrank toward the floor, making themselves smaller targets.

The murmuring stopped. There were movements in the dark and the shuffle of heavy footsteps.

***

Dennis ran his fingers along the wall until he felt a light

switch. He flipped the switch. The hallway was bathed in dim light from a few bulbs scattered along its length.

The lead SWAT grunted as his night vision optics overloaded from the lights. He ripped them off. The second SWAT remained quiet.

Near the end of the hall stood the man Malloy had met in the hotel room, the one known as Jo-Jo or Dennis, depending on to whom you spoke. Dennis reached across his chest and beneath his arm, fumbling for his missing weapon.

Malloy yelled, "Don't!"

The lead SWAT on the other side of the hall let loose a three-shot burst from his MP-5, then another and another. A female screamed from somewhere behind Dennis, around the corner.

Malloy recognized the voice. "Oh, my God. Katrina!" He stepped forward.

The second SWAT, who was closest, grabbed his arm and pulled him back as the lead SWAT across the hall let fly two more three-shot bursts. Dennis dropped to the floor.

Katrina crawled out from the connecting hallway toward Dennis. She fell in a heap next to him.

"Hold your fire!" both SWAT members shouted at each

other.

“Oh, Dennis,” Katrina whispered, “I love you, too. And thank you for…for everything.” She laid her head on his chest as tears fell.

Malloy rushed forward, dragged her off Dennis, and gathered her in his arms. He held her tightly as they both cried.

***

Ahead of Phillips, the lights had flashed on, and shots had been fired. He increased his pace and quickly reached Malloy, holding Katrina.

“Thank God.” Phillips blew a long breath. “One objective obtained.” He reached down and squeezed Katrina’s shoulder. “I was worried about you.” He told Malloy, “EMTs should be in the basement by now. Hopefully, with Sofia and those girls. Take your sister back there, Russ. Make sure she’s okay.”

Phillips looked at Dennis’ motionless body a few feet away. “Another objective obtained.” He stared at Dennis’ empty hands. He knew, even without a gun, Dennis had been dangerous. Dead from a distance was best.

The second SWAT member beckoned Phillips to follow him around the corner. He pointed at a door at the end of another hallway. The lead SWAT stood beside it, talking on his radio.

Phillips rushed forward. “Any idea where this door leads?”

The second SWAT shook his head. “I don’t believe this hallway or this door were on the architectural drawings we reviewed.”

The lead SWAT disconnected his call. “They weren’t.”

“Then we have no other option.” Phillips reached out, turned the handle, and opened the door.

A safety light had been installed above the door frame on the other side. It dimly illuminated the first few steps of a concrete stairwell that extended up into the gloom.

The SWAT members flipped down the scopes to their night vision optics, pushed past Phillips, and began to climb the steps. Phillips followed his human shields.

The three men reached the first landing, also dimly lit by another exit door’s safety light, when a shuffle sounded above. The SWAT members pointed their MP-5s upward and crept up the next flight of stairs.

At the second landing, Phillips pressed his ear to the exit door, shook his head, and they continued toward the third.

They had taken a few steps when Christoph Morton leaned over the railing in the darkness with the AK47 and sprayed the stairwell with bullets. The second SWAT took a bullet to the Kevlar helmet and a few to the ceramic plates in his vest. He stumbled backward down the stairs and collapsed on the landing below.

The lead SWAT cursed and flipped his MP-5 from three-shot bursts to full automatic and sprayed bullets upward. While the lead SWAT changed magazines, Morton fired another burst. Phillips watched the flashes from Morton's rifle, gauging the weapon's approximate location. When the burst ended, Phillips climbed two more steps and flattened his body against the wall.

The lead SWAT fired another salvo, then hurried down the stairs to check on his partner. When Morton reached over and started shooting again, Phillips drew a deep breath and stepped toward the railing. Gripping the Glock, he extended his arms into the fire zone. He aimed for the flashes above and pulled the trigger twice. Morton's AK47 fell and clattered down the stairwell. Something heavy thudded to the floor above them.

Phillips hustled down the steps to join the lead SWAT. He was crouched beside his partner on the landing. The injured man groaned and held his hand to his chest. He didn't appear to be bleeding through his clothes or on the cement. He grimaced and gave them a thumbs-up. Phillips patted his shoulder, turned, and followed the lead SWAT back up the stairs.

On the third landing, Morton lay bleeding. One of Phillips' shots had hit him in the eyebrow and penetrated his forehead, knocking him off balance. The other shot had entered beneath Morton's chin. Most of the back of his head was missing.

Instead of a third landing exit door, a ladder bolted to the wall extended up to a hatch in the roof. Phillips stared at the hatch. "Shit." It was the first word any of them had uttered since entering the stairwell.

Looking up made him think about Sofia and her climbing maneuver at the water tower. And the shape of her ass from his viewpoint below. It was a delightful ass. She might have laughed if she knew he was using it as inspiration. He pulled himself back to the present and the apparent task at hand.

The lead SWAT leaned toward him. "Things have been quiet, we've stayed silent, so I'm gonna check in with the team. I need to inform them about my partner and learn the status of everybody else."

Phillips nodded. "See if the drone is still in the air. Get any help you can. Reynolds must know a way off the roof. We need to get people looking and watching all the doors...and maybe the yard." He glanced again at the hatch and drew a deep breath. "I'm going after him."

"Maybe I should go."

"No, I want you to do the radio work. Do what you have to do. When that's done, and you're sure your partner is okay, come up after me."

"Be careful."

Phillips tucked his Glock back into its holster. He had eleven shots left and an extra clip of thirteen rounds in his Kevlar vest pocket. But he only needed two bullets. One for Damian Reynolds, the other for the scumbag Doc. He reached for the first rung on the ladder.

With every step, Phillips breathed in and out. He felt his heart squeeze. He tried to imagine Sofia one step ahead, the shape of her backside, her legs, her smile as she looked back at him. He paused and reached into his Kevlar vest pocket for his pill bottle, anticipating the chalky taste and dry swallow, then remembered the pills were in the pocket of his coat left in the SUV. *Stupid ass*. No little helper to medicate his mind.

"C'mon. You can do this."

He reached the top rung, his chest tighter than ever, and pushed open the hatch. He locked the lid into its open position, the metal making a slight clinking noise.

The sky was black. Even the stars refused to shine. The icy air blew around him and caught in his lungs as he got his bearings. To his left was a short expanse of eaves, not wide enough for sure footing, followed by an immediate three-story drop. To his right, the roof rose at a steep slant. Several chimneys emerged here and there. A recently shoveled cement sidewalk stretched out below.

Red and blue lights flashed on and off near the front of the house, but he heard no voices, no shouts. He assumed the team was still swarming inside. He glanced back around him on the roof. Tried to make out any movements in the darkness. Hands shaking, he gripped the hatch lid with one hand and placed the other on the slippery shingles. He crawled out onto the roof.

# CHAPTER SEVENTY-FIVE

Doc and Damian Reynolds duckwalked around a five-by-five-foot skylight built into a flat expanse of the roof. "I'm too old for this." Doc was bent over, breathing hard, and he was cold. He hadn't had time to grab his doctor's coat. "Maybe it'd be safer to give ourselves up."

Reynolds reached back and elbowed him in the face, making the large man lose his balance and scuttle a few feet toward the roof's edge. "Shut the fuck up," Reynolds hissed. "If you want to be a pussy and spend the rest of your life bending over for a daily dose of con cocks, go ahead and jump off the roof into those cops' waiting arms."

Doc didn't reply. He felt his nose for blood and looked at his hand. Nothing. He shuffled forward to follow Reynolds. The boss was right. There'd be no more high living. No more girls smiling at him on his exam table, thanking him for his kind ways, his gentle touch. He'd be disbarred, his reputation ruined. The closest he'd come to practicing would be checking out medical journals in a prison library.

The two waddled over to where the top of a metal

ladder jutted onto the roof from a third-floor veranda below. "We're gonna climb down this handy-dandy ladder," Reynolds instructed, "and have ourselves a tea party on the veranda. And if the coast's clear, we go inside, open the closet that leads to a secret door, and get cozy in the safe room."

Doc rubbed his hands on his thighs, trying to warm them. "We have a safe room?"

"Correction, *I* have a safe room. But I'll invite you in just this once." He glanced back over his shoulder and scanned the roof, then gestured for Doc to climb down the ladder. "Ladies first."

Doc scowled and got on his big belly, pointing his polished black shoes at the top rung of the ladder. He slid his body out and downward, his hands fumbling for the metal sides of the ladder, and found a toe hold.

Reynolds peered at him from above. "Hurry up. We don't got all night."

# CHAPTER SEVENTY-SIX

Wes Phillips felt as if his chest was about to explode. He wasn't sure anymore if it was the untreated anxiety or the beginning of a heart attack. *Concentrate. Focus on what you need to do.* His Twelve Step Program raced through his brain. "Just twelve steps out there." By then, the lead SWAT member would arrive to take over.

He forced himself to let go of his grip on the lid and take a few tentative, spider-crawling steps horizontally across the roof. He trained his eyes on the nearest chimney, his focal point. He imagined Sofia crouched beside it, beckoning him forward.

When he finally reached the chimney, he threw his arms around it like a new best friend and paused to catch his breath. Was this fear the last emotion his parents had felt? This out-of-control panic and terror as their motorhome toppled down a mountain. An endless fall. A helpless death.

He hugged the chimney and shook his head. Tried to clear the racing thoughts. *Remember the mission.* He peered into the darkness ahead and detected two shapes near a flattened section of the roof. No, he thought. *No.* He reached for his Glock and unsnapped it from the holster with one smooth motion. “Stop!” he shouted into the wind. “Police!”

# CHAPTER SEVENTY-SEVEN

Damian Reynolds froze and raised a hand. "Hold on. Don't fucking move. I thought I heard someone." He whipped his SIG out from the back of his pants and turned, scanning the darkness again. Waving it in the direction he thought he had heard the voice, he fired once.

"Go, go, go!" Reynolds ordered.

Breathing hard, Doc looked down for the next rung. He descended another step and began to lower his foot again when a shot exploded above him.

"*Fuck!*" Reynolds shouted. His face disappeared, then reappeared over the top of the ladder. "Get your fat ass moving. They're up here."

# CHAPTER SEVENTY-EIGHT

Several SWAT team members helped lead the girls, now wrapped in thick navy blankets, from the basement to a waiting police van. Chief Roxanne Dalestrom and Roni Colburn stood by the van door and guided them into the warm vehicle.

With one arm wrapped around Katrina and the other pressed against his rib cage, Russ Malloy escorted her down the sidewalk. The two moved slowly toward the van.

Eric Martinez strode over and stopped them. "When you get to the hospital, I want you to get checked out, too, Russ. You're clearly hurting, and you aren't fooling anyone."

Malloy nodded. "Yes, sir." He peered back at the house. "Hear anything from Phillips? Did they catch Reynolds and the others?"

Martinez followed his gaze. "I—"

"Sir." One of the SWAT members pulled Martinez to the side. "I just got word from the third floor. Two suspects have fled to the roof, and one of your agents is..."

A shot exploded from the roof. Katrina and the three

men looked up and saw a figure moving at the roof's far end. The SWAT member crouched low and ran toward the backyard, shouting commands into his shoulder mic.

"Is that... *Oh, my God!*" Katrina broke away from her brother's embrace and stumbled down the sidewalk toward the back of the house.

Malloy tried to grab her, but a shooting pain in his side stopped him. He groaned and slumped down beside a snowbank.

"I need a medic!" Martinez shouted toward a waiting ambulance. Curtis Blair, who now stood guard on the front steps, sprinted in his direction.

Martinez hovered over Malloy. "What's going on, Russ? Quit holding back on me." His gaze darted back and forth from Malloy to the high-heeled Katrina, who was slipping and falling on the sidewalk.

"My ribs," Malloy whispered, his breath coming out in small white puffs. "I think something's broken. Could be bleeding internally." He grimaced, both hands now on his ribcage. "Go help my sister. I'll wait here."

# CHAPTER SEVENTY-NINE

Wes Phillips crawled closer to the next chimney, his fingers numb from the cold, and reached its protection just as Damian Reynolds fired an aimless round. His buddy Doc was escaping over the roof on what appeared to be a ladder that led to somewhere below. Phillips raised his Glock with one hand, the other holding onto the chimney, and aimed for Doc's head. The man disappeared into the darkness.

"Damn it." Phillips repositioned his aim for Reynolds. The cold wind gusted around him, and the semi-automatic wavered in his already shaky hand. "Police!" he yelled again. He fired one shot.

Off by at least a foot.

Reynolds swore from across the roof, yelled something unintelligible, and darted for the cover of a chimney.

"It's over, Reynolds," Phillips shouted. "Give it up."

"Fuck you, Stevie. Or whoever you're pretending to be this week." Reynolds peered around the chimney and blew another shot in Phillips' direction. "I should've known you were a cop. You and that cunt Sofia."

Reynolds poked the gun out from the other side of the chimney and pulled the trigger again. "Dennis had a real good time with her." He laughed. "Screwed her every way possible." He laughed again. "Yep. You should've heard her scream and beg for mercy."

Phillips drew a deep breath and let it out slowly. He imagined his gun's muzzle pressed against the center of Reynolds' forehead. He scrambled for the next chimney. Another wild shot from Reynolds whizzed by his ear.

*"Stop!"* Katrina shrieked from below. *"Please!"*

Reynolds groaned. "Ah, not her, too, Stevie. I suppose she's also one of your bitches?"

Phillips didn't respond.

Reynolds let loose another shot. "I've got all night. What about you? You enjoying the view up here? I heard you get a hard-on when it comes to high places." He laughed. "Your little Izzy told me that. 'Course, I had to fuck her brains out after she mentioned your name."

Phillips clenched his jaw and tightened his grip on his gun.

Reynolds sighed. "Okay, Steve-O. I've given this all

some thought. You got me. *Bam.* How 'bout we play this nice and easy? I promise to give myself up in exchange for a shorter sentence and a comfy bed in solitary. Think you can make that happen?"

"I'm not a judge."

"Yeah, well, I'm sure you can do some finagling with all your fine friends."

Phillips blew out a long breath, stared directly ahead, and let go of the chimney. He gripped the Glock with both hands. "I can only make suggestions."

"Fair enough. I'm gonna come out from behind this chimney now, raise my hands. Promise you won't shoot?"

"Drop the gun over the roof. I want to see you do it."

"Only if you drop yours." Reynolds stood slowly, arms raised. He still gripped his gun in one hand yet pointed it at the sky.

"Damian!" Katrina cried from below. "Do what he says."

Reynolds looked down, a mingled expression of love and hate on his face. "This is all your fault," he yelled down at her. "You and that mouth of yours." He swung his gun hand in her direction.

"No, Damian!" Katrina screamed. "I'm… *I'm pregnant!*"

Reynolds froze. "What?"

To the far side of Reynolds, the top of a SWAT helmet popped up from the ladder where Doc had stood, and a muzzle pointed in the direction of Reynolds' head. Too late. Phillips sprang to his feet, steady, sure-footed. He let fly a barrage of bullets, emptying the gun into Reynolds, every shot a kill shot.

For a moment, Reynolds flew airborne, his body spread-eagled, his expression dazed. He fell, bouncing off several leafless tree branches, and crashed onto the sidewalk at Katrina's feet.

She collapsed to the ground, sobbing. "No. Oh, God, no."

Eric Martinez rushed forward and knelt by her side, wrapping his arms around her shivering body. "Come on, Katrina. Let's get you out of here into a warm vehicle."

Katrina shook her head repeatedly, her gaze locked on Damian's blank stare. "No, no, no."

Curtis Blair brushed past them and squatted beside Reynolds. He felt for a pulse. "Bastard's dead."

On the roof, Phillips' vision threatened to blur. He holstered his gun and sank to his heels. Stretching out onto his back, he pressed both palms against the cold shingles. He stared at the sky. One star revealed itself. “Sofia,” he whispered and let the night air fill his lungs.

***

Approaching footsteps on the roof made Phillips turn his head. The lead SWAT had climbed the ladder from the veranda and was hurrying toward him, saying into his shoulder mic, “I got a man down.”

“I’m not down,” Phillips mumbled. “But I want to be.”

The SWAT member knelt beside him. “You okay?” He placed a hand on Phillips’ shoulder, sweeping his gaze over him. “I don’t see any visible blood or gunshot wounds.”

“I’m not hit.” Phillips stared at the sky again. “I’m afraid of heights.”

“Then what the hell are you doing up on the roof? For fuck’s sake, you can’t get much higher.”

“A friend once suggested I focus on what I needed to do, not on what was around me,” Phillips replied. “I’d like to tell her it almost worked. Focusing on something helped.”

“Let’s get you down. You’re starting to babble. Would you prefer the ladder by the hatch or the one to the veranda?”

“The ladder I used had safety bars around it. Did

yours?" Phillips asked.

"No. Your ass will be hanging out there in the wind with nothing to make you feel secure, but it only goes down one floor."

"So does the one I used. Yet it felt like a long way." Phillips blew out a long breath and held out his hand.

The SWAT member took it, pulled, and caught Phillips in his arms. "We're doing fine."

"Easy for you to say." Phillips' cloud of breath mixed with that of the SWAT member's. "You're not afraid of heights."

"I never said I wasn't afraid." The SWAT member kept hold of Phillips' arm, and they turned and shuffled toward the hatch. "Why do you think they make me wear this helmet? Because I fall and land on my head. Humpty Dumpty, ya know?"

Phillips' gaze locked on the roof, watching the forward momentum of his feet. "You're just trying to make me feel better."

"Yeah? Well? Is it working?"

"Not much. You probably shouldn't write comedy."

The SWAT member snorted. "Good to know. And looky

here, we made it to the hatch already."

"That wasn't so bad," Phillips admitted. "But there's something running down my leg and into my shoe."

The SWAT member laughed. "In that case, you go down the ladder first."

"Fair enough. What if I freeze?"

"I go down the other ladder and send a shrink up to get you. Then I get to go home."

Phillips peeked over the edge of the hatch and into the hole it created. "Oh, sweet Jesus. Shouldn't I have a parachute or one of those giant airbags that stuntmen land in?"

"Would you like one? They could set it up on the snow in the yard, then we could jump. Like that rescue scene in *Lethal Weapon*."

"You'd like that, wouldn't you?" Phillips asked.

"I'd love it. Can we?"

Phillips turned and swung a leg over the edge. "Not a chance."

The SWAT member gripped the shoulder areas of Phillips' Kevlar vest. "I've got you by the vest, and if needed, the hair, until you tell me your feet are on that top rung."

Phillips practiced his Twelve Step breathing and swung his other leg over. He felt around for the ladder rung with the tips of his shoes. “Okay, both feet are planted.”

“Take it easy, now. One movement at a time. Remember, you’re getting closer to solid ground with every step.”

*Closer to Sofia*, Phillips thought, descending into the dark hole.

***

A service elevator waited on the second floor when Phillips and the SWAT member finally emerged from the stairwell. Phillips pressed himself into the corner of the elevator, eyes closed, heart still galloping, as they descended.

“You did good work tonight,” the SWAT member told him.

Phillips opened his eyes and looked at him.

“I understand it was a lot of effort on your part that led to this raid and all these arrests and saved lives,” he continued. “That could only be good work.”

Phillips pictured Sofia’s smile and imagined her laugh. “Thank you, but I was part of a good team.”

“And the stuff on the roof... Forget I ever saw it. You

were tired, coming off the adrenaline, needed to move slowly. All perfectly understandable."

Phillips grinned. "Thanks, man." He straightened as the elevator doors groaned open. "That's the best bullshit I heard all night."

***

Phillips rushed out of the house to the closest ambulance. "Where's Sofia Menendez?" he yelled.

EMT Antonio Ortiz was inspecting the bruised throat of one of the girls. Phillips caught the girl's green eyes, the hint of familiarity. *Jane Doe*, he thought. *Thank you, God.*

Antonio pointed behind him. "I think they're bringing her out now."

Phillips turned, saw two EMTs rolling a gurney out the front door, and ran to meet them. A body lay hidden beneath a sheet. His breath caught in his throat. The air around him seemed to drop ten degrees. Phillips swallowed hard, grabbed hold of one corner of the gurney, and helped lift it down the front steps. "Wait a minute." He pulled back the top of the sheet. *Sofia*. Her eyes were closed, her face peaceful.

"This was one tough lady," the EMT beside him said. "A real fighter."

"But there was too much blood loss from the gut wound," the other EMT added. "And an unknown substance in her system. We couldn't stabilize her. We lost her a few minutes ago."

Had it only been a few minutes since Reynolds had paid for what happened to Sofia and all the others? It seemed much longer. But that star...

"Do you want a minute alone?" the first EMT asked.

"Could I?"

"Yeah, of course. Nothing's going to change at this point," the EMT replied. They turned and walked away.

Phillips glanced back down at Sofia. "You said you'd wait, but I was too goddamn slow." His eyes filled with tears. He leaned over, ran his fingers across her cheek, touched her blue lips. "I'm sorry. We were supposed to... I wish..." He had the absurd idea to shake the gurney, to see if it would jar her back to life, but it had been shaken plenty on the steps.

He took her face in both hands. "If I were to say I love you..." His voice cracked. "Would you wake up so you could laugh at me? Tease me? Tell me I don't know what love is? Ask me how I'm smart enough to know I love you when I'm not even smart enough to get into your pants?" He forced a chuckle and wiped his eyes with the back of his hand. "I'd be okay with that." He leaned his forehead against hers. "Please. Laugh at me," he whispered. "Don't leave me."

Martinez and Blair stood ten feet away, pretending to confer with the EMTs. Phillips looked up again at the night sky and its single lonely star. Martinez stepped close and placed a hand on his shoulder. "Hey, Wes, I'm sorry. She was a helluva person, a helluva cop."

Phillips wiped his face again. "Yeah. All the way to the end." He inhaled sharply and looked at Martinez. "What about Russ and Katrina?"

"They're already on their way to the hospital. We sent them in the same ambulance. EMTs are convinced they'll be okay."

"Physically, maybe," Phillips commented. "What about the rest of the girls?"

"All the victims have been loaded into a van. We cranked up the heat, and they're about to head to the hospital, too, accompanied by the chief and Roni." Martinez stared at the van. "From the little we've learned, it sounds like some of them have been imprisoned and repeatedly raped for more than a year."

"Chrissake," Phillips muttered. "What a fucked-up world we live in."

Martinez pointed toward another van. Robert McNellis was shoving a large man into a seat. "McNellis found himself a straggler hiding on the third floor. SWAT had already cleared the room, but McNellis said he had a gut feeling and went back. Found the man crying in a closet, scratching at the walls like a trapped rat."

"Doc?"

"Yep." Martinez jerked his head toward a third van. "And the high rollers from Las Vegas are in there. They were enjoying dinner in one of the main rooms, a girl on each arm, when Larkin and Ellison interrupted the second course. Those men are gonna have a lot of explaining to do down at the station." After a moment, he gently pulled the sheet over Sofia's face and guided Phillips away. He sighed. "I hate to do this, Wes, but we need to talk about what happened. We're going to need your statement."

"I know. We're cops first. Gotta dot the Ts and cross my eyes and fuck the results."

Martinez placed his hand on Phillips' shoulder. "We won here tonight. We saved a lot of girls from sex trafficking and probably death, and we put away some bad guys. We won. Enjoy it."

"For what it's worth. But what's next?"

“We’re not going to think about that now. We’re going to heal and rest, maybe get drunk and salute our friends. Whatever comes next is a different day.”

Phillips glanced back at Sofia’s gurney. “Feels like a different life.”

# CHAPTER EIGHTY

Wes Phillips stared out the car window at his Southeast Minneapolis childhood home. The porch sagged, the siding needed a fresh coat of paint, and several shingles were missing. His father would've been pissed. And who knew what condition his mother's flower garden was in or if it still existed? A heavy blanket of snow covered the area.

The swing set remained in the same spot. A corner in the yard filled with good memories was now an eyesore with its rusty poles and chains and one missing seat.

He thought about his last conversation with Jen. About Alyse reaching out to this newly found brother. Was it his own fault? Maybe he had been too distant from his younger sister these past years. Perhaps this other guy provided something that was lacking in their relationship.

Hell, he could've used a big brother when he was a kid. One who stuck up for him, taught him how to do wheelies, wrestled until he said *Uncle,* and played army men with him instead of dolls.

And maybe this other guy could've used a little brother. Or always wished for two sisters. Or wondered why his biological parents...

*Damn.*

He looked at the time on his cell phone. Turned the key in the ignition.

# CHAPTER EIGHTY-ONE

Porter's was closed for a private party. Eric Martinez had booked the entire bar for his task force and a few friends. On a table near the center of the bar, a framed picture sat beneath a cloth drape, surrounded by roses and carnations. Martinez lifted the drape to reveal a picture of Sofia Menendez. Her pose was similar to a famous Johnny Cash picture. She held her middle finger up, aimed at the camera. Her lips were fixed in a snarl as she hurled an expletive at the photographer.

Martinez turned and faced the crowd. "I took this picture after we wrapped up the last case she assisted with. I told her she was a hell of a cop and actually a sweet person. This is what I got in return." He chuckled and wiped his cheek. "We laughed about this the last time we had lunch when she returned to help us again."

Robert McNellis smiled, holding a glass of Seven-Up. "What was she saying in the picture?"

Martinez cleared his throat. "Her exact words were, 'Hey, bitch, I don't let anyone take my picture.'"

"That's our girl," McNellis mused. "Join me in a toast. To Sofia. The world will not be the same." With a shaky hand, he raised his glass. "To the bitch."

The team shouted, "To the bitch." They all clanked and emptied their glasses and bellied up to the bar for another. Except McNellis. He only sipped his soda.

"Hope you don't mind me cutting out early," McNellis whispered to Martinez. "I gotta go back and see my goddaughter, then do some self-help of my own."

Martinez nodded. "Understood." He placed a hand on McNellis' shoulder. "Give me a call later. We'll talk."

Wes Phillips stood next to Russ Malloy, who was still a little pale and in pain. "I don't think she ever called me a bitch," Phillips revealed. "Other names, though."

"That was because she liked you," Malloy stated. "You may have been the only one."

"I got used to having her around. I'm going to miss her," Phillips murmured, his throat tight. He turned to face Malloy. "And how are you? Really?"

"Couple broken ribs, lots of bruising. But no organ damage, didn't puncture anything." He shrugged. "I'll heal."

Phillips hesitated. "And Katrina?"

"She's got a long road ahead of her. She'll come out of it okay, but it's going to take time. I hope she's patient and strong enough."

"The Katrina I know is strong enough. I'm not sure she's patient, though."

"Hey, I gotta ask you something," Malloy began. "You know all that good-cop, bad-cop shit we pulled?"

"Oh, you mean playing with the bone grinder?"

"Yeah." Malloy glanced at his drink and downed it. "You weren't really gonna..."

"What about you? Were you gonna let me..."

"Hell, no," Malloy replied.

"Well, okay, then."

"Okay."

Martinez came over and handed each of them another drink. "There are a few details you may not have heard yet. I'd like to be the one to share them." He was about to pick up his own glass, but it was empty.

Malloy handed his new drink over. "I shouldn't mix too much more with my pain pills."

Martinez took it and had a long sip. "We found a dead

guy on the second floor of the Summit house. Turns out it was Judge Harold McIntire."

"Jeezus," Malloy exclaimed. "That's why warrants were so hard to get."

"And that's who leaked the information about our undercovers," Martinez added. "He's responsible for the deaths of quite a few good people."

"How did he die?" Phillips asked. "Who stopped him?"

"One of our victims, a girl named Savannah," Martinez told him. "She announced it at the hospital. Showed off her bruises, scratches, and bite marks. Told us how mean and nasty he was and to go ahead and arrest her. She was glad to kill him."

"Wow. My kind of girl," Malloy exclaimed.

Phillips raised his eyebrows. "You didn't. Did you?"

"No, we set her up with counseling, and after she told us her life story, we called Child Protection Services." Martinez took another sip. "Oh, and do you remember Mandy, the stripper?"

They both nodded.

"She was freelancing in the room across the hall with a few of the judge's cronies. She hasn't stopped unloading names to us since. Thanks to her, we're going to chat with all kinds of important people all over the Twin Cities about their relationship with Damian Reynolds."

"What about the Priest Man? And the hotel clerk?" Phillips asked.

"They're asking for a plea bargain. Both said they'd be willing to testify to whomever, whenever." Martinez finished his drink. "Good work. Both of you. This is major, and it's mostly because of you."

Chief Roxanne Dalestrom joined the conversation. "Hey, rookie." She nodded toward Phillips. "You ready to come back to work? It'll be boring after this, but somebody needs to do it."

"Oh, c'mon, Roxanne, give the guy a break." Martinez leaned closer to her. "Tell you what. I'll buy you one of Porter's famous steaks if you give him a week off. With pay."

She snorted. "With pay? What kind of boss do you think I am?"

"A perfectly reasonable one," Martinez replied.

"Does the steak come with sautéed mushrooms and grilled onions?"

"It does."

She looked at Phillips. "I'll tell Waldron you'll be back riding in his squad in a week, rookie." She paused and smiled. "By the way, I heard you did good work." She shook his hand. "Thank you for that." She turned and let Martinez lead her to a secluded table.

Malloy raised his eyebrows and stared at Phillips' hand. "Wow. That moment should go down in your department's history book."

Phillips laughed.

Malloy glanced around at the thinning crowd. "I've got to get back to my sister. Come see us when you can." He patted Phillips' shoulder and left.

Phillips gazed at the picture of Sofia. "Despite your best efforts and your endless harassment and teasing, I did fall in love with you." He raised his glass. "And your ass was spectacular."

# CHAPTER EIGHTY-TWO

Katrina Malloy rolled from her stomach to her back in her hospital bed and found Wes Phillips sleeping in a reclining chair in her room. She watched him for a few minutes. His whole body twitched, jumped in the chair, and he woke.

"Hey."

"Oh, hi." He looked around. "Sorry. I didn't mean to fall asleep."

"It's okay. After what happened, we need all the rest we can get, any time we can get it." She moved around a bit, adjusting her hospital gown beneath the sheets. "I was enjoying watching you sleep. A little smile, an occasional puff of your lip. It was kind of cute. But your dream must have turned. Your eyebrows furrowed, your smile turned into a scowl, and you jumped and woke."

"Yeah, the dreams haven't been the best."

"I'm sorry," Katrina stated. "For both of us. We lost so much."

Phillips nodded.

She turned onto her side to face him. “You know, I meant what I said that night.”

“About being pregnant?”

“Yeah. Are you surprised?”

He was silent for a moment. “What are you going to do?”

“I’m not sure. I might keep it.”

Phillips drummed his fingers on the armrest and looked away.

“It’s not the baby’s fault, Wes.”

He looked back at her and studied her face. “Wouldn’t you think of Reynolds every time—”

“What? No. Oh, God, no. Damian was a user. It took me a while to figure that out. But no. It’s Dennis’ baby. He’s the father. The one who truly cared about me.”

“Ah, Katrina.” Phillips shook his head. “The tales we tell ourselves.”

She sighed. “I’m damaged goods, aren’t I?”

“That pretty much describes both of us.” He pulled the recliner into a seated position. “Russ tells me you’re going on leave.”

"I'm going into treatment, getting cleaned out and up. Then I'm going to try to deal with the trauma."

"And decide about the baby."

"Yeah. Don't tell Russ. I mean, about the baby. He doesn't know yet."

"Shit."

She took his hand. "I don't want to lose you in my life, Wes." She sniffled and wiped away a tear with her other hand. "Thank you for being there. You saved me."

"I only helped."

"I don't mean at the end. Earlier. You saved me when you arrived and cared. You gave me hope that I'd get out of there. I'll never forget that."

Phillips nodded, softly kissed the back of her hand, and stood to pull on his coat. "Take care of yourself, Katrina." He turned and left.

After the door closed, she turned onto her other side and looked out the window. "Goodbye, Wes."

# CHAPTER EIGHTY-THREE

The bag of jellybeans rustled in Wes Phillips' hands as he carried it into Mayhem Books. "How goes the arteries?" Phillips asked Leo, who was perched on his regular stool. He set the bag on the counter.

Leo chuckled, eyeing the candy. "Mmm-mmm, good. You really know how to win a girl over."

"Only the best for you," Phillips replied.

Leo ripped open the plastic wrapper and poured the beans into the jar. He sniffed hard. "Ah, like perfume to the senses."

"Thought you might appreciate a little sugar high. And a big thank you for not blowing my cover last week."

"Yeah, yeah. Yous's business is yous's business, I always say." He nodded toward the Reading Room. "You gonna show?"

"I think so. Might even have something to share this go-around."

“Sure thing, lover boy.” Leo stuffed a wad of candy in his mouth. “And I’m gonna be the next president.”

Phillips looked away, his mind spinning back. When he had returned to the carriage house to retrieve Lucky and pack up his and Sofia’s belongings, the dog greeted him with a pair of panties stuffed in his mouth. Phillips chased him around, but Lucky would run, hide, and growl when he came near.

“To hell with it,” Phillips finally muttered, watching Lucky chew at the crotch. “You enjoy the underwear. I claim the rest of her clothes. And her pillowcase.”

He brought Lucky to the condo, and the dog quickly made himself at home, taking over Bruno’s bed and toys. Every time Phillips stepped out, he’d arrive home to either a wet urine stain on the carpet or more of the leather couch’s armrest chewed up.

Phillips’ thoughts returned to the present. He looked back at Leo. “Say, Lolita wouldn’t be interested in having a boyfriend move in, would she? One who happened to be canine?”

“Answer’s a definite no with a capital N and capital O. Lolita’s a jealous feline. She don’t share me with no one, and I have to say I respect that.”

“So, I’m stuck.”

"Is it a little guy?"

"Small enough you'd barely notice."

"Bring him 'round the store. He can eat jellybeans with me while you rub elbows with them poet-wannabes. But a visit only. You leave, the mutt leaves."

Phillips fingered the gold chain in his pocket. He'd been carrying it around ever since Sofia's abduction. After her death, it held even more meaning. He nodded. He would give it a try. Keep Lucky for Sofia's sake, and maybe for his own. "Any new news in the book business?"

Leo slid his hand under the counter and held up a thick paperback. "Been hidin' this baby away until I'm done with it. I don't like to be one-upped by my customers, if you know what I mean." He pointed to the cover. "A thriller by a new local author. Rumor has it, it's gonna be the next best seller. Yep. A must-read, I says." Leo winked. "'Specially for a pretty boy with a name like Spade."

# AUTHOR NOTES

Characters find me and bring me their stories to tell. They don't realize that writing can be a slow process, that it can take years to get their story into a presentable format. Sometimes, I need help. *In Too Deep* is one of those situations. I went to my regular Wordwhippers Writers Group meeting and asked, "Who wants to try writing a book together?"

My friend Cathy, a.k.a. C. N. Buchholz, said she'd be willing to give it a shot.

That shot gave birth to this series.

Things don't always work like you'd expect. I gave Cathy the basic premise, some character descriptions, and a first chapter. She took off, and the file transferred back and forth until we had a completed novel. It went surprisingly well, too. No fights, no squabbles, neither of us writing the other into the book to suffer a ghastly fate, just writing until we were able to write "The End."

That book is not the one you are reading.

Before getting too deep into edits, Cathy launched the next book, which happened to take place before the book we had finished.

When characters come to us and share a story, why can't they share them in the order we would like to complete them and market them?

It's a control thing, isn't it? A reminder that we are only the translators.

The second book came together easily, too. I was again impressed at how well we worked together.

I thought we were on a roll and brought her a chapter for the third book.

Cathy read it and said, "You realize this is the first book in the series, don't you?"

The only answer I could give her was no. But she was right. And we were off again, and *In Too Deep* was born.

Another Wordwhipper friend, Barbara Schmidt, told us of a contest being presented by the Florida Chapter of the Mystery Writers of America. We entered the required first fifty pages of *In Too Deep*. It was selected as a finalist for their Freddie Award. Being a finalist would allow us to pitch the book to the agents and editors who attended the conference. The catch was the book had to be complete. The mad dash was on. We concentrated on *In Too Deep*, shoving all other work aside, managed a couple marathon writing sessions, and completed the book in three months.

At the Florida conference, we attended author events and breakout sessions, schmoozed with fellow writers, and pitched the book. *In Too Deep* did not win nor did it get picked up by an agent. Such is the publishing world.

We were patient and continued to edit *In Too Deep* and submit other work. Cathy had numerous short stories published in mystery anthologies. She wrote two memoirs and continued her prolific poetry writing.

I had a couple of short stories published, too. Yet I find them more difficult to write than does Cathy. I lean toward lengthy writing and generating a high word count each day. I also work simultaneously on several projects—in my head and on paper. When the stars aligned in my favor last year, my Psychic Guardian Angel Series of paranormal thrillers was picked up by Marlowe and Vane. As I type this, six books have been published and more are on their way.

But it's now time for *In Too Deep* to meet the world. We are excited and thrilled to be presenting our first crime novel for your reading pleasure. Enjoy and stayed tuned for Book Two.

A. W. Powers

Ditto to A. W.'s explanation of the birth of *In Too Deep* and our series. I'll focus my Author Notes on my writing process. Do I have a process? Well, I enjoy creating a story heavy on character. And casting females with strong personas. Although the old school of thought is to place the woman in danger and make her wait until the man rescues her, it's becoming new school to have her kick butt and save herself. Or at least try. I like to mix both methods in my writing and see what my alpha and beta females do.

What about tone of voice, dialogue, facial expressions, mannerisms, and body language? As a writer, I try to be true to each character. I read the character's dialogue out loud as I type. I try to imagine the sound of his or her voice, any accents or inflections, use of contractions or euphemisms. Would they use this word or that word? Would they yell, laugh, or cry?

Yelling may lead to violence. Does violence have a place in the story? Is it necessary to add aggression or cruelty (or worse) to move a story forward, or does it create sensationalism? Unfortunately, violence is a reality in our world. Good people exist, and not so good people exist. This is also true in the fictional universe. *In Too Deep* covers some heavy issues and hopefully it raises awareness of crime that may be occurring in our own neighborhoods. We need to be vigilant in keeping our cities, homes, and children safe. Like the DHS slogan says, “If you see something, say something.”

Violence and animals. *No, no, no.* I’ve owned household pets and farm animals. Currently, I share my home with a Great Pyrenees mix and five black cats. So no, A. W. and I will never allow characters in our books to harm an animal. Or we’ll kick some butt.

Speaking of kicking butt, although A. W. is a power writer, I consider myself a stop-n-go writer. Some days I write, write, write into the early morning hours. The adrenalin flows. The words keep coming. Other days, I find as many distractions as I can to avoid writing. Productive distractions such as arranging my 2000-plus books by genre and alphabetically by author, updating my to-do list of numerous past lists, clicking on YouTube song videos, scrolling through Facebook, or watching episode after episode of Netflix movies. You know, important stuff.

Thankfully, somehow, between A. W.’s prodding and my shuffling, we got ’er done. And we hope we did the book justice. It truly was fun to write.

C. N. Buchholz

# BIOS

C. N. Buchholz is a writer of poetry, memoir, mystery, suspense, thriller, and fiction. She has an avid interest in true crime and stories of survival. Buchholz has been published in poetry anthologies, mystery anthologies, newspapers, and magazines. She lives in the Land of 10,000 Lakes with a pony-size dog, five black cats, and one husband.

William J. Anderson, author, poet and editor writes from his home in Champlin, Minnesota, across the Mississippi River from Anoka, the Halloween Capitol of the World, where he grew up.

Anderson's alter ego, A. W. Powers, created the Psychic Guardian Angel series of paranormal thrillers, published by Marlowe and Vane, and writes fantasy, mysteries and horror. He often wonders how his hometown may have influenced his writing, or if it was the ghost that shared his and his wife's home in North Minneapolis.

More thrills are coming!

**Hit List**

Will be released in 2025.

Check our websites for more information.

Don't forget to sign up for our newsletters.

http://wmjanderson.com/a-w-powers

http://cnbuchholz.com

www.ingramcontent.com/pod-product-compliance
Lightning Source LLC
Chambersburg PA
CBHW022016050726
47499CB00004BA/1020

*9798991443012*